ROSEMARY ROGERS

BOUND BY DESIRE

A new generation
continues the bestselling
saga of Steve and Ginny!

Held Fast By Love

Suddenly, he began to kiss her—fiercely, violently, bending her body back while he held her wrists pinioned behind her so that she was helpless to resist him. Laura didn't care as he unbuttoned and unhooked her silken *pareu* so that it fell from her body before he kicked it impatiently aside, then removed her chemise as well, leaving her naked before him. His lips and his fingers kept searching her and exploring her everywhere.

"Now," he said, "I want you to undress me, very slowly, button by button, just as I have undressed you. And when I'm as naked as you are, bathed in moonlight, then I'll make love to you. Again and again. And you will make love to me."

"SWEET! SAVAGE! SUPER! This is Rosemary Rogers at her absolute best!"
Bertrice Small

"The offspring of *Sweet Savage Love*'s Ginny and Steve Morgan carry on the Rosemary Rogers tradition with glitz and passion only *she* could create."
Patricia Hagan

Other Avon Books by
Rosemary Rogers

THE CROWD PLEASERS
DARK FIRES
THE INSIDERS
LOST LOVE, LAST LOVE
LOVE PLAY
SURRENDER TO LOVE
SWEET SAVAGE LOVE
THE WANTON
WICKED LOVING LIES
THE WILDEST HEART

ROSEMARY ROGERS
BOUND BY DESIRE

AVON
PUBLISHERS OF BARD, CAMELOT, DISCUS AND FLARE BOOKS

AVON BOOKS
A division of
The Hearst Corporation
105 Madison Avenue
New York, New York 10016

Prologue

"Out of the Desert a Flower Blooms"

She whirled, the dance taking her—*letting* it take her. Her body became part of the music and the meaning of the half-sung, half-sobbed flamenco of Spain, and the wildness of the *jarabe* that was all Mexico.

It had been a long time—*too* long since Ginny had danced this way, bare feet on bare earth, naturally. The firelight and the torchlight flamed the cloud of copper-gold hair that fell in ripples to her waist—still as reed-slim as it had been before she had borne her twin children, Franco and Laura, who had, *fortunately,* Ginny thought for a fleeting instant, preceded them to the Hacienda de la Nostalgia.

Had it just been coincidence that while she and Steve were journeying to the Hacienda de la Nostalgia after visiting Renaldo and Missie and their children, that they had run into old friends? *And* that they had stayed to join the ex-Comanchero Sanchez and his sons and some of the vaqueros who had worked for Don Francisco Alvarado for a wild reunion that night? Coincidence or fate—neither of them cared!

"Remember when we all danced at your wedding with Esteban, eh?" Sanchez had reminded her, winking at her when Steve wasn't looking.

"*Dios!* It's been a long time—but you haven't changed!

1

I can still remember how jealous my devoted Concepción was.''

Dancing was losing herself, Ginny thought . . . going back in time to when dancing was all that she had had to help her survive for the fate she had always known had been meant for her—a man she should never have loved and could never resist. *Her husband.*

''Green eyes . . . who is it you are dancing for *now?*'' Half-whispered words shaking her into a breath-drawn stillness for an instant before she responded without hesitation or conscious thought: ''For *you,* Steve, my love, only and always for you!''

Later, he carried her off in his arms to their makeshift bed for the night—out under the stars and a setting quarter moon. And there he made love to her; with words and with touching and feeling and entering until she was filled and fulfilled and trembling within and without her body even as she felt the sweat-slippery vibration of his body against and within hers, and she remembered suddenly how completely desolate she had felt when she had thought once, what seemed now a long time ago, that she would never know *this* and never again feel *this.*

She ought to be angry with him, Ginny thought half-drowsily, still wrapped in his arms and held captive by his legs. He had no right to forcibly abduct her in this fashion; not his *wife!* And no right to treat her as if she were his mistress . . . or his unwilling hostage, as she once had been. But . . . then again, they had had so many beginnings . . . and so many endings that were only new beginnings! The real truth to cling to forever was that they loved each other—and most of all perhaps when they fought each other.

He had carried her off . . . and then set her free to dance—to *choose!* Because he loved her and wanted her to choose freely.

Why should the past matter? That had been learning time for both of them. *Now* mattered, and what was learned from now would grow and spread into the future.

And it was exciting to be abducted by the man you loved! A fulfillment of a fantasy! At least, she realized that now. Whether she had hated him or loved him, Steve had always been her fantasy—as she, perhaps, had been his?

"Steve . . . you are my one love, my only *real* love . . . forever. I looked for ways to hurt you . . ."

"And I did, too, because I was not used to loving a green-eyed temptress! *Bruja!* I think I have let you take possession of my soul—certainly I cannot get you out of my mind, whether I like it or not. We're stuck with each other, *querida.*"

"I'll kill any woman who puts her hands on you!"

"And I'd kill any man who tries to put his hands on you—whether you invite him to do so or not!"

Again they moved together and with each other—swelling and tightening . . . holding.

This time, it was not necessary to say the words "I love you." This time they both *knew.*

Part One—Mexico

The Game of Pretenses

Chapter 1

While Laura Morgan submitted to having her tangled mane of hair combed and brushed by her grumbling maid, her pretty gown buttoned up over a lace corset she didn't need and would remove—yes, and the gown too—as soon as Filomena left her in peace to take her siesta, she let her thoughts wander to her parents, their strange relationship that she could not and perhaps would not ever understand.

What had brought them together? And after their many separations and quarrels, what had brought them back together, and kept them together in the end?

Love? Challenge? What? For some strange reason, and in spite of everything that had happened to them both and the different turns their lives had taken, her parents loved each other, that much Laura was sure of, even if it wasn't the tame, romantic, idyllic kind of love described in the books she read. They *felt* for each other and *sensed* each other in some way . . . and she more than her twin brother, Franco, knew this intuitively, even without understanding the complexity of their relationship.

It was difficult to think about one's parents as lovers, even as separate individuals. Although Laura felt happy for them, that they so obviously enjoyed each other's company, she sometimes felt excluded from their special private sharing. There were even times when she felt sorry for herself—and lonely, in spite of her beloved books and the notebooks that she would write in for hours, secluded in her room or in some cool, private place where the trees clustered closely together, festooned with vines hung with heavily scented flowers that were as yellow as the sunlight that filtered through the branches arching above her.

Since Franco had fallen in love with the pretty, shy Mariella from the village nearby, Laura had begun to feel even more alone, except for her imagination, which could conjure up all kinds of exciting and romantic situations—and the notebooks in which she inscribed all her secret fantasies, writing of herself as if she were someone else.

Laura had to confess to herself disgustedly that since there were so many feelings she had not experienced yet for herself, how could she write about them?

The only lovers she knew were her own parents, and Aunt Missie and Uncle Renaldo. But the love that Missie and Renaldo shared was different—mellower and less stormy; not the kind of passion she sensed her parents felt for each other that would make them fly into rages, act as if they hated each other, just before her father kicked the bedroom door closed behind them. And then, they'd stay locked in there for what seemed like forever.

But *love,* Laura wondered. What was it? How many faces did it wear and how many varied facets were there to an emotion that had been eulogized and written about for centuries? Was love something that caught one up, like a soaring whirlwind, or was it a trap? Laura vowed fiercely to herself that *she* would never, ever allow herself to be caught in a prison formed by one's emotions!

"Well, there you are, ready at last!" Filomena pronounced, stepping back to admire her handiwork. "And today at least, you will look like a young lady when you greet your prospective *novio.* "

In an instant, Laura's volatile temper flared. She swung away from the mirror in which she had been contemplating her new and unusual image, her dark brows drawing together in an angry frown.

"My *novio?* I *have* no fiancé—and I never will unless I decide to choose a man who is to *my* taste. You understand? There is a visitor expected by my father and my

mother this evening—not by *me!* It's nothing to me—I
might not even choose to meet this stranger from California. In any case, I heard bad things about this man when
we were last at the *rancho* in Monterey. And from his own
brother at that! *I* don't intend to be one of his many
women—much less his *novia*—and I've told my parents
so! My great-grandfather and his grandfather had no right
to make such a ridiculous arrangement.'' Seeing Filomena's aghast look, Laura drew in her breath and spoke in a
more controlled fashion: ''Oh, I'm sorry, dear Filomena!
It's not your fault, is it? I—I'm just a little distraught at
the moment—please understand and forgive me?''

She gave the woman a warm hug to mollify her, but
after Filomena left, muttering and grumbling under her
breath, Laura turned back to her mirror and grimaced at
her own reflection. *Lady,* indeed! Ugh! Hair coiled up and
twisted into braids and loops and ringlets. A gown that
was far too tightly nipped in at the waist, making it hard
for her to breathe. How could any woman, lady or not,
stand to wear the garments dictated fashionable so arbi-
trarily by *male* designers who cared nothing for the natural
lines of the female body?

Fashion, etiquette, what was ''done'' and ''not done''
were things as tightly binding as the corsets she detested
and didn't need, and all because of a silly man and a
ridiculously *feudal* arrangement entered into between families while she was still an infant! She knew it was all
nonsense of course; and she could have laughed her so-
called *novio* out of her mind if not for the knowledge that
she had so short a time left *here*—in a place and an environment she loved, among people who loved and understood her.

Still staring unseeingly at herself, Laura blinked back
angry tears. Why must her free, happy life be so suddenly
changed? Why couldn't she stay at home, or with Missie
and Renaldo, instead of being forced to go to Europe to
be molded—no, *forced* would be a better word—into the

image of a fashionable young lady, a chattel put on the marriage market, like a female slave on the auction block?

Her twin brother, Franco, was actually looking forward to his Grand Tour of Europe. He didn't seem to consider poor little Mariella, who loved him, and who he'd said he was "fond of," in his typically male noncommittal fashion. Mariella would probably be married off before Franco returned—if he still wanted to return after he'd experienced the fleshpots of Europe. It was a term Laura liked; it turned her mind from her present dilemma for a moment. "Fleshpots" conjured up all kinds of deliciously decadent images!

There were times when Laura Morgan could not understand either herself or her changing moods and emotions. She was almost eighteen—considered to be on the verge of spinsterhood here in Mexico—and yet she did not look her age at all when she was dressed "comfortably," as *she* preferred to call it, in her usual shabby and unconventional attire that made her look like a young and immature little peasant girl, or a gypsy. And yet, in some ways she was already a woman with knowledge of the world beyond this safe, familiar environment—a world opened to her searching, seeking mind by the books she read so voraciously, most of them borrowed from her uncle Renaldo's extensive library. It was her dear, understanding Tío Renaldo, her father's cousin, who had first encouraged her to put her emotions and burgeoning feelings into words on paper—capturing moments of beauty and uncertainty and wondering about life and what it held for her in word-pictures and little sketches.

She had attended an exclusive young ladies' academy in San Francisco for two years, but had learned much, much more from Tío Renaldo, who was a teacher by vocation, and from her mother who had, Laura more than half-suspected, experienced almost *everything!* From her parents Laura had learned languages, surface sophistication and manners, and how to ride, shoot, use a knife, and defend

herself with her bare hands if needed. She was as skilled at all this as Franco, but what good did it do her *now?*

Abruptly, Laura shook the dark thoughts out of her mind, determined to enjoy this day and riding her chestnut stallion Amigo bareback and barefoot as she usually preferred. How she would miss her Amigo! Who would ride him as far or as freely as she did?

I won't even think about it now, Laura told herself. I'll just live and savor every moment I have left here, and when I write of this day and its feeling in my notebook, I will carry it with me and relive it with nostalgia and sadness forever.

"Oh, *perdición!* Enough!" Laura said aloud, grimacing at her image once more. A stranger looked back at her, a young woman in a constricting, pretty morning gown patterned in colors of orange and green with ribbon threaded through the thin cotton lace eyelets.

Except for her eyes, which were her father's and so dark a blue they could appear black, she could suddenly see her mother in herself—in the gypsyish upward slant of her eyes and brows; her chin, barely clefted, that lifted even now in stubborn defiance. Her hair had an equally defiant curliness, in spite of all poor Filomena's efforts to transform it into some semblance of fashionable decorum with combs that stuck into her scalp and innumerable pins that could not hold back escaping strands and tendrils that clung about her temples and cheeks and even strayed down the slender nape of her neck.

Her hair, almost as dark as her father's when she was younger, had changed under the hot sun of Mexico to reveal coppery strands in its "wild mane," as her disapproving nurse had called it. At least, Laura thought, I have Mama's cheekbones. Abruptly Laura discarded the dress and changed into her favorite riding clothes: a thin cotton *camisa* and a full, faded cotton skirt that enabled her to ride astride in comfort. She didn't care in the least if she *did* show an unconscionable amount of leg. Everyone around here knew her and was used to seeing her ride

dressed this way; besides, no one would dare to criticize
the daughter of *El Padrón* and their *Padrona*.

Filomena would have retired to her room for a nap by
now, Laura thought, leaving her room, so there would be
no scene with her. And Marisa, whom her mother had
adopted as a baby long ago and who insisted on doing the
cooking at the Hacienda de la Nostalgia when ''her'' family was there, could refuse Laura nothing, even if she knew
the girl was up to some mischief that no doubt Filomena
would disapprove of!

Laura was coaxing, wheedling, when she went down to
the kitchen to announce that she was taking Amigo out for
a ride. A little something for Laura to eat and drink when
she stopped to rest the horse?

''Of course,'' Marisa had said immediately. And no—
she would tell no one . . . that is, unless the *señora* herself
asked.

''Not even that detestable brother of mine? *Promise?*''

''No, no, I'll tell *no one* but the *señora*, and then only
if she *asks* me,'' Marisa repeated.

Her lunch and a wineskin tucked into one of the small
leather pouches that hung down on either end of the strap
that she slung before her as she always did when she didn't
bother to put a saddle on Amigo, Laura led her restive
mount away from earshot of the house before she mounted
and kicked her heels against his sides—a signal for a wild
gallop.

Franco watched his sister streak by on that wild stallion
of hers that was almost as untamed as she was, and shook
his head. Laura was incorrigibly headstrong and willful,
and he pitied the man who dared try to tame her.

''Wasn't that your sister?'' His companion raised herself up on one elbow, her brows knitting with puzzlement.
''But I thought—''

''I suppose we all thought that today, at least, my sister
would act like a lady! But you know how Laura is! Angry
at the world when she cannot have her own way, flying at
anyone who attempts to curb her. She doesn't even know

the man who is supposed to be her *novio*. But she'll probably shock him enough so that *he's* the one to back off in
horror! I can't really say that I blame her for this wild ride
today, though. She needs the feeling of still being free
before she has to leave it all behind.''

Was he speaking only for Laura or for himself as well?
he asked himself. Franco's eyes had clouded slightly and
his body had tensed when he'd watched his sister ride by
like a *bruja*, a witch on a broomstick with her wild mane
flying behind her, a banner snapping in the wind. Would
he, too, regret leaving this place with all its memories
when they left for Europe next month? And Mariella—
how could he bear to leave Mariella?

He was with her now in their favorite trysting place—a
tiny, hidden grassy grove protected by trees and thickly
growing vines on two sides and by a tall outcropping of
rocks on the other. A stream of water seeped down from
the rocks to form a small pool at the base.

They could see out through the curtain of vines, but no
passerby in the full sunlight could see them here in their
shadowed green bower.

He and Mariella had been slipping away to meet each
other here for some years now—whenever he was home
from the Eastern prep school, whenever they could manage it. His lovely Mayan Indian, *his* Mariella. He looked
down at her worried face, then silenced her unspoken
questions with his kisses, fierce, tender, demanding—then
tender again, until they both had forgotten everything and
everyone but themselves and this moment.

Laura, on her headlong flight, had not noticed anyone
or anything as she passed—and flight was what it was after
all, she had to admit. Flight from the unknown, flight
from something she had suddenly and unexpectedly found
herself faced with. Yes, it had been a shock.

She remembered staring disbelievingly at her mother
and her father, thinking that of course they had to be teasing her! Fiancé? And this was the first she had been told?

For once her mother, playing with the tasseled edge of her light shawl, said nothing.

"What *are* you talking about, for heaven's sake?" she had said. "I just don't understand! Surely you can't mean—you couldn't have possibly . . ."

"I don't know if you remember your great-grand-father," her papa said, "but he was a man of the old country, never changing his customs, or his ways and his beliefs for that matter."

"But what has all that got to do with *me?*" Or a marriage? A marriage *arranged* for me? You never mentioned such a thing before; nobody ever said—"

"Laura, dear," her mother interrupted quickly. "I don't want you to think that you are being forced into a marriage. Of course not! I hope you know your father and me better than that. What we are trying to explain is that there was a kind of . . . what would *you* call it, Steve?"

"An agreement or a 'family alliance,' " he said straight-faced, catching a wicked glint in his wife's eyes.

Laura's eyes flashed from one parent to the other before she said, almost stamping her foot with frustration, "Stop it, you two, stop it! This is no time to—" She caught herself, sucking in a deep breath before continuing more calmly. "I *still* don't understand and you have not explained *anything* to me!

"Oh, it's something that . . . shall we say, that his grand-father and your father's grandfather arranged between themselves? Naturally they believe in old feudal . . ." Ginny broke off laughing as she encountered her husband's dark look.

"Customs," Steve continued smoothly, his eyes now on Laura's anger-flushed face.

"But Papa—what do you mean when you say that there were certain arrangements made?"

"Yes, like the one your father had with that Ana creature, as I recall," Ginny said sweetly, and smiled just as sweetly, in response to Steve's threatening look.

"I am *trying* to be patient," Laura said tightly, her face

flushing with anger. "But I must confess that I still do not understand anything you're saying. What do you mean by a *fiancé*? And why was I never told before about this silly arrangement which surely has no validity? You're not going to tell me *that*, are you?"

"All we are trying to tell you," Ginny said soothingly, "is that, well, we must try to be, shall we say, *mannerly* about all this. I am positive that Mr. Challenger has no more liking for this arrangement than you do!"

"Mr. Challenger, did you say? Not *Johnny*, surely?"

"No, I'm afraid not. I know how friendly you and John Challenger were when you lived in California. But no, it's his older brother in this case."

"You mean the black sheep? The renegade who—"

"Be careful, young woman," Steve said. "He happens to be a friend of mine!"

"Oh, *that* kind of a friend!" Laura said with her chin tilted up in a fashion that reminded her father far too much of his stubborn wife.

"All I have to say," Steve went on firmly, "is that you will meet Mr. Challenger and you'll be polite to him; and that is *all* you are required to do!"

"Oh, this is impossible, intolerable, and I won't stand for it!" Laura stormed. "How *could* you? He's probably *your* age, Papa, and—"

"Laura, Trent Challenger is only thirty! Not too old to be interesting, I'm sure."

"But far too old for me!"

"Laura," Ginny said tactfully, "you must learn that at some time or other we all have to learn to pretend—at least to be polite if the issue isn't very important. My love, you must know that neither your father nor I has any intention of trying to force you into an engagement—let alone a marriage! All we are asking you to do when Trent Challenger arrives here is to be polite, and if the subject of this arrangement comes up—which it might *not*—he will no doubt have a talk with your father, and then it will all be settled and done with once and for all."

"What do you mean, have a talk with my father?" Laura's voice rose. "What has *Papa* got to do with it? What about *me?*"

Suddenly, she stood up, her expression strangely calm. "Oh, well," she managed to say coldly. "I suppose nothing I say will make any difference anyway." Then she turned and left the room, the door banging shut loudly behind her. All this came back to Laura as she rode Amigo away from the house at a gallop.

To announce to her that she had a fiancé she had never heard about, and whom she must be polite to—this time her parents were going too far. She would *not* meet this Trent Challenger, and if she *had* to, she certainly wouldn't pretend to be polite! She had heard all about him—a gunman, a renegade, some even called him an *outlaw*.

He had *never* come home once he'd left; not even when his mother was dying. It had always been up to poor Johnny to manage things, and now Johnny's bad-penny brother had the nerve to turn up and be announced as her fiancé! Grimly, Laura wondered if he needed money. Perhaps he had been cut off from his inheritance or would be if he didn't marry her as decreed by two old men. She remembered Johnny once telling her that his maternal grandfather was a stern and autocratic old man and, like her great-grandfather, would have no scruples about imposing certain conditions upon his heirs in order that they could inherit. Well, that was no problem of *hers! She* didn't care if her great-grandfather's money came to her or not!

No! Laura thought defiantly now. I *won't* meet him! She would just stay away; she'd visit Anita in the village and stay the night, and her parents would have to make an excuse for her. She'd take the consequences later and be damned!

As she left the house Laura hoped fervently that Trent Challenger didn't intend to stay very long at the Hacienda.

Chapter 2

Trent Challenger, had Laura but known it, had no intention of staying at the Hacienda de la Nostalgia for longer than it would take him to pay his respects to Steve Morgan and his lovely wife, and deliver the packet he had brought with him from Mexico City. He hoped fervently that Laura Morgan would be absent; that way there wouldn't be the strain and awkwardness of a meeting between them. Once his business with Steve had been taken care of he could snatch a few hours' sleep in a bed for a change before leaving first thing in the morning.

He was always leaving one place or another, never staying longer than he had to, never wanting or needing to go back to something or someone. Not any longer. There had been a place he had once called "home," but that had been only while his mother was still alive and holding everything together in her small, fine-boned, and deceptively fragile-looking hands that were really so strong. His mother had managed to be strong in spite of her husband's desertion—to chase after his rich friends and an English title.

As usual, whenever he thought of his father, Trent damned him for a selfish, pretentious bastard, and for his indifferent, cavalier treatment of his mother.

James Challenger, after attending Harvard, had wanted more than anything else a Grand Tour of Europe with his friend Arthur Singleton, son of an English expatriate married to a rich American.

Mamacita—Carmen María Teresa de Avila—came of old Spanish stock. Her family owned almost a million acres of land in the rapidly growing southern part of California, and the aristocratic Don Manuel de Avila was a wise and wily businessman, investing his millions where they would bring back the most profit—in Mexico, all over the United States, even, it was rumored, in Europe and South America.

If Don Manuel had had a weak spot, it was his only daughter, his Carmencita of the dark, sparkling eyes and cascading black hair. She had inherited her mother's almost ethereal beauty, and her father's intelligence and business acumen. For all that, she was as gay and vivacious as any young woman of seventeen—loving to dance and go to parties.

Why, Trent used to wonder bitterly, had she allowed herself to be married to a man she hardly knew, merely because Christian Challenger and Don Manuel had done business together for years and were partners in many investments?

"But my son—I fell in love with your father the very moment I saw him!" His mother had once remonstrated gently with him. "Someday you, too, will understand love, not caring about the risk of pain. He was so handsome, your papa—just come back from Harvard, dressed like an Easterner. It was not his fault. I wanted him, I told my *padre* so, and as usual, he gave in."

James had given in, too, albeit rather sullenly. But on this marriage—a joining of families already joined by friendship, mutual respect, and business—Christian Challenger had been insistent, and implacable. If his eldest son was not "in love" with his wife-to-be, love would come with the passing of time and the sharing of children.

James had been allowed his six months in Europe, and after his wild oats had been sown, he returned for his wedding and the taking up of his responsibilities . . . responsibilities which involved little more than fathering four children—and spending as much time as possible away from the isolated boredom of the Carmel *rancho*.

Ostensibly as a vacation residence for the family, he had purchased a palatial estate surrounded by well-tended grounds, situated in one of the most fashionable and exclusive environs of San Francisco. Leland Stanford, Charlie Crocker, the so-called Silver Kings—Hunt, Fair, and McKay—were his neighbors, along with their polished, sophisticated wives. He rode with them and hunted with them and caroused with them, spending most of his time away from his family, while his wife handled everything: business affairs, the running of the ranch, the account books—everything.

Occasionally, James would visit, for a weekend; if he needed money, a few days longer. It had been these visits, and his father's obsession with tracing his legitimate claim to an ancient English dukedom, that had driven Trent half-mad with frustration and resentment, bordering on hate, for his father's insensitivity where his wife was concerned.

How his mother *glowed*, excited as a young girl, when her husband was expected! And after he had left, with condescending words of advice to his children, she had always had a sad look in her eyes that she tried to hide.

It was partly to escape being shipped off to a "good" Eastern university and partly because he could not stand to see his mother's pain without coming close to killing his father, that Trent had left home at sixteen. And his mother had let him go with understanding, and love—the love she gave so unstintingly and unselfishly, even to her husband who could not understand or appreciate such a feeling.

Damn his father! It would be a good thing if their paths never crossed again—for Trent had learned during the years to kill efficiently and easily, without regret; with a gun, a knife, or his bare hands.

In fact, it was his reputation that had almost got him lynched in New Mexico. The town "boss" had found that his gunnies wouldn't go up against the man known only as Trent, and had arranged to get rid of his most dangerous opponent legally, since he had the sheriff in his pocket. But as it turned out, both the town and the town's boss were cheated out of a lynching and the usual drunken revels that followed such an event. The sheriff was curtly informed by a federal marshal that his prisoner was wanted for questioning by higher authorities—and that was that.

His grandfather, Don Manuel, had had the Pinkertons looking for his errant grandson, and Don Manuel had a friend with influence—a certain Mr. James Bishop. So, Trent had been "rescued," and had learned also that his mother had died. After that, it seemed as if nothing mattered any longer, and all he had left was self-hate for staying away so long and hate for his father.

Don Manuel, who was a wise man and sensed that the rage and bitterness in his favorite grandson must find some release, had raised no objections when Trent was asked to "work" for Mr. Bishop and his associates. For, as Trent was to learn, Mr. Bishop always collected his debts—and used his debtors to serve his ends.

How easily, and how willingly, he'd been drawn into Bishop's spider trap! He'd been tested first, of course, by being given the tough assignments—to seek trouble or to make trouble as the case might be; and to gather as much information as possible. If there was killing that had to be done, he did it knowing that if he was caught there would be no more reprieves. In a way, he had enjoyed the challenge, the adventure—not having time to think too much or dwell on the past with its pain. The *rancho* held too many memories for him, and he had not had the time to become particularly close to his sisters or his younger brother. He didn't care for possessions and shied away from attachments, earning the reputation of being a loner.

No ties—God, how he hated ties—the feeling of being held down, pent in. Love, and especially marriage, were for other men, not for him. Lust and the sating of it when he was in the mood was more than enough. No shackles, as his brave, beautiful mother had been bound, by love and obligation to a man who hadn't cared enough even to pretend!

With an effort, Trent pushed down the ugly, angry thoughts that had suddenly come brooding into his mind like a festering sickness. Black thoughts on a hot, sun-bright day. He had too many other things to think about at the moment, like the sealed letters he was carrying in his saddlebags.

Tomorrow, when he set out again, this time for California, he'd have time enough for introspection. A brief, caustic smile twisted his lips on his bearded face as he recalled what had started off his unpleasant train of thought.

Why did these stiff-backed old Spaniards, used to the autocratic ways of almost a century ago, still insist on arranging for marriages of alliance? His grandfather de Avila, for instance, and his grandfather's friend, Don Francisco Alvarado. Wanting to keep the wealth they had accumulated within certain families? Why, this poor girl—probably a child—who had been chosen without her knowledge or consent as a suitable bride for Don Manuel's eldest grandson was probably scared half to death! A lousy rotten helluva husband *he'd* make for any wide-eyed miss who knew nothing about life or sexuality! She would be relieved, no doubt, when he reassured her that he had no intention of forcing such an unhappy fate upon her, no matter what Mr. Bishop had hinted at during their last meeting! No damn marriage of convenience for him—he'd said so, quite definitely. "She plays a reasonably good poker game," Bishop had offered as a non sequitur from behind his desk just as Trent was leaving.

So? he'd thought at the time, but now he found himself wondering what the girl might be like and who she took after. Steve Morgan's daughter—and Ginny's. Ginny Brandon Morgan of the flashing emerald eyes and shining copper hair, with that promisingly sensuous mouth of hers.

Some years ago, when he first met her at a banquet given by Sam Murdock, one of Morgan's partners and

closest associates, Trent had been unable to take his eyes
off her—off that sweetly promising mouth. He had wanted
her—more than he had ever wanted or thought he could
want a woman, this gypsy enchantress who could even
dance like a true *gitana*. He could even have imagined
himself in love with her, before he found out that she was
the wife of Steve Morgan—and the mother of his children.

Just for the hell of it, Trent found himself wondering if
Laura Luisa Encarnación Morgan bore any resemblance
in looks or nature to her parents. He told himself, shrugging as he lit up a half-chewed cigarillo, that he'd soon
find out—but after he'd been able to take a bath, he hoped.
He'd traveled, with only brief stops to eat or snatch some
sleep, all the way from Mexico City—and today he'd been
riding since before sunup.

He could use some fresh water—and so could the big
black he was riding. "Hey there, Laredo, smell any water,
boy?" There were trees up ahead and brush. All green
instead of burned-out dry. And when Laredo tossed his
head, nostrils flaring, and whickered softly, Trent patted
him on the neck.

"Okay, boy. Looks like you get watered and I get myself cleaned up some."

As a matter of habit, Trent Challenger was careful—
always wary for any sign of possible danger. He'd lived
with danger for so long that caution was second nature to
him by now. Water could mean a stream or a spring bubbling out of rock. Almost always that meant the presence
of animals who drank there—and perhaps humans too.
Most tiny settlements sprang up close to a natural supply
of water.

But in this case, Trent hadn't seen any sign of life yet.
No village noises, no children calling shrilly, no dogs
barking. Not even the bleating of the inevitable goats that
usually roamed free.

Trent rode forward slowly, carefully, until he emerged,
through thick brush and hanging vines, into a small grassy

area where the brush and tree-lined stream widened and deepened slightly.

Laura had ridden until she and Amigo were both tired— and hungry and thirsty as well. The idea of visiting her friend Anita seemed better and better, especially if her handsome older brother was there. It would be fun to flirt with him, now that he had suddenly begun to notice her as a woman. And then let them all fuss at her afterward, and tell her how rudely and irresponsibly she had acted. She did not *care!* She was tired of having everything *arranged* for her!

Amigo snorted; reminding Laura that *he,* at least, was thirsty and could use a well-deserved rest.

Laura was immediately repentant, bending down to stroke his sweat-lathered neck.

"Oh, Amigo! How thoughtless I am! It's time for us *both* to cool off now, I think, eh?"

I love this place, Laura thought. So peaceful, so still— except for birdcalls and the tiny rippling noises of the stream bubbling over rocks and sand. There was grass for Amigo to feed on under the trees, after she had wiped him down with an old, torn petticoat she always carried with her. Once he seemed content, Laura ate her freshly baked sourdough bread with great hunks of goat cheese, and washed down her makeshift meal with red wine from the wineskin she always took with her on such expeditions.

This was one of her favorite places for thinking and writing; lying, sometimes, half in and half out of the water that was too shallow to cover all of her body, while she wrote with her elbows propped up on the bank.

Today there was so much to think about—to savor and to feel.

Feeling the heat, Laura soon wriggled out of her skirt and blouse, and waded into the heavenly cool water wearing only her oldest, shortest chemise. She bent down to soak her hair, scrubbing at her gritty scalp until it felt

clean again before she braided it to hang heavily down
over one shoulder.

Her little stream was far too shallow for a real, soaking
bath, but she could lie down in the water and feel it rippling mind, as ephemeral as darting, opal-winged dragonflies.

Laura let her mind drift into sun-dappled, tranquil la-
ziness—feeling herself like a leaf, floating, floating on the
surface of the stream, going everywhere, and nowhere.

And then, in a moment, everything was shattered, dis-
appearing with the intrusion of a loud, unfamiliar voice
that called: *"Hola, muchacha!* Are you asleep in there or
trying to drown yourself?"

Laura jerked upright with an unpleasant start to find
herself looking up into the bearded face of a stranger riding a dust-coated black stallion that pawed the ground and
looked every bit as dangerous as his rider.

"Oh, so you're alive, I see! Do you do this often?"
And then, impatiently: "Can you speak?" he asked in
Spanish.

He was a tall man with a hard face, his eyes shaded by
the pulled-down brim of a battered flat-crowned black hat.
He could be an outlaw, a mercenary, even a *bandido,* with
his crossed bandoliers, the rifles sheathed on either side
of his saddle. And he carried guns with plain, well-worn
handles as well.

"You have no right to startle me so!" Laura snapped
angrily, finding her voice and answering him in Spanish.
She was unreasonably angry, not scared. This stranger had
intruded on her private place, her private moment, and
she wanted him *gone!* "And keep your big brute of a horse
away from mine!"

She stood up, forgetting that she was wearing next to
nothing until she saw the slight flaring of his nostrils, and
a sudden stillness in him that made her aware that she
might as well have been completely nude, the way her
chemise was plastered wetly against her skin.

Her sun-warmed skin prickled with a chill. Oh, God!

What if . . . "Will you go *away!* Now that you've looked your fill?"

She wouldn't show fear. When he didn't answer right away, Laura took two steps forward, thinking of the gun she had left under her skirt, the gun she always took with her on these excursions. And the knife—but that she had left in the saddlebag!

"Listen, you had better go right now, stranger!" she said boldly. "Get out, quickly! If my family knew, they'd kill you, in spite of all your guns. You look like a *ladrón*— or a *gringo* from the wrong side of the border. We don't like your kind here. Do you understand? What are you doing here anyway?"

"I guess I intended to do the same as you!" the man said with a hateful hint of what might have been amusement in his calm voice. "I wanted to wash off some of this travel dust and water my horse, that's all." He grinned. "And if you're afraid I might rape you, don't worry! I don't waste my time raping little girls," he added contemptuously.

To her horror, he slid from his saddle and began to approach her.

"Don't you *dare* come any closer!" Laura blurted out, glaring at him.

He was taller standing up than he had appeared at first, as tall as her father. And he did look dangerous—even more so now that he was closer to her.

"Listen, little one," he said, pulling the hat off his head and dusting it off against his knee. "Either we can share this water, or *you,* since you've already had your bath, can run home to your mother. *Comprende?*"

"Oh!" Laura gasped, outraged.

She should have choked back her fury, Laura would think later. She should have asked him to at least turn his back while she put on her clothes. Then she would have been able to get her gun. Instead, foolishly, she called him a filthy *gringo* pig—and made a grab for her gun. She actually reached it, grasping it just before a dusty, booted foot almost paralyzed her wrists, forcing her to drop it. Then she found herself harshly hauled up and out of the stream.

"Listen, *muchacha,* I don't like little girls who try to pull dirty little tricks on me!"

He shook her by the shoulders, and Laura was beside herself with fury—throwing caution to the winds.

"Bastardo! Cuchano! Hijo de putana! Let me go! Let me go at once, or you'll be very sorry, I promise you! You'll be *killed—I* will kill you, I'll—"

"So, you have the vocabulary of a *puta* and the temperament of a *loco* she-wolf! And you speak English too," Trent said, reverting to English as well. "That's quite a nice gun you wanted to use on me—and quite a horse you're riding! You steal them—or did some rich *hacendado's* son make you a gift in return for your favors? Now, are you over your temper tantrum yet, little *puta?* Can I release you safely?"

*"Bastardo—*I'm going to kill you!" Laura twisted in his grip, almost getting free as she brought a knee up. But he evaded her easily, with a cruel bark of laughter.

"Some men like your kind of bitch—I *don't!"*

Speechless with fury, almost mindless, Laura got one hand free long enough to try to rake at his face, but her hands only tangled in the thick growth of his beard, and she hated, *hated* his caustic laugh.

"A wildcat, eh? I wonder who knows you're here, all alone. Stop squirming. Look at me, *chica."* He tightened his hold on her wrists until she had to bite back a cry of pain, forcing herself to look upward into his eyes . . . storm-gray . . . icy-silver eyes of a fiend; especially in contrast to his sun-blackened skin and black hair that was as long and as shaggy as his beard.

Laura hung in his grip, gasping for breath, frozen for seconds by those silver-shielded merciless eyes. "Are you going to be sensible and run along while I take a bath now? I don't intend to be long."

"Give me my gun!" Laura said in a choked voice.

"I don't think so, sweetheart. I don't trust you. And I really do want a bath. Either you leave quietly or I'll gag and tether you to a tree until I'm through. Which is it going to be? And don't try my temper again. No more tricks."

She continued to look up into his bearded face, but said nothing. He had been holding her wrists behind her. Now, he loosened his hold slightly, and Laura freed one wrist and slapped him as hard as she could, cursing him and all his ancestors, using words and expressions she could not recall *hearing,* let alone remembering well enough to utter.

"Damn you for a persistent foul-mouthed bitch!" he swore at her, before he sent her sprawling onto her back on the slippery grass, holding her down with his body, her wrists pinioned above her head while his arsenal of weapons dug painfully into her soft flesh. "Is this what you want?"

Hardly believing that this horror could be happening to her, Laura felt her breasts being freed from their damp captivity while she tried to struggle against the inexorable weight of him. He flicked his fingers casually and smartingly over her nipples before he moved his hand downward to the vee between her thighs, merely brushing along and over her flesh before, contemptuously, he cut off her anguished protests with his mouth—kissing her cruelly, kissing her without feeling, kissing painfully and hatefully until she could hardly breathe. Then, at last, he released her and stood over her.

"Listen, *chica,* if I had the time or inclination, I'd give you a try. But right now I have neither! That was just a little show of what I could do to you if you don't behave!" Without giving her a chance to catch her breath, he bent over her the next moment, ripping what remained of her chemise from her body and flinging it aside.

"As I warned you before . . ."

She did not quite realize, at first, what he meant to do with her.

He tethered her to a tree, gagging her first with his grimy neckerchief, and fastening her wrists behind her with his belt.

"Close your eyes if you don't want to look, *chiquita,*" he said as he stripped off his clothes.

He took his time washing himself, the bastard, Laura thought furiously, her eyes tear-filled with pure frustration and rage. She didn't *want* to look at him, at his ugly male nakedness, animal that he was, ugly, uncouth animal! And yet, in spite of herself and her fury, she couldn't help sneaking curious glances at him, *all* of him.

Ah! Disgusting! Horrible! Men were disgusting, with their predatory bestial instincts! He was big—*it* was almost frighteningly large. She never wanted such a mindless *thing* to invade her. And he had thought that *it* was all she wanted—that big, clumsy, ugly thing that men carried between their legs and were so inordinately proud of for some silly reason.

While she was forced to wait, seething, he turned his back on her to face the sun and began to dry himself with *her* skirt, shaking his head like an animal to dry his hair.

"Ah! Feels good!" he pronounced, stretching unselfconsciously before he began to dress with cleaner clothes produced from his saddlebags. A faded blue shirt, an equally faded pair of trousers that fit him far too tightly. He shrugged on the same leather vest he had worn earlier, and then rinsed out the clothes he had been wearing, tying them to the pommel of his saddle where they would dry as he traveled on. Then he put on a fresh pair of socks and his boots. He didn't wear spurs; she had noticed that irrelevantly. What kind of man was he? *Who* was he? And when, if ever, would he set her free? If he chose to, that was.

Laura's eyes spat hatred and defiance at him when at last he walked over to look down at her thoughtfully, reminding her all too painfully of her nakedness and her helplessness.

"Well, washing up sure helped. In some ways, I'm sorry

I can't stick around longer, little wildcat!'' She flinched when his fingers brushed over her nipples again.

Was he going to *leave* her here like this, and just ride on?

The thought seared through Laura's mind, making her begin to struggle to get free.

He had mounted his horse already! He . . . and then he leaned down to her and she saw the knife flash in a sun-ray as he cut her loose.

''You shall keep your horse, *muchacha*. As for the gun, I'll take it for now. You may ask for it, if it's yours, at the *estancia* of Don Esteban Alvarado. *Adiós!*''

Laura's fingers, her whole body, shook so hard from reaction that it took what seemed to her like *ages* until she could free herself of the gag in her mouth.

Had she actually *heard* what he had said, or had she imagined it?

She dressed rapidly, and mounted Amigo, heading toward Anita's. She could not go home yet, could never tell her friend what happened, but she needed her soothing presence as she tried to quiet her mind, her whirling confusion of thoughts.

No—no! It couldn't be *him*—the very man she had been *dreading* to meet, had run away from!

Even her autocratic great-grandfather would never have wanted to arrange a match for her with such a low, unscrupulous scoundrel!

And how Franço would laugh and tease her unmercifully, if she dared to tell him!

No, she'd only succeed in embarrassing herself by recounting her utter humiliation at the hands of that *villain,* that rude, lecherous . . . Ah—it was not to be borne! The memory of how he had treated her, his words, the way he had handled her and made her submit to his hurtful kisses that left her lips still bruised and swollen, was intolerable.

She didn't want to think about it—to remember, *ever!* She didn't want to wonder, in some secret, *terrible* part of her mind what might have happened if . . . if . . .

Laura felt her body tremble—both with revulsion and shame at herself. What was wrong with her? Why did her breasts still tingle as if he were touching them? Why had she let him kiss her so long instead of sinking her teeth into his hard lips that had mocked her before they'd taken hers? Why couldn't she forget what he had looked like naked?

Chapter 3

Trent Challenger was in a black glowering mood when he rode on toward his destination for the night.

That wild little gypsy bitch had made him wary now, just in case she really *had* meant all her threats. He wasn't in the mood to defend himself from a vengeful father and brothers, especially when he hadn't even taken the wench, even when he'd thought he'd sensed a sudden yielding in her there, just before he'd let her go.

Damn her! He didn't know why he was wasting his thoughts on her when he had too many other things to be concerned with.

This ridiculous notion hatched up between his grandfather and Don Francisco Alvarado, for instance. Two old men sitting together smoking their cigars and planning the lives of their descendants. Attempting to *marry* them off when they hadn't even met each other—and never would, if *he* could help it.

But the American Vice-Consul in Mexico City, Mr. Reynolds, had been quite insistent that Trent, and no one else, should carry certain information to Mr. Morgan. After all, Mr. Challenger had an *excellent* excuse for visiting the Hacienda de la Nostalgia, didn't he? Even President Díaz wouldn't question why he would go there before he headed for California again. Damn archaic customs— and damn the ageless Mr. Jim Bishop who sat in the center like a gray spider spinning endless webs of intrigue. Mr.

Bishop knew everyone's weaknesses, it seemed, and used that knowledge for his purposes.

Even his visit to the *rancho* in California—to "settle matters of the family estates"—was part of one of Mr. Bishop's plans, no doubt! What else did Bishop have cooked up?

While Trent Challenger continued to ride with his bitter thoughts and memories for company, Francisco Alvarado Morgan decided reluctantly that it was time to let his lovely Mariella return home, just as he had to do to meet his parents' guest. And, as he had teased his sister only yesterday, his prospective brother-in-law.

In spite of his reluctance to leave their private hiding place and his desire to stay longer—just touching his woman's soft skin and feeling her ready response to him aroused him—he knew *he* must be the one to tear himself away. *She* would have stayed with him all night—given him anything and everything he asked of her out of love for him.

"*Mi corazón*—we must go now before your uncle and aunt become angry with you." Stretching his muscles, Franco came to his feet, bringing her yielding softness with him, and for a moment held her as tightly and closely to him as if he never meant to let her go.

"*Yo te amo, mi Mariella!*" he whispered fiercely before his lips covered hers. "Never forget it, little one—no matter *what*. You understand?"

"*Sí, amor.* Oh Franco, yes—I understand so many things, sometimes too many things for my own heart's sake. But I could no more *not* love you than to tell myself to stop breathing!"

"Come then, I'll see you home," he said gently, wanting her to smile again. And then, to lighten the moment, he teased her. "Shall I tell your uncle that you and I have been discussing my sister's impending wedding? I'll say that you must be one of her bridesmaids!"

"Franco, please, no! Don't tease about it so. *Ay*, poor Laura—how she must hate the thought! He's probably an old man—rich, perhaps, but old and ugly! Please, for me, don't tease her any more and make her angry enough to do something reckless!''

Franco burst out laughing. ''Old and ugly! In that case, poor man! Laura doesn't need provocation to go into one of her famous rages, as you know! Do you think she'll shoot him—or knife him? Will you wager me a kiss on the outcome?''

''Leave me here, please, Franco. It's close enough, and I don't want them thinking . . .'' Mariella blushed under his look and his quizzically lifted eyebrow before bursting out: *''Please . . .* or it will be more difficult for me to slip away to meet you again.''

He kissed her hard and long and passionately before letting her slide from the horse along the length of his body that gave telltale evidence of his desire for her.

''The 'again'—will it be tomorrow, then? If not, I will come looking for you, *chiquita,* and I will carry you off under the scandalized eyes of your aunt and uncle and everyone else!''

The girl clung fiercely to him for an instant before pulling away and forcing a smile. ''Yes, *amor, mañana.* Tomorrow, God willing!''

And then she turned and ran away from him without looking back again—down the narrow path that led between trees and brush to the hollow where the small village nested.

Franco was already well on his way home when he heard that first frantic scream and distant shots. Then another scream that sounded suddenly choked off.

Mariella? God! He wheeled his horse around, freeing his gun from its holster in the same motion, and rode back up the narrow trail until he reached the top of the slope. There was Mariella, still screaming, twisting and turning in the grasp of two men in the uniform of the *Rurales,* their jackets open to the waist, their caps askew. They had ripped part of her blouse away and were playing with her like cats with a terrified, helpless mouse. His father came out in him suddenly, something almost primitive and primeval. He screamed like an Indian warrior as he sent his horse down the slope, firing as he went. One of the men went down; the other he clubbed with the butt of his revolver before, still in motion, he leaned down to scoop Mariella up and sling her body across his saddle.

"Here, Franco—here!" He heard his sister's voice scream to him and rode toward it, toward the house of her friends and his the Velásquez family.

There were shots following him, and he would have stopped to fire back, if not for Mariella. A door to one of the adobe buildings swung open and he rode straight inside; then the door was swiftly closed and barred behind him. Franco slid off his horse, carrying the hysterically sobbing, shaking girl in his arms.

"Look after her, Laura. I'm going back out, I'm going to kill those—"

"No! Franco, no! We need you here! For God's sake—there are too many of them. Drunk, off-duty *Rurales,* dirty pigs! The bastards—looking for some fun and plunder!"

As Laura held tightly onto his arm Franco felt some of the red mist before his eyes melt away, leaving room for sanity.

The women of the Velásquez family had Mariella now. They were whispering to her, trying to soothe her and stop her hysterical sobbing. One of them brought a *rebozo* to cover her exposed breasts.

The men, serious and hard-faced, had few enough weapons—and those old-fashioned.

"That's what I *meant,* Franco!" Laura said. He wrenched his gaze away from Mariella to look into his sister's direct, unfrightened eyes that were as hard as sapphires with fury and frustration.

"We don't have enough weapons here," Laura said now. "And I don't know how much longer we can hold them off. But the walls are thick and we have our wits—and knives and machetes when our bullets run out. Do you have a cartridge belt? A rifle?"

He had been in such a hurry to leave this morning . . . Damn it to hell!

Laura seemed to read his mind and her mouth twisted in a curious grimace.

"*I* have no gun, Franco." *Never* would she admit to him how she had lost it!

"And *I've* only the bullets in my gunbelt and a few left in my gun." He frowned, looking at Laura and *seeing* her suddenly, and noticed that her arm was bandaged. "What happened?"

"It's nothing. A scratch that has been tended to. I sent Juanito with Amigo to the hacienda for help. All we have to do is use our heads and hold out until help can get here."

Franco could take charge now, thank God! Men *did* have their uses sometimes . . .

"Make every shot count—and don't shoot at shadows or hats balanced on sticks!" Franco instructed, and the other men, even though most of them were much older, listened to Don Esteban's son with respect.

Laura's arm throbbed each time she moved it, but she pushed the pain away, concentrating on anger. In running away from one kind of danger, she had come face to face with another. In a way, though, she was glad she had been here to help when those drunken brutes had come skulking down the road. The *Rurales! El Presidente*'s chosen law enforcers who were even worse than the *bandidos* and outlaws they were supposed to catch, especially when they came upon a small, unprotected village such as this.

There was a new volley of shots from outside, then drunken shouts and challenges. Franco went to a slit in the thick walls, and fired twice before twisting away.

"How many?" Laura asked.

"One, at least. I think I wounded the other badly enough to put him out of the fray for some time."

"You were very brave today, *amiga*," Anita whispered to Laura. They had known each other since childhood and no longer stood on ceremony with each other. A pretty,

flashing-eyed girl of about Laura's age, Anita had more
suitors than she could count, but she had always had her
eyes on Franco, who treated her as casually as if she were
another sister. Anita did not like Mariella but she took
pains not to show it. Someday, she planned, Franco would
notice *her!* She had made so many novenas already, and
she had been taking schooling too. Book lessons, from
Don Renaldo Ortega, and from her friend Doña Laura
Luisa, who insisted she was only to be called Luisa by
her.

"I wasn't brave at all, I just couldn't let them find out
I was afraid!" Laura confessed.

They were both thinking, as they turned to look at each
other and touch hands, of that horrifying moment when
they had looked up from getting water at the big stone
cistern to see two men on horses looking down at them.
Grinning—and obviously very drunk.

"Two lovely *señoritas!* What do you say, Pedro? One
for each of us! And they're both pretty, so we're in luck,
aren't we? To find such beauties before the others? A good
thing we rode ahead, now we have the pick—eh, *amigo?*
Heh heh!"

"Here—have a drink—come and take it!" The second
man, loutish, flat-featured, wore the uniform jacket of the
Rurales, and no undershirt. The jacket was unbuttoned to
show an expanse of hairy chest and a dirt-encrusted navel.

"Look, they're surprised, the little *muchachas!* Didn't
expect to see any real men around here, did you? Maybe
we can teach you girls a thing or two!"

Anita had been petrified, unable to utter a word or sound
as her throat seemed to have become paralyzed with fear.

It was Laura, recovering herself and sizing up the mood
of these men, who put herself forward, deliberately swinging her hips and widening her eyes before she fluttered her
lashes in a parody of flirtation.

"You must forgive us poor village girls, handsome *cap-
itanos!*" she said in Spanish. "After all, we're not used
to such—such bold speech! But tell me—"and she smiled

up at the larger one of the two, the one who had spoken first—"why don't you get off your horses and explain what you meant? I don't know about my shy little friend, but *I'm* willing to listen!"

"Aha! A real wild one! And look at those eyes! Bet she doesn't know who her papa was!"

"Well, seems she wouldn't mind being entertained. Want a drink, *muchacha?*"

"Sure, why not? Would you like me to dance for you? My friend plays the guitar. Anita, *por favor,* go get the guitar and hurry back—I don't think these macho *hombres* like to be kept waiting too long." She smiled beguilingly, acting by instinct for survival.

"Come!" she teased, "or have you two strong men suddenly become shy in front of a real woman?" She shrugged, moved back, and kicked Anita in the ankle, waking the girl from her trance.

"Maybe you're afraid that you are not enough to please me?"

"Afraid? Hell, no!"

"Listen to the little *puta! Dios*—she's challenging us!"

"She's hungry for real men. Isn't that it, *chica?*"

"Maybe! A drink, and then when my friend brings her guitar I'll show you how I can dance, eh? Can you take that?"

"She's a real live one! Hey, you! Go bring that guitar. We want to see her dance—see *both* of you dance."

"Yes, hurry, Anita!" Laura said quickly, before she turned to the men with an apologetic smile. "She is a little shy; she hasn't been to the city like I have. But she'll soon prove as entertaining as *I* can be, especially if you're generous enough with your liquor! I can promise you, *señores*—you won't be disappointed!"

Anita left, running on bare feet, not daring to look over her shoulder. Her heart had been pounding so hard she thought she might faint before she got home.

And Luisa—she didn't dare think what might happen to her friend, who had talked so boldly and casually to those two horrible men, holding them off with teasing words and promises. But for how long? And what if . . . ? Anita hadn't wanted to think.

Laura, her mind sharp, continued to taunt and tease. She drank from their wineskins that were filled with pulque—and managed not to choke. And she managed to hold them at bay while they circled around her, leering like dogs after a bitch, until she pretended she would choose one first—the *most* man—before she took the other.

"Show me—yes, show me, *hombres! I* shall be the judge of who is the biggest and the best, *sí?*"

Grinning now, they had begun to unbutton their dirty, dust-grimed pants, asking her to touch, to weigh the quality of what she would be getting soon.

"Ah, I can see it will be hard to choose between you! But wouldn't *you* like, also, to see what you will be getting from *me,* eh? Are you ready?" Laura instinctively *knew* how she must act, what she must do now.

Backing off a few steps, telling them to stay just like that . . . drop those pants down a little farther, *then* she could judge!

She wished she still had her gun, but at least she had the knife. It was in its sheath, snuggled close against her thigh with a soft leather garter—a gift from her mother.

Laura shook her wild hair loose and began, very slowly, to do a dance step without music—lifting her skirt higher, inch by slow inch, until those brutish men were panting and slavering with desire. As she heard hoofbeats—and heard Anita calling to her, Laura quite suddenly turned from teasing coquette into vicious wildcat. She hoisted her skirt up to her thighs, hooking it into the waistband with one hand while the other found the knife.

"And *this* is what you will have from me—*animales*—and *this*—and this!"

Instinct—primitive . . . she had done everything, played her role almost unthinkingly and had killed and maimed for the first time in her life. It was over—she didn't know, could hardly remember afterward what she had done or *how* she had done it. But there was blood dripping from the knife she continued to cling to as she whirled and began to run toward the white adobe hut—to Anita—to join the men who had started to run out before the gunshots exploded. Laura screamed, finding her voice again: "Go back! Go back! There are more of them coming!"

A bullet had grazed her arm just before she reached the shelter of an open door and fell inside into cool darkness contrasting with the brassy glare of the sun outside.

Chapter 4

The drumming of hoofbeats behind him alerted him to possible danger.

Trent reined in and brought his rifle out of its scabbard, holding it against his thigh while he waited for whoever it was to catch up with him.

First, he recognized the golden chestnut with a white blaze on its forehead. *Her?* But it wasn't the gypsy girl riding her big stallion, it was a little boy—not older than seven or eight by the size of him.

"*Hola, muchacho!* Stop!"

"No, no, I must go to *Señor* Alvarado, to *El Padrón*. I cannot stop, I promised—"

"Damn!" Trent suddenly grabbed the reins from the boy, and rode alongside, slowing the stallion's headlong gallop as he spoke in quick, idiomatic mestizo Spanish. "I'm a friend of *Señor* Esteban, so hold on! What in the hell's wrong? And where did you get that horse?"

"It is Doña Luisa's—she sent me with Amigo for help because I am the only one who can ride him!" Unconsciously, in spite of his obvious fear and impatience, a note of pride had crept into the boy's voice, before panic took over again. "Ah, *señor*, there are *many* of them— dirty, drunk *Rurales!* They tried to—they caught my sister and if not for the Doña Luisa—Let me go, *señor!* I promised I would bring help!"

"*Callate*—shut up! Be a man, if you can! Now, you see these guns, these *pistoles?* I can stop the *Rurales* with

40

them until you bring help, but you must show me first where they are and how to get there without them seeing me. *Comprende?* Now—*adelante!* Let's go! And when we get close, then we go slow and quiet. No noise to warn them, eh?''

''The village, it is not too far away, *señor,* and I know a way to get there very quickly. There are many trees and big boulders lying about. They will not see you. *We* did not see *them* until—'' The boy caught his breath quickly before he rushed on. ''Don Franco, who likes Mariella, is there also; the son of Don Esteban, you understand? But you will know that if you know Don Esteban. Ah—*he* would cut those pigs up into little pieces, Don Esteban would—and feed the pieces to the buzzards!''

''I'm sure he would,'' Trent drawled, the thought of battle, of strategy, already singing in his veins, to dispel his earlier tiredness and the black emptiness of his mood.

So, *she* was his supposed-to-be-*novia,* was she? And up to her neck in trouble.

A hard, somewhat cynical smile twisted Trent's mouth for an instant.

Imagine her surprise. At least *he* was now forewarned.

Trent made the frightened boy, whose name, he had ascertained, was Juanito, draw him, in the dust, a rough boundary map of the little hamlet.

''There is only one good road, *señor—here.* There we have cut down some of the trees so that we can take the *carretas* to the market every week. *They* came from there.''

''No other way to get in?''

''Oh, yes! The way I came out! There are very narrow footpaths that only *our* people know of. That is how I led Amigo away without being noticed. He was not by the huts, for Doña Luisa always keeps him in the shade of the trees, farther up, where there is good grass and feed for him. And water too; a small trickle runs through there to the stream where the women wash clothes.''

The boy looked at the big *gringo*'s face—as brown as

his under his dark beard, and as hard as the rock-carved faces of the ancient God-people sometimes found in deep caves. He crossed himself swiftly, as a dart of sunlight through the thickly twined branches made those strange mirror-eyes look red, like fire.

Perhaps he was a devil spirit, this *hombre*—appearing out of the dust, from nowhere it seemed! Still, Juanito felt that *this* devil spirit was on *their* side.

"All right, *muchacho*, you did well! And now, remember what I told you, eh? Walk Amigo until you're out of earshot, hear? After that, ride like hell! And tell Don Esteban that—Oh hell! Tell him Doña Luisa's *novio* is taking care of matters. Now—*get!*"

Ignoring the boy's gaping, wide-eyed look, Trent waved him away harshly and started snaking forward, on his belly at first, until he discerned it was easier to ease through the brush standing up.

He could hear shouts from below, drunken, ribald threats, and sporadic shots.

He took his time, being very careful, until he'd arrived at a place where he could see down. There was no need to worry about being seen because no one was paying any attention. There were a few bodies scattered about—*Rurales* or defenders, he couldn't tell which. But he could see some men hiding, crouched behind a rough wall, who were firing on two of the more strongly built cottages that were huddled close together, perhaps belonging to one family.

There were *Rurales* out in the open or behind stone cisterns, he noticed. They had repeating rifles and pistols, but not the newer-model Winchesters or Colts. This was not very different from the desert warfare he'd become used to in Algeria or Tripoli during his short stint in the Foreign Legion, thanks to Mr. Bishop; or before that in the badlands of New Mexico and Arizona, where he'd built up his reputation as a fast gun for hire—when *he* chose to hire himself out.

Trent's lips drew back from his teeth, like a panther

sensing its kill, as he looked down the barrel of his rifle—and waited. The *Rurale* coyotes were closing in for the kill now, ringing the small, enfortressed houses, laughing and commenting on the fact that the shots from the defenders within were growing fewer and further between.

They advanced closer then, these beast-men—and ever more boldly into the open, becoming more confident now. The sounds of their laughter and their voices drifted upward—the bets they were taking with each other as to which one would take the most women and what they would do with them, especially the bold *ramera* with the eyes of her *gringo* father. Ah, *that* one who had killed one of their friends . . . *that* one was for taming and then using before she was sold into a place where she would be made to service every man who paid a few pesos; and in any way a man desired.

The man who had been talking the most and laughing the loudest had no chance to finish his string of obscenities.

The first shot from Trent's Winchester lifted him off his feet and sent him sprawling, shot through the spine, jerking about like a headless chicken on the dusty earth while he screamed in agony. And almost before his body had hit the dust another man fell sprawling with his head blown off. And the next—and the next . . .

Like the shadow of Nemesis, coldly and systematically the Winchester took them all as Trent moved from one vantage point to another. The few men who tried to shoot back could not see who or what they were shooting at. An *army,* perhaps?

They did not have time to wonder for long before they died—one by one—and without pause it seemed—as Trent changed rifles and kept on shooting, never missing.

One man, drunker than the others, staggered belatedly out of a small hut at the opposite end of the village where he had been enjoying *mas pulque* and a young girl he had clubbed into near-unconsciousness, obviously not under-

standing what had been happening in the space of a few
minutes.

"What is this, eh? Aren't you finished with the miserable peons yet, *amigos?*"

As he stood weaving, his pantalones still gaping open
in front, Trent shot him right *there;* and smiled a wolf-
smile at the man's agonized screams.

Inside one of the two small buildings whose thick walls
and adobe roof had kept them safe from bullets and fire
torches, Laura and Franco looked at each other without
quite comprehending for a few moments that it was over
so fast and so suddenly—the nightmare they had almost
thought they might never wake up from.

After the last shot—except for the screams and moans
from the men who had been deliberately shot to maim
instead of to kill—there seemed to be a strange kind of
suspended pause that hung in the air for some moments,
hung in the minds of all those who had clustered in the
two safest places—the two houses of the same family, con-
nected by underground cellars.

"Is it Papa? But so soon, Franco?"

"Quiet! I don't know! But who else could it be?"

A voice hailed them from above.

"Don't fire—if you've got any shots left! I think I got
all of them. *Hola*—you in there?"

His rifle was still smoking, Laura noticed stupidly. He—
The black-bearded *devil!* She stood at the window to which
she had rushed, and felt suddenly dizzy and incapable of
speech. Vaguely she heard Franco call out cautiously.

"Who are you, and—"

"You Franco? Steve's son? I'm Trent Challenger—and
I was on my way to see your father when I ran into a kid
on a big horse who told me what was going on here. You
going to come out now or what?"

"I'm sorry!" Franco turned to speak swiftly to the men
inside before he unbolted the door and stepped outside,
smiling with relief.

Laura stayed where she was, frozen to the narrow windowsill by her elbow.

Him! she thought. And now we owe our lives to him! I don't want to feel any obligation toward him. I despise his kind of man—and him worst of all! He behaved no better than those filthy *Rurales* earlier . . . only I wasn't carrying my knife then. Damn it! He's the last man on earth I want to be beholden to!

"Laura! Laura! Come on out, sister. What's the matter with you? There's someone here you'll want to meet."

Anita nudged her arm gently.

"Luisa! What is wrong with you? Your brother is calling for you to meet this handsome, oh so dangerous-looking man—a tall *gringo* who killed *all* of them by himself! Come! Or is the wound making you faint? Shall I—"

Cutting off her friend's suddenly anxious words with a look, Laura stiffened her back, sucking in a deep breath.

"I'm fine! I was just thinking . . ."

"Well, you mustn't think too much about bad things that are finished with now! Do go outside, Luisa!"

Soon enough, Laura was to wish she had stayed indoors, pretending to be faint from loss of blood—anything she could think of not to have to face him. But she had been *forced* to—and then, to make matters much worse, he had insisted that she must ride before him on *his* horse— to give them a chance to get acquainted before all the formalities got in the way, he'd said—damn his devious mind!

Laura was furious, as her brother was very well aware; but out of devilment and a sense of curiosity that persisted whenever he caught the clashing glances they exchanged, Franco, too, had added his insistence that his sister must ride on ahead to the house with Trent to explain everything to their parents. And of course, Laura thought resentfully, if she made an issue of refusing she would not only appear rude to the man who had saved their skins, but look foolish as well. It might seem as if she were *afraid* of him, the bastard! Why did it have to be *he* of all people who had come to their rescue?

She sat stiffly in the saddle, hating the touch and heat of his body against hers. What would he have to say to her *now?* They had pretended to be strangers to each other in front of everyone else, which had suited her very well, but why, then, had he insisted on having her ride with him?

She would have much preferred to ride with Franco, but *he* was too busy comforting his still-sobbing Mariella, and he had waved them on, saying he'd join them in time for dinner.

How *could* Franco have been so impervious to her speaking looks and warning frowns? But no—pretending he didn't notice anything, Franco had told her, with a hint of devilry lurking behind his hazel eyes, to go ahead and show Trent the way to the *estancia,* where she should get her arm seen to as soon as possible. "Your first battle souvenir, sister! Mama will be proud of you!"

"Yes, and Papa will be angry that we were both so ill-prepared!" Laura said sourly before she was forced to accept Trent Challenger's hard hands holding her around her waist as he lifted her up before him onto his saddle.

She felt—she wasn't certain exactly how she felt, Laura thought, stiffness freezing her spine, and keeping it stiff.

A few hours earlier he had treated her like a cheap trollop—and she had *longed* to kill him. Now he was responsible for saving her life and she was forced to be polite to him as well as be much too close to him, his arms on either side of her.

"I'm sure glad you ride astride. I can't understand why most women tolerate those sidesaddles."

"Perhaps as a test of *real* horsemanship! Could *you* control a horse sidesaddle, Mr. Challenger? Or jump fences?"

"Probably not!" She could almost *feel* him grin, could picture the amused curve of his hard lips in the bearded face. "I never had to try, though. By the way, your gun?

You should be careful with guns, Miss Laura. Especially when you're taking a bath outdoors. Instead of a dirty *gringo* drifter, those *Rurales* could've surprised you.''

"You're really insufferable, aren't you? You behaved like an utter, despicable . . . well, *you* should know what you are! And you can believe that if you hadn't done what you did for us, I would kill you myself—just like I killed those two filthy *Rurales* pigs who wanted to—wanted me to . . . Oh, *damn!*''

Hating her weakness, Laura was sniffing back tears of rage and frustration when a sudden motion of the horse jarred her against him and sent a sharp pain shooting all the way up her arm. "Oh!" she said on a sharp intake of breath, only to become suddenly and uncomfortably aware that he was leaning his bearded cheek far too close to hers.

"Your arm?" he said curtly. "How bad is it? And what did they put on the wound?''

"It's only a . . . a *scratch!* It bled a little, and we bandaged it up, that's all! There was no time for anything else, and anyway it doesn't really hurt too much!''

He touched the makeshift bandage, where blood had seeped through, and without conscious volition, Laura gasped again.

The next moment she fell against him as he reined his horse to a stop.

"Here, hold still. How much pain can you bear? I have to take the damn bandage off, so hang on to the saddle as hard as you can, and keep that arm up, hear?''

"What on earth do you think you're *doing?*'' What— Oh! That *hurt!*''

How had she suddenly found herself lifted off the saddle, one-armed, and deposited onto her feet? And now, he was . . .

"You're not a doctor! Leave my arm alone—they'll take care of it back home, I tell you! Oh!''

"Grit your teeth. This'll sting a while, but it'll stop blood poisoning. *That* would hurt much worse, I can tell you!''

The bandage, sticky with dried blood, was almost impossible to remove without causing her wound to bleed again. He poured some colorless fluid over it out of a bottle he had produced from one of his saddlebags.

And it *hurt*—it was raw agony for an instant, sending tears springing into her eyes and eliciting a sharp moan from between her lips even if she did clamp her teeth together as he'd advised.

Laura felt her head spin as she fought to keep from humiliating herself even further by fainting into his arms. She was almost relieved at being held up on her feet firmly by an arm clasped about her waist; and then, as the searing pain began to ebb, she felt a bottle being held against her pain-whitened lips. "Here, take a good swig. It'll help."

Still slightly dazed, Laura swallowed obediently and without thinking. The next thing she knew she was sputtering and choking and quite unable to talk, much less protest, before he had her up in the saddle again.

Chapter 5

Laura had insisted that she wear her black silk Lenten gown with the high neck frilled with white lace and long sleeves buttoned up to the elbow, matching white lace trimming at the wrists, to dinner that night.

"But—but it is *not* a gown for a young lady to wear to meet her *novio!*" Filomena had protested in vain.

"He is *not* my *novio,* and I *have* met him already—have you forgotten?"

"Ah, *que vergüenza*—in those disgraceful rags you were wearing, it's a wonder he's still staying on here for dinner!"

"He's here to meet my father, they have business to discuss. And *I* am going to dinner because I don't want anyone to think that a slight loss of blood puts me to bed! Please, Filomena, do not argue with me now!"

"I think your wound has made you light-headed!" Filomena grumbled. "But very well—I'll fetch the ugly black gown, after I have pressed it. Now rest for a few minutes. Drink that herb tea I brewed for you myself—it will make you feel better."

Once Filomena's grumbling soliloquy had receded into silence down the passageway, Laura sat down on her bed with a sigh, studying her freshly bandaged arm.

"Filomena? How is she?"

"We put the special ointment on the wound, Doña Genia. It is not as bad as some I've seen in my day, but—

Ay! Why didn't I stay awake and watch her? Why? I should have known she was up to some mischief when she let me put her in corsets! *Ay!*"

"It's not *your* fault," Ginny said, firmly patting the old woman on the shoulder. "My daughter is as stubborn and self-willed as both her father and I put together! Is she sleeping?"

"Sleeping? No! No, she will not sleep, she says. She will not drink my soothing syrup that will put her to sleep. No, she will go to dinner, she says. And she says also that she will wear her black silk gown—the one with the high neck and the long sleeves—to hide the bandage, she said. And *no* corset!" Filomena's lower lip stuck out and she placed her hand over her heart as if struck. "Not even a corset, Doña Genia! And she told me, 'He is not my *novio* and never will be!' *Ay*, Doña Genia, what can we do?"

Ginny sighed before she said crisply, "Nothing! Bring the dress she wanted, Filomena, and I will go in and talk to her." She shrugged philosophically, and gave the older woman a smile. "She's young and adventurous, and impulsive. But in the end, I'm afraid, and in *her* time, I expect she'll learn."

But not before she's explored—and experienced, and has been hurt—like me! Ginny thought suddenly, pausing for a moment to collect her thoughts after Filomena had waddled off. She remembered herself as she had been at Laura's age: brushed with a veneer of sophistication and daring; wanting to try everything, experience everything, *have* everything that life could offer.

She hadn't bargained on the unexpected, or on Steve—who would change her, and her life forever. Steve—her husband and her lover. Her *friend* and confidant, at last, after all the years of misunderstanding and loss.

Ginny remembered meeting Trent Challenger before; years ago it seemed. He had been young and very intense, and had shown signs of an obvious *tendre* for her, which she had circumvented by treating him like a son—or a favorite cousin, perhaps.

But now—this man who had ridden up to the *hacienda* bearing her daughter before him on his saddle like a prize— this was a *man*, not a youth. A hard, battle-toughened man who reminded her almost too much of Steve when she had first encountered him. One of Jim Bishop's men. And definitely the wrong man for Laura; at least, until Laura was ready for his kind of man; the kind who could turn a woman inside out—make her feel, make her want, and destroy her through her own weakness for him if she let him—or if she didn't fight him back with her own weapons.

But there *was* something, though—an undercurrent, a kind of pull between Laura and Trent Challenger that Ginny could sense; had sensed from the very beginning, when Trent had lifted her daughter down off his horse and had set her down so that she faced *him* first.

How well she remembered from her own experience! And how well she understood the power of a strange, forbidden attraction that could overcome common sense and logic and anything anyone could say, or advise.

Ginny's knock was brief before she pushed the door open, to find her daughter studying herself critically in the mirror.

"Mama?" Laura swung around, clad in nothing but a brief chemise, her face flushing slightly as if her secret thoughts had been surprised.

"Yes, me! I've talked to Filomena, and she's pressing your black dress, even if she doesn't approve of its suitability for this occasion."

"Filomena *always* disapproves. Of everything!" Laura said in a brittle voice that made Ginny raise her eyebrows.

"You seem upset, love. Are you *sure* you want to join us for dinner? Your father and Mr. Challenger are probably going to disappear as soon as they can to talk business, and apart from the recounting of today's happenings, it's likely to be a boring evening for *us*, don't you think?"

"Why? I want to ask Papa and Mr. Challenger what they are going to tell President Díaz about the actions of

his *Rurales!* And I'm sure Franco will want to know what
will be done about such outrages too! Mama, they were
. . . they—I kept thinking, you know, of what *you* might
have done. I stayed with them, those two men, smiling at
them while I pretended . . . And then . . . and then, when
they had . . . when they thought that I—I was *seeing* them,
their grossness . . . then I lifted up my skirt—a little bit
at a time, *teasing* them, you understand, Mama? Before
my fingers reached the knife you gave me—and I killed
them, I think—no, I'm sure of it. Both of them. Very fast.
God—I *killed!* I talked . . . I teased . . . I became someone else . . . acting—and then the acting was over and I
had to . . . to—''

"Sweetheart, I know! I *know!* I've done the same.''
Ginny caught her daughter, who was as tall as she—perhaps slightly taller—in her arms, holding her closely and
fiercely as her mind went back in time.

"I've killed too. A man who—I cannot bear to think
about that time even now, my love. Even now when I
know I'm safe from him. I stabbed him in the throat—
I heard his accursed lifeblood gurgling through the gash I
had made before I ran—'' Abruptly, Ginny brought her
mind back to the present, and her white-faced daughter
who was staring at her as if she'd never known her before.

"Laura, I thought I had managed to forget that part of
my life, but memories are always there! So you killed two
beasts—and you playacted to protect yourself and your
friend because you *had* to. I'm proud of you!''

In the closed circle of her mother's arms, Laura sobbed
for a few minutes like a child before she forced control
upon herself and said: "I don't regret it. Not anymore. I
kept thinking—this is what my mother would do. I kept
pretending that I was *you*, Mama—so beautiful and so
sure. But I guess *you* weren't either, not at *that* time.''

"No one's ever sure, until you suddenly *know* what you
must do,'' Ginny said. She moved to the window before
she said over her shoulder, "Laura, I don't mean to pry,
and you don't have to tell me of course. But . . . I did

sense something there between you and Trent Challenger. He reminds me of your father, at his age—in which case, you should take care!"

Laura stiffened at once, and said jerkily: "So you guessed. I hope I wasn't too transparent; *was* I, Mama?" She sighed, suddenly looking down, before she lifted her head and related the whole story of her first meeting with Trent Challenger, sparing neither herself nor him.

"It was . . . it was the most . . . the strangest feeling! He took me for . . . for some cheap little strumpet, of course. And the way he treated me afterward, what he did . . . I *hate* him for it!"

"Well, but the first time I encountered Steve—I'm afraid that is almost exactly what happened then too. I wandered into the wrong room by mistake, and the wretch thought I was the whore he'd ordered for the night from some madam named Mimi!"

"He did? And—?"

"And he made very *strong* advances! Without giving me a chance to say *anything*, of course. He kissed me so brutally that I became speechless and then . . . he slipped the strap of my evening gown off my shoulder—before he demanded that I should undress—*quickly!*"

Laura's eyes widened with something like shock when she heard her mother's soft and secret giggle.

"Mama! And *did* you?"

"Of course not! Not *that* time! I slapped his face first—then I told him off. And just in good time for *me*, I suppose, the female he'd taken *me* for began knocking at the door. It was one of the few times I have ever seen your father at a loss for words—at least for a few minutes."

"It seems to me," Laura said boldly, "that all men are hypocrites as well as lechers—and bullies as well!"

"Well, they're difficult, I admit. And hard to understand, or even to like at first. But, oh Laura, I wish I could tell you I knew the answers! Only, I don't. Not for you—for me, *now*, yes. But it took me so many painful, wasted years to rediscover what I had always known. I think it was the same for him, for your father. We had to lose each other in order to find each other; and, mostly, to *understand* each other!''

Filomena brought in the black dress and left it spread out on the bed after Ginny told her casually that she would help her daughter to dress for dinner.

''She should be resting in bed!'' Filomena said with down-turned lips. ''Going out with such clothes on—not even anything underneath! And getting mixed up in fighting . . . with guns!'' She muttered something else under her breath before she left, banging the door closed behind her.

Ginny and Laura exchanged looks in the mirror before Ginny smiled, arching her brows slightly. *''No* underwear, my love? I hope you aren't planning to be as reckless as *I* was!''

Laura made an impatient movement and averted her eyes before she said, ''Very well! There's more! He—he ripped my chemise down the front so he could . . . well, it's of no consequence *now*—nothing very much happened beyond that. I suppose he was trying to intimidate me, with his display of brute strength!''

''Hmm. Men do have a way of trying to do that!'' Ginny commented thoughtfully, and then added briskly: ''Well, dear, will you really come down to dinner? You're sure it won't be an embarrassment to you both?''

''He wouldn't be embarrassed!'' Laura swung around, her cheeks flamed by anger. ''He expects *me* to be, so that I'd want to hide from him or avoid him, and I will not do so. That hypocrite! I'll show him. And Mama? After dinner, I think I will ask Mr. Challenger to take a turn about the patio with me, so that I can tell him *exactly* what I think of him, and to assure him that never, never, if he was the last man on earth, would I even *think* of being engaged to him! A man with cheap and easy women wherever he goes, probably! Ugh!''

''Good. I think you *should* make matters perfectly clear to Mr. Challenger—just in case he's laboring under any delusions. I'll tell your father that I think you two ought to have some time alone before they start talking business, in order to set things perfectly straight. And now, my love, do come over here and let me help get you into this ridiculously drab gown!'' Ginny's eyes flashed. ''*I* would have wanted to dazzle him with my prettiest and most flamboyant *toilette*—but then, you are not I, and better so, I suppose, for your sake!''

''Damn it, sister! You look as if you're in mourning!''

Franco burst out in a typically tactless brotherly fashion when Laura and Ginny joined the three men at last. Steve Morgan, at the head of the table, merely raised a quizzical eyebrow at his wife, who gave him a bright, warning smile that made him wonder exactly what was going on between Trent Challenger and his daughter. He hadn't missed the nuances or the barely suppressed tension between them. It had served to remind him that Laura, his hoydenish, tomboy daughter, was growing into a woman. Well able to take care of herself, though, he was sure, what with the tutelage she had received from both him and Ginny.

Ginny, in a pale green dress, very simply cut, looked as seductive as always. She was that kind of woman, and thank God, he was beginning at last to believe that she was all *his*.

''We don't dine very formally out here—as I'm sure you've guessed,'' Ginny murmured to their guest while Steve, showing an uncommon degree of politeness, seated her formally.

They ate in the small *sala* tonight—with the doors leading out to the lamplit patio left wide open on a warm night like this. The perfume of flowers drifted in with every gentle puff of the slight breeze that ruffled vine-hung blossoms, distilling their scent as they opened to the orange quarter moon that hung above the trees like an ancient Druid symbol.

Laura kept her thoughts centered on her too well filled plate, concentrating on forcing herself to eat at least some of the hearty meal set before her rather than thinking about romantic, star-filled nights *or* the man who sat across from her.

Trent Challenger's transformed appearance had shocked her when she walked into the room with her mother. He looked clean, and instead of his sweat-stained trail clothes he wore a dark gray cotton shirt and a broadcloth jacket. His neckerchief of dark blue silk could almost have passed for an Ascot silk—and he had actually trimmed his overly long hair and beard, giving him a far different, more civilized look.

But only on the *surface*, Laura recognized after she had caught his glance that took in her whole, black-encased defense at one glance and ripped it away with the silver daggers of his eyes. False! Even his polite smile was false!

Look at her, the little hypocritical bitch! Trent was thinking. All dressed up in black silk from throat to wrists—like a damn schoolmarm. He kept that description in mind, to taunt her with later. Because, as he knew and *she* knew, there *would* be a later. A confrontation, now that they were on equal terms—and a settlement of sorts. After that, they would not, he hoped fervently, ever have to encounter each other again.

Chapter 6

The waning, yellow-gold moon had already dropped from sight behind the trees, leaving only a faint orange-gold glow filtered between gnarled branches and leaves that moved with the light breeze. Tonight the stars seemed twice as large as usual against the dense darkness of a cloudless night sky, and a myriad of fireflies traced tiny, moving light patterns in and out of the flowering vines that clung to the crumbling adobe walls surrounding the patio and held them inexorably together—wrapped around and about by roots and tendrils until walls and vines seemed one.

Laura and Trent had paced the length and circumference of the patio in silence so far, as if this had been a formal *paseo* in some city square.

Dinner was behind them at last. Everyone had been almost unbearably tactful—even Franco. And she had told her mother firmly that she really needed to have a talk with Mr. Challenger in order to set things straight. But why, Laura wondered almost desperately now, couldn't *he* speak first? Had he no manners and no aptitude for making polite conversation? She halted abruptly—and so did he; but before she had a chance to say what was on her mind and get it over with, he finally spoke.

"Nice night to be outside, don't you think?" he drawled, and then, before she could collect her thoughts again, he was reaching in his pocket. "Do you mind if I roll a smoke? Got into the habit, you see, and prefer my own cigarillos to most cigars.''

"No, of course I don't mind if you smoke," Laura snapped ungraciously, determined to keep to her resolve. "You can smoke all you want out here or indoors with my father and brother. But before we go back inside there are certain things—certain rather awkward matters—that must be discussed and dealt with, don't you agree?"

He had bent his head to light his cigarillo, and as he looked up Laura saw the sheen of his eyes reflect the match flame before it died.

"Oh? And what kind of 'awkward matters' must we deal with so urgently, Miss Morgan? I had hoped that on a perfumed, star-studded night such as this we might— well, make up for the rather different circumstances of our *first* meeting this morning! Do you realize that this is actually the third time we have been together today?"

Struck speechless by his effrontery, Laura could have sworn that she saw the flash of his teeth in a grin before he continued in the same detestable tone of voice.

"I wonder, though—yes, now that I see the difference in you from this morning I really cannot help wondering how it might have turned out if I'd met you first by moonlight!"

It was too much! His arrogance, his impertinence! She had been seething inside all through his sarcastically delivered speech, and now Laura found that she could no longer hold her volatile temper in check.

"This *morning?* Do you *dare* refer to what happened this morning after the vile way you behaved? After you—"

"Oh, for God's sake!" he said impatiently, "how in the hell was I to know who you were? Especially when you used that gutter language on me—language, I might add, that no well brought-up young lady is supposed to understand, let alone use on a stranger. You acted like a little whore—and I took you for one. Maybe you should let what might have happened—if I'd been less tired—be a lesson to you for future reference—Miss Laura, ma'am!"

"You're an abominable monster!" Laura burst out, her voice shaking with rage. "There was no excuse for your actions! I wish I had *killed* you!"

"In which case, my dear, you'd probably be the plaything of those randy *Rurales* right now!" And then, while she was still gasping with outrage, he said, "Ah, what the hell! What do you want to hear—apologies? For what? You slapped *me* first—and I kissed you to shut you up. Fair enough?"

"I don't—I won't listen to any more!" Laura flung at him, hating him. "I only came outside here with you to tell you—I *meant* to do so politely until you—Oh, damn you! All I meant to make perfectly clear to you was that I certainly don't intend to go along with this ridiculous *farce*—this so-called engagement that I knew nothing about until just today! And what's more, I hope that we never have to run into each other ever again! Goodnight and goodbye, Mr. Challenger."

At least she had managed to recover her senses at last, and, finally, to make her voice emerge as cold as ice flung in his despicable face. Fearing that if he said one more word to her, she would lose her temper again, Laura whirled about with a swishing of her decorously long taffeta skirts. Suddenly she felt her arm seized and was swung around like a doll to face him again.

"Don't you believe in goodnight and goodbye kisses, Miss Morgan? As your thankful ex-fiancé I claim the right."

To her credit, Laura was to think later, she *had* tried to free herself. To escape from the constriction of his arms. She had tried—and if he had been cruel, hateful, hurting, perhaps she would have been able to avoid what suddenly had seemed to her to be inevitable. His lips were teasing, cajoling, seeking, taking, until her head fell back against his arm and she *let* him kiss her; wanted and learned to kiss him back, with all thought, all reason, falling away while he kissed her, and continued to kiss her—in so many different ways that she could never have imagined before.

In her room, much later, voices, and the tang of cigar
smoke from the men on the patio drifted in through her
open window, until Laura closed it firmly.

But even then, for some uncountable reason, she found
it difficult to fall asleep. As soon as she closed her eyes,
her mind was assailed by all kinds of strange thoughts and
images she couldn't dispel. Angry at herself, Laura made
up scenes and speeches, imagining all the cutting things
she should have and might have said to Trent Challenger
to demolish his bloated male ego.

She should not have engaged in pointless recriminations
that only seemed to amuse him! She should have told him
coldly, clearly, and concisely what she had to say at the
very beginning; and having made her point, she should
have turned on her heel and left him standing there alone
and thoroughly set down!

Why *hadn't* she done just that? Why, damn him, had
she allowed him to kiss her—and for such an inordinate
length of time too—until sheer lack of breath had made
her clasp at his shoulders in order to keep from losing her
balance completely? Oh—how she disliked the brute! How
she longed to forget the whole sordid incident and her own
treacherous weakness that he had taken such advantage of!

Laura woke up much later than was usual for her—and
then closed her eyes quickly against the brassy brightness
of the sun shining into her eyes.

Filomena must have been in her room to open the shut-
ters, she thought drowsily. But why hadn't she called to
her loudly as she usually did?

Her head ached, Laura realized. She turned onto her
stomach and rubbed her eyes, kicking off the thin sheet
with which a disapproving Filomena must have covered
her while she lay sleeping. *Convention!* What was *right,*
what was *proper* for a young lady. Filomena was full of
such lectures and always had been, since Laura and Franco were young children.

Laura sat up, stretching and grimacing at the heat of the

sun on her body—like hot hands . . . Her spine stiffened at such ridiculous imagery, and she was suddenly completely awake, remembering last evening.

I'll show him, Laura thought, getting out of bed to begin her perfunctory ablutions at the washbasin in a screened-off corner of her room. Filomena had left two pitchers of fresh water for her—icy cold, of course—and clean, fluffy washcloths and towels.

Naked and glowing from scrubbing herself, Laura called impatiently downstairs through her slightly cracked door: "Filomena! *Filomena*—where *are* you, old woman? I need your help with dressing, *por favor!*"

She had decided, contradictorily, to wear the same cool morning dress that Filomena had buttoned and hooked her into yesterday. Let the grumpy old thing grumble and make comments under her breath. It looked like a beautiful day, and she was hungry—and ready to face anybody *and* face them down, if necessary!

Her mother and father never emerged from their rooms in the original "little *hacienda*" for their breakfast before eleven at the earliest—and sometimes much later—so Laura was sure of not being too late, if only Filomena would hurry!

"Filomena! Where *are* you? Must I run downstairs half-dressed to find you?"

"I'm coming! Such impatience! I'm not as fast on my feet as I used to be, you should know."

Knowing exactly how to get round her old nurse, Laura gave the woman a hug as she pushed open the door and lumbered in, panting from climbing the stairs.

"I'm sorry, Filomena, but the smell of food has made me *so* hungry . . . and I hardly ate at all last night."

"Yes—I am sure you didn't!" Filomena said. "All that wine! *I* noticed how much you had! Far too much for a young girl your age. I told your mother too. Wine goes to the head and inflames the senses! And—*what* will you be wearing under that dress you threw aside yesterday, eh?"

Laura had slipped into her gown already, and now she turned about to face the mirror.

"I'm wearing one of my new chemises! Can't you see? And *no* corset! I couldn't eat a morsel all laced up. If I breathe in—*so*—and hold my breath, the dress will fit quite well! Please do hurry. And don't waste time scolding me— you'll have no one to scold when I've left for Europe, you know! You'll miss me *then!*"

"Hah! Miss you, indeed—miss trouble and worry? I feel pity for those who will have the responsibility of watching over you and turning you into a lady while the *Padrón* and the *Padrona* are traveling about on their own. Be still now, if you want me to fasten you into the gown. I had to press it again, you know! The young these days! I swear by the Blessed Virgin I don't know what you will come to—and us with you!"

"Oh, Filomena, hush! *You* were probably just as wild— or *worse,* when you were my age! Didn't you say once—"

"Enough—enough! Never mind what I said. *I* wasn't supposed to be a lady, I was a poor peon's daughter, and had to make the best living I could! *There!*"

With Filomena glowering behind her, lower lip protruding ominously, Laura examined her reflection in the mirror, pinched her cheeks lightly, and twisted her thick braid of hair into a heavy coil atop her head, leaving her neck bare except for tiny, escaping curls that clung to her nape.

"Are they already breakfasting, Mama and Papa? Oh, how hungry I am! I hope there's lots of food."

Filomena followed Laura out of the room, still grumbling as was her wont.

"Of course there's food! And drink. Too much, as usual! And why are you in such a hurry that you almost fall over your skirts? Lift them up with one hand, like a lady!"

"Filomena!" All the same, Laura did slow her too precipitate rush, and lifted her skirts. It would be intolerable to trip over them and fall—to end, probably, in an undignified heap of billowing material at *his* feet!

"And if your hurry wasn't just your appetite for breakfast, but to see *him*, that hard-faced *gringo ladrón*, you could save yourself the trouble. *He* left before six this morning—and your brother along with him. So much the better—you're too young and inexperienced to get mixed up with *his* kind!''

"Oh! What do you know?'' Laura blurted out before she turned her back on the muttering old witch and walked stiffly toward the small *sala*.

So he'd left already! And with Franco. Not that it mattered to her at all, except that she'd not had a chance to put him down *first*. It didn't matter one bit—good riddance! And the end to an unpleasant and disturbing incident that she would be able to put out of her mind completely now.

But then . . . why did she feel so unaccountably let down and disappointed because he hadn't had the courtesy to say goodbye? A sudden, unwanted, unlooked-for thought flashed across Laura's mind before she shut it away, angry at herself.

What if *she* had been the one to go with him to California, instead of Franco?

Laura sipped purposefully at her hot, black coffee, not caring if it burned her mouth. So Trent Challenger had left already, his ''business'' with her father taken care of, no doubt—as well as his business with *her*. After all, what else was there to keep him now that he had accomplished everything he'd come here to do?

Let Franco go adventuring and learn bad habits. *She* was going to Europe to travel and broaden her horizons. And hopefully, to learn a great deal on her own. While he . . . but why should she care what Trent Challenger would be doing, or where he would be journeying? In spite of the undeniable physical attraction that had suddenly flared up between them last night, they really had *nothing* in common at all.

Laura sipped again at the bitter black coffee and felt it scald her mouth—almost welcoming the pain that took her mind away from other things . . . like sensations she had never experienced before that took her from herself. Kisses that forced certain responses from her; the feeling of not being in control of her emotions; of being carried away on a whirlwind, tossed helplessly this way and that.

"I'll *never* let myself be at the mercy of feelings, emotions, I don't understand—ever again!" Laura vowed to herself, even while a darkly primitive part of her being continued to wonder and want what might have happened . . . if . . . if they had both been less civilized, perhaps—or less chaperoned?

Her mother had said bluntly and honestly: "He's almost too like your father, Laura—in the early days. Be careful—*don't* scratch beneath the surface—*don't* feel obliged to find out, to explore! Damn your curiosity! You might find it leads you to something you didn't bargain for!"

"But *you* did, Mama! And you had been brought up in *France,* in society—you knew nothing about the rough side of life here, as I do!"

"And you, love, know almost nothing about men—yet! I don't want you hurt, you understand that? Just go into everything with your eyes open, able to weigh the risks and the rewards, Laura. You are too much like me, I'm afraid—and that is what frightens me sometimes!"

"I can look after myself, Mama! And I will . . . always!"

Part Two—Paris

La Belle Epoque

Chapter 7

It was good to return to Paris, Laura thought; and to her little house that *Grande-tante* Céline had left to her mother, and that her mother, knowing her daughter's love for Paris, had given to her for a twenty-first birthday present.

"I was so happy here, with Tante Céline and Oncle Albert—and yes, my cousin Pierre, too, of course," Mama had said. "I used to have quite a *tendresse* for Pierre, when I was sixteen or so!"

"And did he return your feelings?"

Her mother had smiled a trifle wickedly, Laura remembered. "Mmm, yes, I think he had begun to become quite interested in me, especially since all his friends were. But by then, of course, all I could think of was traveling to America to meet my father—and dreaming of all the adventures that lay ahead!"

And now it's my turn, Laura thought, looking out the window at the rain. How it poured down! But she didn't mind it today. She was tired from traveling; it would be good to rest, to relax, to be alone with herself for a change so that she could think. Tomorrow, of course, all her friends would come calling; she would be expected to visit her uncle Pierre and his wife Lorna, and . . . oh, but she didn't want to think about all that just now. Not about everything she had to do or was supposed to do, but about what she wanted and planned to do now that she was back in Paris. Alone, legally of age, and independently wealthy, thanks to the fact that she had understanding parents.

"We keep crossing each other's paths!" she had learned to say lightly when she encountered her parents on her travels. As usual, they were completely unpredictable; and now she would not be encountering them again for almost a year since they had decided, on a mere whim, to explore India.

Turning away from the window and the rain, Laura crossed the room, drawn to the fire and its moving, leaping flames, the sparks hissing up the chimney. The rain was peaceful, steady. But fire and flame were excitement and challenge. Contrasts—like people, like all the different countries she had traveled through and explored and learned about during the past three years. Unbelievable, almost, that it had been that long since she had left the safe, familiar security of California and Mexico for Europe; full, then, of contradictory emotions she could not quite express even to herself. Feelings of doubt, of uncertainty mixed with a kind of fear of the unknown and unfamiliar.

But now—yes, she was a different person now. She had learned along the way and had changed. She wanted and needed to learn *more;* to experience everything she had not yet experienced; to feel new emotions and to discover, at the same time, how to control them. Ah yes! She wanted everything—everything she could get from life. But then . . . Laura sighed and sank down into a chair, gazing, with a frown, into the fire. Damn it, why was there always a *"but"*?

For three hectic years she and Franco had traveled throughout Europe—sometimes with and often without their parents; stopping in one place sometimes for a month or two, but then always moving on afterward; always with new tutors, language teachers, music teachers, dancing instructors. Everywhere they went Laura felt as if she'd been in a hothouse kind of schoolroom, somewhat like a cultured orchid. She'd even attended lectures by Professor

Freud, who preached such revolutionary theories in Vienna!

In fact, she had been exposed not only to the intellectual levels of society, but also, recently, to the more frivolous and earthy side of Parisian life as well!

She had met everyone who was anyone, and had acquired the kind of poise and sophistication that made her one of the leaders of the fashionable set unafraid of voicing her own opinions and ideas instead of being just a follower of the crowd.

It was, she realized, only because she was daring enough and rich enough not to have to care about convention! And at least, Laura reminded herself consolingly, she had also learned to hide her emotions.

As Laura had half expected, her friend Céleste de Fornay called far too early the next day, arousing her out of a dream-laced sleep.

"Ooh! Why did Adèle let you in? I told her—"

"You told her to tell anyone who called that you were fatigued by your journey and not to be disturbed. But *I* am not just anyone! And I knew, of course, that this would be the only opportunity I would have of seeing you alone today and hearing about everything that has happened during the last . . . has it been a whole *year?* Well, it is high time you came back from the wilderness of wherever you have been traveling last! Everyone has missed you, even the Baroness Adolphe de Rothschild and the rest of the Amazones. So now—tell me *everything!* I swear I won't tell a soul. Ernesto—that little Italian prince, what happened? Was there anyone else? Anyone, I mean, who was *interesting!* Well?"

"*Bon Dieu,* Céleste, at least give me time to wake up enough so that I can answer *some* of your questions!" Sitting up in bed under her friend's unsympathetic brown eyes, Laura yawned and massaged her temples. "Coffee— that's what I need. I'm never very coherent soon after I've been waked up!'' Laura shot an accusing glance at Céleste, who merely shrugged before she thrust a tray at her.

"Coffee—a whole potful of it. And also freshly baked croissants with butter and marmalade. Enough for now?''

"But how can I possibly relate or remember *everything?*'' Laura complained. "And it's been less than six months since I was last in Paris, and then we met in—was it Monaco? Or Aix? God, I've been moving around so fast and so often that I've lost track of time! Anyway, it hasn't been *that* long, I'm sure.''

"Long enough, *ma petite!* But at least you've arrived here in time for the Season. There will be so much happening! So many new and interesting people to meet. But first—Ernesto. Start with him. He seemed nice enough, in addition to being very rich and very eager! Did you manage to get rid of his dragon mama? Did you—?''

"Ernesto! Oh please, Céleste. He—it was a disaster!''

"But,'' Céleste pursued inexorably, "I heard that you two had disappeared together for at least a week. Long enough to make his mama frantic with worry!''

"Yes,'' Laura said wryly. "But then she decided to unbend, after the Princess di Paoli—she's an old and *very* close friend of my father's that my mother positively *dislikes*—well, I suppose she mentioned the fact that I was—was, well, an heiress! Ugh!''

"But that could not have been a disaster! Mama didn't mind after that?''

"No,'' Laura admitted. "But *I* did! I didn't expect . . . after all, Italian men are supposed to be so *passionate!* Everybody says so. You've told me that too! And he was so . . . well, he seemed so self-assured, and he was—is—so damned handsome, after all! I thought it might be an exciting and romantic interlude, just . . . well . . .''

"Well? So?''

"Well,'' Laura confessed ruefully, "I felt . . . I felt as if I were supposed to be the leader of an expedition! I mean, he expected me to—to—''

"Hmm!'' Céleste said knowingly, "to be the one to

lead the way, eh? To be the one in charge, to tell him what to do and how and when to do it? To be, in a word, like his mama!''

"How on earth did you guess? And why didn't you *warn* me?''

Céleste de Fornay ignored the annoyance in her friend's voice as she shrugged one shoulder, her carefully plucked brows lifting. "But why should I warn you, *chérie?* Isn't it better to learn from experience? And besides, you did not ask me for advice.'' She laughed lightly. "So—no more Ernesto! You returned him to his mama, yes? And then?''

"Really, Céleste, you would make a good lawyer—or an inquisitor!'' Laura said tartly. She had no intention of saying anything more—not yet, and not until she was ready. Madame de Fornay, being worldly-wise as well as understanding, did not press Laura any further. She genuinely liked this young woman, and had begun to think of her almost as a protégée.

Céleste de Fornay was from a family of the *haute bourgeoisie,* and because she was of the upper middle-class and her father was a successful lawyer, she had had both an excellent education and many opportunities to meet eligible young men. She was intelligent, clever, and quite lovely; but she had made the mistake of falling in love with the oldest son of a baron, who happened to be married. She had married her lover's younger brother—an intellectual and a poet who was also an alcoholic and an avowed homosexual. It was a marriage of convenience for them both, and it pleased their families while not changing their lives in the least. Before Aristide died, he had given Céleste entrée to all of the most fashionable *salons* in Paris, and had introduced her to many of his rich and influential friends from some of France's oldest and most illustrious families—such as Comte Robert de Montesquiou-Fezensac, who reigned as prince of society salons. It had not taken poor Aristide long to die from his excesses—and Céleste had everything she wanted: his name, money, and an entrée to society. She had made the most of it, of course, and of every opportunity that came her way, although she was always most discreet in taking a lover or accepting a protector.

"Life is to be enjoyed and savored, what else?" Céleste had once said, laughing, to Laura's brother Franco, who was so different from Laura herself, even if they were twins. He was always scowling and serious; and she loved to tease him. She was also a little bit intrigued by Franco—he was so handsome and there was something in the way he walked and carried himself that made Céleste sense he would be a good lover. But no, he would never rise to her bait and would lecture instead on the frivolity and irresponsibility of modern women until his sister was goaded into losing her temper with him—and then their discussion would turn into a shouting match at which point Céleste would leave discreetly.

"He's such a hypocrite!" Laura would storm afterward. "I can hardly recognize him or believe he's my brother sometimes. And when he starts preaching at me about my shocking behavior and the company I keep—well, it's more than I can stand!"

Céleste wondered, as she left her friend's house, how long it would take for her brother to show up. A slight smile curved her lips. No doubt he had heard all the rumors of his sister's doings during the past few months—and no doubt he would be angry! Such a typical male—and especially since *he* had been paying such assiduous court to Laura's timid American friend who had been married off by her parents to the Earl of Sedgewick, a very noted lecher with very strange sexual preferences! It was not surprising that the Earl had been posted as Ambassador to Turkey soon after their marriage, while his wife traveled about Europe chaperoned by her mother-in-law. It was such a pity, this traffic in American heiresses who were sold into marriage by their families who paid millions of dollars for a title!

Céleste really was like a whirlwind, Laura thought a

trifle ruefully as Adéle helped her to dress after her friend
left. Within the space of less than an hour, Céleste had
contrived to bring her abreast of all the latest town gossip,
and to relate the newest *on-dit* that were going the rounds.
Céleste had also reminded her, unfortunately, of all the
silly obligations she must fulfill and get out of the way
before she could really begin to enjoy herself again.

"If ma'amzelle would please draw in her breath? Yes?
And again, once more? Ah!"

Draw *in* her breath? Laura felt as if her power to breathe
were being cut off completely. Corsets! How she hated
having to wear one in order to be in fashion and to look
ravishing in her clothes. It wasn't natural for a female to
have an eighteen-inch waist, and to have to suffer such
discomfort merely to have the kind of "hourglass" figure
that men seemed to adore. No doubt because they preferred women to sound breathless—as if they were overcome by the mere proximity of a man—and because a
woman so tightly laced up could hardly manage to eat
more than a little bird—something that men preferred to
attribute to their mere *presence!* Everything a woman did—
the way she acted, the way she dressed, walked, spoke
. . . and even what she *read*—was ordained *by* men and
for men. It was all so disgusting and denigrating to the
female sex!

Laura studied herself critically in the full-length mirror
that took up one whole wall of her dressing room. Why,
feeling as she did, did she still conform? To *use*, instead
of *being* used, her mind shot back at her. Well, here she
stood, already layered with undergarments even before she
had been buttoned and laced into her gown! Silk, lace-
trimmed chemise against her skin to protect it from the
horrid tight corset she detested. Then a lace-trimmed corset cover, and over that two petticoats—one of Japanese
silk and the other taffeta for that rustling *frou-frou* sound
that men found so enchanting when a female walked by.

Laura sipped on her tiny silver-chased glass of sherry
before replacing it on the silver tray that was always kept

on the table in her powder-blue and silver dressing room, and stared back at her reflection. *Had* she changed during the past nine or ten months? And if she had—in what way? She had reacquired the dark-gold color that the sun always brought out in her skin; in this case the sun of Italy and of North Africa. It suited her, even if a pale complexion was supposed to be fashionable these days.

Laura thought suddenly, still looking back at herself: God! How long have I been traveling about? Homeless— but learning along the way! And learning what? About people, about life—about myself, mostly.

One more sherry, Laura thought, and I won't mind anything that Lorna says to me, even the way in which she always subtly compares me with my mother! No, and she wouldn't care about any criticism from Franco either— Franco with his newly acquired stuffiness!

Adèle returned to help Laura into her blue-gray princess gown trimmed with black Persian lamb and blue-black velvet ribbon that fit her as closely as a glove before the skirt flared out slightly to make walking easier. The gown was new, and in the latest fashion—it had been delivered only the day before from the House of Worth, where they had her measurements.

Laura adjusted her small toque hat trimmed with fur and ribbon and black aigrettes, then fastened it in place with gold hatpins, grimacing at herself in the mirror as she did so. Her hair had been drawn up atop her head in a Grecian knot with small, curling tendrils escaping artfully to caress her forehead, her temples, and the nape of her slender neck. She was, in fact, every inch a young lady of fashion, and looked—as even *she* had to admit—almost startlingly like her mother, except for the difference in the coloring of their eyes and hair. She was tired of hearing everyone who knew them both say so too, Laura thought, wanting to be taken for herself and not just her mother's daughter!

Downstairs, pulling on her ivory-colored suede gloves, Laura took one last look at herself in the mirror that graced the hatstand in the small entrance hall. She looked well enough, considering the boring afternoon she faced. The evening would be better, and much more fun, she resolved. And after today and tonight were over with, then she would have time to herself, to relax, to do only what she pleased and exactly *as* she pleased.

The whole of the Paris season stretched before her. She was so tired of traveling and of traipsing all over from place to place, from city to city, and from one country to another until she had almost lost track of where she was or what she was doing or supposed to be doing wherever she was! Settling back in her smart new carriage, Laura yawned slightly, putting one gloved hand up to her carefully rouged mouth to smother it. She was still tired—and, so far, quite bored! What a change from her expectations when she had first arrived in Europe—one part of her excited at the newness of everything and the other a trifle sullen and resentful at having been snatched out of her familiar, comfortable environment willy-nilly—without being consulted about her own inclinations.

How long had it been since she had left California? The three years that had elapsed seemed to have flown by without her realizing it. A hothouse schoolroom orchid. Well, at least she had learned. But had she *blossomed?*

Chapter 8

Last night, when she had fallen asleep, the rain had been blowing in spattering gusts against her window. This afternoon, the sun was showing itself and reflecting off puddles and dancing droplets of water that the breeze shook off green leaves. The air smelled fresh and clean and Laura suddenly felt invigorated.

She had spent almost three years on her so-called Grand Tour—usually reserved for young *men*, of course—and now, no more tutors, no more lessons in languages and deportment and dancing and . . . well, she had certainly led all of her poor tutors and female companions a dance, hadn't she? Laura acknowledged it to herself without regret. Her parents had seen to it that she had the right introductions everywhere before letting her go off on her own—once they felt that she was able to take care of herself. There were times, though, when Laura wasn't certain whether she appreciated their attitude or not! And one thing she *did* resent was the fact that they had decided to go off to India on their own without even asking her if she might want to go along too. What an adventure India would have been! But instead she had had to settle for a month in Egypt studying pyramids and camels and two weeks in Tangier after that.

Tangier. Romantic-sounding—but such a dirty and primitive place, for all its European population. All the same . . . it had had its own kind of fascination.

Laura suddenly felt a small, cold chill run down her

spine, making her suddenly sit up straighter and close her eyes for a moment. Tangier . . . she must rehearse what she would say to everyone, how she would describe it. She had made notes and sketches; Frank Harris would no doubt be interested in *those,* and so would her uncle Pierre who had given her a letter of introduction to the French Ambassador there. She wondered if he knew anything about Tangier apart from the dirt and the smells and the squalor—from which most of the foreign embassies tried to remove themselves in their heavily guarded villas outside the town itself.

Yes, she could tell everyone a great deal about her two-week stay in Tangier that had made her quite relieved to think of returning to civilization again. A great deal—but *not* everything! Laura inhaled the fresh spring air as deeply as she could with whalebone digging into her. For now, Paris lay ahead of her to reexperience and she would wipe everything but anticipation out of her mind—once this duty call was out of the way.

Laura had intended to spend only a very short time with the Dumonts and she had her excuses prepared in advance, but in the end she found herself quite enjoying her visit as she discovered in a more relaxed and informal environment another side to her uncle Pierre. Even Lorna Dumont seemed different and much more human on this occasion.

"Juliette's at her dancing class and I must pick her up in half an hour," Lorna said a trifle distractedly soon after Laura had arrived. "But I do hope you can stay until we come back? She has been *so* excited about seeing you again since you telephoned this morning!"

"Before our daughter, who is at that inquisitive age, arrives with all her questions, you may give us adults the unexpurgated version of your latest exploits, eh?" Pierre said. "Tell me—what about this Italian *conte* you eloped with? Or did you?"

"Pierre! Really—and you *promised. . . !*" Lorna exclaimed.

"I promised Lorna I wouldn't embarrass you, but you're

not embarrassed, are you, Laura? In any case, everyone you know is going to ask you questions—why not practice your answers on your relatives?''

Laura found herself responding quite naturally to this new, teasing side of her uncle Pierre with a saucy grin.

"Oh, well, you see . . . it wasn't really an elopement at all! *How* people *do* love to gossip! Why, Ernesto's mama was with us. At least . . ." Laura added in a normal voice after a theatrical pause for effect, *"that* is the story that his mama and I agreed upon. Do you think anyone will believe it?''

Pierre Dumont chuckled, shaking his head, but Lorna Dumont's smile looked a trifle strained.

"Lorna's rather *distraite* these days, I'm afraid!" Uncle Pierre said after his wife had left them. "Her mother is arriving this week on her annual visit, and the prospect always makes my poor Lorna quite nervous, having to make so many plans and arrange for expeditions to Aix and Biarritz, Trouville—even Monte Carlo! Madame Prendergast loves to gamble!'' And then he looked up from pouring more sherry into their glasses to ask: "And you, Laura? What are your plans for the next few months?''

Laura gave him an almost impish smile, her dimple showing. "The usual things I enjoy doing, of course! But you don't have to worry about me *this* time, Uncle Pierre. I think I've sown most of my wild oats!''

"Well, thank God for that! No more *chahut* then? Kicking up your legs on a stage to show your drawers like La Goulue?''

"Oh, *no!*'' Laura said demurely, glancing up from under the screen of her long lashes. "I only learned the cancan to prove I could do it—even the splits and the cartwheels! No, this season I've decided to take belly-dancing lessons. I've been told it's quite the thing these days, and good for the figure as well!''

Pierre Dumont decided wisely *not* to tell his wife about the belly-dancing lessons. Lorna would *not* have been amused, he thought ruefully—wondering if Laura had really meant it or had been pulling his leg. She reminded him more and more of her mother, his equally reckless and headstrong cousin Ginette, who had never cared a fig for convention!

In his Paris apartment, Franco Morgan was thinking the same thing about his sister. Damn it, when would she stop acting on every mad, thoughtless, selfish whim without bothering to consider the *consequences?* Laura needed above all to learn self-discipline—to learn *control* and caution for her own sake if not for the sake of those who genuinely cared about her and worried for her reputation even if *she* did not. He had tried to explain his feelings to their parents before they had left—but then of course, Franco recalled ruefully, he had only managed to annoy his mother by mentioning that, after all, Laura should remember she was a *female*, and supposed to be a lady!

"Oh, indeed?" his mother had said coldly, her eyes narrowing at him before she had exchanged a glance with his father, who had only quirked one eyebrow at her. "I wonder, my son, what you must think of *me* in that case? Nobody can accuse me of being exactly conventional or, to use your term, Franco, a lady! If I had been what everyone wanted and expected me to be, you would not be standing here at this moment being so priggish and so stuffy that . . . that I am positively ashamed of you!"

It was still a particularly unpleasant memory, Franco thought rather unhappily. He loved his mother and admired her tremendously and he could hardly stand her anger—let alone her contempt! She had a way of reducing him to adolescence again; of wanting and needing her approval above all things, although as a man he could never admit it—not even to himself at most times. And she was honest—she had always been so, and there were times he found her directness almost unnerving!

Franco had not realized that he had been pacing back and forth from one end of the room to another until he was brought up short by his own scowling reflection in a mirror.

Oh, hell! In the end he had made up with his mother, of course, and had promised to be less critical of his sister, to try and get along with her. Franco ran his fingers distractedly through his hair as he stared rather shamefacedly back at himself, remembering that he had made the same promise to Ena.

As usual, the thought of Ena had the effect of cooling his temper. Helena—Ena—Lady Ayre, Countess of Sedgewick, with a daunting mother-in-law and an absent husband. Lovely, unhappy, innocent Helena . . . forced into a loveless marriage by her father who had coveted a title for his daughter to set the seal on his newly acquired status as a millionaire, and who didn't give a damn about *her* feelings as long as *he* could compare himself to the Astors and the Vanderbilts. How could a brutish, self-seeking man like Patrick Driscoll have produced a daughter like Helena? So lovely, so fragile, so . . .

Damn, he sounded like a lovesick calf, Franco thought. But how could he—how could anyone for that matter—help loving Helena? He had fallen in love with her almost from the moment his sister had introduced them; *he,* who had begun to pride himself on his detachment and cynicism. And he had been the only man, he knew, who had been able to cut through the coldly formal indifference of manner that Helena had built around her feelings for protection—to find at last fires hidden deep beneath the ice.

He had to admit, with an uncomfortable sense of what was almost guilt, that it was Laura he had to thank for his unlocking of the puzzle and the mystery that was Helena. If Helena had not formed an almost instant friendship with his sister, and had not trusted and confided in her, she might never have trusted *him,* or let down her guard. "Rapunzel, Rapunzel," he had teased her after a while. And God! When she had let down her guinea-gold hair for him and opened the floodgates of all the emotions and passion in her that even she had not known she possessed, he had been lost—wanting to drown in her, to know her, to *have* her. Even if he had to kill her husband to possess her. Helena—his Helen of Troy! What in the hell was he going to do about her in the end? The poet and the warrior, the cynic and the idealist waged a constant battle within him.

In a way, Franco was glad that his sister had finally returned to Paris to cause a distraction—as she usually did! Laura was everything Helena was not. She was stubborn, opinionated, and self-centered; one of the new breed of independent women who delighted in shocking everyone. And yet there were moments when, perversely, he could almost wish that Ena could be a little bit more like Laura—more sure of herself and a little less afraid.

Franco Morgan had no way of knowing it, but his Ena's thoughts almost echoed his at that moment. Laura had finally arrived in Paris—Laura, her closest friend, her *only* real friend. Franco's sister. Oh God, Helena thought now, almost feverishly, why am I not more like Laura? As strong and as indomitable as Laura?

Helena was the present Countess of Sedgewick. Wife of Archibald Ayre, Earl of Sedgewick, who had allowed her the honor of using his title in exchange for the millions her father had paid to get his daughter into "high society."

She *longed* to be plain Ena Driscoll again—even to be living in the shack she'd been conceived and born in, before her father had struck it rich in the silver mines of the Comstock, and her mother had decided her daughter must be educated and taken out in Paris and London and Vienna.

She'd been dangled before Dukes and Earls and Marquesses and Comtes and Contes and Principes—all bidding for her dowry—until it had made her ill; and in the end she'd been taken to the waters at Baden-Baden when her misery had begun to show in her face and the thinness of her body.

It was then that her father had brought Archie back one evening—and it was all settled, without her wanting it or expecting it. No one, not even Ma (whom she must remember to call Maman) had warned her—told her anything. It had taken about a month—with her locked in her room, slapped and beaten, and existing on gruel and water—before she had surrendered.

She hated and feared Archie, but strangely enough, once she had met his mother, she had felt safer. The Dowager Countess was someone to be reckoned with—outspoken and forthright, protecting her from Archie, and advising her. More of a mother to her than Ma had ever been!

And now, at last, she had found a woman-friend of her own—a fellow American heiress, so different from herself! More spirited and independent than she had ever been, never pushed into anything she did not want to do.

Laura Morgan's still devilishly handsome father had known Helena's father long ago—that was how Helena and Laura had first become acquainted; later they became friends because they *liked* each other. Even Lady Honoria, Ena's *"Belle-mère,"* had grudgingly admitted that she quite liked the girl—she had spirit, at least!

And then . . . there was Franco, Laura's twin brother. But as always, when she thought of Franco, Helena tried to push his disturbing image out of her mind. Franco . . . as naked and beautiful as a young satyr when he showed his wanting for her. He had made her *want*—made her feel—made her into a woman! He *loved* her, he treated her like a goddess, so tenderly, sweetly; overcoming, in the end, all the defenses and coldness that Archie had instilled in her from his first rape of her unsuspecting, inexperienced body to the next and the next, just before he had left for Istanbul as British Ambassador.

"Oh—I don't care!" Helena thought wildly. "I'm *loving* at last—I know at last that I can love and *feel!* I *must* learn to live for the moment and not worry about the future. Nothing matters but the present!"

Chapter 9

"My dear," one of Lady Honoria's friends had once whispered of Laura over the dowager's silver tea service, "it seems she prefers to frequent the company of the *demimonde* . . . *and* the kind of place where women of *that* kind are usually sent! If this latest American heiress, this Miss Morgan, has no one to advise her as to the impropriety of her associations . . ."

"Bosh!" The Dowager Countess of Sedgewick had never been one to mince words, her forthright comments often causing her more delicate-minded friends to wince. "What year d'you think this is? Almost the end of our century, my dears—new times, new ideas, whether we like it or not. Everything's changing, and the girl's part of it. Fortune or not, she's no hypocrite, at least, and she's made it clear she's not like the rest of them from across the Atlantic—letting themselves be bartered away in exchange for a title! I like her. So does Ena."

The Dowager Countess of Sedgewick was very decided in her opinions, although there were *degrees*. She either tolerated certain people, or she took one to her liking (which was very seldom), or else she positively disliked, which meant *most* people. It was therefore fortunate, as Helena, her daughter-in-law, thought quite often, that her formidable mother-in-law had actually liked her friend Laura.

"So your madcap friend is back in Paris, is she?" Lady Honoria asked her daughter-in-law that afternoon. "I wonder what other scandalous mischief she's been up to since that silly little Italian! Never could stand his mother, y'know!"

Oh yes, Helena thought again as she felt a shaft of pale spring sunshine warm her cheek; she was so glad that Belle-mère did not mind her friendship with Laura. And now that Laura had come back to Paris and would be here for the rest of the season, she could see more, oh, much more of Franco!

Miss Edge, Lady Honoria's faithful and self-effacing companion of some twenty years, made a clucking sound with her tongue as she shook her head, bringing Ena's guilty attention back to her mother-in-law who fixed her with a shrewd glance before snorting, "Hmph! Think *I* hadn't heard all the details? News travels fast, my girl! And just wait until I confront that young hussy! I'll get everything out of her, don't you worry. And she'll have a piece of my mind too. Hmph!"

The dowager snorted again before she continued: "What Miss Laura needs, and her parents obviously haven't taught her, is—restraint! She has to learn to be more *discreet!* All important, my dear, if one wants to be accepted in society. After all, why flaunt your private life in the face of the public if by exercising good sense you can have your cake and eat it too? Eh?"

Helena could not help the color that rose in her cheeks when she caught her mother-in-law's almost knowing look. Could it be possible that Honoria was giving her a subtle warning with a tacit *approval* of her affair with Franco?

Laura would know, Helena thought, trying to compose her features. Laura was everything she wished *she* could be: strong, unafraid, and worldly-wise. Why, Laura was the only young woman who had, from the beginning, actually stood up to Lady Honoria—not in the least intimidated by her, and even daring to argue. It was like a game they both played—each understanding what the other was about. Lady Honoria lectured and Laura pretended to listen—for a while at least, before she gave her own usually outrageous views on whatever the subject happened to be. Helena knew that she could never be so bold; she was still slightly afraid of her mother-in-law, and Lady Honoria knew it, of course. She seemed to know everything!

"So! You've been getting yourself talked about as usual!" Lady Honoria barked, barely waiting until Laura had been greeted and seated before she launched her attack. "You won't get away with defying convention forever, my girl, and you'd better learn that before it's too late!"

"But—too late for what, Ma'am?" Laura responded with deliberately wide-eyed innocence that made the dowager raise her lorgnette for effect as she looked down her long nose at Laura.

"Come, come! Don't disappoint me by playing coy at this late stage, m'dear! I want to hear *everything*—the *truth*, mind you! I'm tired of hearing everything second-hand! And if you'd have had the gumption to ask me for advice, I could have given you the history of the family! Weak stock—the men, especially. Easily ruled by their women! And surely *that* wouldn't be enough of a challenge for *you*, eh? Well? And mind you—I expect to hear everything *else* you've been up to after you've finished explaining your silliness! If you had to have an affair, you could at least have chosen better!"

While Lady Honoria and Laura embarked on one of their duels of wits and words which they both seemed to enjoy, Miss Edge twittered in the background and Helena looked out of the window while she thought about Franco. She hoped fervently and, she had to admit, selfishly, that he and Laura had not quarreled once again, for that would spoil everything! And it was no use preaching to Laura— she had tried to tell Franco that. Why, her surface-fierce mother-in-law seemed to understand Laura better than her own brother did.

Lady Honoria felt quite stimulated after Miss Morgan had taken her polite, unruffled leave, explaining that she

had promised to show her friend Mr. Frank Harris some
of her recent writings and sketches. She thoroughly enjoyed an argument, especially with an opponent who could
cleverly parry her verbal thrusts—and even fight back! It
was a pity, she thought sometimes, that her poor little Ena
was not a little more assertive, although perhaps it was
just as well for all their sakes that Helena was so *biddable,*
and had been trained all her life to be obedient and to do
what was expected of her.

If Ena had had half the spirit that her friend Laura Morgan had, she would never have been foolish enough to let
herself be married off to Archie.

Lady Honoria had never been able to like her son, although they had learned to tolerate each other, and she
took pleasure in the thought that she had always been able
to intimidate him. She had disliked her husband, too, and
had been relieved when he had conveniently managed to
kill himself with his excesses. If she had been born into a
different generation, she might have been like Laura Morgan; but in her time one did what was expected of one
and learned to be clever about one's indiscretions! She had
had many lovers in her time—picking and choosing them
according to *her* will and inclination and discarding them
when they bored her. But never, ever, had she been *obvious!* It was a lesson, she thought, that Miss Morgan
would do well to learn. To be *circumspect,* at the very
least. What *would* the girl be up to next?

Whatever the case, the dowager had to admit with an
inward chuckle, it would not be *dull.* Whatever Laura
Morgan did was always interesting! And perhaps one of
the reasons that she quite *liked* the chit was because Laura
dared to be everything that she, Honoria Mayhew, had
dreamed of being when she was young and less intimidated by the weight of *consequences!* Oh yes—even in *her*
day, and in the wildest set, one always considered consequences, and if not, there was always the example of poor
Caro Lamb who had thrown everything to the wind in her
impetuous pursuit of that silly posturer Byron.

Unfortunately and unhappily, the poor, foolish creature had ended up risking everything for nothing! Laura Morgan, though, was different. It would be interesting to watch how she turned out.

Chapter 10

"Oh Lord! I'm so exhausted! Duty calls and debates
. . . I felt as if I were in the fencing academy!"

Flopping back on the paper-cluttered couch, Laura sent
her hat spinning across the room as she kicked up her
shapely, silk-stockinged legs in a deliberate parody of the
chahut before continuing, with hardly a pause: "Questions! I'm so tired of questions! Thank God I can feel
comfortable with *you,* at least!"

Frank Harris was one of Laura's new friends—introduced to her by Franco of all people! He was a journalist
and a novelist, well thought of and respected in literary
circles. And now, sitting across from his visitor, Harris
had to take a deep breath before he managed to say
sternly: "Well, I'm glad *you're* comfortable, but I'll have
you know that I'm not! In fact, I'm not even able, right
now, to stand up and pour out some wine for you! Please
do put those legs down and out of my sight—unless you
meant to give me permission at long last, to—"

"No!" Laura sat bolt upright, snatching her skirts
down about her ankles and reminding him of a rebellious, half-sullen child. *"Do* stop teasing me, Frank! I
feel . . . well . . . *serious* about this. About what I've
been writing recently. And I want you to—That is, I need
you to tell me what you really think, Frank! I want people to take me seriously! Yes, even my brother, who just
talks a lot about changes that are needed and must happen but . . . but it's all theory, all talk! Don't you see,

Frank? Perhaps, if I do it in the right way—even if I'm using the format of a novel—maybe I can reach more people!''

So she wanted to be taken seriously, did she? Frank Harris had wished, on more than one occasion, that Miss Morgan would take *him* more seriously—take him as a lover, in fact! He enjoyed, even savored, making love to women. Especially those women who were challenging to him and not too easy to conquer. Laura Morgan, as he'd discovered, could not be categorized or easily pigeon-holed either. She was a talented and observant writer; she was rich, an heiress who could have practically any man she wanted. Unfairly enough, she was beautiful as well. And there were other words, other phrases, too, that could be used to describe her. Teasing—intriguing—promising—provocative—*naïve?* How much did Laura really know about sex? Now *that*, Frank thought, was the real puzzle.

''Besides,'' Laura went on, ''I've *heard* all about your prowess as a lover, and I also know that you write about your experiences and experiments—and in great detail too! I don't mind—and in fact I rather admire you for being honest! But personally, I'd rather write about than be written about—please try to understand! And I'd rather keep you as a friend and a confidant for always, instead of a sometime or one-time lover! I feel so comfortable with you, Frank,'' she went on to say. ''I can talk to you about everything—I even listen to your advice and act upon it occasionally, don't I? And anyway, I'm not ready for a lover just yet. There are things other than sex and sensuality that I want to find out about first.''

''Well, then, can I inquire of you, as a *friend*, mind you, have you experienced sex—sexuality—sensuality—anything of the sort yet? You give the impression of knowing and having experienced everything—or almost everything. And yet I have the feeling, call it instinct if you will, that you—that you're a fake, Laura dear. Or, perhaps, merely a very good actress.''

He looked down with a sense of resignation mixed with definite interest at the untidy pile of papers she had just dropped on his already cluttered desk.

"I'm trying something new in my writing—*that's* what's important," Laura told him, blue eyes storm-dark. "You must promise to be honest with me or I'll never forgive you." Then she rushed out in much the same way she'd stormed into his shabby, cluttered little room. Damn her for her indifference! Well, perhaps he'd find some answers to her puzzle as he read, Frank thought ruefully.

She was more than just a puzzle, she was . . . unexpected! Definitely *not* the average kind of female who could be read easily enough after a while. How could he possibly forget the night when he, still hopeful, had accompanied Laura to one of the new café cabarets in Montmartre?

In those days she had been emulating George Sand and Rachilde. She had been dressed in men's clothing; very fashionably, of course, since it was none other than Robert de Montesquiou who had seen to the cut and fit of her apparel. Thank God her brother had never found out!

And if Frank had not genuinely *liked* Laura—well, he would probably have found several reasons for never seeing her again! After all, there were limits to what a man would put up with!

There had been three men there who looked like retired prize fighters, thick-set and ham-handed in addition to being drunk and obnoxious.

"Here's one of the 'New' women!" one of them growled, looking Laura over from her silk hat and thin cigar to her expensively shod feet. "Let's teach her a lesson. To respect *men*, eh?"

Frank always carried his sword case with him on his little private expeditions, but Laura had not given him a chance to show that he could use it.

Arrogantly, as if she had in fact *been* a man, she had looked them over coolly and contemptuously, gesturing

him back into his chair with his sword cane still gripped
in his hand.

They'd been angry and full of hate—he'd noticed that
right away—but Laura had not seemed to care.

"Are you *sure* you want to continue this?" She had
taunted the one who had spoken first. "Perhaps I should
warn you . . ."

"Of what, eh? That you're a—"

Her next movement was deceptive—almost like a ma-
gician's sleight of hand. *She* stood still, letting the first
man advance on her before, by merely shifting her balance, she used one hand, like a matador in a bullring.
As the man fell, she watched the other two through narrowed eyes.

"Well? Does any other *man* want to prove himself
against a woman?"

The one who had started, in a frenzy of rage, to pull
a knife, had fallen back screaming with pain—his wrist
seemingly paralyzed. The other two, after one look at
Laura's smile and her face, turned around and ran for it.

"Shall we go now?" Laura said coolly to Frank, who
was almost dumbstruck, unable to believe what he had
seen with his own eyes. "It's beginning to become *boring* here, don't you think so, Frank?"

No wonder she'd intimidated him, the little bitch!

It seemed as if, no matter where she was and what she
did or *didn't* do, Laura had a way of attracting attention
to herself!

If only, as Frank was to think ruefully on too many
occasions, if only the little wretch could settle down to
some extent at least—or if only *he* could have the strength
of mind to resist the challenge she presented, and the
craving to know what she was really like beneath the
surface sophistication. She was reckless enough—and had
proved it—to flout convention and the rules that were
supposed to govern her behavior; and she had managed
to get away with it! Not only that, she had *talent*—a real
talent as a writer that could match or better any journalist

or novelist he could think of, including himself. If she concentrated all her energies on writing of her observations and discoveries about people, and what lay under the brittle-bright surface of so-called *society,* with all its rigid rules, manners, and mores . . . But how much did little Laura actually know of real life? How much had she actually *experienced,* for all her bold talk and equally bold behavior?

At least, Frank consoled himself when Laura frustrated him, well, dammit, at least he seemed to be the only man she confided in, and *trusted!* And perhaps someday he would be the man to break through the barriers she had erected about herself and discover the real, passionately female side of Laura Morgan. After all, there had to be a time when she would be ready to yield—even if it was only through curiosity!

Frank liked her latest "scribbles" as she airily called her self-expression, and had promised her that he would get them published as a series of articles under the nom de plume of the initials "L.M."

"It won't do for anyone to know that you're a woman. I'm sorry, Laura, but you do want to be taken seriously, don't you? Well, I'm afraid that this is the only way—at least for now. You have something to say—and you say it very strongly too—about the unfairness and injustice of the double standard that is prevalent and tacitly acceded to in our society. If you write as a woman, you'd be ignored or scoffed at—face the fact! But if L.M. is a man, that's a different kettle of fish. You see? It's unfair, of course, but it's reality. And," Frank added with a chuckle, "you'll probably be challenged to a duel—or rather, Monsieur L.M. will be. I gather that duels are becoming fashionable again!"

"What fun, and how exciting!" Laura returned lightly, before she declared that she had to hurry—she was to meet some friends in the Bois de Boulogne; to ride together and observe and *be* observed.

"Oh, I can understand how busy you are, now that you've come back for another taste of Paris!" Frank said.

Was he being solemn or sarcastic? Laura decided that she didn't care. Not at the moment, when she had so many things to look forward to.

True, she had promised herself to be "more serious" as she put it; to concentrate more on her writing and to cut down her social activities to a minimum. But unfortunately, her rediscovered friends had other ideas, and insisted that she simply *must* go here or there, attend this or that entertainment. How else could she write with sincerity and truth about life, after all? It was easier to let herself be swept along, forgetting time, "musts," and "have-to's," on the crest of a wave of activities and events. And why not? There was nothing and no one to stop her—even her brother seemed determined to get along with her this time, in spite of the fact that she had once again become the subject of a great deal of speculative gossip and conjecture.

But then, as she knew, Franco actually seemed to have fallen madly in love with Helena, who simply did not have the courage to fly in the face of convention, although she was brave enough to spend long afternoons with him in Laura's house, while she was supposed to be out shopping with Laura, or driving with her in the country to visit places of historical interest.

At this point in *her* life, Laura spun in time with a dizzying whirl of activities that kept her busy, but didn't quite reach far enough inside her feelings.

Yes, she might dance to the music and enjoy the dancing as everyone else did, but she had discovered that she did not necessarily *respond* in the same way that everyone else she knew did.

But now, at least for now, Laura decided to think only for the moment, and only of pleasure. After all, hadn't

Frank Harris told her that her articles had actually been sold, and would be published soon—not only in France but in England too? She felt elated this afternoon, and ready for *anything*.

Chapter 11

"Laura! *Chérie!* We had almost given you up! Do come along—it's the Palais de la Glace first, and then we have to talk about new clothes—and costumes for the ball . . .''

"Céleste, you're going far too fast. What *are* you talking about? What ball—what costumes?''

"Don't you read your invitations? Or your mail? But my dear, naturally I am talking about the Bal des Quat'zarts—it's going to be *so* amusing; and the costumes I've heard are all designed to be so very provocative! So therefore ours must be too! And then, after we get tired of *that* grand show *and* the party at the Moulin Rouge, why then we shall be going to Danielle's house—she is giving one of her famous gambling parties, and even better, no one has to unmask! It sounds like fun—yes?''

"Oh, but you *must* come, my dear," another friend, Liane, interjected in her huskily seductive voice, brushing a loose strand of hair back from one temple. "You'll bring a breath of fresh air into the same old circle of people, I'm sure! And wear something *daring!* Give *everyone* something they will talk about for weeks! *I* only wish I wasn't saddled, for the moment, with that *boring* little Baron from Belgium—although he's *rich* at least, and will do until my young Arab princeling makes up his mind to be bold enough to keep me in the fashion I *insist* upon!''

Laura couldn't help laughing—she always enjoyed Liane's world-weary contributions to her far-too-limited knowledge of the *real* world, a world she had just begun to discover and savor. Why, these women of the *demi-monde* were the only women who were really honest and had the courage of their convictions! They were knowing, intelligent, and *interesting*. Above all, they were *free* and insisted upon remaining themselves instead of moving about in a closed and gloomily shuttered atmosphere of rigid conventionality.

A masked costume ball—beginning on horse-drawn floats along the streets of Montmartre, and then moving on to the Moulin Rouge, after which a select few would go to Danielle Goulet's house on the Avenue Chabanais for still more dancing and drinking and carousing—and gambling.

"At least I feel lucky, and strong enough to cope with almost anything—or anyone, for that matter," Laura said, her sudden, spontaneous laugh showing even white teeth. "Perhaps Danielle will have a poker table—I've heard she likes American card games such as faro and poker!" It all sounded like fun, much excitement, and tremendous grist for her writing!

"You Americans are *so* damned *athletic!*" Liane complained later. "Is there *any* sport you don't excel at?"

"Well . . . I'm only a fair skier, and playing tennis in silly long skirts is no fun at all! Also, I've only recently learned to skate on ice—I was brought up in much warmer climates, you know!"

Céleste laughed merrily. "But you can *fence* as well as any man—and you can shoot a gun without flinching, yes? Don't *ever* let the man you decide you want find out any of this! The idiots *do* seem to prefer the helpless types they feel they can *protect*—or so they like to think," she added, with a shrewdly knowing wink in Laura's direction. "So, you *are* coming with us, are you not? I can promise you that at least it will not be a *dull* evening! You might even find a man . . ."

"*Or* even one of the New Women!" Liane put in.

"Yes—or a woman, of course—but someone you could *really* be interested in. If you've never felt *love*, as you've

said, then it's high time you did; or *passion* at least—
although only for a very short time, you understand.
Something to enjoy for a moment, to savor, and then to
fling aside when you're ready to move on to something or
someone else new and more exciting! That's *my* philoso-
phy, at least! And—it's amazing how many men *want* to
be controlled and ordered about by a really strong
woman!''

"Oh yes—unless the man's foolish enough to fall *into*
love . . . and then . . . watch out!" Liane said.

Fascinated, Laura listened—and learned from the lightly
cynical conversation that flowed between her experienced
friends.

Perhaps, she thought determinedly and quite seriously
later, I *should* take a lover and learn—but without letting
him know what a silly novice I really am! Oh, stupid! It
would happen in the end—she *knew* it would happen.

Before they separated that afternoon the three young
women discussed at length an elaborate art exhibition that
was to be presented at the well-known Durand-Ruel Gallery by Joseph Péladan, founder of the Society of the Rosy
Cross. It was bound to be quite a show, even though the
detestable man refused to show any work by a woman.

"Oh, but you must come, Laura! And you *must* look
fiercely ravishing in blue-black and silver. The very gown
you helped design, the moon-goddess gown, remember?"
Céleste said.

Liane added: "And, my dear, I have an escort for you
in mind—an Indian Prince, *very* rich of course—and very
timid of striking, dominant-seeming European women!
You'll have no trouble at all with him, I assure you. He
likes to worship at a shrine—as *he* put it with that strange
accent of his—and won't dare *touch* unless he's given permission!"

"But at least," Céleste said practically, "he will pay
for everything! The art salon exhibit and, afterward, dinner at Maxim's . . . Le Moulin Rouge—perhaps Le Chat
Noir? We'll see, shan't we? But—you *will* join us?"

"Perhaps," Liane put in mischievously, "perhaps your handsome English journalist friend will follow us there? If *you* won't have him, I might . . . but only once—to see if he's as good as I hear he is at giving pleasure to a woman—almost as well as another woman could, or so I've heard!"

"Poor Frank! Should I warn him?" Laura was laughing by now. "I wouldn't miss your conquest of him for the world!"

"He's bound to be there, of course." Liane yawned behind a slender, gloved hand. "He goes *everywhere*. And you say that *he* is a writer too? Is he a good lover?"

Laura shrugged negligently, refusing to commit herself. A shrug could pass for almost any kind of an answer.

Chapter 12

"Listen to *this!* During the course of about three months, the subject of this book—the companion to Lady M.—insists that she was, in spite of being . . . oh yes, at least she admits to looking 'extremely plain' . . . well, in spite of *that* drawback and the ugliest, dowdiest wardrobe one can imagine, she found herself—and her *virtue*—constantly threatened on all fronts by almost everyone she encountered. Footmen, railway porters, young lordlings, even their bored ladies! Can you believe in anything so ridiculous and so obviously exaggerated!"

"Obviously, my friend, there are many people who *do*—hence the success of this latest *roman à clef,* not to mention the money our formerly poor ex-companion is now inundated with, no doubt! But the story *does* have a ring of truth to it, doesn't it?" Frank Harris stroked his luxuriant moustache before continuing slyly, "Perhaps that is why it has become so popular! And even *you* must admit, especially after your impassioned speech, that you have *read* it—this piece of drivel, as you call it. After all, if *you're* not personally concerned or feel you've been slandered, what's to worry about?"

Yes—what indeed? A grim-lipped silence or casual disclaimer was sometimes the best way out of an awkward situation. And, as Trent Challenger reminded himself, his friend Frank Harris was a journalist—a fact that transcended even friendship.

"What's the matter, Trent? You're still looking posi-

tively *dour*. Recognize yourself in that piece of drivel? It's
not like you, old man, to become so *heated* about such a
thing—even that divorce case everyone was laying bets
on.''

"I noticed that your *Saturday Review* gave the whole
sordid incident a tremendous amount of publicity, my
friend. You're fortunate I didn't challenge *you* to an exchange of pistol shots, as well as the lady's husband. The
thought *did* cross my mind at the time, you know!''

"Dammit, Trent, I *am* your friend—so don't climb on
your high horse with me or give me that icy look either!''
Frank Harris gave one of his infectious laughs before he
clapped his friend's shoulder, continuing: "Look here,
shall we go out for an evening of fun tonight? Dinner at
Maxim's, and entertainment at the Moulin Rouge—what
do you say?''

Swearing at himself inwardly, Trent gave a shrug and a
grimace of almost-apology. "You have reminded me of
why I happen to be in such a vile mood—and I don't mean
to take it out on you, my friend. I've promised the United
States Ambassador to join him in his box tonight at some
silly arts exhibition—and I'm not in the right mood for
that kind of thing! But''—and his eyebrow lifted suddenly
as Trent gave one of his rare grins—"why don't *you* come
along too? Afterward, we can go wherever you suggest!''

In the end, they went to M. Péladan's exhibition together—and it was there that he saw *her*.

He saw her from the U. S. Ambassador's box—without
being seen by her. He didn't recognize her at first—how
could he have? Damn, she was so different! Exquisitely
groomed, bejeweled, laughing; a pretty flower among
other pretty flowers!

"Well, since I happen to be acquainted with Liane de
Pougy, I suppose I'll have to ask her to introduce me to
that sparkling young creature with her!'' Trent drawled.

"Oh, but that's . . . hmm . . . it wouldn't *do*—that's
Laura Morgan. Moves in rather a fast crowd, and I've

heard she's *writing*—anonymously, of course! But Mr. Morgan—her father, that is—told me he thought his girl could learn to take care of herself, and one can only hope for the best, eh?'' the Ambassador said.

"*Laura!* Why, the little—'' Trent barely stopped himself in time, knowing the Ambassador's rather strait-laced views and manners. Laura Morgan? How much had she learned and experienced during the past four years? He thought that perhaps he'd enjoy finding out, memories of their last meetings suddenly returning to his mind.

He was determined, in any case, to find out just how much she had changed. And, of course, he *did* know Liane de Pougy quite well, after all!

Later on, after dinner at Maxim's and entertainment at the Moulin Rouge, Trent found himself feeling slightly guilty for quarreling with Frank, who, after all, had nothing to do with the surprising surge of anger he had felt on seeing Laura Morgan—the *new* Laura Morgan with her courtesan friends and their men—and *other* men as well—all dancing attendance on her as if she were actually one of *them!* She might as well be part of the *demi-monde,* he thought, a *grande horizontale*—the flirtatious bitch, the little slut that she had become.

Noticing the direction of his friend's eyes, Frank had chuckled. "Aha! Laura Morgan again, eh? You were watching her before. Well, I could introduce you if you want.''

"*That* won't be necessary,'' Trent said shortly, puffing on his cigar far too strongly before he laid it down in the ornate ashtray. "We have met before, although I wish you wouldn't mention it to her. She might not want to remember.''

Frank gave him a sideways look, and he touched his moustache. "Oh, so it's that way!''

"What way do you mean?'' Trent said touchily. "We *have* met. Long ago. She was almost a child at the time, and just as . . . well, she was quite young and immature at the time. Perhaps sixteen or seventeen? And almost—''

"Ah, there's a lot of almosts here—"

"If you don't stop that, Frank, I'm liable to challenge you to a duel, which you know you can't win, because I'm a much better shot."

"Ah, *touché, touché!*" Frank chuckled. "Very well. So if you only want to watch Miss Morgan at a distance, please do so. As you said, you can always get an introduction from Liane if you choose to."

"I think I choose to just observe her for a while, *first*. Did I mention, by the way, that we did not get on too well at our first meeting? Or our second either."

"Ah, you've met so many times?"

"Yes."

"I see," Frank said, in an ultrasolemn voice. "Hmm, well, it all sounds very interesting, shall we say. And full of possibilities."

"Oh, hell! When will you stop talking like a fucking journalist?" Trent said in a disgusted tone of voice. "I tell you, Frank, the girl, or girl-woman, is really not my type. The problem is—"

"Yes? There is a problem?"

"Frank, shut up. Let me finish. No, on the other hand, I'm not going to finish. You've learned enough for the moment. I told you—I *have* known Miss Morgan. A long time ago, a *very* long time ago. I know her father and her mother much better. And that's all you're going to get out of me. What's more, friend, if I see a word of this in print, then I will have to kill you, won't I?" At which point, Trent smiled his baretooth, tiger grin, as Frank called it.

"Ah well, I've no desire to be killed at an early age, before I've enjoyed all the pleasures life has to offer, so therefore I will be, I promise you, my friend, *discreet* for as long as I can stand it! But mind you, I would really like, and maybe just for my memoirs, to have as many details as you can give me as time goes along. For instance, how far do you think you can get with Miss Morgan? It seems to me that she's a very independent type of young lady, not at all the usual American heiress, not at all the *usual* beauty either.''

"Oh yes, I can tell *that* much at least from the company she keeps and the makeup she wears!''

Frank laughed. "Trent, really. If I did not know you better, I would think you sounded like a jealous husband.''

"Oh, I do, do I?'' Trent growled with a dangerous look in his eyes.

Frank put one hand up placatingly. "Forget what I said. I didn't mean it.''

At which Trent let his rigid shoulders relax for a minute before he shrugged. "Ah, well, I suppose the little wench always could rub me the wrong way. Anyhow, I *did* promise her parents I would keep an eye on her.''

"Oh certainly, certainly, of course!'' Frank said solemnly, receiving in response a narrowing of his companion's eyes, and a hardening of his mouth. "No offense meant,'' Frank said hastily.

"None taken,'' Trent said wryly, "but I would really rather *not* be recognized by Miss Morgan—for the moment, that is.''

"Quite so,'' Frank said, "quite so. Now, would you like to stay here, or shall we make our way to one of the more Bohemian places?''

"It's clear to see she's quite happy in the company of her friends, so why shouldn't we leave?''

Trent wondered afterward why he had been so unaccountably annoyed at the sight of her with some of the most famous courtesans in Paris; dressed and made up like one of them and laughing and giggling with a man whom he recognized as a minor Indian nabob. What, he thought gloweringly, was the matter with the little bitch? What kind of game did she think she was playing this time? And yet all the same he had to admit, albeit unwillingly, that she *had* certainly changed. She was not only a woman now, she was a temptress. She had learned how to dress, how to arrange her hair, and how to be seductive. It made

him angry, and—damn it—it made him want her, really
want her. Want to teach her a lesson, in fact, about playing
with fire!

"My dear," Liane said to Laura on the next occasion
they were together, riding in the Bois, "I haven't had the
chance to tell you before, but I've been made an offer! For
you, that is."

"You have? Really?" Laura said, turning her face toward her friend, her eyes sparkling. "Oh, Liane, you're
not serious, are you?"

"Of course I am, darling. Aren't I always?"

"Yes, hmm, well . . . I *guess* . . . *!*"

"Of course I can't divulge his name. He insisted on
that; but I could tell that he was serious about it. He has
promised to put you up in a house, in a most fashionable
section of town, and money's no object. You shall have
your own servants, he promised. And you will be able to
decorate your apartments as you wish. He will even draw
up a contract, to be agreed upon by your lawyers. You
shall have carriages—as many as you please; even a horseless carriage, if you want one. He sounded *most* generous."

"But *who* is he? Why would he do all this?"

"I presume, or so I've been told, that he saw us together
at Monsieur Péladan's Review, where M. Satie performed
so magnificently, and then afterward he observed us at Le
Moulin Rouge. Oh, I don't know, that's how one meets
men, as far as I know. He said you deserved better than
your escort that evening and he was ready to give you the
best. *Chérie*, I am merely conveying the message. And
I'm not even sure who he is except my friend tells me he's
extremely rich, good-looking, and an English milord in
the bargain. It sounds interesting, *non?* And are you not
always looking for interesting things to write about?"

"Yes, *but*—" Laura said, not knowing whether she
should be flattered or insulted. She just wished she knew
what this *he* looked like; *who* he was. Of course it was

interesting—of course it was. But at the same time she could not admit to Liane how woefully ignorant she was of certain facts of life.

"Well," Laura said uncertainly, "I'm not sure. In fact, it's something that I'd have to think about, even if it does sound intriguing! But, I can't go with a man, or agree to anything right away—not with someone who might be a *hunchback* or syphilitic, for all I know."

Liane gave one of her deep, sultry laughs. "Ah, *petite!* I am positive that he could not be anything of the kind! If you don't want him, *I* would be willing—but, *alors,* he wants *you,* and I've said I would speak to you. Although I think I already knew then what your answer would be." At which she laughed again, before saying: "But think, *chère amie,* you could write about this, couldn't you? And since you're independent you can leave him anytime you please. But—it's only a thought, of course. What you do is your decision, after all. I just relay a message."

"Are you sure," Laura pursued suspiciously, "that you *really* don't know who it is? Now you've got me intrigued. Are you sure, Liane? Are you *sure?*"

"But of course I'm sure. Because if I knew, I would tell you if it was somebody I knew. I would tell you if he was good in bed or not! Or worth keeping or not. But I don't know. I must admit it intrigues me too. Perhaps if he can't have you, he might want me. I'm getting tired of waiting for my Prince to become a King."

"Oh, well," Laura said hastily, "just let me think about it. Tell your friend that I am considering the man's offer. Although I would like more details before I could possibly commit myself, even to a meeting. Even though," she added, half in an undertone, "I am *dying* to know what he looks like."

So, he had made her an offer, and she, the slut that she must have become, was actually, cold-bloodedly, "considering" it! Not only that, she was already thinking of the legal side of it. She couldn't be serious, surely, or was this all part of a plot so that she could write some story, some stupid exposé type of article? Trent felt he should pay a friendly visit to Frank Harris before Frank left for London.

"Well, you never did tell me what transpired," Frank Harris said when they next met.

"Why, I made an offer for her," Trent said shortly, shrugging off his caped evening coat. "After all, since she chooses to masquerade as a *demi-mondaine* I thought I would treat her as such. And I'm surprised that, as a very serious journalist—or so *you* say—she has not yet answered my offer, which I made in all good faith, I assure you."

"You are surely joshing me," Harris said, his eyebrows rising. "Honestly, Trent old man, tell me you are joshing me. You did not!"

"Of course I did. I'm serious about anything I do—part of the time at least. She intrigues me. And I suppose I wanted to see how far she would go. I mean, you could get *two* articles out of this, instead of just one—her version and mine. If she takes me up on my offer, at least! I wonder if she might? Even if in the pursuit of . . . shall we say, art for art's sake?"

"You are priceless, my friend!" Frank sounded incredulous. "Does she *know* who you are?"

"Of course not! I specifically told Liane to be very cagey about that. No, as far as she's concerned, I'm an English milor' who set eyes on her, fell madly in love with her immediately, and decided she needed to be set up in the style to which one would think she had become accustomed to by now."

"I can't believe it!

"Well, do believe it! I'm still waiting for an answer. All I got from Liane the last time I talked to her was that she says 'Maybe'—she's thinking about it."

"She *is?* Liane said that Laura is actually thinking about it? Well, by God! I mean, she wouldn't let *me* get anywhere close to her."

"Oh? Maybe you don't have enough money to offer her, or maybe she's just playing it safe. Frank, knowing your reputation—"

"Hah!" Harris snorted. "You're a fine one to talk, my friend. My reputation, indeed. Hah!"

"Just don't write me up, Frank. Remember, any duel I'd always win."

"That's what I keep thinking about," Harris said dourly. "Well, at least you can keep me posted, and I swear, I swear," he said, putting one hand up emphatically, "not a word will pass my lips. Not a word will I write. *Yet.* I just want to know what happens. So you will promise me to tell me what transpires, won't you? Now that you've teased me to this extent."

"Perhaps. If she gives in, I'll tell you. If she doesn't . . . but we shall see." At which point, Trent took his leave, wondering as he did, how exactly he really felt and why there were so many conflicting emotions playing against the screen of his mind.

"But who is this man? Who *is* he? How do I know that he's not disfigured—no, Liane, you wouldn't do that, would you?"

"Of course not, *chérie,*" Liane said in an offended tone of voice. And then she smiled, shook her head, shrugged her shoulder. "I suppose you do not understand yet. To you it's all a game. To me, to *us,* to my friends, it is a way of life, we're just part of the life. And so—it is up to you. But you had best be honored, I think. Once you sign a legal document—"

"*Legal?* These things are legal?"

"As legal as marriage," Liane laughed, her laughter echoed by the other woman who lounged in the window seat of Laura's salon, her skirt tucked up almost to her knees, one slim ankle trailing down to the floor. This was Justine, Justine with the copper-gold hair that reminded Laura of her mother's except that it was a darker shade, almost a bronze.

Justine was very popular these days. She had just signed a contract with a minor King and was waiting for her new apartment to be furnished exactly the way she had demanded it should be in the agreement that had been drawn up. "I'll be getting one of those new horseless carriages," Justine volunteered between popping grapes into her mouth.

If you're serious about this," Liane said, cocking an eyebrow at Laura, "then you should ask for at least two of these new, what do they call them, motor cars, if you can stand the noise and the smell. As Justine says, it is *quite* the fashionable thing these days. It's like having a telephone."

Laura chewed thoughtfully on her bottom lip before speaking. "Isn't it time to *see* this person? I mean, after all, I have to find out what he looks like and who he is too."

"That can be arranged, but I assure you, *chérie*, if he was not out of the—how do you say it?—top drawer?"

"Yes."

"I would not even have told you about this offer. But he's of the English nobility—"

"Titled?"

"An old title, I understand. And very, very rich, as I've mentioned. Also"—she gave a soft, murmurous laugh—"a very good lover . . ."

"Indeed?"

"And he is not too old. So, you see, it is now up to you what you will do about this."

Yes, it was indeed up to her what she would do about this, but Laura hovered between uncertainty and curiosity. Who *was* this man? English? Most Englishmen weren't her type at all. They were rather too effeminate, she thought. She did not particularly care for their drawling Oxford accents, but—there were always exceptions, she supposed. Like Frank Harris, whom she quite liked.

On the one hand, Laura's writer's curiosity warred with her sense of caution. She had nobody she dared talk to about this. Frank Harris was planning to return to London and was expecting to see her there, as he had reminded her several times. And in a way that was a relief because Frank had been getting rather insistent in his attentions to her, even though he was too much of a gentleman to push too hard. But still, one couldn't tell! In a way, she was quite attracted to Frank, though she did not have the least desire to be just one more of the many conquests that he recorded in detail in his diaries the next day.

Oh no, when I lose my virginity, Laura would think sometimes, it will be like Roman candles going off—like rockets, like bells ringing madly. After *that*, who cares? I just want to like it the very *first* time!

"Oh, by the way," Liane then said, "*he* will be at the ball, and afterward at Danielle's house too. He told me to say that he was sure you would find each other so that both of you might finally decide whether or not the arrangement would work."

"Well, you're certainly making it all very mysterious!" Laura said, almost snapping in exasperation.

Liane merely gave one of her indolent shrugs. "My dear, he was insistent, and he pays well. He's *too* handsome, I'll tell you *that* much. Who knows?"

"Oh yes, who knows?" Laura said flippantly, wondering exactly how she was going to extricate herself from this mess—or whether she would go ahead with it. How much of her was a journalist, and how much a scared virgin? She was curious—she admitted that much to herself. And she could always back out at the last moment, couldn't she? After she'd met this man and heard all the details of his proposition. Who could he be? Someone she'd met? She'd felt, at times, as if she were being watched, even followed. She had said as much to Frank and he had scoffed.

A few days later, everything else was wiped out of her mind by something *really* exciting. She learned that she— that is, Monsieur L.M.—had been challenged to a duel by an angry, hot-headed young Vicomte who imagined himself and his family maligned by the most recent article she'd had published.

"Well! Now you've really made your mark!" Frank had congratulated her. "And think how foolish that young hothead will feel when he's informed that the piece of filth he refers to was written by a member of the endangered female sex he wants to protect and defend from such ideas! Let *me* compose the letter we'll send him, won't you?"

"But Frank!" Laura said sweetly as she practiced a wide-eyed and innocent stare on him. "I've already *accepted* the challenge, of course—you should have *known* I would! And you had better not breathe a *word*, or you'll be the one facing my Colt revolver, I promise you!"

He knew that once Laura had made up her mind, there was no deterring her. Not only was she determined to fight a duel, but she had actually asked him to be one of her seconds.

"I suppose I'll have to have Franco as the other—if he doesn't fuss too much!"

Chapter 13

"You *are* going to meet him, *chérie?*" her friends said. "For the honor of womanhood . . ."

"And *sisterhood!* Oh—capital! I haven't heard anything so amusing for months—*years*, perhaps! Shall we charge admission, do you think?"

She was deluged with questions—with suggestions—with encouragement. She was about to become a symbol of the liberated female who was the equal, if not the superior, of an arrogant, blustering man! The Amazons would be there in full force—taking careful cover in the forest, of course.

"It's beginning to sound like a circus sideshow, I'm afraid," Laura confessed wryly to Frank Harris, who had finally volunteered to be one of her seconds. "But then it *is* exciting." And suddenly she began to laugh, remembering Buffalo Bill's Wild West Show that had taken Paris by storm. Why not? Yes—why not indeed? Even Franco, for all his angry protests, had, she felt, begun to be amused by the whole idea, once he'd had time to get used to it.

He had exploded with anger at first, of course—just as she had expected.

"Be serious! Fight a duel? You, a woman? Damn it, Laura, this is going too far!" But in the end, just as she had known he would, he gave in.

While Laura felt triumphant, her brother tried to keep his reservations to himself, at this point.

Franco had known very well that his sister would go ahead and have things her own way in the end, no matter how much he might protest and remonstrate with her. Damn Laura and her hotheadedness—her stubborn willfulness!

Of course he wasn't afraid that she would be hurt or even slightly injured by participating in this silly duel that she had decided to think of as a *symbol* of some kind. No, as he had consoled Ena, who had been quite distraught when he had last seen her, it was not Laura he worried about, but her unfortunate adversary—not to mention the possible consequences if she was reckless and mindless enough to kill the poor devil! With Laura, one could never tell. She was completely unpredictable, and she needed curbing along with a liberal and much-needed dose of self-discipline.

He felt that he had tried hard to communicate with his sister and to maintain an amicable relationship with her. But to no avail! Laura was far too headstrong to be reasoned with and their parents could not be reached, even by cable. He was in enough trouble himself to leave Paris somewhat precipitously.

How in the hell could he have known that some of the friends he had made—self-proclaimed socialist anarchists—would actually go as far as they had? He didn't believe in extreme measures, which always seemed to produce a backlash that slowed down or even blocked what they wanted to achieve.

Stupidity! What was the point in exploding bombs in public places and killing innocent bystanders in addition to their intended victims? What were they thinking to prove? He believed in change, yes, but in peaceful revolution. The revolution of the pen and the mind rather than brute force and terrorism. The answer lay in opening people's minds to the truth and to compassion for the downtrodden and less fortunate masses.

But in any case, he had been advised, been *told*, in fact, that he would be wise to leave Paris within the week.

To go to England and live a dilettante life of pleasure until things died down. He would be escorting Helena and her mother-in-law, of course—but he also had to leave his recalcitrant sister to her own devices and her foolish mistakes!

Just as well, maybe. Laura had a way of annoying him and making him lose his temper, thereby granting *her* the advantage! Well, he wasn't responsible for her; although he might possibly pick her up when she fell, as she was bound to do in the end! In the meantime, it helped to relieve some of his inner tension to talk out his conflicting feelings with a friend in whose discretion he could trust, Franco thought.

He had met Trent Challenger again under the auspices of the ubiquitous, all-seeing, all-knowing Mr. Bishop; and had discovered in so doing how much they had in common, especially when the subject of Mr. Bishop came up. The man seemed to have a finger in every pie and know of every intrigue and *possibility* that might arise. And he had instructed Laura in the fine art of playing poker! Mr. Bishop might be the one person that Laura would listen to! But first, he'd talk to Trent. For some inexplicable reason Trent seemed interested in Laura—even *intrigued* in some oblique fashion. Surprising, given their first meeting, which had seemed to induce only mutual dislike and verbal sparring; their so-called betrothal that neither of them had had any hand in. Yet for all his apparent interest, Trent was unwilling to meet and be reintroduced to Laura.

Franco thought: Now that would be a real duel. Between two of a kind, bound to clash and quarrel. And with what results in the end?

"It's my sister again. Laura's always up to something deliberately outrageous, and of course she's too stubborn to listen to reason!"

"Oh? And this time—what?" Trent was a good poker

player, almost as good as Mr. Bishop, and he had obviously trained himself to betray no emotion.

"She's been challenged to a duel, of all things—and of course she's accepted!"

"And so?"

"Well, it's ridiculous, of course! These deliberately provocative articles she's been writing under those initials—knowing Laura, she probably expected the outcome! Not only that, she's damn well relishing it! And so are her friends, all of them—the *grandes horizontales* as well as those mannish Amazones. They're encouraging her—and *she's* quite excited about it. Not only that, she doesn't want this poor wretch of a Vicomte, who's in for a tremendous shock, to know that he's going to be fighting a duel with a woman! And she expects *me* to be one of her seconds! To tell you the truth, I don't quite know how to deal with Laura any longer. If I try to advise her, she displays a childish contrariness! And so, damn it—Well, what am I supposed to do? I can't stop her from going ahead with this particular piece of bravado—that would be quite useless. And I also have problems of my own to cope with."

Franco had started to pace about his book-lined study by now, wishing that Trent would volunteer some comment or contribute some idea that might lead to a solution of this problem of Laura!

"*Are* you going to be her second? Does she have another one lined up yet?"

"Well, I said I would be—she might have picked one of her ill-chosen friends otherwise! But I'm supposed to leave for London, as you know. Our mutual friend was quite insistent about it." Franco ran his fingers through his hair distractedly. He added, hoping to provoke some reaction, "I believe she's asked Frank Harris to be her other second. And he's probably going to be fool enough to agree, especially since he seems to be quite taken with Laura. *I* can't see it, of course, but he says he's quite *fascinated* by her! Now, look here Trent . . ." Franco stopped his pacing to glare at his friend before continuing strongly, "I'm sure you know why I'm telling you all this, and I'm going to come to the point. Will *you* keep an eye on things? It's customary to have a doctor present, I believe, and perhaps you—"

"Everyone will be all muffled up or masked, I suppose? Considering that duels are supposed to be illegal. And your sister . . . ?"

"Oh, Laura isn't about to spoil her fun by letting anybody know she's a female, I'm sure of that much at least. Not unless *she's* ready to unmask—and I'm positive she'll do it very effectively too!"

"Well, perhaps I can be the customary doctor. I'd like to watch this masquerade in any case. And I have done quite a bit of horse-doctoring in my time, so I suppose I could manage . . . if necessary. Hopefully, she'll keep her head, and intimidate her adversary rather than execute him! Don't worry," he added thoughtfully, "I promise to keep an eye on your sister. Maybe she needs to be given her head for a while, until she gets tired of running around in circles, not certain what fence to jump first. She reminds me of a wild mare, with neither bit nor bridle nor stallion to guide her! She's a wayward runaway from the *civilized* way of life, but then, considering—"

Franco gave a crack of laughter. "What you're talking about sounds very much like *The Taming of the Shrew*. Is that what you intend to do?"

"Perhaps. But I'll let her get tired out first, and as soon as I have her *halfway* tamed . . . well, we'll see . . ."

She had been the one to be challenged, even if the hotheaded young Saint-André had taken it for granted that L.M. was a male.

Therefore, since she had the choice of weapons, Laura had not had any qualms about naming Colt .45's—and a shoot-out Western-style. So many paces toward each other . . . a draw from a holster or belt . . . and, *voilà!* The end to a disagreement!

Laura's friends were fascinated by her expertise with revolvers. And they were impressed and amused by her choice of costume for this duel: tight-fitting fringed buckskin breeches, a leather vest, a fringed buckskin jacket, and a Western-style hat to go with the outlaw bandanna she wore to disguise her features. She even wore boots that reached past her calves.

It was really quite *dramatic,* Laura thought. Actually fighting a duel—even if it was with an *idiot!* The Vicomte de Saint-André had hung around her for a while. She had no intention of letting him, or anyone else, know that she was a female. Anyone, that was, except for a few close friends.

It was almost exciting, this experience, as well as being amusing. Pistols for two at dawn, with a mist almost obscuring everything. Her opponent was a mere shadow—a wavering shape that seemed not quite real. Their seconds were muffled up and caped—she could hardly recognize Franco. And as for this doctor friend of his he'd drummed up out of bed—he was probably another of his revolutionary socialist friends who despised the effete habits of the *bourgeoisie* and preferred to use bombs instead of guns or rapiers!

Surely she's going too far with this stupid masquerade, Trent thought wrathfully when he first saw Laura's "costume" as she discarded, languidly, the long, muffling cloak she had been wearing.

That outfit! Who did she think she was, Annie Oakley? And that slouching walk of hers—all business, and danger, with the butts of the Colt revolvers sticking out of low-slung holsters about her slim hips. But of course she knew exactly what she was doing, the little witch-cat!

In the end—well, of course the way the farcical event ended was quite predictable! She had drawn with dazzling speed, only *one* of her guns, before shooting circles

around her dazed, and by now fear-frozen, opponent.
Barely missing him . . . also on purpose, of course.

"And I have the *other* gun as well . . . you see?" She
had actually taunted him. "I don't want to *have* to kill
you, you know. Just to prove how very *silly* you are to
believe everything you read. Now—do you want to fire
at me while I move in and out of this precious mist—or
delope? *Or*—must I hurt you? I *could* shoot the gun out
of your hand, you know, or else—"

"Please, don't show off!" came a muffled voice from
one of her seconds. Or was it the doctor? Laura didn't
care. She faced her adversary boldly and almost carelessly—turned sideways to him, with one smoking gun
already thrust back into a holster, and her fingers hovering almost caressingly over the butt of the other.

Saint-André's seconds whispered to him urgently, anxious to be gone before the mist vanished under the rising
sun. And he, obviously petrified with fear, nodded his
head rather sullenly.

"Good! Then you will delope for honor's sake? And
pray, *do* feel only that you have been gallant and sensible
about doing so, sir—for you surely wouldn't want it
known that you had challenged a *woman* to a duel . . .
or much worse, had been *killed* or injured by her?"

Oh, Trent thought cynically, she certainly had a sense
of the dramatic, the little vixen! Her next move was pure
theater! Off came the hat, and down came the cascading
ripples of her long, luxuriant hair, at which point the
poor Vicomte fainted into the arms of his seconds—to be
carried off quickly, with many fearful backward glances.

And Laura stood there laughing, accepting the congratulations of her friends and drinking toast after toast
from the flasks of brandy that they had thoughtfully
brought along.

By the time they were ready to leave, she discovered
that her seconds, *and* the surly, taciturn doctor as well,
had disappeared. No doubt to avoid any touch of scandal!

Franco would naturally have wanted to leave the scene of the crime as soon as he could!

Laura's dark brows knitted together in a frown before she smoothed it out and laughed instead at a sally by one of her Amazone friends. Yes, the duel *had* been amusing and she felt as if she'd *achieved* something in the name of womanhood!

Chapter 14

She had actually fought a duel and proved a point—now she had to deal with the slightly let-down feeling that inevitably followed the building up of excitement, Laura recognized. She still had a masked ball to look forward to; and in the meantime she had decided to start shopping for clothes, jewelry, and underwear in preparation for the Season in London. Dull and stuffy London—she had already made up her mind that she would probably feel not only bored but restricted as well!

Lady Honoria, her favorite and perhaps most respected adversary, had already issued stern warnings as to behavior and comportment.

"Paris, my dear, is *one* thing—you can get away with a great deal in the free and easy atmosphere that prevails here—at least for a *time,* while you are still the latest rage and your escapades can be written off as being due to youthful ignorance. But you will find that the rules of conduct are much stricter in England—and society is less forgiving! I do hope that you will have the *sense,* not to mention intelligence, to conform—or at least to practice discretion! I'd be disappointed if you weren't clever enough to do so!"

Conform? Well, she could try, at least. A new and different challenge should prove interesting—and Frank would be there, too, of course. He had already promised her introductions to all kinds of fascinating people, such as Oscar Wilde, whose plays were creating such a stir, for instance.

Better still, as far as *she* was concerned, Franco was leaving for London within the week, and she wouldn't have to put up with him breathing down her neck all the time—and his constant criticism of her.

With the thought of London in her mind, Laura embarked with Helena and Lady Honoria, and on certain occasions, her disapproving Tante Lorna as well, on a veritable shopping spree.

"My dear! You act as if you are buying a whole *trousseau!*" Lorna Dumont said to Laura. "And *are* you by any chance?"

"Oh no!" Laura said with limpid eyes. "This is fun, and I like the feeling that I'm indulging myself. After all," she added wickedly, "this wardrobe won't be wasted on just *one* man!"

"Oh *really*, Laura! You are growing more and more like your mother!" Lorna had not been able to prevent herself from exclaiming.

"Mmm, yes! I guess that's how she got my father—and managed to hold on to him too!" she said with a small laugh, directed partly at the *look* on Lorna's face. "Just wait until you see the lingerie I've specially ordered! *That* should be enough to catch any man I happen to want!"

"And *that*, miss, is enough!" Lady Honoria interrupted peremptorily. "Are we not supposed to be at fittings in ten minutes' time?"

The gowns and cloaks and hats, as well as the lingerie that Laura selected, turned out to be exquisite. She and Helena, whenever they were seen out in one of their new gowns designed by Worth or by La Ferrière, would be the envy of all the other women.

"The London Season will begin soon, and Belle-mère says we should go back early to the country house first, and then to London to make sure everything is ready. You will come soon, won't you? And stay with us at Sedgewick House?''

Helena's voice sounded almost desperate, and Laura patted her small, cold hand reassuringly.

Of course I will. Haven't I promised? But I can't leave Paris until after the Bal des Quat'zarts. I just *have* to experience it! And then, when I come to England, I can write about it—and the rest I've learned about gay, naughty Paris!''

"Oh, Laura! You always try to make light of everything, but are you *sure* you'll be safe? I've heard that people go quite crazy during occasions like that—carnival—floats—masked balls—''

"Stop, please do, Ena dear. You're beginning to sound quite like my brother! *He* is always preaching gloom and doom at me until I could scream! And *that,* in case he ever wonders aloud, is why I do my best to avoid his company!''

Helena flushed and lowered her head slightly at the mention of Franco, who had offered to escort her and her mother-in-law to England where, he'd said airily, he had business of his own to look after. She was aware of his growing annoyance with his sister, but she'd always remained stubbornly loyal to Laura who, after all, had been so loyal and protective of *her.* All she wished for was that Laura's natural recklessness wouldn't lead her into more trouble than she could handle, as her Irish grandma used to say.

"You *will* be careful? You promise?'' Helena said almost wistfully—wondering how it would feel to be as strong and as daring as her friend. And oh, if she was, she would have run off by now with Franco to Italy—or to Egypt—or even to India or Ceylon; to live a free, unbound life! But of course she lacked the courage to *do* anything— as always—or else she would have escaped from her father's tyranny, her mother's ambitions for her, as well as her marriage, a long time ago!

I'm a coward, of course—and Laura's not! That's the

greatest difference between us, Helena thought. But she worried all the same, even if she kept Laura's confidence and revealed none of her concerns to Franco.

"I can look after myself very well!" Laura told her friend bracingly when they parted—boxes and trunks and bandeaux standing all over the apartment waiting for the movers to take them to the ferry.

"And I'll see you very soon—I promise! In the meantime, I'm sure my uncle Pierre will *try* at least to keep an eye on me!" Grimacing slightly, Laura added: "I'm supposed to have dinner with them tonight. And they want me to go with them to Monte Carlo next week, but *that* I'm going to get out of, without saying anything about the ball! Can you imagine how shocked they'd be? My mother's told me that her cousin Pierre was quite a gay blade in his time—and her very first infatuation! I'm sure I can't imagine *how* he could have been!"

"Well, everyone changes with the years, I suppose," Helena said softly, wondering if *she* would change—or if Franco would, in the end. Life was so uncertain for the uncertain!

Helena had been melancholy when they parted. The dowager had warned Laura again to be careful of what she *dared*—for her own sake. Franco—well, Franco had delivered the usual sermons that he had developed a predilection for of late!

"But I *will* come to England soon! Immediately after the ball. And I *do* promise to be on my best behavior. *No* gossip! I'll be terribly discreet—I promise! And I'll leave calling cards with Pierre and Tante Lorna every day."

Pierre Dumont not only had to put up with his wife's complaints about Laura's behavior, he also felt he had to take upon himself the task of apologizing to his close friend the Comte d'Arlingen, who had once been engaged to his cousin Ginny, for the fact that Ginny's *daughter* had fought a duel with his son!

"Oh, don't apologize, old friend! Eduard has been

needing to be taught to cool his head and his temper for a long time now, and I'm glad it was a *woman* who showed him up as being far too silly! I've sent him off to South America for a while to cool his heals and get over being the laughingstock of all Paris!''

But even as he laughed and passed the whole matter off with a casual shrug, Michel Rémy found himself intrigued; especially after the reports and rumors he'd heard about Ginette's little girl—now an heiress and *not* so little, and a beauty into the bargain, they said.

That was the reason the Comte d'Arlingen had made arrangements to have business in London where he would carefully arrange to meet Miss Laura Morgan—the latest American heiress to appear on the marriage market—although she, it was rumored, was not to be bartered and pushed into a match by her parents, who had trained her to be independent. They said she intended to make her *own* match—*if* she felt so inclined—and that a title mattered not in the least to her. It was also rumored that she had said she valued understanding and *intellect* above all other considerations!

How much like Ginette she was beginning to sound! And, from pictures he had seen in the magazines, she took after her mother in looks as well! He could not wait to meet her—and meet her he would, in the end.

At first, once everyone had left, Laura felt almost a sense of relief—she no longer needed to make excuses to anyone. Now, at last, she was really on her own—and should be reveling in the feeling of being able to be herself, without any hindrances. So why on earth should she feel, all of a sudden, slightly *bereft?* Like Paris itself, Laura told herself dramatically; with the season ending and everyone drifting away to be swept up in the activities and excitement of another fashionable season in another place.

Tout-Paris was not the *real* Paris left to the Parisians

themselves. There was the ball to look forward to, and
more time for her writing.

And then—there also remained the irritating puzzle of
the mysterious Mr. X. How *dared* he anyhow! Especially
since he had already apparently retreated into indifference!
Or was it that Liane, when she found herself challenged,
had decided to try to fascinate him herself?

Damn it—and damn them all, even her so-called protective friends, to whom she was an innocent, inexperienced child! She wanted to hold her own!

"And so, *ma petite,* you're thinking you are ready? Not
even a trifle afraid of the unknown and the unexperienced?
You're *sure?*"

Sometimes, Laura thought with annoyance, Céleste
could be most aggravating with her ability to read Laura's
mind. Perhaps they all regarded her with a somewhat con-
temptuous affection, as a mere dilettante! Well, she *was*
ready! And she told Céleste so; sounding far too defiant,
she thought later.

Oh, damn, Laura thought. Why did she have to mark
time for a whole week before the wild celebration of the
Bal des Quat'zarts? How should she occupy herself?

As usual, it was Céleste who came up with a suggestion, delivered over the telephone in her typically languid
tone of voice that sounded as if she were just waking up,
no matter the hour!

"Oh, Laura! I had almost forgotten until Justine and
Liane reminded me—and then I thought at once that perhaps *you* might find it interesting to go with us this evening, to Armand de Fleury's house, you know. He's just
returning from spending almost a whole *year* in India—or
was it Tibet? I'm not sure, *chérie,* but you'll find out—if
you want to come, that is. *He's* the one they call the Mysterious Marquis! A fascinating man . . . and his salon is
only open to friends after midnight." Céleste then added,
"You *did* say, didn't you, that you were ready for . . .
mmm . . . experience? Well, if you really meant it, my
dear, I think you might enjoy this evening!"

It all sounded terribly intriguing and of course she'd go, Laura decided. It would save her from *boredom!* She had been squinting with frustration down at the blank sheet of paper in front of her for hours now.

She *had* meant to write, but nothing seemed to come into her mind. Perhaps what she needed was some diversion to inspire her; and for Céleste to have sounded almost enthusiastic meant that the evening would prove quite interesting, if not inspirational.

"Don't be surprised at anything you see or hear, my dear!" Liane whispered in Laura's ear after they had all fitted themselves and their elaborate gowns into the carriage. "And if you're *shocked* by anything, please—you mustn't show it! We're bound to meet all kinds of interesting people with open, free minds. Rachilde will be there, and Madame Willy probably; you know, that quaint young thing who writes quite well and calls herself Colette. Oh no—you won't be bored, I promise you!"

"If you happen to recognize anyone you know, pretend you don't!" Justine added, giggling. "It's much more intriguing that way, don't you think? Regarding even your friends or lovers as strangers you've just encountered. But you'll see for yourself."

In the end, and especially after all the whispered confidences, Laura had not known *what* to expect!

The Mysterious Marquis lived in a chateau in the environs of Paris, surrounded by dark woods and carefully tended parkland.

"It's very old, this place!" Liane said. "You must ask Armand about this ancestress of his who slept with almost *everyone* who was anyone powerful during the Reign of Terror. She had no discrimination, only the will to survive!"

What had been her first impression? Laura found it difficult to remember later. Darkness—the cloying smell of incense everywhere—a slightly built, ascetic-looking man sitting cross-legged in what she learned was the lotus position, wearing a loincloth and a turban.

Nothing was like anything she had expected or imagined! Rooms leading into other rooms, all dimly lit by hanging lamps—tapestried walls—stone stairwells leading to more rooms and cold turrets. She could *never* find her way about, Laura had decided even before being formally introduced to their host.

"Welcome, friends, to the Temple of Fulfillment! Please, make yourselves comfortable. I have been talking of some of my experiences and a few of the truths I think I have learned—but don't feel obliged to listen! Speak to whomever you please—have food and drink—indulge your every wish and desire!"

And what did *that* mean? But while she wondered, Laura found herself staying extremely close to her familiar friends.

"He's been different since he came back from India," Liane told her. "He lived in a cave, meditating, or so I understand, for *months* on end. He's fascinating—and a complete hedonist of course! A friend of Richard Burton, who was another explorer of the senses. Armand believes that by indulging the physical senses one can discover the real power of the mind! His theory is interesting, yes?"

"Only a theory?" Laura questioned with manufactured boldness while she tried to collect her thoughts and her impressions at the same time; wondering why she was here, how she was supposed to react to what she had seen and heard, and to what lengths she was prepared to go to experience what the evening had to offer.

They had all been smoking some sweetly acrid substance she was told was hashish through bubbling water pipes while they sat on cushions that were strewn everywhere on the floor. There were no chairs or full-sized tables. The exotically different-tasting food that kept appearing before them was supposed to be eaten with the fingers of the right hand, never allowing the food to touch the palm. This room was as dark as a fakir's cave or the interior of a Hindu temple lit only by a few hanging lamps.

She had asked a question, Laura remembered suddenly when Céleste—or was it Liane—touched her face with stroking fingers.

"Theory? Are you really bold enough to find out? To go beyond questioning to find *answers*, perhaps?"

She didn't know yet—no response seemed to be expected of her now, at this moment. Then the music started to insinuate itself into her head; strangely haunting music quite unlike anything she'd heard before. Even the instruments were different—sitar, via, softly insistent drumming tabla pulsing like heartbeats, her own heartbeats. The sounds seemed to underline the message and the meaning of sensuality and of letting go . . . of everything but her own instincts and emotions and locked-in questions that she had kept dammed and hidden.

Laura felt almost disembodied, although sensation ran in little tremors beneath her skin. There was nothing to be ashamed of—nothing to be afraid of. Her mind stopped its arguments with her body, her senses, her *feelings*. She was ready, at last, to explore the dark caves of her own sensuality; the primitive, instinctual part of her woman-self. Her real, *natural* self.

She was standing up—the pins that had held her hair in fashionable bondage were suddenly, magically pulled out and tossed away, letting the heavy, rippling length of her wealth of copper-stranded hair fall down to her waist. And then, as she stood with the music still wrapping itself around her senses and her mind, Laura felt herself grow lighter as the restriction of her clothes—silk and brocade-trimmed gown, taffeta and lace petticoats, and even at last, really freeing her, the tightly laced, embroidered corsets she had always hated—were being gently, lovingly removed with soft hands and kisses. She felt herself wrapped about and protected and understood by the affection and caring she sensed. Ready, not at all apprehensive now—only eager to find out and feel more.

Then, suddenly, she found herself lying back on some kind of a padded platform or deeply cushioned Maharaja's bed of pleasure. Her eyes were closed, shutting out thought in order to feel with her flesh, her senses. Her warm skin was caressed by deep-piled velvet—dark midnight-blue shot through with bronze and deep crimson—and Laura let the tide take her now.

There were only a few dim red-gold lanterns hanging in the far corners of a distant tapestried room that kept expanding and retracting like herself—the inside of herself.

She remembered what she had been told earlier about tantric yoga—the yoga of the senses: holding back to let the feeling of pleasure grow and grow, and be kept and held on to for as long as possible to intensify it.

Oils, perfumed with musk and jasmine, were being gently, slowly, and savoringly massaged into her skin until she, under the glowing jeweled lights, glowed like a jewel herself.

Soft bodies, soft flesh so like hers moved against her, stretched against her, found and explored her with soft, languorous whispers.

"Your breasts are so perfect—I'd like to sculpt you just like this . . . lovely Laura!"

"Mmm—darling, darling girl! Mmm, yes—touch me, too—kiss me—do you like me?"

She hardly cared at that moment who whispered lovingly against her heated flesh. Everything that was happening seemed so natural, almost inevitable! There could be nothing wrong with this—with giving in to feelings and to sensation, leading up to satiation in the end, she supposed, with that part of her mind that was still capable of thinking. Along with the hampering layers of clothing that closed her in she willingly cast aside the last vestiges of inhibition.

She hugged, touched, kissed, and explored with her mouth, her tongue, her sensitive fingers just as *she* was being explored. She had never experienced such intimacy before, such identification with her own sex—her innate sexuality!

Whoever she married—*if* she married—would have to understand. That is, if she told him of tonight.

Frank would understand. But then she'd rather enjoy him as a friend and confidant instead of having to put up with him as a jealous lover or a husband!

Frank Harris, sitting cross-legged in the shadows and watching Laura's initiation ceremony, felt that he had to have her! Now, while she was ready . . . and still poised on the very brink of the ultimate discovery. If he didn't take her *now*—it would never happen; and he would probably regret it for the rest of his life! Laura . . . little neophyte . . . daring . . . courageous . . . *wondering!* And now she was ready at last!

He started to rise, in spite of the hard throbbing between his thighs, when he felt himself pushed back against the cushions.

"No!" Trent said with barely tamped-down fury underlying that one curt word. "Sorry, Frank—but I intend to go first. After all, I'm expected to marry the little bitch—after I've got her halfway tamed! It won't do, having her feel compelled to *confess* to me at some later date. Understand?"

Well, of course he understood, Frank thought resentfully as he watched his so-called *friend* almost knife his way up to the sacrificial altar. He should have guessed. And he wasn't brave enough or foolish enough to fight Trent for Laura. There was something there. Hidden by both of them. A familiarity. *What?*

God, she was a born whore, Trent was thinking, and a teasing *cocotte* on the surface. She needed to be married and ridden like a wild mare until she was tired out and admitted to being mastered.

What in hell was she doing here in the first place? Learning about life from her lesbian friends to the throbbing background of sensual Indian ragas?

It was high time she learned that she couldn't flirt with

danger without experiencing it! Let them get her ready for him. She had better be. He was going to do exactly what he should have done four years ago in Mexico when he'd caught her naked and dripping in the stream!

"So—is *this* what you really enjoy? Being a nautch girl in a Hindu temple; dancing sex, giving sex? You've experienced one side of sensuality already—I hope you're ready for the *other* version!"

All of a sudden—all of a sudden instead of being *led* to something gently and tenderly, she was being—man-handled! Rough, ugly words breaking through enchantment—rough hands moving her about. Who *was* he? This man who had suddenly scattered and scared away her friends to take possession of her for himself, just as if she had been conquered territory? She didn't have to do anything she didn't want; or to submit to anything distasteful. All she had to do was cry out in protest and anger as she rejected his rough invasion of her dreamlike trance.

She opened her mouth to give vent to her rage and then he kissed it—covering and smothering *everything* after a while. Thoughts, protests, rebellion . . .

He was no more than a naked man-shape looming over her, subduing her struggles with knowing, gently teasing caresses. She couldn't see his face—almost didn't want to. A satyr—cunningly arousing her, teasing her, taking her to peaks of sensation she hadn't dreamed existed! And of course this all had to be—it *must,* for her sake, be a dream!

"Is *this* how you want it? And this . . . and this? To be watched while you're being seduced, to be told how beautiful your body is—your breasts, with those rose-pointed, hard little nipples, your belly, your thighs, your—"

"Oh no—oh, please stop! Please—"

"Enough of pretense! And you want this, don't you? Aren't you honest enough to admit it? To *ask* for what you really want?"

"Oh God . . . I hate you! I hate what you're doing to me . . . making me feel!" Her voice was a scream caught in a whisper as her body, quite apart from her questioning, protesting mind, began to arch and convulse. Why didn't he set her free? Why was he continuing to torture her?

"Say it, Laura. Say you want to be fucked. Tell me you want this as much as I do—damn you!"

It seemed as if he had explored and memorized every part of her body—her skin—making it his, taking possession of her like a conquering barbarian, leaving her helpless in the ugly grip of her own emotions.

The words almost stuck to her tongue, refusing to leave her mouth. She gave in grudgingly, hating him, his power over her as he rocked her with him—with the force of his fiercely implacable desire.

"Now, my lovely, passionate, gold-skinned bitch! Tell me you want it!"

And, oh God, she *did!* Feelings and desire overcame all her defenses, all her inner anger rising and almost exploding within her.

"Yes—oh, damn *you!* Yes—please—*yes!*

The first, fierce thrust made her scream. It had been fast, brutal, leaving her no time for anticipation or for agonizing in her mind.

But after that first sword thrust piercing through stubborn membrane she felt freed. Laura thought she heard, as if from very far away, muted applause and voices. Nothing mattered. She was aware only of what she had been waiting for, holding in, keeping back. She heard herself cry out and cry out and cry as she felt from the inside to the outside of herself the cresting and breaking and the crashing that did not seem to stop.

Chapter 15

Laura woke up with a splitting headache the next day; and with absolutely no recollection of how she had got back home or who had brought her back. She drank almost a whole pot of scaldingly hot, strong black coffee before she decided that it was, perhaps, better *not* to wonder and not to remember too much of what had or *might* have taken place the night before.

She had had far too much to drink of that fearfully strong liquor called arrack, on top of wine and brandy. And she had smoked hashish for the first time—a powerful and mind-altering drug, as she ought to have remembered from what she had read. What she had *thought* she had experienced, therefore, had to be nothing more than a drug- and alcohol-induced nightmare or a dream state; her wild imagination taking strange and weird directions.

None of it had actually happened, of course. She had been caught up in some fantastical nightmare; and she didn't want to and would not let herself believe anything else—if only for the sake of her own sanity.

She went about her day as usual, and met with her friends . . . nothing was mentioned of the night before. Everything and everyone seemed the same as always, and Laura herself did not want to know or face what she wasn't ready or prepared to think about or to accept. No! She would think only about pleasure and enjoyment . . . the future.

After the exciting masked Bal that she was determined

to attend and to enjoy, there would be the new challenge and experience of London. Pretending to conform while getting away with as much as she could. Hmm! Perhaps London might *not* be so boring after all!

The night of the Bal, as she was getting dressed, Laura thought about Helena, whom she missed, but whom she would be seeing again soon. Helena had helped her choose her costume, and had been both thrilled and shocked that Laura could be so daring as to wear so little!

"You wouldn't really be seen this way in *public*, would you? Oh, Laura! What will people say?"

Poor Ena—when would she learn that it did not really matter what people might say? She had accompanied Laura on her expeditions to the Rue du Caire where they bought trinkets impulsively at small *souks*, or markets; and had even, upon Laura's insistence, ventured into some of the small Arab cafés to sample couscous and spiced lamb, drink mint tea, and watch the serpentine undulations of belly dancers. Of course Helena had positively refused Laura's pleadings to take lessons.

"Oh, please! You know it wouldn't do for *me!*" Helena had protested. *"You* are strong enough and brave enough to do anything you want—and to get away with it too! I couldn't. I wish so much that I could be more like *you*, but I'm not, you know. I'm a coward—I can't help worrying about *consequences*, and I can't help the way I am!"

Poor, trapped Helena, who worried too much and cared too much. Perhaps it was the difference in their natures and outlooks that kept them friends!

Laura studied her reflection critically now—kohl-rimmed eyes with sparkling eyelids that caught every gleam of light. She had reddened her lips and flushed her cheekbones just enough to emphasize them. Her costume, all shimmering multicolored gauze overlaid by layer upon layer of shining gold and silver disks, moved and tinkled seductively with every provocative swing of her hips as she practiced before the mirror. She put on her exquisitely bejeweled headdress that was meant more to flatter than to conceal in spite of the transparent veil attached to it that came as far down as her mouth. She was rubied and emeralded everywhere—even to the shining jewel in her navel! But of course, as a slight sop to modesty, she wore close-fitting, gold-flecked, and all but transparent silk tights.

Snatching up her muffling domino and face mask, Laura couldn't help wondering with mixed amusement and defiance if she might be one of the revelers tonight who would be arrested on the orders of that silly old puritan fanatic Bérenger, who had been rightly and cleverly nicknamed *Père le Pudeur* by every artist and freethinker in Montmartre. "Father Prude"—how amusing!

Well, if any poor fool of a gendarme attempted to arrest *her,* she would put up quite a fight! And then her long-suffering uncle Pierre would have to bail her out of jail; and, poor dear, attempt to make excuses to Lorna! It all depended on when, and under what circumstances, she decided to disrobe and unmask! *If* she felt like doing so at all.

In the end, after the endless-seeming parade and the shaky floats that threatened to tip everybody out onto the street, Laura found herself slightly disappointed. It was too crowded everywhere—even the Moulin Rouge, where it could have been gay enough if one could only catch a glimpse of the stage or hear the words of any of the songs.

At least she had managed to catch up with some of her friends—and they left the crowds and the crush behind them early, and with relief.

"Oh, *Bon Dieu!* I felt as if I were going *mad!*" Liane sighed, fanning herself. "So now we go to Danielle's house—at least we will enjoy ourselves *there* in a more select company!"

Danielle's apartments on the fashionable Avenue Chabanais were luxuriously and elegantly appointed—every room, salon, and *petit-salon* was sumptuously furnished, as well as spacious and comfortable.

Danielle herself was welcoming and lovely. As the hostess, she was the only member of the party who was neither masked nor costumed.

She was a tall, willowy blonde, with lustrous dark eyes that contrasted stunningly with her coloring and complexion. It was rumored that her father was an Ottoman Turk, but her actual origins were unknown. It was obvious, in any case, that she was not only educated and accomplished but beautifully dressed and attractive as well. It was rumored, Laura had heard, that Danielle was harder on her *male* servants than she was on her maids. But she *was* a charming hostess, and she was protected by—financed by—at least *three* very, very rich and famous men, all of whom knew about the others and didn't seem to mind, being as enthralled as they were by the lovely Danielle.

After they had entered and had been hugged and warmly greeted by their hostess, Laura found herself descending a flight of shallow steps, at the head of which stood two masked and motionless footmen, each holding a seven-branched candelabrum. All the other guests—and there must have been at least fifty or more, Laura guessed—had already been informed of the "rules" as well as the privileges and advantages of this extravagant fête—or party-game, as Laura termed it in *her* mind.

What did it matter? It all seemed like such *fun*—and Paris, her friends, this evening and many others before it, had provided her with a veritable wealth of experience; not to mention invaluable material for her magazine articles in the future!

Everyone here mingled freely together, seeming to know each other. There was dancing in the drawing room, and an enormous buffet of hot and cold refreshments in the dining salon.

Laura was fascinated by the gathering of people that Danielle had brought together tonight—all masked and

cleverly costumed. She noticed that the flimsy costumes
of some of the women displayed much more bare flesh
than even hers did. The *theme*, Céleste had told her, was
that everyone should come as whoever or whatever they
secretly wanted to be. Fantasy fulfillment, she had called
it. What a very clever idea—and of course it was calcu-
lated to make one wonder about who or what lay behind
the fantasy façade and their masks! She had to admit to
herself that she was quite curious.

They had been taken on a rather cursory tour of some
of the rooms, then left to their own devices, free to follow
their own inclinations. But at least the rooms that Laura
had been shown were lighted by electricity, and one could
see clearly as well as *be* seen to advantage!

There were not many other belly dancers—thank goodness for *that*, Laura thought as her eyes scanned her fellow
guests with interest. Liane had chosen to be Madame Ré-
camier, commenting that all she must look for now was
the proper divan to recline upon while she waited to receive whichever admirers she might choose to receive—or
reject, of course. Céleste was Lucretia Borgia—mysterious, alluring, and dangerous—playing her role to the hilt.
Justine said she had always wanted to be a ballerina—her
costume showed her pretty legs off to their greatest advantage. And Angèle, who was quite young and innocent
looking, made a pretty little nymph, constantly looking
over her shoulder to discover a satyr or an Olympian god
to pursue her and carry her off over his shoulder. She was
a new acquaintance, an actress, and Laura liked her for
her directness and honesty. She was looking for a "protector"—but of course he had to be extremely rich, and
not too jealous, because she liked to sleep with anyone
she pleased whenever she felt like it—whether they were
princes or grooms. Or a handsome and well-built footman
with strong legs. She was eyeing one now as the four young
women drifted about carrying their glasses of champagne
while they were making up their minds what they wanted

to do first. Eventually, they would all separate to follow their own inclinations.

Laura had already made up her mind that she would only go as far and dare as much as *she* really wanted. She did not relish the feeling of not being in control of herself; and whatever had happened or *not* happened before, on an occasion she did not choose to recall, would never be repeated again! Tonight she was here only as an observer and not as a participant in any hashish-induced orgy. Or so she told herself. No, she would not even enter the small chamber she had been shown, with red satin quilted walls, where the cloying, pervasive odor of hashish was far too strong for her liking.

"Well, I don't blame you, chérie!" Céleste agreed when Laura shook her head. "Sometimes it's good if you are in a certain mood, and sometimes—well, I think that tonight I would prefer to feel strong and full of energy. Now this . . ."

Until Céleste gestured, Laura had not noticed the tall footman standing motionless in one of the alcoves that flanked the door to the chamber they had just left. It was easy to mistake the footmen for statues! This one held out a silver tray patterned by lines and circles of what looked like white, crystalline powder.

"This, I promise you, my dear," Céleste continued, correctly interpreting Laura's rather doubtful silence, "is not at all like hashish. With the smoke you become—how shall I put it?—you go more inside yourself. This is cocaine, and it is a completely different, and opposite experience! You will feel so alive, so . . . well, you will see, if you're brave enough. This Professor Freud whom you admire so much—he has said that this makes his brain much more clear. So . . ."

Also arranged on one side of the silver tray were what looked like thin silver reeds, each about the length of her little finger. Laura watched, fascinated in spite of herself, as Céleste picked one up and bent her head—inhaling deeply.

"Mmm! This is good! And exactly what I need this evening! Now I am ready for anything and everything, I assure you!" She inhaled more of the powder before throwing back her head with a laugh that challenged Laura. "If you are brave enough . . ." she had said. Laura felt as if her honor were somehow at stake.

"Well, now that you've shown me how I'm supposed to do this, of course I must try—and see what it does for me!"

Picking up another little silver reed, Laura tried to follow her friend's example, encouraged by Céleste's instructions.

"Let *out* your breath first and then breathe in. Yes, like that! And now, close *that* nostril and do the same thing with the other. You'll learn exactly how—and how much, too—soon enough!"

Laura gasped sharply at the unusual sensation, blinking her eyes before they had time to water. If only she wouldn't disgrace herself by sneezing or having to blow her nose, she would manage to pass this latest test well enough! She felt slightly light-headed, but also suddenly acutely aware of everything and everyone around her. Even the tempting strains of music that carried here from the ballroom. Céleste had been right—cocaine was very different from hashish. But then, why did anyone need to experiment with either?

Laura decided to ask Céleste the next time they were alone and could talk seriously. Why take refuge in doing something you didn't really need, or even want to do, just because it happened to be in fashion? So unnecessary—even silly.

Well—later! She would have time to think, time to talk and ponder over everything she had experienced and learned. Time to sit down with herself and write too. But now, right now the music called to her as she felt suddenly and deliciously chased-through by a surge of pure energy and self-confidence!

"I think you want to dance—you are tapping your feet

in time to the music!'' Céleste said, her eyes gleaming bright through the slits in her mask. Shall we go? Let's see what we find—and if we lose each other in this excitement, we'll find each other again later. Yes?''

In the gold ballroom they burst into, there were no gilt chairs set against the walls for chaperones or hopeful spinsters. The high, domed ceiling was delicately painted in pastel shades depicting cherubs, cupids, and nymphs caught in bacchanalian orgies with Grecian gods, satyrs, and centaurs. The walls were mirrored and paneled alternately—each panel an intricately brocaded tapestry showing more orgiastic scenes of voluptuous abandonment to every pleasure of the senses.

Everyone was dancing—changing partners at will or whirling from one partner to another; all changing, moving patterns against the polished floor, reflected in every mirror.

Both of them, even while they still paused on the threshold, were seized and swept onto the floor to dance and be carried away by the music and by sensation.

The anonymity of the masks and costumes gave a feeling of security and freedom. There was to be no traditional unmasking at a prescribed hour, thank goodness. Clever, wise Danielle!

The lightness and the looseness of her costume made Laura feel so free and gay and unencumbered.

She danced—oh, she could have continued to dance forever if the empty feeling in her stomach had not suddenly reminded her that she had not eaten for hours! The thought of the dining salon with its tempting buffet was suddenly too much to resist. And she did not need an escort to fill her plate for her—she could nibble at whatever she fancied and eat standing up if she chose. Wonderful! She did not even need to offer an excuse to her current partner—a Roman emperor—she could not recall which one! Probably Caligula, from the things he kept suggesting to her.

"Oh, but I'm sorry I can't be your horse or one of the wives of your senators! And as for the rack—no, I'm afraid not! That is, unless *you* were stretched out upon it and *I* was the one giving the commands to stretch you more—and more—and more! But since we're from different centuries—thank you and goodnight! I really *have* to find my friends now . . ."

Laura turned out of his arms with the music, allowing him one teasing wiggle of her hips before she made for the doors, only to be stopped by the devil himself. Satan—Lucifer?

At this point, as hungry as she had begun to feel, Laura didn't particularly care which title he preferred to use. She wasn't interested in dancing with the devil—she needed food and drink. Only, when she tried impatiently to free herself from his grip, she found herself whirled around to end up, quite shockingly, in his far too tight and intimate embrace. How *could* that have happened unless he had known of and *used* a certain pressure point, a certain technique that most Occidentals did not know unless they'd studied it?

His costume was almost too close-fitting—red and black. She couldn't help but feel, when he pressed her against himself, what he no doubt wanted her to feel! Well, she wouldn't let him intimidate her!

"I had to leave out the tail and the pitchfork. Too awkward and cumbersome. I happen to believe in improvisation. Seizing the main chance."

"So I have noticed!" Laura snapped back acidly. "But I should tell you, *Lucifer,* that I don't enjoy being seized, as you put it, against my will. I was leaving. I'm tired of dancing. And I don't wish to dance with *you*. Do I make myself clear?"

From the time he had spoken to her, she had been plagued by a nagging sense of unpleasant familiarity. Déjà vu? Oh no, not that! She had too vivid an imagination, that was it.

"Clear enough, little lost soul, but you pretend too much!" Her unwanted partner taunted her while he whirled her around so quickly and energetically that it was all she could do to keep her balance and her breath. "But surely you've heard that the devil always gets his due?"

Stung into real annoyance, Laura managed to say quite flippantly: "Oh, really! And what do you think to get from me, Lucifer? My soul?"

"Hmm . . . well, *that* of course. Among other things. *Many* other things. I might want, and demand, *everything* of you someday. But—not yet. Not quite yet! You'll just have to wait and wonder, won't you?"

"Dear God! You really *are* carried away by the role you are playing, aren't you? And by your inflated opinion of yourself! Why, I—"

"Never mind! Before you say anything you might regret later I'll let you go. For the moment, though, little one. You've already lost your soul to me whether you know it or not!"

He danced her as far as the opened double doors and Laura escaped from him thankfully, without deigning to glance back or say another word. He—whoever he was— was best avoided! That rasping voice, the too familiar way in which he'd spoken to her—she was neither ready nor prepared to face what her mind and her memory told her. In fact, if she had not been halted by Céleste's hand on her arm as she left the ballroom almost too precipitously, she would probably have gone home to sense and safety and the forgetfulness of sleep. But of course she couldn't let anyone, even Céleste, think she was running away!

"Oh, Laura! I saw you dancing with the devil! You looked as if you needed to be rescued, and I was almost prepared to be your savior! Was my instinct right?"

"He's an unsufferable creature, whoever he is! I should never have allowed him to dance with me. Who is he, Céleste? I must make it a point to avoid him for the rest of the evening!"

"Well, I can't tell you who he is—I don't recognize him! But he must be rich, and *someone,* or he wouldn't be here. But listen—never mind *him!* I'm glad I found you because I think you might enjoy gambling tonight. The stakes are getting higher and higher, and I know that when *you* gamble you are usually lucky! What do you say? All the most interesting people are there already. Those who, of course, have a great deal of money to throw away. You could win or lose a fortune—or anything else you care to wager instead. There are no *real* rules, you understand?'' Céleste gave a soft chuckle as she took Laura along with her. ''My dear, you'll enjoy this! Liane has already lost herself to some Turkish Pasha—at least, I think that's who he was! She's usually lucky—maybe she preferred to lose this time!''

Why not, Laura thought, letting Céleste sweep her along. On the way they consumed more champagne. Lots more champagne—and even a little more cocaine for confidence and energy.

Chapter 16

The gambling salon was quite large and lavishly appointed, and the air was full of smoke from cigars and cigarettes. The only illumination here, apart from the leaping red flames in the fireplace, came from the green-shaded lamps that overhung each gaming table. As Laura soon found out, if one was thirsty or cared for refreshment, an attentive footman was instantly on hand, summoned by the mere lifting of an eyebrow or a slight motion of the hand.

At first, Laura felt it was enough just to walk slowly about the room, pausing at one table or another and listening, curiously at first and then with amazement, to a whole plethora of different accents and languages and inflections. It was fascinating—to be anonymous among other people who were equally anonymous.

She played almost every table in the end. Chemin de fer, roulette, baccarat, even *vingt-et-un*. Sometimes she won, sometimes she lost—but only a little. She enjoyed the feeling of being alone; of being unattached and free to choose or *not* to as she pleased. Except that she seemed, in the end, to have lost *all* of her friends, including Céleste, who had disappeared somewhere with someone.

She had almost decided to go exploring again when, unfortunately, the devil himself appeared at her shoulder, making her jump in spite of herself.

"Did I manage to frighten you at last? I thought, since you've tried everything else, you might want to know they're setting up a poker table over in that corner by the fire. You have an American accent, and I wondered . . .''

"So have *you!*" Laura retorted grimly, glaring at him as she wished she could see beneath that mocking, derisive devil mask.

"Have I?" he drawled in that obviously, *false,* rasping tone he had used from the beginning, as if he sought to disguise his real voice. And then he added with a shrug, beginning to turn away, "I suppose I should have suspected you'd back out, you false siren. Poker is *hardly* a female's game, is it?"

It was the last thing, or the worst thing, he could have said, bringing all of Laura's Amazon, *female* instincts to the fore. Poker? It was her favorite game, since Mr. Bishop had condescended to teach her a few tricks several years ago when he had been visiting the ranch. Hah! Not a *female's* game? She could even beat Franco—and sometimes even her father!

"Yes, I do happen to enjoy playing poker. And I hope *you* can, too, Lucifer! I'll best you."

"Fierce talk from a supposedly submissive little Turkish dancer, who's supposed to dance in order to please men. *Do* you? Please men, I mean. You seem to be a trifle vinegar-tongued for that."

"And *you,*" Laura said between tightly gritted teeth, "are . . . are . . . a trifle too overdone and *pompous* to be a *believable* Lucifer! Well,—do *you* play poker? Or was this all a ploy to hold me in an inane and insensible conversation?"

Oh, but she had been *such* a *fool,* Laura was to think bitterly afterward. Primed with far too much champagne; and feeling far too careless and self-confident. She had allowed her opponent to goad her into losing both her temper and her normal control—a mistake Mr. Bishop had often warned her against.

They had been playing, as Laura discovered soon enough, for different stakes than the usual. One round for money—and then the next round, and the next, for what-

ever one chose to wager. Any bet was accepted. Possessions—houses, horses, hounds, or even mistresses or lovers
perhaps. Laura pushed and taunted and challenged; had in
the end wagered herself. Against *him* and all he possessed,
whatever *that* was. And she had lost. *Lost!* God, what *had*
she lost? And what would it mean to her? What would he
claim of her?

Laura felt numb when she rose from the card table,
hardly aware of the buzz of speculative voices around her.
Had *everyone* gathered around to watch the outcome of
this particular game? Humiliation swept over her, making
her straighten her back and hold her head high, even when
she felt long, steely fingers tighten about her wrist, drawing her inexorably to her feet.

She heard also, it seemed, from a distance, *his* voice
announcing in a too matter-of-fact way: "If you'll excuse
us? Mademoiselle Egypte and I have some urgent business
matters to discuss."

Laura felt, *knew*, that all eyes were fixed on her at this
particular moment. Wondering—weighing! Oh God, that
thought alone was enough to enable her, somehow, to
maintain an air of casual insouciance—of almost indifference. Oh, but she couldn't stand for them to guess the
frightening mixture of emotions that churned beneath the
all too brittle and breakable surface of her manufactured
poise.

She was numb with shock, not even able to wonder yet
what the consequences of her recklessness might be. She
had to pretend, somehow, that it was all fun and part of
playing the game. The dangerous game she had deliberately entered into knowing very well what risks she was
taking. Well, she was going to pay for her foolhardiness!
But she wouldn't let anyone know what she felt and feared.

"Oh—it's too bad—and it's so early yet!" Laura managed to say lightly, although her mouth was dry, and she
felt she needed more champagne. She wished that he didn't
insist on almost *dragging* her along with him, making it

difficult for her to maintain either her balance or her outward composure. Where was he taking her? She couldn't help feeling like one of the Sabine women—carried off as part of the spoils by a conquering warlord!

"I can't keep up with you, damn you!" she protested between her gritted teeth. "And there's really no need for *force,* you know! You're bruising my wrist!"

All of a sudden, Laura felt an icy blast of the night air almost paralyze her with shock, rendering her incapable of speech while she tried to catch her breath.

For God's sake—where *was* he taking her? And what did he intend to do with her? She felt frozen—numb. Didn't he realize that he had just dragged her out of a heated, firelit room into the cold without a wrap or a coat to protect her?

And then suddenly she felt the heavy warmth of a fur robe encase her as it was wrapped around her.

"There's no room for ice maidens in hell," she heard him say as she was lifted off her feet and bundled into the closed carriage that was waiting outside. "I like my women warm and willing and accomplished as well. Are you warm enough yet? Or are your teeth still chattering from cold?"

He was holding her against him, halfway draped across his lap, as if she were an unwieldy package. And she was helpless, or she would have used her nails and every other art of self-defense she had learned against him, Laura thought, struggling to free herself from the closely enveloping folds of fur that held her immobilized.

"Stop wriggling around—you'll have time and opportunity for that soon enough, I assure you. And we'll be alone this time. You won't change your mind and want to renege on your bet if you're not under public scrutiny, will you?" He paused a moment. "No—I think you have too much pride and too much arrogance to try to back out of anything you've committed yourself to!"

"Stop—stop—stop!" She found her voice at last. You don't have to *say* all this to me—to gloat—to . . . Oh! I know we struck a bargain of sorts when you won and I lost! And I'll pay, but there are limits! And you cannot control my feelings. Whatever you want—*do* it—get it over and done with! I can't and won't pretend to *feel* anything but hate and disgust for you, understand that. You may have won the right to use my body, Lucifer, but you'll never possess my soul! Or *me* for that matter!

He said then, his voice a silky cutting saw: "Don't be too sure! Not of anything, even yourself! That's why you lost yourself to me tonight, because you were far too sure of yourself; and too certain perhaps that I would be too much of a 'gentleman' to collect! But do try to remember, if you can, that what I might actually decide to take right *now* is another matter! I might *try* you out now and *have* you later. That is, if you're worth it—and if I still wanted to!"

"Never!" She fought him back fiercely. "And don't think that I don't know by now who you are—and that I don't hate you all the more for *what* you are!"

"We'll both find out about *that*, won't we? But in the meantime, while you're so—*available*—in spite of all your brave words and frenzied squirming, *I* intend to discover some things for myself!"

Oh God—what had she let herself in for? To what lengths would the *fiend* dare to go this time? And for how long must she submit to this deliberate humiliation he seemed to enjoy subjecting her to?

Here they were, in a hired carriage with a coachman sitting up in front. And without showing a trace of decency or consideration for her, he was teasing her, playing with her, treating her as if she'd been a waterfront whore who, for a few francs, would do anything and submit to any degradation. Intolerable! Impossible that this could actually be happening to her, and worse—that she should be forced to endure it!

He had removed her from his lap and put her on the unpleasantly narrow seat of the jolting, jouncing vehicle. And he was holding her down with his weight—one leg suddenly thrust between her thighs in order to keep them apart.

Her arms were still pinioned, but *he*—his weight and nearness almost smothering her—had insinuated a hand beneath the furry robe. She was forced to feel his teasing, probing, exploring fingers run riot wherever they pleased, without being able to do anything to stop him.

She had worn nothing under the tightly fitting silk tights—and now she regretted her daring as he began to deliberately stroke her with his thumb, from the V of her parted thighs, down, exploring further, too much further, far too familiarly. Teasing—*tantalizing,* damn him—pressing into her just far enough so as not to rip the delicate fabric.

She hated it, hated *him!* And wished he'd finish with it. She wouldn't plead for mercy. She wouldn't! She wouldn't give in—would never give him the satisfaction of feeling her surrender. And yet, she could hardly help herself or prevent the reaction of her body and her senses after a while—or the feeling that her will was being taken away from her.

He leaned over her—kissed her moist, open mouth as he pleased, his lips moving along her tear-wet cheeks to her temples and back in time to smother her small, involuntary gasps and moans.

He spoke to her; talked to her in the crudest language— and in all the languages she knew—as a man would address a whore he'd paid for.

"How's *this?* And this? How many men since the last time? Would it excite you to have me take you *here* for a change from the ordinary?"

The silken fabric of her tights ripped at last under his harshly demanding fingers, leaving her open to his further plundering. Nothing mattered any longer—she couldn't help herself any longer or fight against the rising, surging tide of pure feeling that was engulfing her to the exclusion of everything else.

How could such a thing happen? How could she possibly lose all control over herself, *expose* herself and her vulnerability to such a brute—beast?

She thought that he would take her cruelly and callously as he had done once before. He'd made her ready, had her wanting and waiting . . .

And then, he suddenly stopped *everything*—withdrawing from her, even patting her abstractedly on the cheek before he said to the coachman: "Oh yes—this *is* the correct address, Marcel. Thank you. And please wait for me while I see Mademoiselle to her door!"

She was in a disbelieving rage—that he had actually done *this*. Had he actually said, "And that's enough of a lesson for tonight, my sweet houri. Perhaps there'll be another at a later time, when I'm in the mood, hmm?" Did he consider this a victory or a kind of revenge—and for what? She didn't say another word to him. *He* said nothing more to her. Like a statue, a creature chilled into stone, Laura somehow managed to open the door. Adèle would be waiting for her. Tomorrow she would leave Paris. She did not want to think further as the door closed behind her. *Finis!* The end to a bad dream!

Part Three—London

Champagne and Chandeliers

Chapter 17

"Laura! Laura dear, please do wake up! You have us all worried—even Belle-mère, who is threatening to come up herself with a doctor in tow—and I *know* you wouldn't want that! Unless you're really ill, that is—and I hope not! But it's not like you to sleep for almost a day and a half without any real nourishment except for champagne and caviar! Can't you tell me if there's anything wrong? Laura! Stop trying to hide under the covers! What are you trying to hide *from?*"

Laura had never heard Ena sound so firmly insistent— and how could Ena have guessed anything when all she had said when she had arrived at Sedgewick House was that she was exhausted and needed to sleep?

"Ooh!" Laura moaned. "My head aches so!"

"It's the champagne, I imagine. Or you have influenza and need a doctor." Helena sounded quite unsympathetic.

"Ena . . . oh, please be patient! I *am* trying to wake up, and my head does hurt. But no doctor please—just coffee?"

"Coffee and croissants. Freshly baked. And I'm going to sit right here with you to make sure you eat too! Belle- mère is positively bursting with curiosity, and we're sup- posed to go for the usual drive through the park to see and be seen! I thought I'd give you enough time to prepare yourself!"

Laura forced her eyes open to look up at her friend's

face, concern dispelling for the moment all the nightmares she'd been trying to escape from.

"Ena . . . ?"

"No, please, I really can't talk about it now. Any more than you, I suppose, care to speak of what is obviously disturbing you." And then Helena leaned forward to hug her friend spontaneously before she added in a rather shaky voice: "But oh, Laura, you can't know how *glad* I am that you're here! You're the only person I can really confide in!"

Very well, Laura thought to herself a short while later as she soaked in a tub of hot water perfumed with bath salts. Very well—the past was the past and from now on she would think only of the future and what was before her. Mistakes were meant to be learned from and she would never repeat those she had made. No, never again! At least she wasn't in the same predicament as Ena, who had no control over her own life and lived, unhappily, by the so-called rules.

"So! You've decided to rejoin the living at last, eh?" Lady Honoria greeted Laura when she came downstairs, making her proper, polite apologies that might have fooled anyone else but this particular gimlet-eyed dowager. "High time, too—you've missed a lot already. And—" she added significantly, "don't you think you can fool *me,* miss! I wasn't born yesterday, you know!"

Fortunately, Lady Honoria decided to postpone her questions until later. There was a correct time for everything—and they must not be too late when they joined the rest of the fashionable set in their slow stately progress through the park. "To see and be seen," Helena had told Laura before—and she had certainly been correct. It seemed as if their carriage stopped every few minutes for introductions or nods of acknowledgment.

Lady Honoria seemed pleased at the stares they received. "Well!" she commented. "I must say you two young fillies are certainly attracting a great deal of attention, especially from the gentlemen. And most of the ladies are jealous of your Paris gowns and style. Of course, it's only to be expected. And you, Miss Morgan, will soon be one of the P.B.'s, I suppose. I have already noticed some of the usual hoi polloi standing on benches to ogle at you! Just don't let it go to your head, d'you hear? Keep that air of cool reserve and you could probably have your pick of any eligible male.''

"Oh, but I doubt that I'll want any one of them. Not those I've seen so far, at least!'' Laura responded lightly, twirling her silk parasol. Her wandering eyes caught another pair of eyes—bright brown and intense. Fixed upon her face with a look that seemed to know and recognize her. Was it possible that she had met him before? He was well-dressed and quite good-looking, with silvered temples and sideburns. He had an air of self-assurance that she could not help but like, even as he surveyed her with interest and perhaps . . . a little more than that? In fact, he couldn't seem to take his eyes off her. She was both flattered and intrigued, permitting him a half-smile before she turned her head away with an assumed air of indifference.

"Aha!'' Lady Honoria suddenly pronounced, bringing Laura to attention. "Don't think I didn't notice *that* exchange of looks! I was known as an accomplished flirt myself when I was much younger! Do you know him?'' She went on without giving Laura a chance to say anything. "Well, it's plain enough you don't, or he'd have made some excuse to come up to us in order to get reacquainted. He's a French Count. In the diplomatic service, I believe, which means nothing of course. He's recently widowed and on the lookout for a rich wife. He might be a good lover, I suppose, but you have to realize, my dear, that one of the differences between men and women is that the older *they* are, the less *able* they are. And I'm sure you know what I mean. *Women,* of course, have usually only just begun to awaken when their husbands start to go to sleep early! Not that it isn't convenient sometimes,'' she added with a darting glance at Helena.

''There's nothing like a younger man as a lover—as long as a woman is clever enough not to be found out! *That,* my dears, is the one sin society will never forgive or forget!''

Laura had the impression, while Lady Honoria delivered her frank and unexpected speech, that it had been directed more at Helena than herself. A warning, perhaps? Had poor Ena been too rash, too open? They had not had time to talk in private yet.

Knowing the dowager's love of an argument, Laura was prepared to engage in a debate with her when their carriage came to a halt in its slow pace—this time to acknowledge the occupants of a lighter and much more sporting vehicle driven by a young man with a female companion who, it turned out, was his sister; the kind of English beauty that every man admired.

Helena had gone quite stiff beside her—Laura had time to notice that much before she was introduced to the rather dashing-looking pair.

Lady Sabina Westbridge was a sparklingly lovely young woman dressed in the very height of fashion in a gown that emphasized both her figure and her femininity. She was almost too perfect, Laura thought, studying her critically. Like a porcelain figurine, meant to be placed on a shelf and admired.

Silver-gold hair and large cerulean-blue eyes shaded by dark brown lashes and arched eyebrows. Her complexion was porcelain, flushed with rose along her delicate cheekbones. The kind of woman, Laura decided nastily on sight, that every other woman would dislike and mistrust! But she *seemed* nice enough; until she professed herself to be overjoyed at finally meeting Miss Morgan—having heard *so* much about her from her *brother.*

No wonder Helena disliked the artificial creature! And what was dear brother Franco about, to pay attention to anyone so obvious?

Laura's carefully composed features gave no clues to her real thoughts, although she could not help but notice that Lady Westbridge's brother, Mr. Forrester, was an uncommonly handsome man, with the athletic build and grace of a fencer. He interested her simply because she was ready to have her mind diverted at this point—and *he* seemed to be more than interested in her, asking Lady Honoria's permission almost immediately to call on her.

"Oh, he's smooth-mannered and has a winning way, that young man," Lady Honoria said as soon as they were alone again. "And he's just as beautiful to look at as he's dangerous to any unwary female. Be careful, my dear, not that I need to tell *you* that, I suppose. You seem to be level-headed enough on the whole."

After which pronouncement Lady Honoria declared she was not only tired of riding up and down the Row, but was positively starved as well.

As they proceeded back to Sedgewick House, Lady Honoria had the opportunity to observe the two young women seated opposite her. The Dark and the Fair, they would no doubt be dubbed within the next few months. Both lovely, both fashionably and flatteringly gowned. Helena, her daughter-in-law, ash-blond and fair-complexioned; and Laura Morgan, golden-skinned from the southern sun, with her dark, copper-struck hair. Perhaps it was because they were both American that these two had struck up a friendship, for all that they were opposites in so many ways. Perhaps the influence of the fiercely independent Laura, or the flattering attention of Laura's brother (before he had taken to dangling after that silly Sabina Westbridge, that was) might help her self-esteem and strengthen her personality.

Poor little Ena! Perhaps, in time, she'd learn how to have her cake and eat it too—without giving herself away. She could take a few lessons from her friend, who gave away nothing—or *almost* nothing—even under the most adroit questioning.

Even if she allowed it grudgingly, the dowager was honest enough to acknowledge when she was bested. In fact, she was to think with amazement afterward, it was *she* who had been flattered and persuaded into divulging all the very latest London gossip, without learning even a tidbit of importance about Laura's more recent doings in Paris!

"Oh—" Laura had said with a negligent shrug and a mischievous half-smile. "I've written everything down in my journals, of course, and if Mr. Harris was really serious about wanting to publish my anecdotes, then you will be able to read everything I have to say about life— even if it *is* a trifle fictionalized!"

"Hah!" Lady Honoria snorted, leaning forward to fix Laura's innocent-seeming look with her gimlet eyes. "I wonder how much you'll leave *out,* young lady! Or will you reveal a little bit *too* much? Be careful, my dear. I've warned you before, and as you'll soon discover for yourself, London is not in the least as gay and easy-going as Paris; and society here is unforgiving, if you should happen to slip!"

"You mean in *public?*" Laura inquired with an outwardly innocent look. "Well, of course I wouldn't be quite so foolish, I assure you!" Her eyes sparkling, she added: "And I promise I shall take your advice and be *very* discreet. I might flirt—for I do enjoy flirting—but I certainly don't intend to cause any unnecessary gossip."

"Hmm—well, we'll see, won't we?" was all Lady Honoria had said, in a rather skeptical tone of voice. Nevertheless, she could not help her lips from twitching in the beginning of a smile as she thought of that brief exchange. Damn it, she *liked* Laura Morgan's style and honesty; even if the girl still had a lot to learn about life and the importance of discretion.

It was quite inevitable, of course, that this latest young American heiress would be the subject of critical scrutiny and discussion in drawing rooms and clubs now that she had arrived in London. And there would naturally be whispered rumors about her unconventional behavior and her independent attitude. But then one had to think about the example set by her parents, who had managed some-how to escape social ostracism in spite of everything.

Well, at least they had breeding and a certain air about them, those two, Lady Honoria reflected while she pre-tended to doze. As for Laura—she had already decided to take the girl under her wing and make her into the success of the Season. It was a challenge, of course, but then she had always relished a challenge because she hated being bored. She had a feeling that she was definitely going to enjoy seeing how things would turn out in the end. She might even manage to get the girl married off—*suitably*, of course, and to a man capable of holding his own *and* holding her as well. Hmm—now who could she think of?

Miss Edge, her dear patient companion and friend Izzy, might have some suggestions. She kept up with everything that was going on and should probably be able to produce, at a moment's notice, a roster of all the available and most eligible bachelors in London. And she herself, Lady Hon-oria decided, would see to it that her protégée was invited everywhere and attended every fashionable event that was worth attending. *And* that she met the right people.

Planning—strategy—*arranging* matters so that nothing would seem too obviously contrived. Lady Honoria felt like a general on the eve of battle. And fortunately, Miss Morgan had looks as well as spirit and intelligence. Every-one they had encountered or who had seen Laura Morgan today would be wondering who she was by now, and anx-ious to find out more about her. And that was all to the good!

Chapter 18

"So that's the latest American heiress, is it? The unconventional one they've all been talking about? She's better looking than I'd have imagined—and bridle-shy as well. I do think, dear sister, that she might be worth breaking in!"

"If you can manage to get close enough, dear brother!" Lady Sabina enunciated coldly. There were times when she almost *hated* Reggie—and of course he knew it, as he had always known all her moods, damn him!

His moods varied, too, and he could be ugly . . . but this time he merely laughed and patted her hand carelessly.

"No need to be jealous, my love. Didn't I . . . er . . . facilitate things so you could get as cosy as you are now with her brother, Frank Morgan? He might still be pursuing his sweet Helena if I hadn't proved she was just another unfaithful wife—unfaithful on as many occasions as possible!" Reggie Forrester smiled engagingly at his sister, enjoying the pink flush that rose in her cheeks. Porcelain. She was pale porcelain all over—porcelain and dusty rose. Quite lovely. No one else knew her as well as *he* did—least of all her short-lived husband, Gervase, Lord Westbridge, who had married her, given her his name, a title, and a heavily mortgaged estate before he had conveniently expired on their wedding night.

"Perhaps *she'll* be the one to teach you a lesson, brother Reggie!" Lady Sabina said in a brittle voice, looking straight ahead. He laughed softly beside her.

"Perhaps. And perhaps not. I'm growing tired of the too-easy conquests. A contest is what I need! Wish me good hunting, dear sister. And we shall both celebrate when I run down my quarry."

Sabina merely shrugged with an air of indifference. "You'll do as you please anyhow, won't you?" she murmured. Then, with a sidewise look at him, she added: "But before all your concentration is taken up with your latest quarry—I have heard that the *latest* Duke of Royse, also an American of course, has just arrived in England to claim his title and his estate—and whatever else there is leftover. He is supposed to be very rich—much richer than his father was. Shouldn't we arrange to meet him?"

Lady Westbridge knew her brother well—and knew his greed, which was almost as strong as hers. There were few enough Dukes in any case—and almost none who had not been ruined by taxes and death duties. Perhaps . . . ? She felt clever at having managed to turn Reggie's attention away from her current lover, whom *he* thought she controlled, and *she* knew she did not—and never could. Worse, she was almost on the verge of feeling herself in *love* with Frank. The very thought terrified her, although she would not have missed her assignation with him this evening for the world. Let Reggie go his way and pursue whom he pleased as long as he let her do as *she* pleased while lending her respectability with his presence as a protective escort.

Franco Morgan had been likened by the few people who really *knew* him to a coiled, lethal spring-mechanism hidden under a smiling, rather bored façade.

At first, he made it easy for those he met to brush him aside—or cultivate him, as the case might be—as the typical rich young American discovering Europe's decadence and pleasures—naïve and gullible in most ways, especially with regard to women. The women found out differently first; and Lady Sabina was only one of them. The men—those who had a sense for danger—soon learned to steer a

respectful path around him, unless they wanted trouble of
the violent kind.

The only woman in all of Europe that Franco really
wanted was Helena . . . the fair Helena . . . Helen of Troy
married to her Menelaus for his bloody English title, without love, without feeling—the bitch! But *he* wasn't a lovesick Paris who would make a fool of himself for her—only
to lose her in the end, all over again, to her diplomat
husband, the Earl. No, give him the Sabinas—the Profes-
sional Beauties or P.B.'s whose languishing looks on penny
postcards graced many a middle-class mantelpiece.
Women who took lovers and changed them almost as often
as they changed clothes in one day.

"Frank? Franco dearest—you *did* say, did you not, that
you wanted me to wake you up?"

It was not Helena but Sabina who leaned over him, her
pale ringlets brushing his face and bare chest. Sabina, who
was always available, in place of Helena, who was *not*.

"Not quite so abruptly, sweet Sabina! I had hoped you
might use your imagination."

As she had half hoped and half feared, one strong arm
suddenly tugged her down on top of him before he rolled
over, losing the bedcovers in the process, and had her
pinned down—captive to a naked, brown-skinned satyr.

"Ohh—Franco—no! I can't stay—I—Reggie would sus-
pect—my *corsets* . . ."

"Fuck your precious brother *and* your damned corsets!
Why do you wear them unless it's because you want them
unlaced? Well, dammit—I'm no ladies' maid, Lady Sabina! You can keep your corset *and* your pretty frilled
corset-cover. I'll help you only to slip off your drawers."

He talked to her crudely because he had discovered that
she enjoyed that; to be talked to and treated as if she were
a slut, which, of course, she was!

Under his hands, in spite of her pretense at squirming
and little gasping moans of protest, her rose-tipped breasts
were freed from the constriction of her high-necked gown,
and her silken undergarment ripped out of the way, leaving

her wet and open to him. "Oh! Oh, you beast! You brute, to use me so! Oh, damn you, Franco! Yes—*yes!*"

He didn't hurt her, and yet he gave her such exquisite pleasure that she almost felt turned inside out. Every part of her body felt sensitive and aware of him and every brush of his skin, his fingers, his mouth, filled her with longing. She had never felt this before—and that was precisely what frightened her so much. She was used to being in control of the men she slept with, never being touched herself in any way by the wild frenzy of their emotions. Now she didn't even belong to herself. For the moment—or for as long as Frank Morgan chose to toy with her and use her— she was nothing more than a plaything to him, as she was very well aware. Damn him!

Afterward Sabina felt the urge to get at *him* somehow; to pay him back for the humiliation she seemed constantly to invite him to inflict upon her. He'd never told her, even once, that he loved her. He'd never implied that he might ask her to marry him, as she had hoped and half expected in the beginning, when they had started their affair. She had really thought at that time that she could control him and get whatever she wanted from him—but it had been the other way around, and God, she almost hated him for it!

Rearranging her hair before the mirror while he remained lazily sprawled across the disordered bed, Sabina murmured: "Reggie thinks I should be more serious about my future. He's looking for a suitable match for me, he says—and has suggested the latest Duke of Royse as a likely prospect. An American, and a bachelor. Reggie's planning to introduce us . . . What do you think, darling? Will he like me? Remember that you *promised* you'd never ever, say anything about *us* to anyone. You wouldn't, would you?"

She had hoped for jealousy—even anger at the thought that she might be ready to discard him so casually. But instead—instead he merely crossed his arms behind his head and grinned at her.

"The Duke of . . . Oh yes! I'd forgotten that poor Trent has suddenly been burdened with a *title,* of all things! It just doesn't seem to fit him, or the kind of man he is. But I could very easily arrange for you to meet him, sweet, delicious Sabina. I'd be a trifle jealous, of course, if you prefer Trent over me, but . . . *c'est la guerre!* You know I don't believe in ties of any kind, and I certainly don't want to stand in your way."

"You *know* him?" For once, Franco thought, he had actually startled her into a perfectly *natural* reaction. Her eyes had widened and her lips pouted. "And you didn't *tell* me, you beast! You let me go on and on . . . but are you serious or are you just teasing and testing me?"

"You've made me realize that I don't have any right to be selfish about you, my sweet. After all, we made no commitments to each other from the start, did we? And so I won't try to hold you, darling Sabina, no matter how much I might miss you!" He didn't want to overdo the drama, Franco thought—feeling both relieved and amused as he imagined the possible consequences. Sabina and Trent! By all means, let Trent take over the burden that his mistress had become. But he almost pitied little Sabina in a way!

Sabina, trying to control her emotions from showing too obviously, felt a churning mixture of feelings inside herself. Part regret, part anger, part anticipation, and part release from a situation and a relationship that had begun to prove far too dangerous for her. She *had* to be practical after all. It was something that had been dinned into her for almost as long as she could remember. If Franco actually knew the Duke of Royse, and could arrange for her to meet him *first,* before any other female had a chance to set her cap for him, well . . . who knew what might transpire? And perhaps she could still continue to see Franco occasionally—very secretly, of course!

He had finally uncoiled the length of his body out of bed to hug her, kiss her, pat her bottom, and to reassure and promise her that he would arrange for her to meet his friend. Nothing *too* obvious, perhaps a private dinner party? And she must bring her brother along, of course, as her escort.

As he started to open the door for her with studied politeness, Sabina remembered something she'd meant to mention before. Laura. Reggie would be quite furious with her if she didn't say *something!*

"Oh! I'd meant to tell you before you distracted me," Sabina said, turning around. "I was introduced to your sister this afternoon while Reggie and I were taking a ride through the park. And he told me that it was a *coup de foudre!* That one glance at her was all it took to dazzle him. And that is *quite* unlike my brother, you know! Your sister Laura is, I must say, quite lovely. She's staying at Sedgewick House for the Season under the eagle eyes of the Dowager Countess, with her friend Helena—although I'm sure you know *that* already!" And then, catching a flicker of amazement in his eyes, Sabina pursued curiously: "Or *didn't* you know? I'm sorry if I've divulged some secret, or some surprise . . ."

Franco said slowly: "My *sister?* Well, by God, she might have *told* me—the contrary little bitch! I'd thought she was going to savor the fleshpots of Paris for at least two more weeks, or so, she said. In fact, she seemed quite determined about it. Are you *sure* it was Laura?"

"Well, of *course* I'm sure it was your sister! And Reggie, poor dear, was immediately infatuated by her. He's already wangled an invitation to a soirée she'll be attending at Lord and Lady Chamlers's house—he means to pursue her quite seriously, I think." She gave a negligent shrug of a silk-clad shoulder. "Perhaps you should warn her that Reggie, well . . ."

The very last thing Sabina expected was an unabashed and spontaneous burst of laughter.

"Good God! It's poor *Reggie* who should be warned! Laura is . . . Well, if he's persistent enough in his attentions, I suppose he'll find out soon enough—although you might warn him not to expect anything run-of-the-mill or

conventional from my sister! She's hot-tempered, opinionated, too stubborn for her own good, and—a damn good
shot, an excellent fencer, and well—I actually pity any
man who thinks he can take her on! You can tell your
brother he's welcome to try to pay his compliments to
Laura or try anything else for that matter—but at his own
risk!''

While Sabina was occupied with the current object of
her interest, her brother had been busy, too, finding out
as much as he possibly could about the fascinating young
American heiress he had been fortunate enough to meet
before too many other aspiring fortune hunters had had
their chance. Not that it was just the millions of dollars
she could award to some fortunate man that made her so
attractive. No, dammit, he had sensed something in her—
something about her that actually intrigued and attracted
him enough to be curious about her. To wonder what it
might be like to uncover her, to explore her, and in the
end to find and conquer her—destroying and forcing down
all her light, polite barriers and breaking through the surface of self-contained sophistication she presented.

Women were, so to speak, Reggie Forrester's *forte,* and
he enjoyed penetrating them—discovering what was hidden under the layers upon layers of clothing and conventionality that polite society called for. The greater the lady,
the more of a whore. And he'd proved it, too—over and
over. He actually preferred whores to the so-called ladies;
they were honest, at least, and a man always got from
them what he wanted—and paid for. Even if it was only
information.

The younger son of an impoverished Baronet, Reggie
had learned very early to find his own way through the
maze of ''society,'' and to use every weakness he uncov-
ered and every advantage that his good looks, his birth
and breeding, and his lovely sister afforded him. He had
had his sister when they were both still in the nursery—
before any other man who yearned after her silver-blond,

snow-queen beauty. Had her, and their red-haired Irish
governess as well. Maura—what a voluptuous creature she
had been, with her spectacles taken off and her ugly, constricting clothes shed to reveal the lush promise of her
body. An explorer's paradise, her body had been, before
she became pregnant, and his father had sent her away to
the country to bear the child he had thought was *his*.

After Maura there had been others—and always there
had been Sabina, his silver-pure sister, whom he took as
often as he wanted, even if it was only, on some occasions, to teach her a lesson. Especially when she seemed
to become carried away by her silly emotions—this *affaire
de coeur* with Frank Morgan, for instance. Laura Morgan's twin—but how different they were in looks! As for
temperament—that remained to be seen. Frank (or Franco, as Sabina called him) was one of the very few men
that Reggie steered clear of and even grudgingly respected
as being an extremely dangerous adversary, and a much
more useful ally.

When he and Sabina had parted company, Reggie had
gone first to his club, and then to visit an old friend, Mrs.
Cornelius, who presided over an extremely discreet and
distinguished establishment known for its beautiful and
accomplished young ladies—actresses and music hall ar-
tistes who "lodged" there and would provide, if paid well
enough, "entertainment" for the few select guests Francine Cornelius allowed in her house.

Francine had always had what she termed "a soft spot"
for Reggie, whom she considered a *protégé* in some ways.
And he had provided her with some of her best girls, real
ladies who had been sweet-talked by some man and gone
astray, or young women of education and poor families
who preferred *this* life to the dreary existence of a governess or paid companion.

None of Mrs. C.'s young ladies had been forced into
the profession they had chosen—they were the cream of

the crop, willing and accomplished and polished too. All of them.

It was not often that a gentleman called in the afternoon, but Reggie was different. Francine saw him herself, in a flowing, Liberty silk tea gown, her abundant brown-gold hair hanging down her back. She was lovely indeed, he thought. Just as lovely and young looking as she had been ten years earlier when he had first seen her riding in the park—the mistress of one of his father's friends. He had taken her from the old goat in the end and had enjoyed her, talked to her, and helped set her up in business. And she had never forgotten. He was always made welcome when he visited.

"Well, Reggie-boy!" Francine greeted him with a perfumed hug after he had been shown in to her private parlor. "Is it really *me* you've come to see this time, or would you like other company as well? I'm afraid Dorina is out of town with her latest Prince, but Leanna is sleeping in—and she might not mind being awakened by *you!*"

"I'm here this afternoon for you, of course, and a cosy talk afterward. I need some information, and who else would I come to? You know everyone and everything that goes on, don't you, my love? But first . . ."

His hands brushed over her and against her before his fingers pushed aside the silk of her flowing gown and pressed into her, making her catch her breath sharply. He certainly had a way about him, the bastard. And he was just about the only man who wasn't charged the earth for her favors.

Reggie felt quite at ease and at home here in Francine's opulent parlor that led into her even more opulent Turkish bedroom. He was completely in charge as he pushed her back onto the ottoman, enjoying the way the silken folds of her gown fell away to leave her bare and open to him. Any other man would have to pay through the nose for this privilege! Francine was the best there was, after all, and *he* was the only man who could have her any time, any way—and for nothing!

After the lovemaking they talked like old friends and Reggie learned a great deal. Francine had friends everywhere and she always seemed to know everything about everyone—in London and in Paris. Reggie learned, for instance, that Laura Morgan had an interesting, adventurous, and unconventional attitude toward life, and did not enjoy conforming. He wondered what she was doing being chaperoned by Lady Honoria who was certainly known for her insistence on what was proper and correct. He also asked a few questions about this latest American Duke of Royse.

"Royse? Yes, he's been here, but briefly. He's a hard one to figure. Not a man to underestimate, Reggie! A real tough one. Not at all like his father—as different as chalk and cheese. And if you're thinking of your pretty sister for him, forget it. For *her* sake. I know men, my dear, and he's not the kind to settle down and beget heirs. He's an angry man with something eating at him from inside that makes him dangerous. *Very* dangerous, if you rubbed him the wrong way, I'd guess."

So much for sweet sister Sabina's aspirations—but perhaps the little slut deserved to find out for herself, Reggie thought as he hailed a hansom to take him back to their lodgings. *He* was much more preoccupied with Laura Morgan, who intrigued him even more than she had after their meeting, now that he had learned something about her. She was a secret waiting to be discovered and *he* wanted to be the one to do the uncovering. Reggie had no doubt of his power over women, so why should Laura Morgan be an exception to the others. He had always found that once he'd managed to get a woman into bed with him, he could have anything from her that he wanted!

Michel Rémy, Comte d'Arlingen, smiled slightly to himself while his valet carefully trimmed his beard.

He had finally encountered the young woman that he had come to London to see. Laura Louise Morgan—fruit of Virginie's continued liaison with that arrogant upstart

outlaw who had somehow managed to capture her heart
as well as her body.

And of all things, Ginny's daughter was the same young
Amazone who had actually fought a duel with his son and
come off the victor! How like Ginette!

How much of Ginny's spirit did she have, and how much
of Ginny's sexuality? He was determined to find out! There
were such infinite possibilities! His eyes narrowed slightly
at the thought of *some* of them; and the gossip he now
remembered reading in the yellow press of Paris about this
particular young woman who had occupied his thoughts
from the first moment he had seen her—without knowing
who she was.

He had been compelled from the beginning to find out
as much as possible about the dark-haired, flashing-eyed
young siren who had held his overly bold stare with an
equally unabashed and unafraid boldness in the park. A
femme du monde, he'd heard, as young as she might be,
or so he had thought at first, while making his discreet
inquiries. He had learned what he had more than half suspected already. The young woman had indeed been Ginette's young daughter, grown into lovely womanhood.
And what an amazing "coincidence," to be sure, that he
had just "happened" to be in London on a diplomatic
mission at this time! In fact, what a time he had had *arranging* it, after he'd heard about the duel the chit had
fought with his hotheaded milksop of a son—besting him,
of course, as her mother would have done. Ah—his fickle,
false Ginette! He still had a score to settle with *her!*

"La Belle Laure"—he had heard her called that, without being too interested at the time in either gossip or
American heiresses who indulged in willful escapades. But
now . . . ah yes, *now* he was definitely interested and intrigued. After all, she must have something of Ginette in
her, apart from her gypsy eyes and stubbornly cleft chin.
Faithless Ginette, whom he had once thought of as *his*,
and had even wanted to marry in spite of everything in
her past. He wondered now how much experience of men

Ginette's lovely young daughter had gained already. He was determined to find out for himself—before any other man in London could do so, he hoped.

He had, in fact, been clever enough to make sure she would be invited to the reception and dinner at the French Embassy that was considered one of the most glittering events of the London season; *and* he had arranged to be seated next to Miss Morgan at the dinner.

He was quite certain that she'd be there—her hostess, the Dowager Countess of Sedgewick, would doubtless make sure of it!

And then? What would or might happen remained to be seen, of course, but Michel had a certain *feeling* about it. Like mother, like daughter? He could hardly wait to find out.

Chapter 19

"You should have let me keep on sleeping, fortified with champagne and caviar!" Laura complained to her friend. "Good heavens, Ena—how many times have you been through this? How could you possibly *endure* it? And how many more engagements has your belle-mère accepted for us today? I'm exhausted—just from changing clothes!"

"Well, tonight there's the famous French Reception, as everyone's beginning to call it. I think the Prince of Wales is supposed to put in an appearance too. It should be quite interesting, Laura. Really. So don't give me that . . . that world-weary look of yours! You might actually enjoy yourself!"

Laura had come to London expecting to be bored, bored, bored! But as it turned out, she had begun to enjoy herself—especially after she had been presented to the Comte d'Arlingen!

"You've had too much wine and champagne to be able to keep your balance, my girl!" Lady Honoria commented disapprovingly when they were on their way back to Sedgewick House from the French Embassy. "And don't think for a moment that I didn't know what was going on either! He had everything arranged, no doubt, that slippery Frenchman of yours; and *you,* miss, gave him far too much of your time—and far too many smiles! What did you think you were doing, anyway? Hah! I'm already aware that you enjoy playing with fire, just to see if you can get away without being burned, but playing with a *man* is something else! Or was it *he* who was toying with you? Are you aware—''

''Oh yes, Ma'am,'' Laura broke in quite composedly. ''If you mean, am I aware of the fact that Michel Rémy was once my mother's fiancé a long time ago—yes, of course. I told him I knew all about their relationship too!'' Her eyes met the challenge of the dowager's stare without wavering before she added, ''And of course *he* knows it was his son I fought that duel with—and he was merely *amused!* I quite like him, as a matter of fact. He's intelligent and informed, and—''

''Hah! And just as accomplished a flirt as you are, I suppose!'' Lady Honoria snapped impatiently. ''But that isn't everything, you know! I'm sure you find him intriguing—just as he must find *you* intriguing. Especially in view of the *past,* I suppose. But you'd be much better off looking toward the future—if you have enough sense to realize it—and keeping your wits about you, for God's sake! There are times when we all have to learn to be *pragmatic,* as you'll find out soon enough. And you can do much better than that French Count. In fact,'' the dowager continued, while she fixed Laura with her eyes, ''you are in a position, my dear, to pick and choose! Don't disappoint me by choosing too soon and too tamely!''

Lady Honoria leaned back and closed her eyes to indicate that the subject was closed as far as she was concerned. At least for the moment. She was allowing Laura time to ponder and to consider. Impulsiveness had its inevitable consequences, and the sooner that lesson was learned the better. She hoped, because she liked the girl, that the self-sufficient Miss Morgan would be able to keep her head—not to mention her balance—during the next few months. Ah well, whether she did or not was part of the game of life; and who could possibly predict what the turn of a card or a chance circumstance might bring about? As one grew older, she thought with satisfaction, one grew more detached, more of an observer of life rather than a participant. Well, she had delivered her warning; what Laura did afterward was up to her. She only hoped that the girl would not disappoint her by making a fool of herself.

Lady Honoria was able to sleep soundly that night, once she had had her hot chocolate, but neither Helena nor Laura found it easy to drift off into the comforting numbness of the deep, dreamless sleep they both craved.

Helena, in the privacy of her bedroom, was tormented by thoughts, memories, and indecision. She didn't know why, and especially tonight, she had to keep thinking of Franco. What did he expect of her? It seemed as if she had spent her life trying to please everyone else. Only Franco hadn't been satisfied and had wanted more—_all_ of her. By marrying Archie, she had pleased everyone, except herself. Archie had seemed glad to discover that she wasn't going to be a demanding wife—and he was by no means a demanding husband. In any case, they had not had too many opportunities to be really alone with each other; not even on their honeymoon, during which they had spent most of their time traveling from one European country to another.

They had stayed at villas and in castles, or at the best hotels. She had understood what was expected of her, and had learned to accept her role without asking too many questions. After all, it _was_ a kind of exchange, wasn't it? Her father's money for an English title. And if she hadn't met Franco, who was so very different from the other men she had taken as lovers while Archie was away in remote parts of the world—why, she might just have remained content with the life and the bargain she had made, and the boundaries within which she was expected to live.

She had always been told that discretion was all that mattered, even by her mother-in-law who had surely known of her short-lived liaison with Franco. Laura had told her strongly to forget about Franco or, if she couldn't, to make her mind up once and for all.

"You've got to stop caring about what other people might say or think, Ena," Laura had whispered to her. "For heaven's sake! What do you *really* want? Do you really enjoy this life that you are living? Are you happy, Ena? Are you really happy? Have you ever thought of what would really make *you* happy?"

Helena was almost afraid to think about the answers.

Wanting and needing in a purely physical sense was something she had never experienced or known about until Franco had taught her. She had had other lovers before him; some of them Archie had introduced to her and suggested she take because they might prove useful. But she had never really *felt* anything (like a good whore, Franco had sworn at her once); not until *he* had touched her and talked to her, and explored her, wanting to *know* her and everything about her. Goddamn him, *that* was his power over her! That was why, try as she might, she couldn't put him out of her mind, or go back to being the detached, sophisticated, and slightly bored woman of the world she'd thought she had become.

Damn him—damn him! He'd put his hands on her and opened something up in her that she hadn't known existed before. Why had he spoiled everything afterward?

"Helena—come away with me," he had insisted. "Anywhere in the world—as long as we're together. Archie can divorce you on whatever grounds he chooses— who cares? For God's sake! Your father made his millions by grubbing for gold and silver; and my father was a mercenary and a speculator. Does being a fucking Countess mean that much to you?"

He had refused to listen to reason, or to good sense, she thought. But then, he wasn't like any man she had ever known before! He had refused to make any compromises, even though she had begged him to try to do so— for *her* sake. He hadn't even attempted to understand her position, her obligations. He had torn her soul apart; and in order to save herself, to bring herself back to sanity, in the end she had deliberately flaunted another lover in his face.

But why, she wondered miserably now, had she chosen that despicable cad Reggie Forrester of all people?

By taking on Reggie, she'd lost Franco. And *he,* without a qualm, so it seemed, had transferred his attentions to Reggie's sister Sabina. Just as if nothing important or meaningful had ever existed between them! Just as if he hadn't really cared or felt anything he'd said he did for her.

Oh, she had been right, of course, and *sensible,* to put an end to their affair by taking the initiative herself before it went too far for safety.

She was the Countess of Sedgewick, after all. The wife of a man that everyone predicted would someday be one of the major statesmen of the British Empire. She should be happy. Or at least content with what she had! Shouldn't she? She had everything that any woman could have wished for on the surface—and yet she had nothing she really wanted!

Helena buried her face against a lace-trimmed pillow. She fell asleep at last through sheer exhaustion, with tears spiking her lashes and staining her cheeks.

In *her* room, Laura found it hard to fall asleep, for all that she kept reminding herself that she had promised to go riding with the Comte d'Arlingen early in the morning. Why was she so restless? Her soft silk nightgown had risen above her thighs and she pulled it down impatiently, wondering why she wore the nightgown at all. Because it might shock the maid who brought in her coffee and croissants in the morning? I don't know, Laura thought . . . I don't know why I am so restless and so wakeful. Michel Rémy, Mama's ex-lover. She could not help wondering what, or how much, had happened between them. Perhaps that was the reason he interested her—in some perverse way.

"I must admit that at first I was curious about you; in fact, more than just curious—intrigued. But now that I have met you and have had the opportunity to talk to you, I find myself interested in *you*. No longer just because you are Ginette's daughter but because I find you a fascinating woman yourself!''

She remembered his words all too clearly. And she imagined her mother with Michel. What would it feel like if she . . . She tried to blot out the image that had almost crept into her mind, but, damn it, Michel Rémy *did* interest her! She did not know yet and did not even want to guess how far she wanted to yield or, on the other hand, whether she would tease and tempt like her mother—and not do anything at all.

She drifted off into fitful sleep, but other images pressed themselves against her mind to make her even more restless and uneasy. Too many other images she wanted to avoid, to escape, and to forget. Somehow and in some way as she moved between dream and dreamlessness she was herself and her mother, one and then the other. There was something between her mother and her father that she could not understand. When she thought about them, she imagined herself, as always, waiting outside their bedroom door until they were finished. She remembered always wondering, and not wanting to ask. She never wanted their kind of violent, almost volcanic relationship for herself; she had always, consciously or not, told herself that.

Images. Arguments, angry words, and then the slamming of the door that they disappeared behind; only to reappear hours later with different looks, as if nothing at all had happened. No, not for her, never for her! But then, how much was she *them?* Like her father, like her mother? She had to find out, even if she was afraid of what she might discover.

As the night wore on and the fitful dreams continued, Laura tossed restlessly in her sleep, kicking free of covers one moment only to pull them about her chilled shoulders the next, as the fire burned itself out into ashes.

Roads traveled, hotels and houses, places seen and left behind for new places, new experiences. Opera—La

Scala—Bayreuth—Paris—Vienna—Russia. Lectures and learning.

Herself—changing, it seemed, each time she looked at herself in a mirror. So many different mirrors . . . different faces . . . masks . . . no! She half woke up, shivering again; and at last sank deeper and deeper into the comfortably secure darkness of dreamless sleep.

Chapter 20

"I'll be damned if I acknowledge her presence in town, especially since she didn't even have the decency to tell me herself!" Franco said angrily as his long legs carried him from one side of the firelit study to the other where he fingered velvet drapes.

"Although of course I've heard that my dear sister keeps herself busy enough," he continued. "Both she and her close friend the Countess of Sedgewick! She's only been in London a few weeks, and already she's the talk of the town, with all the fortune hunters dangling after her, including our dear little Sabina's brother Reggie. Not to mention the Comte d'Arlingen. And *that* is going a little bit too far, I think! I mean, Laura *knows*, although it's obvious Lady Honoria doesn't or she wouldn't allow it. To tell you the truth"—and Franco turned around abruptly to face his friend and the fire that crackled behind him—"I'm tired of hearing about Laura's latest escapades from everyone else!"

"Like our mutual acquaintance, the lovely and obliging Lady Westbridge!" Trent Challenger said in a voice that gave nothing away. "You were right about her—she's most *informative* as well as being uncommonly obliging."

"Oh—that she is!" Franco gave an unwilling grin. "But really, Trent! I *am* her brother, after all! What am I supposed to do?"

"Maybe you should call on her," Trent said expressionlessly. "She just might need some brotherly advice, don't you think?"

"She'd never take it!" Franco stated, and soon left. After Trent had seen him out, he found himself thinking far too much about Franco's errant sister.

"The lovely Laura," she was already being called by the yellow press. Damn her, Trent thought. She had been in London for less than a month and she had already managed to get herself talked about *and* written about! The latest P.B.—her figure and face displayed on penny postcards for public scrutiny and speculation, although she was, of course, corseted and closely clad up to the neck. It was that Mona Lisa half-smile that gave her away, though, making her seem both mysterious and beckoning at the same time. A promise and a challenge that could be a threat to those who did not actually know what she was like underneath all the layers of her silken garments that could be taken off far too easily and with hardly any resistance on *her* part to reveal not only her body but the depths of her passion and sensuality as well. Damn her!

And then Trent damned himself as well, swearing under his breath in the Spanish that came so naturally to him. She had been ready and ripe for taking; and it was he who had been fool enough to do so, instead of leaving her to the first comer, male or female—it couldn't have mattered to *her!* Too obviously she had been waiting for it and wanting it—practically *begging* for it, in fact, the little bitch! And now, conveniently deflowered and experienced in artful deception and playing whatever role she chose to play, Laura Morgan had suddenly become the current toast of London, pursued by almost every male in heat who lusted after her fortune—and her as well, perhaps. A mistake he regretted now, and would probably have to pay for by marrying the troublesome vixen himself in the end, before anyone else did so. Like Reggie Forrester, for instance, whose sister he'd been bedding of late, thanks to Franco. And then of course there was Michel Rémy, Comte d'Arlingen, an ex-lover of Ginny Morgan's who also happened to be the father of that poor, silly young Vicomte Laura had almost killed while she carelessly demolished his pride.

"I can't do anything with my sister," Franco had stated earlier. "I wish *you* would! As I recall—"

"Oh shit! There are certain things I wish you *didn't* recall!"

"Have you changed your mind about wanting to marry her, then? Not that I'd blame you! She's impossibly stubborn and unreasonable; and I actually pity all of those poor devils who imagine that they're in love with her!"

Franco had also added that his sister would be in for a shock when she realized that the Duke of Royse they were all talking about was actually an old acquaintance.

Damn! Trent thought angrily, wondering again, as he had too many times already, why he'd gone along with what Mr. Bishop and his strong-willed grandfather had demanded of him. He was the Duke of Royse by an ironic accident of fate and because of his father's social-climbing ambitions. Unfortunately, he was saddled with all the responsibilities that went along with the bloody title as well. Death duties, tenants, extensive properties in Ireland as well as in England. And the seat in the House of Lords that Bishop thought would prove "useful."

When he had been informed that his father had died of a heart attack, Trent had felt nothing.

His response to the solemnly delivered information that *he* was now the Duke of Royse was the same as his great-grandfather Dominic's had been: *"Fuck the bloody title!"*

It had been Bishop who told him, naturally! The ubiquitous, all-knowing Mr. James Bishop and the Foreign Office of the United States of America had, it seemed, different ideas and schemes. And as for the extent of their planning and how *he* was to be used by them, that only became apparent when it was too late—and he was far too committed.

"Expediency, Challenger! Um—Your *Grace,* isn't it now? We need you *here* at this point, you see. There is a great deal going on in Europe, especially in England at this time. And you will not only have a seat in the House of Lords, but the entrée into polite society as well. All you have to do, really, is to keep your eyes and ears open—*feel* things out at first. And later, perhaps, you might give a few speeches in the House on occasion? Oh, and by the way, Parkhurst, at the Embassy, will be getting in touch with you from time to time—and you with him, no doubt! Whenever it's necessary.''

Mr. Bishop had pushed his chair back when Trent said angrily, ''But, dammit, what about the rest of it? I'm *American*, remember? If I wasn't, I wouldn't be involved in all these undercover machinations of yours! And as you know very well, I'd have to renounce my American citizenship in order to claim the damn title as well as the seat in the House of Lords—which would give me the opportunity to make usefully diplomatic speeches. That would achieve—what?''

''Oh, it *that's* your worry, it's all been taken care of already. *Sub rosa,* of course. Once this is all over . . . well then, you can make your choice, hmm? As far as *we're* concerned, you're an American for as long as you choose to be; but *not* on the surface—not as far as anyone else knows. You take my meaning?''

''Hah!'' Trent had said sourly, squinting at Bishop through arctic eyes. ''And I suppose *that's* all the guarantee I'm going to get?''

''I've never broken my word yet,'' Mr. Bishop had said coolly. ''Well—I shall be hearing from you then? And in the meantime, I'm sure you'll find ways to enjoy yourself. Goodbye for now, Challenger—or, as I should say, Your Grace, the Duke of Royse.''

Well, God damn Mr. Bishop, his cool assumptions and his calculatedly offhand orders! Trent thought now. Then he smiled in a particularly ugly fashion. He had been advised—indeed, *encouraged*—to enjoy himself and his new status—something Bishop would, of course, use to his advantage. Well, he'd play his role to the hilt. Why the hell not? Nothing to lose and perhaps a few things to gain!

In any case—there was Laura Morgan, and their inevitable meeting. Something he could look forward to for a change because he couldn't guess at the outcome or at his reactions or hers for that matter.

It was strangely annoying—the way that Sabina's silver-gold and rose image could be so easily stamped out of his imagination by the flamed darkness that was Laura. He remembered far too well the heavy fall of her hair that reached to her waist, the color and silken feel of her skin; how she had felt, *everywhere*.

His dark brows drawn together in a frown that gave his face even more of a saturnine look, Trent's long legs carried him from one end of the library to the other. Damn it, he thought, what was he doing, letting her remain in his mind like a poisoned splinter. He'd meet her sooner or later, and in the meantime there were too many other things that had to be taken care of. Business—all kinds of lengthy legalities that he hated to waste his time upon. Trent was almost relieved when Hodges, the butler he had inherited from his father, knocked at the door before entering to announce that Mr. Weatherby had arrived.

"Oh yes, of course, I've been expecting him. Show him in, Hodges, and you might bring in some port and whatever it's customary to serve on an occasion like this!"

Mr. Hodges gave a slight, dignified inclination of his head before withdrawing. The new Duke, he thought, was not at all like his father. Not in looks, certainly; rumor had it below-stairs that His Grace's mother had been a Spaniard. But for all his fierce dark looks the present Duke of Royse was a *gentleman* at least, and that was something! It was even rumored that Lady Margaret might be coming back to the house, to act as His Grace's hostess during the Season.

Mr. Weatherby, his solicitor, had come laden with worn leather briefcases containing innumerable documents that were laced through with Latin phrases. Mr. Weatherby, an older man with silver hair and drooping Dundreary whiskers, was a stickler for etiquette and what he considered to be his duty—namely the detailed explanation of everything concerned with the estate that had been left to this young man by his father, the late Duke.

Shit! Trent thought later after consuming what must have been at least his fourth or fifth glass of the excellent Scotch whisky that Hodges had produced. What in hell had he got himself into anyway? Shooting boxes, an enormous mansion surrounded by parklands and tenant cottages somewhere in Cornwall, and this town house in London as well, not to mention other property in Ireland that included a castle, of all things! It was too much to consider right now—although he had listened politely to Mr. Weatherby and had asked what he hoped were the right questions. Thank God that Mr. Weatherby had assured him that he would, of course, continue to look after matters for His Grace if that was what His Grace desired. Always pleased to oblige! Mr. Weatherby had also mentioned that he had written to Lady Margaret Sinclair, the Dowager Duchess of Royse, and had received her reply stating that of course she would be glad to receive His Grace the present Duke at any time it was convenient to *him.*

Another thing to be taken care of! It wasn't her fault, of course, and he knew it. It was his father he blamed for everything, and his father was no longer alive to be accused and confronted with his sins. Oh hell! Trent had been staring abstractedly into the fire that he had ordered to be lighted earlier, the flames making him remember, suddenly, camp fires that had warmed him at times when he needed warmth; the feeling of *space* around himself. Big country, big endless skies, and places waiting to be found, everywhere.

So what was he doing *here?* In London, England—trying to get used to playing the part of a goddamn Duke, of all things. He must have been crazy to let Bishop talk him into this stupid masquerade when there were other things, much more exciting things, that he would rather be doing, other places where he'd much rather be.

"Lady Westbridge, Your Grace. She said you were expecting her." Hodges's face was impassive as it always was.

"Oh yes, thank you. She is supposed to help me with all these damned cards and invitations that have been piling up on my desk!"

"Yes, Your Grace. Of course. But if Your Grace would consider hiring a secretary . . ."

"I haven't had the time to think about it yet," Trent said impatiently and wondered for a fleeting moment if Hodges's face would show any reaction even if he proceeded to seize Sabina in his arms the moment she was shown in and threw her down on her back to lie sprawled against the red-patterned Persian rug before he began to make forceful love to her right there. But hell! Probably not in front of poor Hodges after all, although he did have the feeling that Sabina herself might not mind! He'd found out that Sabina *was* uncommonly obliging; and in more ways than one!

Chapter 21

Breakfast in bed was a daily morning ritual that the Dowager Countess of Sedgewick insisted upon. She enjoyed lying back in comfort while she went through all the calling cards and invitations that had been delivered the previous day, and taking sips of her nice hot tea between the comments and instructions she directed at her patient companion.

"Hah! Our Miss Morgan's brother has finally unbent enough to leave his card. Well, it's high time, too, and I shall have a few words to say to that young man. After all . . . Izzy, pray do ring for Mannering at once! I think Laura should be warned that her brother will be calling this afternoon, and I've no doubt they'll probably have a great deal to say to each other, too—considering the way she's been carrying on of late!"

Mr. Mannering entered the bedroom of the dowager with a carefully controlled expression on his ruddy face. A rotund, silver-haired man of indeterminate age who had been butler since the time of the late Earl of Sedgewick, he was an absolute autocrat below-stairs and carried himself with an air of haughty superiority and aloofness that put most people in their proper place. The only person who had ever managed to actually intimidate him was Lady Honoria, with her unexpected directness and her blunt way of speaking.

"I'm afraid *The Times* was delivered later than usual this morning, Your Ladyship," he said. "I will make a point of seeing that it doesn't happen again, of course. Is there—?''

''Mannering! I'm not yet ready to read *The Times,* as you very well know, and that is *not* why I asked Miss Edge to send for you! What's the matter with you this morning? I want to see Miss Morgan, and as soon as possible. At least, before she goes off somewhere before I can tell her—''
Lady Honoria broke off suddenly, her shrewd eyes narrowing before she demanded irascibly, ''Why are you standing there dithering? For God's sake, wipe that look off your face, Mannering, and come right out with whatever you have to say! Where's Miss Morgan?''

Mr. Mannering had to clear his throat awkwardly before he could find his voice again.

''I am sorry, Your Ladyship, to have to be the one to inform you that . . . the young lady is not . . . that is to say, she has not returned yet.''

''Returned? Returned from where? It's not yet ten in the morning! I wish you would stop stuttering and trying to evade me! Come to the point, for heaven's sake, Mannering!''

Mr. Mannering took a deep breath. ''The young lady, I'm afraid, has gone to ride in the park. By herself, too, I am sorry to report. And . . . well, Your Ladyship, I have to confess that this is *not* the first occasion she has insisted on doing so! I have attempted to reason with her—to point out the danger and the imprudence of such rash behavior— but to no avail, I'm sorry to say!''

Once he had begun, Mr. Mannering found himself almost relieved to be able to express his real feelings, which came out in a burst of speech.

''The young lady told me she always carried a small pistol with her, in one of the pockets of her—that American costume she wears, those divided skirts so that she doesn't have to ride sidesaddle, she informed me! *And* she leaves the house at about six in the morning too! Perhaps I should have said something before, but, after all, the young lady is a *guest* of Your Ladyship! And beyond saying all I could to try and dissuade her, what else could I have done? The young lady seems to have a mind of her own, unfortunately.''

Miss Edge found herself holding her breath while she waited almost fearfully for Lady Honoria's reaction to this latest dreadful indiscretion of Laura's. She liked the girl, but oh, goodness! Such recklessness . . . where would it lead to?

Surprisingly, Lady Honoria actually chuckled, before she pretended it was a cough, and then said, ''Hmmph! Well—I suppose these early-morning rides are better than *other* indiscretions I could think of! Thank you, Mannering. And please be sure that Miss Morgan is told I wish to speak with her as soon as she returns.'' She picked up the copy of *The Times* that Mannering had brought up to her, dismissing him with a slight inclination of her head.

''Hmm!'' the dowager pronounced as she lowered her newspaper soon after the long-suffering Mr. Mannering was out of earshot. *''I've* never seen any reason to make a fuss about small things! Nothing wrong with going riding very early, before anyone else is out! I used to do it myself sometimes—but without a pistol for protection! No, Izzy, it's the *important* issues one should try to deal with as soon as possible, and get them out of the way! And now, let's see, we have Miss Morgan's brother calling this afternoon, the opera this evening, *and* supper at Lady Chalmers's later! Do *I* have any appointments I've forgotten about before then?''

Miss Edge produced the gold-engraved leather-bound appointment book from a drawer in the escritoire and began to turn the pages. Appointments, luncheons, suppers, and even riding engagements for any member of the household were all meticulously recorded in here; the Dowager Countess always insisted on knowing what everyone was up to, as she put it.

Now Miss Edge looked up, dismayed. ''Oh! If Miss Laura's brother is calling at four—*you* are promised at three-thirty to have tea with Mrs. Prentiss at Lyons! Although I suppose—''

''Nonsense, nonsense, what does that matter? It's not me he's coming to see, it's his sister. And what about *her?*''

''She has fittings at Madame Fleur's on Regent Street at . . . let me make sure . . . two o'clock. And after that—''

''Never mind. When I talk to her, we'll make arrangements. My daughter-in-law will receive the young man and keep him entertained in case Miss Morgan is late—as she usually is, I've discovered!''

And if she is today—we'll see! Lady Honoria thought later. She was tired of seeing her daughter-in-law practically moping about all the time; and since gossip had it that Lady Westbridge was now being taken everywhere by the Duke of Royse . . . well, who knows? Ena needed something in her life to keep her entertained. It wouldn't be a bad notion at all if Laura *was* slightly delayed by some other engagement. Lady Honoria thoroughly enjoyed *arranging* things . . . and people.

This was all Trent's idea, Franco thought angrily. Actually having to leave his card and make an appointment to see his own sister!

And then, on top of everything, the *concession* he'd made, to be told that she had not returned yet from an earlier engagement!

Franco had been ready to leave a curtly pungent message with the high-nosed butler at Sedgewick House before taking *his* leave when the man had informed him that while his sister was delayed, the Countess would receive him.

The Countess. Not the *Dowager* Countess, but *Helena?* And she was waiting to receive him! How? In the way she always had before, sitting alone before a silver tea tray, waiting to pour? Damn! Franco thought, but it was the way he had suddenly pictured her in his mind that made him decide to stay—and his tardy, foolhardy, rude sister be damned!

When Laura finally rushed into the pastel-patterned morning room, she looked and felt like a storm wind in her cloud-gray riding habit that was cut in a severely masculine style; the open jacket worn over a turquoise vest, and a pleated, high-collared white silk shirt. She had the appearance, as usual, Franco thought disapprovingly, of a gypsy! Her hair was escaping from the pins that were supposed to subdue it, curling and clinging in disheveled strands against her flushed cheeks and the slender nape of her neck.

"I'm sorry! I *really* am! But the fittings took *ages,* and then—" She stopped suddenly as her eyes took in the two of them: her brother's saturnine expression and Ena's flushed cheeks. And then she gave a light laugh before saying mischievously, "Oh, but I'd almost forgotten how well we know each other's worst traits by now! You aren't going to lecture me again, are you, Franco! Please don't try!"

All the same, and in spite of the light kiss she gave him and her equally careless words, Franco could not control his rising temper, not even when Ena reached out to touch his arm warningly, before she said quickly that she would leave them together in privacy now.

"You could have let me know that you were here, dammit, before I had to hear it from other people and *read* about you in the yellow press! You're the talk of the town, I gather, and the latest P.B.! But this isn't Paris, you know, and there are limits to what you can get away with *here.* For God's sake, Laura! Don't you realize that you can't flout convention forever? I wish to God that you would understand that—if you are capable of thinking of anything beyond satisfying your every little whim with no regard for anyone but yourself!"

Why did they always have to quarrel? Laura wondered impatiently, tapping her riding crop against the top of one polished boot. She'd thought he might have changed for the better since he'd been in England, but no—he was as moralistic as ever. She didn't understand how he could have changed so much in the space of so few years, but now she was *glad* that she had contrived to keep out of his way so far—*especially* since she had heard that he was said to be quite enamored of that simpering Sabina creature whom she couldn't abide!

Laura drawled, in a purposely affected tone of voice: "Why, I hadn't noticed before, but Franco, you *do* look very much like Papa when you are in a rage!

"And *you*—"

"I'm too much like Mama?"

Laura infuriated her brother even further by the coolly insouciant shrug she gave before saying, with a note of impatience in her voice, "Oh, for heaven's sake, Franco! We're both too much like our parents, don't you think, to be anything but rebels, so *do* stop trying to preach sermons to me—before I retaliate by preaching at you about your latest misdoings! And," she added sweetly, before her brother's temper could explode in her face, "just because your sweet Sabina threw you over in such a hurry for this American Duke everyone's speculating about—why take it out on *me*? Haven't you heard, that what's sauce for the goose is sauce for the gander?"

"Fair or not, I'm afraid that realistically that's not so, sister mine! At least, not within the social group with which we associate!"

Franco felt like seizing her by the shoulders and shaking her—but he hadn't been able to get away with that since they were both very young; and if they ended up having a wrestling match right *here, that* wouldn't do either. But hell! What was he to do? He hated these explosive arguments of theirs as much as Laura did.

"*Social* group?" Laura flung back at him furiously. "Ha! Look who's talking! I thought you believed in revolution and change! Or so you pronounce and preach! I'm sorry to find out that you're a typical bourgeois male after all! Yes you are! Believing in *two* sets of rules and stan-

dards of conduct—one for women and one for *you*, the
privileged class! Oh, *damn* you, Franco, but you make me
so *angry* . . . !'' Laura had to pause to take a deep breath
while her brother watched her with his jaws clamped together.

"I don't know how Ena is able to put up with you, you
know! And I hope you did not upset her either; she doesn't
deserve *that*, on top of everything else she's forced to tolerate.''

"Ena's not *forced* to tolerate anything at all," Franco
said in a suddenly controlled voice that matched his sister's. "Ena—well, damn it, the fact is that she's so used
to being locked in a cage that she doesn't even know the
door's unlocked, that all she has to do is push it open and
walk out if she wants to!''

It had been a long time since they had been honest with
each other, Laura thought. But having heard the bitterness
in her brother's voice, she made hers light and playful.

"Hmm—I guess that Helena and I will be going out
shopping *much* more often from now on. And stay for
ages!" And then, impulsively, "Oh, Franco, I don't *mind*,
you know! Just be happy, both of you!'' Then she added
firmly: "And *do* try to stop criticizing me at every turn—
that way we'll get along much better together, don't you
see? Just as we used to.''

After Franco left, Laura went upstairs to rap lightly at
the door of Ena's little private sitting room that adjoined
her bedroom.

"Oh, Laura! You didn't quarrel *too* fiercely, did you?''
Ena's eyes were wide with apprehension. "I hope not,
because you see I—''

"Yes, I know!'' Laura said briskly. "Don't worry, for
heaven's sake! And Franco told me that he's been invited
to Lady Chalmers's supper tonight, too, after the opera. I
think he also said that he hoped you'd reserve at least two
waltzes for him!''

Helena's face had already begun to glow with pleasure
and anticipation, Laura noticed. And at the same time she

thought, Poor trapped Ena! Not able to reach out far enough to take something she wanted that could be hers!

"Oh, Laura! I'm so happy! And perhaps we'll finally get to see the Duke of Royse—and he'll want to meet with you!" Helena said, her sudden joy spilling over. "I'm quite sure you could *devastate* him if you really wanted to!"

"Hah," Laura retorted, sounding very much like Lady Honoria for an instant. "Well, I'm sorry if I might disappoint your expectations, Ena, but I've heard enough about this so-called American Duke to make me sick! I feel as if I despise the wretch already!" Laura's expressive face showed her disgust; her brows were drawn together, and her mouth turned down at the corners as if she had tasted something sour.

"But Laura," Helena persisted, "I've heard he's actually very handsome, in a dark and dangerous sort of way. Like Heathcliff in Miss Brontë's *Wuthering Heights!*"

"Oh? I don't believe it! Any man who has the bad taste to take on Lady Westbridge from my brother—Oh, I'm *sorry,* Ena, but, well . . . And then, on top of that—how could *any* man of honor renounce his American citizenship merely to snatch at a title? Duke of Royse, indeed! I've no doubt he and sweet Sabina deserve each other!"

Helena was in a mischievous mood, and even the reference to Lady Westbridge could not upset her now that she knew she had Franco's attention again. She had watched Laura walking back and forth across the room and speaking out; and now, knowing how much Laura loved a challenge, she said teasingly: "But Laura, don't you think it would be *fun* to take his attention away from Lady Westbridge? Just to *prove* you could do it? I *know* you can! I can just picture the look on her face! Laura, *please!*"

"Is this a dare?" But then Laura couldn't help smiling at the thought. She had somehow taken an instant dislike to the platinum-plated Lady Westbridge, and the mental picture that Helena had painted of the look on Sabina's face . . . well, it might be worth it! "Maybe I'll condescend to *flirt* with him at least. To annoy that little—Well, perhaps to prove I can best her at her own game. *Maybe.* Depending on my mood, of course. *You* watch for the results, Ena!''

Chapter 22

The two young women, Helena, Countess of Sedgewick and her friend Miss Laura Morgan, created quite a sensation as they alighted from their carriage before the Opera House, along with Lady Honoria, resplendent in black silk shot through with purple and royal blue trimmed with fur. Even the usual crowd of onlookers who always gathered to watch and comment on the dress and demeanor of the *haute monde*, and to exchange whispered bits of gossip, grew silent for a few moments—a tribute seldom given except to the established and well-known P.B.s.

They made perfect foils for each other—Helena with her gleaming, dark-gold hair and topaz eyes, and Laura with her dark hair threaded through with copper-gold strands that caught the light every time she turned her head. Even their gowns, created especially for them by the House of Worth, formed a pleasing and almost tantalizing contrast. Laura's turquoise and gold silk with a subtle hint of crimson woven into the fabric to match the fire-opals that had been one of her parents' gifts on the occasion of her twenty-first birthday; and Helena's gown of darker gold silk, shading into emerald-green to match the magnificent Sedgewick emeralds that had been gifted to her on the occasion of her marriage.

On this resplendent occasion the ladies were accompanied by Lord Anthony Grey and his sister Lady Evelyn. Lady Honoria had, some time before, insisted that Laura needed to meet more suitable young men. Lord Anthony, the son of a Marquess, was considered eminently suitable, and his sister Lady Evelyn was intelligent and well-read, as well as being possessed of a bubbling personality, a sense of humor, and a pretty smile.

Surprisingly enough, to both Helena and Laura, Lady Honoria had actually given grudging permission to Reggie Forrester to join them in their box. She whispered in an undertone to Laura once they had settled in: "I thought he might prove useful in fetching us champagne and refreshments! And in any case it would be awkward to have only one male escort for four Ladies." Then she added: "And where is your Frenchman tonight? I thought we were expecting him to join us?"

"He had to go to Paris—diplomatic business, he told me," Laura whispered. "But he's expected back by tonight—and I'm sure he will be."

"Hmmph! *Sure,* are you? Well, take it for what it's worth—*I* wouldn't be too sure of what any man says, even when he's swearing undying devotion! Rather trust those who *don't* swear to anything, myself—but then *I* learned too late! Nothing like keeping 'em dangling, though—and you're doing a good job of *that,* at least!"

This small exchange with Lady Honoria, who sat at one side of her, kept Laura from being too conscious of the fact that they had become the cynosure of almost every eye in the house. Opera glasses and lorgnettes were turned on them, and she felt, angrily, as if they were in a cage at the zoo! Then, she followed Lady Honoria's example and picked up *her* opera glasses to study those who were studying them.

Soon enough, the lights were lowered and the orchestra began playing the overture to *La Traviata,* and Laura leaned back in her chair, anticipating with enjoyment seeing again one of her favorite operas. Lord Anthony on her other side whispered to her: "So you like *La Traviata* too. I have always enjoyed it myself."

"Yes," Laura said to him, "but I have often wondered why it is only *women* who are supposed to fall. Poor Violetta—if only she had been less weak and less at the mercy of men. Less *noble* and more pragmatic!''

Lord Anthony, who was known as a bookish man, gave a soft chuckle in appreciation of her words before turning back again to watch the stage. He liked Miss Morgan; she had wit as well as mettle, and he found that he enjoyed her company more and more each time they met.

Reggie Forrester was seated behind Laura, and he had been trying not to show his annoyance at the exchange between her and Lord Anthony Grey. He wondered why he even continued to dangle behind her, but then, he had always been stubborn when he wanted something, and he knew that he wanted Laura Morgan.

He fixed his eyes on the slender nape of her jewel-encircled neck, with curling tendrils of hair escaping from the high-piled and coiled evening coiffure that was held in place by tiny, bejeweled golden combs. He'd like to see her hair come down—for him. He'd like to conquer her and have her and *own* her—breaking her in like a wild mare to suit his tastes and his fancy. Yes, *he,* and not the Frenchman, would tame her arrogant spirit in the end; no matter what he had to do in order to get her, *and* have her fortune in his power. But in the meantime, he had to be careful; had to be patient and wait for the right time and the right opportunity to present itself. He would make himself her friend, and make her believe that she could trust him. Water wore down rocks in the end! And damn it all, he wanted her, bitch or not, more than he had ever wanted any other woman in his life!

Helena had been looking for Franco, even though she knew he did not enjoy the opera, and would probably not be there. She wished that her mother-in-law had not allowed Reggie Forrester to join them in their box, because his presence made her feel uncomfortable and even *guilty,* in some strange way.

With a sigh that her observant mother-in-law did not miss, Helena straightened her shoulders and shifted in her chair, determined not to indulge in unhappy introspection any longer.

Lady Honoria shifted in her chair, too, adjusting the folds of her ample skirts and wishing impatiently that it was time for the end of the first act. She was well aware why Helena had seemed so thoughtful and preoccupied of late, and even felt a flash of pity for the poor girl—torn between a charming lover who had brought out her sexuality, and a marriage of convenience. Ah well—Helena would learn to adjust, as *she* had in her time. If a woman was careful enough and discreet enough, she could enjoy having her cake and eating too, just as men did! Perhaps, in time, Helena would learn to manipulate her lovers and would-be lovers as Laura Morgan seemed to do, the clever little minx!

Lady Honoria was relieved to be able to stand up and move about during the intermission as she shepherded the three young ladies who were in her charge in the direction of the Ladies' Retiring Rooms. Reggie Forrester and Lord Grey would bring light refreshments and chilled champagne to their box. Both Laura and Helena would have paused to acknowledge friends and acquaintances if the dowager had not swept them along with her.

"All you need to do is to nod your head and smile. That's all anyone expects in a crush like this!" But their little procession did indeed come to a standstill when the Prince of Wales came up to them and requested that Lady Honoria present the ladies to him. His slightly protuberant blue eyes seemed to be fixed on Laura's décolletage, after he had looked her up and down.

"Hmm!" he said after the introductions had been made. "Think I remember your mother—you take after her. There's a portrait by that fellow Alma-Tadema that she modeled for once—quite some time ago! I bought it though. Have it at Sandringham. You'll have to visit, and see it for yourself sometime. Soon, I hope!"

Helena was excited and overwhelmed, her cheeks pink with pleasure; Lady Evelyn giggled softly and told Laura she was *in*. But the dowager and Laura herself were more composed and cynical.

"Well—and now you'll have even more eager swains panting after you, my dear! Sets the royal seal of approval on you—as if you need it!" Lady Honoria gave Laura a knowing, sidewise look that spoke volumes before she added: "And now he'll be at Lady Chalmers's supper for certain—with his eye on *you*. Know what you're going to do about it?"

"No—not yet. But I suppose I will . . . improvise—if the occasion arises." Laura gave a soft gurgle of laughter, glad of Lady Honoria's understanding, before continuing in a more thoughtful voice. "I have heard that he's a gallant and attentive lover! And if His Royal Highness *does* deign to proposition me, I just *might* decide to succumb!"

Chapter 23

Lady Chalmers's little supper party was, as she had hoped, quite a success!

The Prince of Wales had promised to come, and *did;* and the Dowager Countess of Sedgewick, an old friend of her mother's, arrived with her American daughter-in-law and the already famous Miss Laura Morgan, who was the latest and most elusive American heiress.

"Not at *all* what we might have imagined, of course," people whispered behind their fans, but still, Lady Randolph Churchill, who was also an American, had vouched for her; and although she was already being pursued by suitors on all sides, she appeared to be, in spite of rumors to the contrary, a polite, polished, and well-bred young lady!

Lord Chalmers had pronounced that he approved of the girl, as did the autocratic Lady Lenox, Amelia Chalmers's mother, especially since she had talked privately with her close friend Lady Honoria.

After an excellent cold repast had been enjoyed by the guests, Lady Lenox proceeded to take charge of the evening's entertainment, which was provided by a group of musicians concealed behind an antique Chinese screen at one end of the ballroom.

"*Do* dance, all of you young people!" Lady Lenox commanded when she saw that everyone was waiting for someone else to take the floor first. "I tell you, things were different when I was your age! A private evening like this would be a time for fun and games! Don't you agree, Honoria? *You* remember, I'm sure!''

Laura was sorry that Lord Anthony could not stay very long at the supper party. She was beginning to feel, she whispered to Helena, as if she were a nice juicy *bone*. While Michel, who *had* returned from Paris in time for the dinner, and Reggie glowered at each other before pouring compliments upon her.

She liked Lord Anthony; and besides, he created no complications for her. She remembered that before Jenny Churchill had introduced them, there had been a chuckle in her voice as she whispered, ''Darling, I know he is young and quite earnest, but he is nice, and he's certainly not a fortune hunter. You might enjoy him, or at least having him squire you about. I assure you he's considered quite a catch.''

From the beginning, Lord Anthony had shown her, and had even told her, that he found her refreshing and different from most of the young ladies of his acquaintance. ''You're like a breath of fresh air,'' he said to her once, his eyes twinkling. And she liked him, just as he had begun to like her more than a little—her intelligence and her wit, as well as her beauty and her spontaneity. He had made a habit, when they were together, of asking her all kinds of questions about America, which he told her he was eager to visit. In fact, he told her he was planning perhaps one day to buy a ranch there, like so many other Englishmen had already done, including the husband of Jennie Churchill's sister, Carita.

Lord Anthony, Laura had found, was an impeccably polite escort. His father was a Marquess, and, of course, a member of the Marlborough House Set; he owned racehorses and was a member of the Jockey Club. True, Lord Anthony was the Eton and Oxford type, but he also loved the outdoors and tramping the moors; and he had invited her—along with Lady Honoria and Ena, of course, he added hastily at the time—to his manor house in the Cotswolds. Laura thought sometimes it was his love of horses and the outdoors that attracted her most to him, but all the same he was pleasant and unassuming, and comfortable to be with.

The Duke of Royse arrived late, with Lady Sabina Westbridge on his arm, and there was a little stir when he entered, especially since he had not been seen too much in public. Everyone had been curious; no one knew quite what to expect. James Sinclair, the former Duke, had been known as a capital fellow, but his son was an unknown quantity; there were even rumors to the effect that he had been brought up on a ranch in the American West and was quite wild!

The politenesses over with, Trent Challenger looked about the room—and there she was, as he had expected. A sparklingly jeweled butterfly surrounded by the flattering attentions of her admirers while she contrived to dazzle them all—even the Prince of Wales, it seemed!

He studied her coldly, narrowly, with his eyes looking like sharp splinters of glass, while his partner for the evening chattered on lightly by his side, satin-gloved fingers resting on his arm. Lady Sabina, at least, was predictable; and being so, gave him time to *think*—and even, perhaps, to plan.

For her part, Sabina had not failed to notice, with a flash of anger, that Reggie was, as usual, dancing attendance on that brazen hussy Laura Morgan—even if he was only *one* swain out of several. She wasn't accustomed to seeing her brother quite so obsessed by any female in the past, rich or not. He was disgusting in his outward devotion which certainly didn't seem to be having any tangible results.

She, at least, Sabina thought with a touch of malice, had managed to capture the attention of the American Duke, at least for the time being. She was the envy of all the other women, particularly those looking to be married well and wealthily.

They all thought that she had him fast; after all, she

was the only lady he had been seen escorting about town and in the country ever since he had made his first appearance in London.

But what they would never know was that appearances were only appearances after all. They would never know how detached he was from any real feeling for her; or for anyone, it seemed. He was not only almost frighteningly *cold* sometimes, but he could be hard as well. And he was nobody's fool, no matter what Reggie wanted to imagine. Their first "chance" meeting in the country that had been arranged by Franco; his outward show of attention—it meant nothing at all, and she had known it almost from the outset. He had kissed her, more than that in time . . . *his* own cool time. On their first occasion alone, he had her disrobed and disconcerted. He had begun to caress her—calculatingly and diabolically slowly—until she had not been able to help losing control of herself and had reached one wild sexual climax after another without the actual entry of his body into hers. Only his tongue and his fingers . . .

Oh! He was an utter *brute,* Sabina thought beneath her sparkling, vivacious mask. A wild, mad, cruel beast who could make her, without any physical force, perform for him like a whore—*serve* him like a slut. He managed to keep her tantalized and hanging on the edge until it suited him to allow her to be satisfied, the bastard! And somehow, he seemed to have found out her every hidden fantasy and desire, using her weakness to keep her his sex-slave!

Sabina's breath caught in her throat sharply as she thought of that very afternoon, when he had had her pose for him in varying stages of deshabille and undress, pretending modesty, then acting licentious, like a "tableau vivant." Oh, what a wild beast!

Her stream of madly crazy thought was interrupted just then, when Trent said: "Would you care to try some of the champagne punch, my love? I've been warned that it's laced with Jamaican rum—but at least it might help to dispel your suddenly pensive mood. Are you tired? Should I take you home early?''

"Thank you, no," Sabina managed to respond coolly enough, pulling her pride like a cloak of armor about her. Did he think that she hadn't caught the straying of his eyes in one particular direction? Then unable to help herself she added: "But pray do not let me prevent you from going in the same direction in which your gaze has been straying for so long now! Would you like an introduction to our latest American heiress?"

"You know her then?" He actually had the effrontery to smile at her, not at all taken aback by her barb.

"I've met the fabled 'fortune,' of course I'll be happy to present you—if we can get close enough, that is. I see that now that the Prince of Wales has left her side, her French Comte has taken his place. Well?"

"Well? Shall it be a glass of punch, or a waltz? And actually, I've *met* Miss Morgan before—several years ago, in fact. We were engaged to be married at one time." As Sabina's eyes widened and the color came and went underneath her porcelain skin, her companion's smile thinned, becoming sardonic as was his voice. "A family arrangement, you understand, my sweet. Fortunately for both of us, we decided to give ourselves time to consider . . . other people and other things, such as life in general—and its enjoyment."

For perhaps the first time he had shocked her into silence; and when he offered his arm with exaggerated gallantry, Lady Westbridge took it without a word, hardly caring where he was leading her. Was he teasing her? Or could it really be true? And did Franco know—more importantly, did Reggie? Damn the man! Damn all men! Why had she been trained and brought up to cater to them anyway? Laura Morgan did not—that much was obvious. The slut went her own way, doing just as she pleased—and had managed to get away with it, too, so far!

Recovering herself slightly, Lady Sabina snapped:

"Oh, *really!* This is almost too much! Since you two are such *old* friends, why don't you ask Miss Morgan for a dance?"

Trent's eyes narrowed again as they traveled over the subject of their conversation. "I might just do that after all," he drawled. "But not yet. I should give her other suitors their turn first, don't you think? And after all, I'm here with *you*, my dear!"

Laura found herself wondering if perhaps the Prince of Wales had confused her with her mother. It was well-known that he never dallied with women who were unmarried—to be on the safe side, of course. But . . . he *had* hinted that once she was married, perhaps they might attend the same house parties and move within the same circle of friends—a group that was referred to within fashionable circles as the Marlborough House Set. He had, however, acted as if her marriage were something that was already foreordained—or imminently forthcoming—and she could not understand what could have put such an idea into his head! If it was her dear brother Franco who had been dropping hints to "protect" his sister's reputation, then they would soon be quarreling and on the outs again!

By then she had quite forgotten about the so-called American Duke who had been expected to arrive with Lady Sabina Westbridge. What with having to put up with Michel and Reggie glowering at each other, on top of the attentions of the Prince of Wales and his puzzling hints, Laura had begun to feel positively *besieged*, and not quite ready for such a situation. She had, in fact, been wondering if she should plead a headache and withdraw herself from the front line, when she looked up suddenly to find her brother standing before her with a suspiciously amused glimmer in his hazel eyes. She should have been warned by that look! And *then*, as she was to tell herself later, perhaps she would have been forearmed in some way for the *shock* of the introduction!

"Oh, Laura! *Here* you are—and here's an old acquaintance of ours, in quite different circumstances this time, but I'm sure you'll remember Trent Challenger? He saved our lives some years ago in Mexico. But, let me do the honors *formally,* for a change, to prove that I've acquired some manners during my stay in Europe! My sister Laura—the Duke of Royse!"

She only needed to meet his diamond-hard eyes to feel recognition like a lightning-jolt through her whole body. She put out her hand to be kissed as stiffly as if she had been a mechanical doll, before she could recover her composure somewhat.

"*You!*" Laura said, putting a world of meaning into that one word.

"What a greeting, and after such a polite introduction! You look extremely well, Lorelei—and not at all like a Mexican water nymph any longer!" Just as if she had been a rudely backward child, he gave a shrug and a smile as if to actually apologize for her bad manners to her two stunned-looking admirers, who stood transfixed on either side of her.

For a moment she thought—but then she decided it was better *not* to think about *that.* This was only the same obnoxious Trent Challenger she had unfortunately encountered in Mexico, with his references to "water nymphs" and "Loreleis," and he could not possibly be that—that *other* one, for all that for a moment the timbre of his voice had struck her with unpleasant familiarity. But no, it wasn't *possible* and he probably couldn't speak a *word* of French! No, of course not. She'd heard that he'd only recently arrived in England from America, and hadn't been seen too much in public because he was busy with estate matters. *And* Sabina Westbridge, of course, but *that* was no surprise. The man was just as annoying as she remembered him to be—and Laura was determined to put him in his place as soon as the right opportunity presented itself.

But how quickly and how smoothly he maneuvered

everything and everyone—including herself, Laura thought furiously later. She attempted to use Lady Sabina as an excuse for refusing him a dance, but Sabina, all sugary sweetness and smiles, vowed that she didn't in the least mind *one* dance between two old acquaintances while she renewed her friendship with her own brother, whom she had neither seen nor talked to for so long—in fact, not since he had met Miss Morgan!

And then Franco, scheming traitor that he was, promptly proceeded to engage the reluctant Comte d'Arlingen in some kind of political discussion almost immediately—leaving her no choice but to accept the offer that had sounded far too like a *command* for her liking.

"Oh, but I insist, as an old family friend!" he said, drawing her away from her friends. "And I've not yet been fortunate enough to find out how well you . . . *waltz,* have I? Although I've heard, of course, that you're most accomplished at *everything* you do!"

And what had he meant by *that?* Laura wondered angrily.

There were certain words she would have loved to have flung in his face, if they had not been in so public a situation, and with H.R.H. still present, Laura thought furiously. And she was determined to attack first, once he had swung her into his arms that kept her, she felt insanely, in far too close confinement against the hard, muscular length of his body.

"I see that *you* haven't learned to dance politely yet!" she snapped. "You might loosen your hold on me—unless your little blond temptress has accustomed you to holding a female so close that she cannot escape from your grip. And how dare you, in all good conscience, call yourself a *Duke?* You still call yourself an American, I presume? We don't acknowledge silly titles, as you should know, unless you're one of these Anglophiles who renounce their citizenship for a Sir or a Lord or Your Grace before their name! In fact, you—'' He swung her around so fast at that moment, holding her so closely in his arms, that Laura lost her breath—and almost her balance as well. Damn him! she thought. *Damn* him! And at the same moment *he* was damning her for that cutting little speech that had hit far too close to home!

Laura felt that everything was whirling about her, and she was practically *forced* into clinging tightly to him until at last the room came back into focus, along with her poise. He was saying something, in that drawling, sarcastic manner that she had learned to hate from the time of their first unpleasant encounter . . . which was exactly what he was referring to *now,* the unprincipled blackguard! In fact, it was *he* who was doing the attacking and putting *her* on the defensive!

"In fact, I—what? What would you have me do about you, or *with* you, Lorelei? Apart from the proximity of your whaleboned and corseted body at this moment, I must say that there have been several times in the past years when I've wondered—quite *idly,* of course—what might have happened if I'd taken advantage of the naked, elemental gypsy-peasant creature I had so conveniently fastened to a tree—and don't imagine that I didn't notice how you watched *me* while I took my bath. Be honest— if you can still remember how to be, my dear. Haven't *you* wondered too?"

He was trying to confuse her, of course . . . and to . . . to *bait* her! But why, *why?* Oh, but she wouldn't let him—bastard that he was!

"If we weren't in public, and under the scrutiny of far too many people, *Your Grace,* I would . . . why, I'd like to—"

"You'd like to what? Be made love to, slowly and lingeringly—once the corsets have come off, of course—or would you like instead to tap me over the wrist with that pretty fan of yours because of certain incidents we are both remembering at this moment? I'd be sorry to learn, sweet gypsy, that you've turned hypocrite as well as lady of fashion."

"I won't let you play with me this way, as if . . . Well,

I won't allow myself to be baited by you any longer, Trent Challenger—or whatever you're calling yourself now! Call *me* what you like and think whatever you want to. Your opinions *and* your recently acquired title mean nothing at all to me—do you understand?'' Laura's voice had turned cuttingly cold—almost as cold as those glacier-eyes of his.

Trent could not help smiling to himself in spite of his justifiable annoyance at what she had let herself become. A flittering, fluttering, empty-headed little social butterfly dancing in the sunshine of attention from royalty and the usual fortune hunters. So she refused to allow herself to be—how had she put it—baited? Then bait her and play with her he would, for as long as she continued to intrigue him with the mass of contradictions she presented. This wasn't yet the time to pull in the line—hauling *her* in, wet and dripping on the other end of it. He would take his time and enjoy the ensuing battle before she was netted and forced to admit defeat—the bold, far too self-confident, and daring little hellion!

''I really do not choose to dance with you or to be forcibly held by you any longer! Have you forgotten that you are supposed to be the escort of Lady Westbridge? Talk to my brother, do—instead of inflicting *me* with ugly memories. After all, he and you have a great deal in *common!*''

This time she actually drew a laugh from him—his storm-gray eyes actually lightening for an instant to silver.

''*Touché*, little gypsy-witch! You *have* learned a few things, haven't you? It makes you much more interesting, you know.''

Before she could react, Laura found herself pulled again far too closely against his body and whirled about maliciously from one end of the room to the other, so that in the end, before he handed her back to Michel, her understandable dizziness prevented her from protesting or slapping his face as he well deserved when he bent his head and brushed her parted lips with his—with a little *too* much force!

"You're out of breath, my precious!" Michel murmured, putting a protective arm about her waist. "Did he annoy you?"

"He—he presumed far too much on a slight acquaintance and his friendship with my parents, that is all!" Laura turned a brilliant smile on Michel before surrendering herself gladly to his arms for the dance he requested. At least *he* wouldn't make her feel so dizzy that she could hardly stand up.

From across the room, where she stood with her brother, Sabina had not missed anything, including Laura Morgan's anger *or* the familiar way in which Trent had treated her. Reggie had been angry—directing his anger at *her* for not advising him ahead of time that the Duke of Royse and his latest quarry knew each other well—perhaps too well! But it wasn't *her* fault—she had been as much taken by surprise as her brother had been!

"Shouldn't you retrieve Miss Morgan now that Royse has decided to release the poor creature?" Sabina had said cattily just before Trent sauntered up to them. What a cad the man was, after all—like most Americans who were only to be tolerated because they were rich! All the same, hiding her jealousy and the smart of anger, Sabina managed to give her escort one of her sweetest smiles as she took his arm with possessive fingers, while her brother stamped off to wait for Miss Morgan to tire of dancing with her French count.

With a restraint and a lightness she was far from feeling, Sabina said, "You bad man! It seemed as if you managed to make poor Miss Morgan quite *angry!*"

But all she got in reply from the Duke, with a most peculiar smile, was: "Yes I did, didn't I?"

* * *

Trent Challenger-Sinclair did not feel obliged to inform Sabina of his thoughts and his feeling—that Miss Laura Morgan would soon be much, much angrier when she discovered what he had planned for her—and for her future.

And as for the pretty, empty-headed Sabina Westbridge, Trent was already beginning to tire of her, especially since of late she had begun to cling too closely, expect too much, and even insinuate that her ''reputation,'' such as it was, he thought sardonically, might be compromised by their being seen so constantly in each other's company.

Trent didn't care for arguments with women—and especially not for the scenes some females could create out of spite.

He had several matters that needed attending to—and *that* was a good enough reason, Trent thought later that night, as he smoked his cigar and savored a glass of excellent cognac, for him to get away from London for a while to attend to the business that had brought him here in the first place.

He looked forward to doing so too. Visiting Ireland, especially, and the birthplace of his great-grandfather—and before that . . . well, there were other visits to be made.

He had asked Mr. Weatherby, when they had last met, to arrange a meeting with Lady Margaret, the Dowager Duchess of Royse, his stepmother. He felt, with a certain sense of what was almost guilt, that there were matters that should be resolved between them.

But first, there were other matters to be resolved, involving Mr. Bishop for one, and Laura Morgan for another. What in hell was he *really* going to do about her? What did he *want* to do with her in the end? He wondered, eyes narrowing as his brows drew together, whether she actually didn't *know* that it was he who had had her for the first time and had *almost* taken her for the second time in Paris. If she *did*—she was certainly a consummate actress! And if she *didn't?* Well—he'd find out in the end. He meant to tear away her carefully constructed defenses and show her to herself as what she was—if nothing else!

Chapter 24

It was unfortunate, Laura thought in the days that followed that unpleasant encounter at Lady Chalmers's that she should have to keep running into Trent Challenger, or the Duke of Royse, as he now called himself, on almost every occasion she went out in public; or so it seemed to her. She tried to avoid him of course, and in fact she would have enjoyed cutting him dead whenever they saw each other, but Lady Honoria had reminded her that that would not do!

"Want them all to think there was, or *is,* something between you that makes you afraid to face him, eh?" she said bluntly. "Thought you'd have more gumption, my girl! Only thing to do with men is—outface 'em! Smile sweetly—disarm them with their own weapons by neither running away nor fighting them! You take my meaning?"

But as much as she tried to ignore him, it seemed impossible; that was, unless *he* was ignoring *her!* Sometimes he would make a point of coming up to her and engaging her in pointless conversation, especially if she happened to be with some of her gentlemen friends. On other occasions he infuriated her by merely giving her a polite inclination of his head before he turned back to whatever or whoever seemed to be holding his complete attention at the time.

She had come to the point where she almost dreaded going out anywhere because she was bound to see *him* there as well, usually accompanied by Lady Westbridge of course. And far too often their glances as well as their words clashed. Even Lady Honoria had remarked upon it.

"Such a coincidence, isn't it, that we keep meeting Royse almost everywhere we go—or *is* it a coincidence? And didn't I hear that you two were once supposed to be betrothed?"

"As I told you, Ma'am," Laura retorted, "that was *ages* ago—some silly old-fashioned arrangement between our grandparents. Of course neither of us took it seriously."

"Hmm!" Lady Honoria said shrewdly. "Perhaps *he* did not take this *'arrangement'* as lightly as you think! Well, have you thought of that?"

It was something that Laura didn't really want to think about, as a matter of fact. Whenever they spoke together—which was only when she was *forced* to do so by politeness because they were in public—she had a nagging sense of unpleasant familiarity that she was not ready to face. In any case, when he chose to acknowledge her presence he certainly treated her with far too much familiarity; and it only served to amuse him if she showed her annoyance.

Whenever she was alone she had to tell herself that it couldn't have been *him,* it *couldn't* have been! *That* would be intolerable! He was only, she scoffed at herself, that bastard Trent Challenger whom she had met once in Mexico and learned to despise utterly, just as she despised him now—a gun-wolf in an English Duke's clothing! *Why* couldn't he just leave her alone? After all, he had the more than obliging Lady Westbridge to play his little games with! What kind of game was he trying to play with *her?* What did he want from her? But she did not even want to think of answers to *that.*

Helena was no help when Laura complained to her. "I can't *stand* the man! You don't know how frustrated it makes me feel to have to be—*polite* to him, merely for form's sake."

"What I *have* noticed," Helena said, "is that whenever you two meet, you are always *jousting* with each other!

You know, I feel that in some way you . . . well, *attract* each other! Now, don't be angry with me for saying so, Laura, but I really think that's the case.''

"Honestly, Ena!" Laura said, narrowing her eyes. "I don't see why you should think that. Joust with him, indeed! Why, he is the last man in the world that I—'' and then she added suddenly, "Oh God! I hope that *you're* the only one who thinks that way, because I would be quite mortified otherwise!''

Ena said soothingly, "Oh no, it's just *me,* I'm sure! And that's only because I know you so well! And anyhow it's obvious that you're making Lady Westbridge furiously jealous! You've surely observed those little venomous looks she shoots in your direction!''

Laura tried to make sure that she was escorted by one or the other of her so-called admirers wherever she went. Michel Rémy was still an ardent suitor, and Lord Anthony accompanied her to interesting places, went riding with her as often as possible, sometimes with his sister accompanying them. And then, of course, there was Reggie Forrester, as assiduous as ever in his quiet pursuit of her in spite of the rivals in his way.

All the same it seemed to Laura as if there were no way of avoiding *him.* Wherever she turned, there he was, smiling that sarcastic, rather twisted, *knowing* smile of his, and, whenever possible, making it a point to annoy her with his caustic comments that covered sly innuendos. How she wished he'd stay out of her way and leave her alone to enjoy her first London season.

But the London Season, Laura soon discovered ruefully, consisted of much the same round of activities that she had gone through in Paris, except of course that in Queen Victoria's London one had to be *so* much more circumspect. So much more *caution* (or hypocrisy, as Laura thought stormily) to be exercised in order *not* to be found out enjoying something that society decreed forbidden.

All the more reason, she would think sometimes, to *taste* of forbidden fruit!

Trent Challenger? She didn't know why she thought about *him* of all people!

Laura had found that in between the almost endless round of activities she was engaged in, at least *writing*—sometimes in the privacy of her room, and sometimes on her early morning rides to the park—helped give her a sense of objectivity, and gave her something *real* to do that she sorely needed at this time.

After all the telephone calls they'd exchanged during the past time-crowded weeks, Laura had finally *made* the time to visit Frank Harris in his office. She came laden with scribbled pages, and thanks to him some of her pieces had already been accepted by the *Saturday Review* and *The Pall Mall Gazette;* she had even been published in the recent issue of *Titbits*—a gossip rag, it was true, but they paid quite well! And she had begun to have *fun* writing "fiction" that was based on real life and real persons and events—leaving the avid reading public to *guess* who was being referred to!

Frank seemed to like her new work. Frank also seemed to like *her,* almost too much. Why, he had even tried to seduce her again, seeming to forget that his first casual attempts in Paris had met with no success.

Laura had been in his office one day and was just rising to leave when he caught her hand to stay her and said abruptly, "Laura, why don't you go to bed with me? I have a small flat close by, and we can be *very* private there, I promise you! *Do* come with me, Laura dear—without stopping to think or hesitate! I swear I'll make you happy!"

"Frank, I *can't* do it and you know that. I've told you before that I want you as a *friend,* and that I look upon you as a friend. If we went now to your flat and made love, I think it would spoil everything—at least for *me* it would. I have too many men to deal with as it is! *Do* understand, won't you? I don't know! It's just not the right time, maybe! And it's not that I think you won't be a good lover—I know you *are* from what I've heard and from what I've *read*. But *no,* not for me, not now.''

"Damn it, Laura," he growled disgustedly, dropping her hand, "somehow I knew you'd say that. Well, if that's the way it has to be, that's the way it has to be, I suppose! But remember I'm always here if you want me or need me. Or if you should change your mind, or just need to talk to a friend or to be held close by somebody who cares for you—here I am, and you know it.''

Then Frank's eyes suddenly narrowed on her as his tone changed. "But I'd like to know something—as a *journalist,* that is. How *does* it feel to be pursued? Maybe that should be the subject of your next article! Of course," he added hastily, under her glowering look, "you'd use a different pseudonym, and no one would know who the writer was! But all the same—" And then he laughed. "Frankly, I really *would* like to know how you deal with it. This artificial life, I mean. And how you deal with Trent. Because I happen to know he's not easy to handle.''

"That," Laura said in a stiff voice, "is nobody's business but mine.''

Frank held up one hand. "Very well, very well. It seems to me it's the same answer I've been getting from Trent . . . No, no," he added, seeing the expression on her face. "I'm not going to delve any further or say any more. You two have to work out your problems, I suppose . . . or is it solutions?''

"Oh, *damn* you, Frank," she said forcefully.

"Well," Frank said hopefully, "if you want to make him jealous, you could always . . .''

"I have no intention of trying to make him jealous. I don't *want* to make him jealous. I don't want *him.* And I wish you'd stop it, Frank, or we won't be friends any longer!''

"I'm sorry, I'm sorry! Not another *word* on the subject of our dark Duke, I assure you!" Harris swore solemnly, although there was a twinkle in his eyes that Laura didn't *quite* like, and she frowned at him forbiddingly.

"I *hope* not! Dark Duke, indeed! Sounds like the title of a—" And then, her eyes widening, she began to smile quite dangerously. "Yes! Oh yes, I *have* it! Oh, dear *dear* Frank!" She leaned over his desk and actually kissed him, taking him utterly by surprise. Then she whirled away, laughing. *"Yes,* of course—a gothic novel! *The Dark Duke. I* will write it—and *you* will see that it's published! You *will,* won't you, Frank? Promise me!"

Chapter 25

It was true that ever since she had last talked to Frank Harris she had been toying with the idea of writing something gothic—something really satirical that would lampoon *him*. But now, Laura thought furiously, the bastard had really gone too far, and since she was too angry to sleep she was determined to sit up and *write* instead. Write something that would hold him up to public ridicule.

They had just returned to Sedgewick House from a soireé given by Lord and Lady Latimer, and of course she had encountered him there as usual, unencumbered on this occasion by Lady Westbridge. Both Ena and Lady Honoria had commented on that fact, especially since he kept looking, almost *glowering*, in fact, in her direction.

"It doesn't make any difference to me how he *looks* at me," Laura had said lightly. "I only wish that he doesn't ask me to dance!"

But that, unfortunately, was exactly what he had done and just at the *wrong* moment when Lord Anthony had left her side in order to fetch her a glass of punch. Lady Honoria had already warned her that common courtesy demanded she not refuse, especially since the Duke was a friend of her family's. All right, she had thought furiously. I won't let him outface me! I won't let him see how *uneasy* he makes me, damn him.

So he had danced with her and had acted decorously for a change, she thought with surprise, until he spun her into one of the small alcoves leading off the ballroom. And

then, before she knew it, he had her leaned up against the
wall in order to kiss her! While she was still too startled
to react, the wretch had put one hand up and actually
dared to touch her breasts, his fingers lingering over her
nipples! Oh, she would have killed him if she could have!
She would have at least slapped his dark, enigmatic face
if he hadn't, just as suddenly as he had taken her off the
floor, grasped both her wrists to lead her back out and
under public scrutiny again.

Lady Honoria had remarked how flushed she had become, and Laura had said only that it was far too hot for
her. How she hated him and that damn knowing smile on
his face when he bowed to her with false politeness afterward.

Laura remembered now, working herself up into more
of a rage, that on some occasions when they had met and
he had taken her hand politely, as if to kiss the back of it,
he had instead turned it around the kissed her palm in a
far too intimate way that made her gasp involuntarily before she could snatch her hand from him. And there had
been the other time when he had, against her will, pretended to read her palm, tracing the lines on it—telling
her that her lines of fate and heart were intertwined.

"There's something between you two," Ena had said
then. "I don't know what it is, but you seem to strike
sparks from each other."

Laura had been pacing around the room and now she
stopped in mid-stride, wondering why Ena had said that
and whether she could possibly be *right!* And then she
thought, angry at herself, of *course* not! We don't even
like each other, but he's the type of man who would delight
in tormenting the object of his dislike! But *why?* And Laura knew the answer in spite of herself. Because there *was*
something between them; something she didn't quite understand; some dark alchemy that she hated feeling in herself, almost as much as she hated *him* and what seemed
to be his suddenly constant and intrusive presence in her
life.

Very well, then! Laura thought with sudden determination. Very well, I'll *exorcise* him! I'll have my revenge and he won't like it and I won't care! And with her dark thoughts and her words suddenly flowing, she sat down at the escritoire and began to scribble furiously.

Two days later, Frank Harris, with his eyebrows raised and his mouth twitching, turned the closely written pages of the untidy manuscript that had just been all but thrown upon his cluttered desk, while Laura watched him anxiously and questioningly from across it.

"Hmm!" he said. "Let's see now—yes, *this* page! '. . . the swarthy face of the Duke loomed over the trembling young woman. She wanted to, *tried* to, scream—but no sound emerged from her paralyzed throat! She could only stare at him in helpless terror, as if mesmerized by his darkling presence.

" '*Oh! Now* at last she knew what all the warnings had meant! Warnings and hints that she had willfully disregarded. Now she realized the horrors of being at the mercy of a beast of prey—knew that even the fact that she was of gentle birth and impeccable lineage could not save her from his licentious clutches . . . for he had her alone, defenseless, and in his power!

" 'With a growl that sounded animal-like, the dark Duke took one step forward; and then his strong, cruel fingers ripped away her high-necked white nightrobe—exposing her fully to his lecherous gaze—and even worse!!

" ' "Now, my lady fair, you shall in truth be compromised—and lost to the realms of polite society—unless you put matters right! *After* I have done with you! You have a fortune—and I can use it! So—after this *private* wedding night of ours, and after you have learned to submit your will to mine in all ways—we shall be formally married—and continue in *this* fashion privately!" ' "

Frank Harris leaned back in his chair and gave vent to a burst of laughter.

"By God, Laura! And I can guess which particular dark-

visaged Duke you had in mind! But are you serious about
this?''

''I hope *you're* serious, Frank!'' Laura retorted, an angry flush staining her cheeks. ''It's my first attempt at
gothic fiction, as you know, and I had hoped for an honest
evaluation from you—instead of raised eyebrows and . . .
and *laughter*, of all things! For heaven's sake, tell me if
you don't like it! Is it badly written or rather too strong
for the public? Is that it?''

Frank pulled at his moustache before lifting his eyes
from the next page to meet hers, without being able to
help the smile twitching at one corner of his mouth.

''Well . . . I suppose that since you *are* a female, you
can't be expected to come on stronger, eh? *I* would, but
then, *I'm* not a female—thank God!''

''Naturally not!'' Laura retorted acerbically, at which
he grinned.

''*Vive la différence*, hmm? Don't *glare* at me so, love.
I like it—I *do* like it! Even if you are taking rather a risk,
aren't you? I mean, if Royse—'' He stopped hastily, seeing
the look she gave him. ''But then of course we would
publish under a pseudonym. And perhaps—perhaps you
might change to the first person? 'He ripped *my* flimsy
nightrobe, *my* last remaining defense, down to the waist—
baring *me* to his predatory eyes and hands,' et cetera, et
cetera. You know what I mean!''

''I *don't,* actually!'' Laura said, tight-lipped and
haughty, before she broke down and was forced to laugh
at the vivid word-picture her friend had just dramatically
described.

''Well,'' Frank Harris said calmly, deliberately looking
away from her as he concentrated on lighting up a cigar,
''at least you'll allay my curiosity one of these days, won't
you? By telling me exactly what happens after Royse hears
about this? But do leave *my* part in this out when he con-
fronts you, I beg of you!''

''I'll tell *him* nothing and *you* only as much as I must!''
Laura was all merriment suddenly. ''But then, it's not

finished yet, like the Season! And so there will be more to follow. In the meantime, if it *is* published in installments—*TitBits,* you think?—then everyone will try to guess, won't they? And that will help the sales, too, I'd imagine!''

"Laura," Frank said unbelievingly, "you're incredible!"

"Do you think so, Frank?" Laura said ingenuously. "Why, I'm flattered! I do hope you like the rest of my novel, and that you *will* find someone to publish it *soon*, as you promised." And then she added with a dismayed glance at the clock, "Oh! I've got to run! I've been told that Lady Honoria wished to see me as soon as possible— and even *I* wouldn't want to keep her waiting!"

Laura was a few minutes late, as it turned out, and when she was shown into Lady Honoria's boudoir, the dowager looked her up and down disapprovingly.

"Well! You're late as usual. And where have you been *this* time?" Lady Honoria demanded.

"I was delivering a . . . manuscript to Mr. Harris. Part of my very first novel, or attempt at one, as a matter of fact," Laura replied lightly.

"Well, at least you're here at last! So—sit down, sit down, for heaven's sake, you make me nervous when you're standing up there fidgeting about! And what I have to tell you is going to need thought and a great deal of planning."

Lady Honoria looked Laura over suspiciously. Laura thought ruefully that aside from her great-grandfather, Lady H. was the only person that she had been even the slightest bit in awe of.

Lady Honoria continued. "I hope your latest writings are not *too* scandalous because I have plans for you. I have decided that we should have a grand affair here, at Sedgewick House, and in your honor. A good way to repay everyone else for the invitations we have accepted."

As usual, Lady Honoria did not make suggestions, only

pronouncements. And her pronouncements usually became facts.

"There's no use arguing with my belle-mère, Laura," Ena later said philosophically. Her eyes sparkled with mischief as she glanced sideways at her dismayed-looking friend. "You ought to be used to her by now, and realize that she will _always_ have her own way in the end! And anyway—she _likes_ you! Couldn't you see how excited and energetic she was at the thought of planning a reception for you? You can't disappoint her—what's more, she won't let you."

"But Ena, for heaven's sake! I don't know the first thing about planning such an event. I can't even think of any particular names I'd want on the guest list. I'm just not used to this kind of thing, Ena!"

"You know you don't have to worry about that," Ena said. "By now I'm sure Belle-mère and Miss Edge have everything arranged between them—in fact, I have a feeling the invitations might have been sent out already!" She added teasingly, "And just think of the _theme_ for the reception—Roses of the South! I think that is so apt. Belle-mère told me she thinks roses suit you—so lovely, and so prickly too!"

It seemed Laura had no choice in the matter. She was shown the guest list in the end, of course, and did not recognize most of the names on it. She only wished, rebelliously _and_ a trifle apprehensively at the same time, that Lady Honoria had not seen fit to invite . . . what was she supposed to call him anyway? Royse? Well, _he_ had been invited, of all people; _not_ to mention Lady Sabina Westbridge as well!

By this time Laura had grown almost resigned to meeting him everywhere. At Ascot, at Epsom Downs—she couldn't avoid him, it seemed.

There were some things, even about herself, that she didn't quite understand, and perhaps didn't want to recognize. A secret sensual side of herself that she didn't want to acknowledge but was _there_ all the same, lurking in hiding, waiting to betray her. Oh, damn him! Why was it that she always *felt* his presence and the silver burn of his eyes on her, seeming to go *into* her through all the layers of her clothing, even before she actually *saw* him?

There was no one that Laura could really talk to about these feelings. Ena was lost in a world of her own—alternately happy and miserable, depending on Franco. She had confided once that when Franco had impulsively suggested that she should leave everything and everyone behind and go with him wherever he went, she had been afraid, and had drawn back, and *that* was what had made him angry with her. But now when he had suddenly told her that he was willing to have her on *her* terms—she didn't know why that should still make her unhappy!

Preparations for the ball went ahead with a frenzy—and so did Laura's interminable round of social activities in which she tried to *bury* herself—succeeding for the most part until by some ill-chance she happened to run into that damned Royse!

Helena had been right, she found to her relief. The dowager and Miss Edge had everything well in hand—musicians, extra footmen, the buffet which would take up one whole end of the enormous ballroom. Laura was reminded of a stage production, and said as much to Ena, who merely laughed, knowing her mother-in-law and her ways.

"Wait until *the* night!" Ena threatened. "You'll feel like a Princess, Laura—just waiting for her Prince . . . or might it be a Duke?"

"Ena! Oh . . . if you weren't my very best friend, I'd . . . I know you're teasing, but the very mention of that *wretch* is enough to put me in a rage! I wish he'd tire of his little game and let me alone!" Laura's face was flushed and her eyes flashed blue fire. "Maybe I'll just become engaged to someone that night! Michel—he's proposed of course, and I put him off. And I think Lord Anthony might be on the verge; I'm sure I could manage to push him over the edge if I wanted to!"

"But *do* you want to?" Ena asked bluntly.

Sometimes Ena had a disconcerting way of seeing right through her, Laura had to allow grudgingly. No, she didn't want to, not really! She enjoyed Anthony's company and that of his sister; and they shared a great deal in common, what with their love of horses, the same books, the opera—but . . .

Oh! Laura thought angrily. Why do I always feel, with all of them, as if there's something *missing?*" What *was* it? Fire? Passion? The secret something that her parents had that she resented and *envied* at the same time? If only she knew! But she'd already had the experience of being burned by the fires of passion, and that had been lesson enough, Laura vowed to herself before she forced that subject out of her mind to concentrate on her dress for the ball.

Chapter 26

The night had arrived at last; and Laura, feeling unaccountably nervous, had first to be inspected by Lady Honoria before they went downstairs and prepared to receive their guests.

Lady Honoria was quite pleased as she surveyed her charge. The girl was really quite exquisite! She had chosen to wear a ruby choker that emphasized her slender neck, with only plain ruby studs in her ears. Her *ciel*-blue satin gown was enriched by bead embroidery all over the skirt in a crimson briar-rose design that was also repeated on the wraparound bodice with its pointed waist. The skirt and the shoulder straps of the gown were edged by more beading in a rose design of crimson, green, and gold; and she carried a black lace fan also similarly embroidered in silk.

Yes, Lady Honoria thought as she had Laura turn about before her just once more, the girl was going to create quite a stir tonight—and set some male hearts beating faster!

"And now you, Ena!" The dowager commanded, while Helena, too, turned herself about twice, being used to this kind of "inspection" from her mother-in-law.

She had chosen to wear a pale green peau de soie gown with gold silk roses at her shoulders and stitched down one side of her skirt. There were diamonds in her ears, dangling down almost to her shoulders, encircling her neck, and on her wrists. She hoped Franco would appreciate the way she looked tonight. She had dressed and jeweled herself for *him!*

The inspection over, Lady Honoria, resplendent in purple velvet and satin, gave the command to descend.

"I know this must seem quite an ordeal!" Ena whispered in Laura's ear as they went down the curving staircase in the dowager's wake. "But you'll begin to enjoy yourself soon enough."

"I'm sure I will—especially if *Royse* doesn't come!" Laura whispered back. "I *do* wish that he hadn't been invited! I hate the man!"

Lady Honoria overheard and paused to look up at her and say: "Hah! Then you'd better be careful, my dear. Hate *and* love are both strong emotions, and one can so easily merge into the other!"

No! Laura thought, although she said nothing out loud. Not as far as *he* is concerned. The fact was that she actually felt *uneasy* when she was near to him—near enough for him to murmur ridiculous things about satyrs and water nymphs while he held her *far* too closely and . . . and then she was saved from thinking along *those* lines any longer as Lady Honoria arranged them in the order in which they would meet their guests.

The grand ballroom at Sedgewick House had been magnificently decorated with festoons and tall vases of red roses, their delicious perfume filling the air under the newly polished gold and crystal chandeliers.

The massive carved wooden doors leading into the ballroom had been flung wide open, and it was here, at the head of the marble steps leading down into the ballroom, that Lady Honoria, flanked by Helena and Laura, received their guests for the first half hour. Afterward, any latecomers would be announced by Mr. Mannering, who looked resplendently pompous tonight.

"Now remember, my dear," Lady Honoria warned Laura behind her fan as they prepared to mingle with their guests at last. "You must not seem to favor any one young man with your attentions; and before dancing more than once with your favorite swain, you should give at least one chance to any of the other gentlemen who might ask; or sit out a dance or two in between to *converse*. I'll introduce you again to those here whom I think you might give some of your time to. The old guard, particularly! You must try to impress them with your manners, your politeness, and—be agreeable, do, girl! Pray don't come out with any of your startlingly *modern* notions on women's suffrage and the like!''

Laura would have liked to grimace, but she was only too aware of being watched, and *studied*. Why had she let Lady Honoria steamroller her into facing such an ordeal? But it was much too late for regret as she accompanied the dowager on her majestic progress around the room.

The ballroom was all light and color and gaiety once the music had begun and the dancers made patterns against the polished floor—women in glittering colors with their trains looped up over silk-gloved wrists, their jewels and headdresses sparkling under the chandeliers and throwing off shimmers of light. Their beauty and brightness were emphasized in contrast with the severe black and white evening attire of their partners.

These were the *crème de la crème* of the aristocracy and the *haute monde* who could afford to dance their nights away and spend their days indulging in whatever activities pleased them. What, Franco thought suddenly, was he doing here in a world that suddenly seemed unreal? Helena's world—the world she seemed afraid to leave.

Forget it! he told himself then. He was here, and Helena had saved as many waltzes as she could for him. And now he must find his popular sister and claim at least one dance with her, if he could manage to extricate her from her mob of admirers. He wondered, as he made his way purposefully toward his butterfly-bright sister, where the devil Trent was tonight?

It was the same question Helena had whispered to Laura

a little earlier. "I wonder what has kept Royse? I know he accepted for tonight."

"I don't care if he comes or not!" Laura retorted. "In fact, I shall be quite relieved if he stays away and spares me the annoyance of his presence!"

All the same, and much to her own annoyance, she had caught herself looking over the heads of the others in the crowd for a certain tall figure, with darkly curling hair and a saturnine face, its harsh planes thrown into prominence by black sideburns that came down to the hard jawline, and the villainous moustache he affected now and then. Oh—what on earth was the matter with her? Too much champagne, making her light-headed. Lady Honoria had, in fact, warned her sternly *not* to imbibe any more and to stick to the punch if she didn't want to end up disgracing herself!

Laura turned her attention, even more sparkling than usual, to the three men who stood attentively at her side while she sat plying her fan and swearing that she really did need to rest for a while. She had just refused young Mr. Carruthers's offer to fetch her a glass of punch, and Reggie Forrester's offer to fan her, and Michel Rémy's offer to escort her outside onto one of the terraces for some fresh air—when, thankfully, her brother appeared.

"Afraid I'm going to exercise my brotherly privilege, gentlemen, and force my sister out onto the floor with me whether she likes it or not! Well, Laura?"

"I suppose I'm offered no choice! Please excuse me, won't you? And *do* dance with some of the other ladies here or Lady Honoria will give me a good lecture tomorrow about monopolizing the attentions of the most charming and handsome gentlemen here!"

"Very charmingly done, sister dear!" Franco chuckled when he had her on the crowded floor. "How on earth do you do it, though? Managing to keep so many suitors and would-be suitors by your side without having to commit yourself? You females have never ceased to amaze me!"

"Well, *you* did a very adroit job of rescuing me, brother

dear!" Then Laura made a small grimace. "Good heavens! What an evening! And what one has to go through for social approval!"

"Do you *need* it? You sound like Ena."

"I won't hear *anything* against Ena! You don't understand how it is with her and the way she was brought up."

"Very well," Franco said with surprising calmness. "We'll leave it at that, shall we? Ena wasn't brought up like we were, to think for ourselves—I've already accepted *that!*"

Laura thought that she really did not want to be on the outs with Franco again. For Ena's sake and her own peace of mind too; so she changed the subject to something trivial until the dance was over.

And then, over the music, she heard Mannering announce in a stentorian voice: "His Grace, the Duke of Royse and Lady Westbridge."

"So Trent's decided to show up at last!" Franco exclaimed. Suddenly, with a few turns he maneuvered her, willy-nilly and out of breath, to the bottom of the marble steps at the very moment the music ended.

Damn her brother!

"Aren't you going to greet your guests, Laura?" Franco prompted her in that hateful tone of voice she knew too well hid laughter.

"Miss Morgan! My—our apologies for being so late!" Royse said with a mock-polite inclination of his head in her direction.

He didn't bother to explain *why* he was late, Laura noticed before she managed to compose herself enough to respond coolly: "But how *good* of you both to come at all! I'm sure we're all delighted. Lady Westbridge, Your . . . Your *Grace*—let me take you to Lady Honoria."

"Oh come, Laura! I've been longing for a dance with Sabina—and have never been able to manage it with Trent about! So why not be slightly shocking and change partners for this dance?" Franco's eyes were glowing—he was actually having fun for the first time this evening surrounded by this stilted, formal crowd and the "protocol" that was demanded. "Besides, I'm sure Trent won't mind dancing this one at least with my wayward sister!"

Lady Westbridge was gowned in blue satin, garnished with blue sapphires that were the color of her eyes. When Franco took her masterfully by the wrist Sabina found herself with no choice but to accede. Royse had not protested, after all, and she couldn't possibly afford to make a scene.

"Are you wayward?" Trent asked softly as he took her hand and kept fast hold of it. "But you can't stand here *gaping* at me, my sweet Lorelei—*not* in front of all these people!"

He allowed her no time to protest, before he forced her back in the crowd of dancers who were all, Laura felt, watching and commenting and . . . oh damn! *Speculating*, as well, probably! It was best, perhaps, not to say a word. She'd have enough to say in explanation of Lady Honoria later, she was sure! But *he* seemed determined to *sting* her into speech.

"Hmm. No questions as to why I'm so late? No accusations? Not even an expression of relief to see me here finally?"

Laura made a small, furiously expressive sound between her gritted teeth. She wouldn't let him provoke her this time. She *wouldn't!* But why did he *persist* in doing this to her? *Why?* What were his motives?

"You're doing an uncommonly good job on *this* occasion to keep your temper, I must say, Lorelei. And your silence—except for that little tiger-growl I heard escape from you a few seconds ago. I admire your control, you know; although—well, I'm afraid it challenges me, in some strange way I can't understand myself! You make me wonder why you always manage to arouse all of the most rampantly wicked and evil impulses in me!"

Trent didn't know himself why he so much enjoyed deliberately baiting her. As little as he liked to admit it, he hated the fact that she seemed to be able to provoke him to anger as well. There was unfinished business between them that had to be resolved one way or another and he knew that by now—even if *she* didn't know it, or wouldn't yet admit it.

The rose-patterned, rose-festooned, and rose-perfumed room seemed to spin around and around as Laura's breath caught in her throat. Oh, Lady Honoria had been right about too much champagne! She only wanted to sit down somewhere at this point, alone. She wouldn't, no, she *couldn't* allow herself to swoon in his arms!

Her face had become unaccountably pale and she almost missed a step, so that he had to hold her up. Oh damn! Trent swore to himself before he said to her in quite a different tone of voice from that he had used before: "Laura? Laura—for God's sake! What's wrong with you?"

"Nothing, nothing!" she managed to say after breathing in deeply. "It's just that—oh, it's just been too difficult an evening for me to cope with! And then on top of it all *you* . . . well, it's just been too much for me. There, I admit it—does that please you? Stop tormenting me—I don't know why you're doing it, I don't know what your reasons are—all I wish for is that you would leave me alone!" She had to blink back tears of frustration and anger in admitting her own weakness to him, and Trent could not help but notice, damning himself for choosing the wrong place and the wrong time to tease her.

Trent said harshly: "I'm going to take you back to your friends soon, Laura. And I assure you that I won't force myself upon you for the rest of the evening." Then he added in a steely undertone, "For Christ's sake, don't blink teary-eyed at me because it won't work on *me,* as you ought to know by now! We've got unanswered questions to settle between us, whether you want to admit it or not! I'll have to leave you to your many ardent admirers for the time being, though, since I have to leave town for a few days." He quickly reverted to his usual bantering tone. "Try not to miss me too much, Lorelei. I intend to see you when I get back. In fact, there will be a reception at Royse House that Lady Honoria has already accepted for you—supervised by my stepmother, Lady Margaret, the Dowager Duchess of Royse.''

It was only after he had deposited her with Lady Honoria that Laura felt as if she had regained her proper senses.

"Well, well!" Lady Honoria exclaimed when he had stalked away. "It was a trifle irregular, I suppose, his seizing you for a dance soon after he had arrived, but I don't suppose it will do much harm in the end. He certainly managed to make all your other young men quite jealous, and that doesn't hurt, you know! Besides, I didn't seem to notice that you objected too much, hmm?" Before Laura could protest hotly, she added, "I suppose you can go back to the others now. The Comte d'Arlingen is already making his way here, looking for you! And I've noticed that Lord Anthony has been glancing several times in this direction as well. So, make up your mind, my dear, make up your mind! Now that you have so many men dangling after you, the rest is up to you, so go on, enjoy yourself!''

Laura was sure afterward that she *had* enjoyed herself tremendously, especially as His Grace the Duke of Royse had decided to devote his attentions to his partner, Lady Westbridge. And Laura had been invited by Mr. Carruthers to take a turn with him around the park in his new phaeton, and asked by Lord Anthony to help him choose some new Thoroughbreds for his stable. Reggie Forrester had whispered in her ear that he must talk to her in private, and Michel had told her that he had a surprise for her! By the time the endless-seeming evening was over, Laura was so exhausted that she could hardly think, much less remember what she had promised to do within the next few days and with whom!

"Well, my dear," Lady Honoria announced the next day, "you were certainly a huge success! *Two* dances with the Prince of Wales—and then of course there was Royse. You should have seen Lady Sabina's face while he danced with you! Her eyes were like glittering pieces of glass! Hah! No wonder she dragged him off as soon as she could. That creature . . . well, I'm afraid I can neither like nor trust her, even if she *is* accepted everywhere!" And then, consulting the notes that Miss Edge had placed before her, Lady Honoria continued in a brisk voice. "Now that that's behind us, we must make plans for the rest of the season. There are several invitations here—"

"But Ma'am!" Laura could not help interjecting at this point. "Oh, I do apologize for interrupting, but I was told something about an invitation to a reception at Royse House. And if that is true, I really don't feel that I want to—"

"Nonsense!" Lady Honoria shot a sharp look in Laura's direction before saying firmly: "Now look here, my dear, Lady Margaret happens to be an old and dear friend of mine and this will be her reentry into society, so to speak! She was brave enough to throw her cap over the windmill for James Sinclair—the last Duke of Royse and *your* Duke's father! And this was before his first wife had died, and he was able to marry Margaret!"

She looked forbiddingly from Laura to Helena before adding with a note of finality in her voice: "I have accepted that particular invitation. It is for Margaret's sake and I want you to understand that. And you, miss," she stared directly at Laura for an instant, "I don't want to hear any excuses or any nonsense out of you—no matter what you might feel about Royse. We'll go and then we'll return. Nothing lost—but a great deal to gain, at least for my friend!"

It was not until she and Ena were in the privacy of Ena's little flower-patterned sitting room that Laura could give vent to her rebellious thoughts. "Oh, damn! I think I *do* understand about Lady Margaret and all the rest, but Ena, I don't want to be constantly thrown in his path. Why can't anybody seem to understand that?"

"I'm sorry, Laura," Helena said, "but perhaps it's because you aren't convincing enough when you say you can't stand Royse!''

Laura stared blankly at her friend for some moments, thunderstruck, before she recovered herself sufficiently to say in what she hoped was a cool and unaffected voice: ''Good heavens, Ena! I do hope that there are no other people who think the same way you do. If so, I should feel quite mortified!''

Her brows drew together in a black look, but when she spoke, her voice was different, less sure. ''Do you think it is obvious to everyone? Oh God, Ena, I just don't know! I just don't know how to react to him! And I do hate him— I *do!* It's just—it's just that I feel out of my depth with him, and, oh *damn* it, Ena, I'm not used to that, as you should know by now!''

Laura managed a travesty of a laugh, but she spoke seriously. ''I really don't know what it is! I know I don't like him and I know that I wish he would stop—well, *singling* me out. But he does and I don't know why! I've asked him and he won't tell me! But all the same I feel— no, I *sense*—that in some way he's actually pursuing me! But why? Why?''

Laura didn't understand why she had let that outburst escape her, and to Helena of all people, who could never understand the dark depths of her instincts and her fear.

''Oh, Laura, I never understood—'' Helena began when Laura cut her off quickly with a sharp laugh and a non-chalant shrug of her shoulders.

''Oh, heavens! I'm a writer, you know, and sometimes I suppose I let my imagination and sense of drama run away with me! Please forget what I said, Ena. And as for Royse, since I will have to be seeing him more often than I choose during the next few weeks, I will just have to face him and learn to outface him as well! So now, do take that *look* off your face and try to think of an excuse for the two of us to escape from the house together this after-noon by ourselves. I think that we both need an invigorating ride in the park to clear our heads of everything that is worrisome and unnecessary, don't you? And who knows who we might run into. Didn't you say something earlier about meeting Franco?''

Chapter 27

Michel Rémy, Comte d'Arlingen, was overjoyed to hear that the Duke of Royse had left town and would not be back for at least a few days. Even if Laura would still be surrounded by the usual crowd of admirers, he felt more confident of himself with Royse out of the way. Somehow that man seemed to have a strange and disruptive effect upon Laura, even if he *was* supposed to be an old friend of the family and an ex-fiancé at that!

Bah! Michel thought. Those others don't worry me! That Lord Grey is far too quiet and sober to suit the taste of Ginette's daughter, and that M. Forrester, well, he is of no account of course! A mere fortune hunter obviously, but of course Laura knows it and only keeps him dangling about her skirts in order to make other men jealous! She is so much a *cocotte,* just like her mother!

The Count had decided to make the most of this golden opportunity. He had invited Laura to a private exhibition at the French Embassy of some interesting old artifacts that had recently been discovered in a cave in one of the southern provinces of France. He knew it was exactly the kind of thing that she would be interested in. And after that he had already arranged that they should have a light, and *very* private, meal. After that, well, it remained to be seen, did it not? Anything was possible, and he did not believe in waiting so that others could gain the advantage first. He would talk to her, he would caress her, he would make the suggestion to her again that perhaps when she was ready they could be married. In any case, he intended to make love to her—and he had a feeling that if he went about it cautiously enough and patiently enough, she would succumb.

"Well?" Helena demanded.

"Well what? What do you want to know?" Laura questioned, laughing at the expression on Ena's face.

"Oh Laura, you know very well what I mean!" Ena exclaimed. "Your Count. Michel. What happened?"

"Oh," Laura said with an exaggerated sigh of boredom, "the usual thing, of course! He took me to see this private exhibition and then for refreshments in his apartments— Don't look so shocked, Ena! There was nothing wrong with it, I can promise you, although in between the courses he made the usual passes. And tried to ply me with as much wine as he could. However, I managed to keep my head."

"And what does that mean?"

"It means that I managed to say no *without* saying no, if you know what I mean! I'm afraid I rather enjoy playing these little games," Laura confessed ruefully. Then her eyes narrowed slightly. "Unless I find myself pitted against that boor Trent Challenger—Royse! You can't know how relieved I am, and how much lighter I feel, to know that he is out of town! I hope he never returns—he seems to spoil everything for me when he is about."

She *should* feel more at ease now that he was away. She didn't have to look for that arrogantly held dark head at every gathering she attended; nor have to face that certain look he almost always seemed to give her. She should *not* have felt so unaccountably annoyed, therefore, by the information Reggie Forrester had dropped casually when they had gone riding together yesterday in the park.

"Royse is out of town, as I suppose you know, and I'm afraid my impulsive sister went with him! It will only be a matter of time, I think, before there's an announcement in *The Times!*" Reggie had said, fingering his golden moustache. He frowned slightly. "I don't know that I quite like it! I know my sister's of age, and unfortunately widowed at that, but in some ways she's quite the naïve innocent—and it's plain to see Royse isn't. He had better not be playing with her affections."

At the time, Laura had had to restrain herself from laughing out loud, as she wondered if poor Reggie *really* didn't know! She felt tempted to tell him what *she* knew of Trent Challenger, now, of course, the Duke of Royse, but decided against it. She could hardly feel, try as she would, any sympathy for Lady Westbridge—and in fact she almost relished the thought that Sabina would learn the lesson that countless other gullible females must have learned before her!

Thank God, Laura thought, *she* wasn't among the poor fools who allowed themselves to be affected by him and by the things he probably said or promised them. She told herself again that it was such a relief to feel that when she went out now, she would not have to become tense at the thought of running into him. She should make the most of this respite. Why, then, did she actually feel as if there were something missing? But damn him, he was with that silly simpering slut Sabina right now, and they deserved each other! Laura felt sorry for Reggie if he really imagined that his sister had the chance of becoming the Duchess of Royse! Poor Reggie. Poor Sabina!

Reggie Forrester also felt sorry for himself. His pride, he felt, had been mortally injured by all the damned men dangling after Laura Morgan. Why, today she had only allowed him a scant half hour's turn about the park with her before she pleaded another engagement and left him. Goddamn it, he thought balefully, what should he do now—drop out of the running? If only the arrogant little bitch would give him a chance to show her how good a lover he was, then he knew he'd have her under his thumb, as he had had so many other women before!

It was in a disgruntled mood that Reggie went to Francine for consolation, as usual.

"So," she said, "how is it going with you and that little American heiress? Are you going to get her?"

Reggie scowled. "Damnation! That doesn't seem too bloody likely at the moment. She has too many other men hanging after her—and she seems to enjoy all the attention. What am I supposed to do? *I* don't have any money, as you well know, not like her other suitors."

"My poor Reggie," Francine murmured, nuzzling her lips against his neck. "But after all, there are always ways and means to get around everything," she added thoughtfully.

"What ways? Francine, you don't know what she's like, this Laura Morgan. She is an American, and if that wasn't bad enough, she is the kind of typical American female with money who is far too strong, far too self-confident, and far too independent—damn her."

He moved sulkily against Francine as they reclined together on the chaise in her silk parlor. "Francine, I know that I'm only being used by her and I don't like that—I'm not used to it! If only I could get the bitch into bed, things would be different—but no, I'm only used by her as an occasional escort when it's convenient to *her.*"

Francine's hand began moving caressingly over his groin. She gave a small laugh. "Oh no, you're so used to being in charge, aren't you, darling?"

"Yes, goddamn it, I am! And I don't like having women play games with me! If there was only something I could do—some way in which I could get her into a position where she wasn't always surrounded by other people. If I could get her *alone . . .*"

Francine's hand kept on stroking him, but almost negligently, her mind spinning. "Tell me more about her, Reggie-boy. Whatever you know. What does she like to do? Where does she usually go? Is she ever alone?"

At that Reggie sat up abruptly, and studied the small

smile that curved her lips. "What are you getting at, Francine?"

"Darling, does she ever go *any*where alone?"

Reggie knew Francine well enough by now to know that there was always a purpose behind her most casual-seeming questions. He said slowly: "As a matter of fact, there are a few occasions when she does go off on her own. She likes early-morning rides in the park by herself. And . . . so?" Reggie looked inquiringly at his companion as her catlike smile widened.

"Well, my dear Reggie, just think of the consequences of such recklessness, hmm? And the infinite possibilities if certain things might be *arranged!*"

"Such as?" And now Reggie was intrigued, his eyes narrowing down into hers. "Come on, tell me what you mean."

"Well, when I said that certain things could be arranged . . . consider this. We know that the park, especially in the early hours of the morning, can be a dangerous place, what with all the ruffians who loiter about there! It can be especially dangerous for a young woman alone. And what do you think might happen if your Miss Laura goes riding one morning as usual, and all of a sudden she is snatched off the back of her horse and—*abducted?*"

"Abducted?" Reggie repeated disbelievingly.

And now it was Francine's turn to sit up and stare at him. She said impatiently, "But do you not see what I am getting at? Let us suppose that she *is* abducted, and then taken somewhere—somewhere private, to some place where she might be . . . shall we say, *disciplined?* In the same way that a wild mare is disciplined and tamed until she begins crying and begging for her master as she nuzzles his hand!"

"Surely you can't be serious?"

"Well, if you don't think such a thing is possible . . ." Francine turned away with a casual shrug to pour from the bottle of champagne beside the chaise.

But as she had expected, Reggie pulled her around to

face him. "Francine!" He kissed her long and passionately. "My God, Francine, how clever you are!"

"You want her money?"

"Yes."

"And you want to tame her?"

"Yes! Yes! I would like to tame the little bitch, there is nothing in the world I'd like better!"

"So," Francine said, smiling, "then we are in agreement? I assure you that it will not take more than a month before she is yours."

"But where and *when,* do I come in?" Reggie questioned impatiently, eager to hear more.

"You? Why, you *rescue* her, of course! Who would want to marry her after what she's been through? Although of course nobody else will know that *you* have been the man to master her." She shrugged silken shoulders before she said thoughtfully, "It can't be *here,* of course, but I have friends and I know of places, very private places where she could be taken."

Reggie started to stroke his moustache, and then suddenly he smiled, and they clinked their glasses together. "Francine, I swear that you are a genius! Of course, that's it. That's it! Naturally, nobody will want to marry her afterward, and so . . ."

"Of course, there will be a few inquiries," she said. "But I have connections with certain people who will do anything for money."

She looked at him, with her eyebrows arched. "Of course, once *you* have married her, and I can arrange for that, too, before she is released—then you will have control of her money, and I take my share, yes, my dear?"

"You'll get more than your share—including *me.*"

"So we have a bargain then?"

He laughed suddenly, throwing his head back. Goddamn the little bitch, he thought. She did need to be tamed. He looked down at Francine, then poured the champagne between her breasts, and leaned over to lap it up.

"My dear, you can ask for anything, and you'll get it. Once I get control of her and her fortune."

When he left Francine, Reggie Forrester could hardly contain his feelings of elation *and* anticipation. His mind was filled with images of Laura in every conceivable attitude and position—helpless, stripped naked before him for his pleasure, her arrogance broken by the whip until she crawled to him on her hands and knees to kiss his hands, begging him for mercy! Laura—soon to be his slave-wife; his obedient, submissive, and infinitely obliging *wife* with all of her fortune in his control and she under his command! Francine had promised that in a few days her plan would be put into operation.

He could hardly wait!

While Reggie Forrester was planning her future, Laura had been keeping herself busy. Too busy, Lady Honoria thought. That wise lady had not failed to notice how Laura's eyes would search about the room wherever they went. Nor how her gaiety seemed to have almost a feverish quality. Well, there's nothing like bringing matters to a head, she thought, and that was exactly what she intended to do.

Laura and Helena were told that they were to go out shopping for hats and ribbons and bolts of fabric that would be made up into new gowns for them both; any lady of fashion could not be seen in the same gown on more than one fashionable occasion—so Lady Honoria announced. "And on the way, of course, since it is the right time of the afternoon, we will leave our calling cards wherever necessary." Laura and Ena exchanged resigned glances. Leaving off calling cards could be an interminable process—and so boring too.

Laura felt as if she actually might doze off when she heard the coachman announce: "Royse House, Your Ladyships." And then she sat upright with a startled look that Lady Honoria did not miss.

"Royse House? But Ena, why should we leave our cards

here when there is no one home to receive them?" Laura whispered to her friend.

Lady Honoria did not miss that, either, and gave her a forbidding look before she said: "We are stopping here to leave a card, naturally. It's customary, you know, especially since we have been invited to a reception here in less than a week from now."

"But, Ma'am," Laura said impulsively, "I thought . . . well, I understood that—"

"*I* have been informed," Lady Honoria interrupted, "that my friend Lady Margaret has already arrived in town."

While Laura was still trying to digest *that* particular piece of information, which shocked her for some reason, the footman who had taken in the cards came out immediately with a smile to say that Lady Margaret hoped that her friend and her companions would join her at tea.

"Well, good! We'll be glad to come in," Lady Honoria stated before Laura had the chance to protest.

Laura's mind was a whirl of conflicting thoughts as she followed reluctantly in Lady Honoria's wake, with Ena alongside her.

If Lady Margaret, *his* stepmother, was here already, did that mean that he had already returned to London? And how was it that Lady Honoria had known, while she had not! What did this visit *mean?*

It was a relief to Laura to find only two ladies there to greet them, with no signs of a dark, glowering Duke of Royse! Thank goodness!

Lady Margaret Sinclair was a small woman, but her erect carriage and high-piled silver-gold hair gave an illusion of height. She had a warm face and a real smile as she held out her hands to greet them, her eyes sparkling with genuine pleasure. Laura liked her immediately. Miss Letitia Renfrew, Lady Margaret's companion, was all twitters and nervous giggles as she professed herself quite overwhelmed that Lady Honoria had decided to join them for tea along with the Countess of Sedgewick and Miss Morgan.

"So good of the dear Duke—the present Duke, I mean—to ask us here!" Miss Renfrew said in a nervous rush of words as she made sure everyone was seated comfortably. "We were quite nervous, you know, when we heard he was coming to call. Lady Margaret was even more nervous than I was, I'm sure, although she didn't show it!"

Lady Margaret hushed her before turning to the others and saying quietly, "But she is right, you know! I did not know what to expect when I received the letter from Mr. Weatherby saying that Royse wished to call upon me. I had thought at one time that he might resent me. He was so devoted to his mother, you know."

"Come, Margaret," Lady Honoria demanded. "You must tell me the whole of it, for all I've heard so far is rumors!"

She looked around at the prettily decorated room that had been Lady Margaret's own sitting room before and had not been changed at all. "You're to be hostess at Royse again, eh? Good! I'm glad that Royse had the decency to think of it! And now you will make your reentry into society."

At this moment the butler entered, bearing a huge tray on which were piled all kinds of little sandwiches cut in different shapes and *petits fours*. Conversation ceased while Lady Margaret poured tea.

"No milk or sugar for me, please," Laura said automatically when she saw Lady Margaret smile at her understandingly. It was only then that she noticed the wedge of lemon on her saucer.

"I rather thought that being from America you, too, might prefer your tea with lemon instead of the milk and sugar we English use," Lady Margaret said. "My stepson is the same way, you know. He has told me that the only way he can possibly stand to drink tea is with a squeeze of lemon in it!"

At that moment Lady Honoria's shrewd eyes noticed the

suddenly unguarded expression on Laura's face, and made
a mental note of it before leaning closer to Lady Margaret
and saying in a significant way: "I feel that you and I have
a great deal to discuss. And I expect you to give me all
the details about this reception that you're giving. Who's
coming?"

While the two older ladies embarked on a lengthy discussion, Laura and Ena took tiny nibbles of their sandwiches and small sips of tea, replying politely to the small
talk that Miss Renfrew felt obliged to engage them in.

Laura's thoughts were a jumbled mixture of emotions
that she did not feel ready to sort out yet. Lady Margaret
hadn't mentioned it, but had Royse also returned to town?
Or was he secluded somewhere in one of his country
homes with Sabina? And why should she care! She didn't!
He was an annoying distraction in her life—preventing her
from really enjoying her social life with his dark, diabol-
ical presence! She hoped he hadn't returned to town yet.
She wished—

"Laura!" Lady Honoria's commanding voice brought
Laura back to sudden attention with a guilty flush rising
in her cheeks.

Looking sharply at her as if she had been able to guess
her thoughts, Lady Honoria said: "Miss Renfrew has just
been kind enough to offer to show you and Ena some of
the new paintings Royse has brought back with him from
Paris. Perhaps you two might enjoy viewing them in the
gallery." She added impatiently, "My dear, where on
earth has your attention been wandering!"

"Oh, I am sorry, but I . . ." Laura started to stammer
as she rose from her seat, her face now positively flaming
with embarrassment. At that very unfortunate moment the
object of her wandering attention strode into the room—
booted and still in his riding clothes with his eyes going
arrow-straight to her face before he quickly made polite
apologies to the ladies for the informality of his attire.

As he stood there, Laura was almost transfixed for some
moments. She was rescued by Lady Margaret who said:

"Royse, Miss Renfrew was just about to show the Countess of Sedgewick and Miss Morgan through the gallery to
see those new paintings you have hung. I thought you
wouldn't mind."

Why, Laura thought rebelliously, did *he* have to take
over in his usual high-handed fashion by drawling that he
would enjoy giving the ladies a personally guided tour of
the gallery and some of the rooms in the house that they
might be interested in seeing. "I like watching the reactions of people to this new school of art," he said, his
eyes lingering for a moment on Laura's face. "There are
so many different interpretations and feelings that these
paintings can evoke in people."

"Oh no," Laura began to say frostily. "I wouldn't
dream of imposing . . ." But at the exact same moment
Ena said eagerly that she would *love* to see the new paintings.

It was all decided when Lady Honoria said briskly,
"That's very kind of you, Royse. Margaret and I can get
on with our talk while you're doing the honors!"

There was no help for it, Laura supposed resentfully.
With exaggerated politeness, Royse showed them room
after room on the ground floor, each more magnificently
furnished than the other; then he led them to a private
stairway that went directly to a long and well-lighted gallery.

"This is lit by the new electricity, isn't it?" Helena
inquired interestedly.

"Yes, it was one of the first things I had done to this
house. And these particular canvases—this, and this—had
to be properly lighted in order to bring out the excitement
and the color in them; or to emphasize the darkness like
this one and this one."

Strangely enough, Laura understood what he meant, as
she stood transfixed before a small canvas by Vincent van
Gogh where light and color and thick layers of paint sliced
with a palette knife formed images that were like thoughts.
Not picture-pastel pretty but alive and vital and almost

leaping out at one from the canvas with its broad statement.

"You like that particular painting, don't you? I thought you would."

Somehow, without her realizing it, he had come to stand behind her—*far* too close behind her; his long legs encased in shiny high-topped riding boots almost brushing hers. Why, Laura thought almost frantically, did she always have to react this way when he was close to her? She could almost feel the warmth of his body reaching out to her though her clothing.

Trying to maintain an air of cool composure, Laura swung about to face him, her stubborn chin slightly tilted. "It is a very good example of Vincent van Gogh's work," she said rather stiltedly, considering the fact that he had not stepped back to give her space. He seemed to loom over her, those gray-glacier eyes boring into hers and through hers to send a small *frisson* up her spine.

Where was Ena? Where was her ally? As if he could read her mind, he said, "Your friend, I see, seems to prefer Gaugin." Indeed, a few feet away Ena seemed to be gazing enrapturedly at paintings of Polynesian beauties.

The silence stretched between them until it was so taut that Laura couldn't stand it. For some reason, her breathing had become faster and she wanted more than anything to get away. He had no right to keep on just *looking* at her in that peculiar way of his, without even saying a single word. Somehow she had to get away!

Laura managed to produce a falsely bright brittle smile which she directed at him. "This has been so kind of you! I really enjoyed the gallery, but I must confess that I am rather tired and we do have fittings to go to in a little while." And then she called, more sharply than she intended, "Ena, are you ready to go?"

"Was that supposed to be a call for help?" Royse whispered with his lips close to her ear. Then he straightened and moved away from her with a distantly polite bow as Helena came hurrying over to them.

Downstairs, Lady Honoria proclaimed that it was high
time they returned. "I was beginning to think that you
had managed to get yourselves lost and had forgotten that
you have an appointment for fittings in less than a quarter
of an hour."

Lady Honoria took her leave from Lady Margaret, Laura and Ena politely thanking her, and only Ena thanking
Royse.

"I like her," Lady Margaret said to her stepson after
her guests had left. "I mean Miss Morgan. In fact," she
added with sudden boldness, "Lady Honoria seems to
think that you two have a decided partiality for each
other!" She went on more timidly. "What I mean to say
is that, well, even at first acquaintance I could not help
but observe that Miss Morgan was *changed* after your arrival. And oh, I do hope you will not mind my saying so,
but it seemed as if you, too, seemed in some way *affected*
by her very presence in the same room!" Her level gaze
met Trent's dark look. "I really don't think that if you did
not *like* her you would glower so!"

At that Trent's expression lightened and he gave an unwilling laugh. "Am I glowering?" He turned to look at
himself in the ornate mirror over the mantelpiece. "Oh! I
suppose I am!" He turned again to Lady Margaret. "I
must confess that she has a habit of getting under my skin
like a burr and of making me angry."

"But I think that *you* have a habit of making her angry
too," Lady Margaret said quietly.

"Do I?" And then Trent said almost without pausing,
"I suppose I do. I enjoy annoying her, for some reason.
I guess the two of us are like flint and tinder—we extract
sparks from each other."

"Well, even *I* noticed that," Miss Renfrew said from
the corner where she sat knitting; at which Trent directed
one of his glowering looks at her, making her turn quickly
back to her knitting again.

"Oh damn!" And then recollecting himself, "I beg your
pardon, Ma'am, but the truth is," he added with a sudden

burst of honesty as he ran fingers through his rumpled night-black hair, "that I don't really know what to do with her, or do *about* her for that matter!"

The two ladies exchanged meaningful glances before Lady Margaret said soothingly, "I'm sure that in the end there will be some solution for both of you. And," she added quite cunningly for *her,* "didn't you tell me once that there was some kind of an engagement between you?" For a moment Lady Margaret thought she might have gone too far when she saw him stiffen and his brows draw together in what she thought of as his "black look," but then he shrugged, and his lips twisted in an almost-smile.

"That's right. And who knows? I might actually end up *marrying* the wench in the end—even if it means dragging her off by force!" His eyes narrowed in a particularly dangerous way, as if he were talking to himself, before he added in a silky-sharp voice, "I think that our Miss Morgan is a shrew that definitely needs taming!"

Miss Renfrew could not help gasping at *that,* and dropped a ball of wool, which the Duke obligingly retrieved for her. Then he made his excuses and, as Miss Renfrew whispered to Lady Margaret afterward, positively *stamped* upstairs while calling for his valet in an unconscionably loud voice.

"Do you think he has actually fallen in love with the girl?" Miss Renfrew whispered.

Lady Margaret looked thoughtful. "Perhaps. Honoria thinks that there is something there. And I suppose there is," she said on a sigh. "One can only hope, Lettie, that they do not *hurt* each other too much before discovering their true feelings!"

Upstairs, in his room, Trent swore to himself savagely. They were all performers! He—and *she*—playing their roles to the hilt! The Duke of Royse and the American Heiress. What a good title for a play by Oscar Wilde!

Christ, there were times when he would enjoy strangling her! Then again, there were times . . .

When Trent left Royse House later that evening, he was

still in a darkly introspective mood that he was determined to shake off before the night ended. And in the morning, very early, he would try out the new gray stallion he had just purchased at Tattersalls. A sweet runner. God! How he missed the space and the endless distances he had left behind him for *this!*

Chapter 28

On this particular morning, Laura felt as if she had to escape from everything and everyone, even if it was only for a short while. She loved the feeling of freedom when she went for a canter in the park very early in the morning, a mist hanging from the trees dewing every blade of grass, muting and blending colors and shapes together in a soft, gauze-wrapped stillness and peacefulness.

She hadn't slept well the previous night, her fitful slumber haunted by nightmares of dragons with fiery tongues that licked out to wrap themselves around her body. She had felt pursued, besieged—and she wanted to feel free enough to think clearly.

At Sedgewick House her groom brought around her horse from the mews, and as usual he did not have to help her mount.

"Cor! Wonder if that's how all American ladies ride!" one of the stable boys exclaimed.

"Oh no," Duffy the groom replied a trifle proudly, "but I do know this young lady carries a pistol with her, too, in the pocket of that divided riding skirt she wears. Why, Mr. Mannering himself told me that milady herself told *him* that the young lady can shoot that pistol just as well as Miss Annie Oakley in that Buffalo Bill Wild West Show."

"Well, I never!" the boy said in an awed voice as he gazed after the young lady who dared to ride astride in those outlandish leather divided skirts—and who carried a pistol as well!

When she rode into the park Laura had no idea what time it was and didn't care. It was still misty, and she felt the dampness against her face and in her hair, a transparent gauze curtain that seemed to envelop her. She loved this time of the morning—the freshness of the air each time she took a breath, the green smell of grass and leaves, the faint perfume from hidden violets. Oh yes, this was what she needed!

She rode first at a canter and then at a gallop down the usually frequented paths and then down unfamiliar avenues, eventually slowing down until she finally brought her mare to a stop at her favorite place where a willow tree hung over a curve in the Serpentine.

Laura dismounted and went to sit against the tree, her pencil and notebook resting on her lap; but there was not enough light to write by yet, and in any case she did not feel inspired. It didn't matter, Laura thought almost dreamily. She could watch the dragonflies skimming over the slowly rippling, misted silver surface of the water while she let her mind suspend thought and flow between consciousness and unconsciousness; thinking and not thinking! It was peaceful—*so* peaceful at this time of the morning! But within a few hours this place, the whole park, would be all harsh sounds and sights and colors—nothing like this!

Laura would have stayed in her dream-drowse if she hadn't been jolted back to awareness when Freya, her highstrung mare, suddenly started to paw and stamp restlessly, head tossing, and snorting. Laura stood up quickly to pat Freya's neck, whispering in her ear to calm her. And then, instinctively sensing all of a sudden what her horse had already felt, Laura swung around and saw them. Two men, big, ugly-looking and burly; one had a cudgel, the other a rope knotted at one end—the usual weapons of the ruffians that hung about the park after dark and early in the morning. She had been warned before and often enough! But there was no time now to remember warnings.

Laura felt her derringer snuggled like a friend against her thigh—but they were coming in now, too quickly for her to have time to draw it. Hardly thinking, acting on pure instinct, Laura went for *them*—taking them completely by surprise. Her divided skirt made it easy for her to kick the one who was closest to her in the groin before she pivoted like a matador, ducking under the upraised cudgel of the other, with one hand paralyzing his wrist so that the weapon went flying while the side of her other hand caught him in the Adam's apple and sent him sprawling to the ground alongside his still-writhing companion.

When they had recovered sufficiently to be able to sit up, groaning, she had her gun pointed at them—as cool as a cucumber, one of them said afterward, with her eyes looking as deadly as the gun.

"Run along now, boys—and feel lucky I've given you a chance to live! Unless you'd like me to shoot a few holes in you? You wouldn't be the first scum I've had to kill—and I'm an *excellent* shot—you might want to remember that!" While they continued to stare at her, dumbfounded, she said dangerously, "Go! Before I change my mind! And go *running!*" And they did run, too, daring to look back only once!

They were gone, but Laura felt as if the privacy and peace of mind she usually found in the park at this hour had been violated and spoiled for her forever.

It only made it worse when she heard a sarcastic voice that she recognized too well assail her.

"I must say you handled that very well! I'm sorry I didn't come galloping to your rescue—but I didn't doubt you'd be able to manage just two of them by yourself."

"Oh damn! *You* again. What are you doing here? *Stalking* me as usual?" With reaction to the incident setting in, and seeing *him* sitting on his gray stallion grinning down at her—it was too much for her to take!

He slid off his horse and she poised herself quite in-

stinctively in a fighting stance, as if he were a foe she had
to defend herself against. He laughed.

"Why are you all set to duel with me, I wonder—when
I haven't even challenged you yet? And what are you afraid
of, Lorelei—me, or yourself?"

"I don't need your spears flung at me this morning!
You saw that I'm quite capable of taking care of myself,
didn't you? So why—"

"Why?" The lightly mocking tone had suddenly disappeared from his voice as he took one long stride that
brought him close to her—catching her off guard.

"Damn you!" he exploded. "What in God's name are
you doing here at this hour? Were you looking for adventure? New exciting experiences to write about?"

Abruptly, without her knowing how, he had her pinned
up against a tree, reminding her far too vividly of another
time—in Mexico. He was strong enough, damn him, to
hold both her wrists behind the tree while he leaned against
her and *into* her, it seemed, until . . . until she felt smothered, breathless, helpless.

"Let me give you a demonstration of what *might* have
happened, Lorelei," he whispered harshly. "Perhaps it's
the kind of excitement you really enjoy!"

And then he began kissing her, taking his time about it,
too—lips traveling from her temples to her earlobes and
up again to find her eyelids, the bridge of her nose, her
damp cheeks, the line of her jaw, the cleft of her chin,
and then, finally, when she felt she could hardly *bear* it
anymore, he seemed to discover her mouth. The hardness
of his lips bruised the softness of hers, forcing them open.
By this time Laura was past all reason as the serpent of
sensuality she had already discovered within herself uncoiled, and she moaned softly in her throat as she arched
her body forward to press against his. Wanting . . . *wanting!*

She hadn't noticed that he'd freed her wrists until she
found herself clutching at his shoulders—touching his
hair—holding him and feeling the muscles of his back

move under her hands before she pulled his head fiercely down to her upturned face again, not *caring*—wanting him to do more than tease the hardened nipples of her breasts that longed to be free from the constraint of her tight bodice.

It was *he*, finally, who had to halt what was happening. *He* who had to free himself from her entangling arms and almost forcibly hold her away from him.

His voice was harsh over his uneven breathing. "Oh *Christ!* I could couple with you right here, right now if the sun wasn't becoming bright enough to burn away the mist and bring other people out. Your suitors might not understand the liberties that old friends can indulge in with each other!"

His caustic words were like a pitcher full of cold water thrown at her, and Laura felt as if she had suddenly escaped from the grip of a nightmare into cold reality.

"Oh! Oh *God!*" Realization struck with all the force of a blow, bringing her out of the trance she'd been in, filling her with shame and embarrassment.

"Pull yourself together!" he said coldly. "What in hell's the matter with you? If you want to finish what just started, I can take you, *now,* to a private house not far from here." His voice turned suddenly, devilishly, caressing, as he touched her tear-wet face. "Lorelei!" She stared up at him, unable to speak. "I *want* you, damn you! And I know you want me just as much. Why play games of pretense with each other?"

"Oh no! Oh *no!*" The words came out of her throat in torn gasps.

He seized her roughly by the shoulders. "Laura, stop hiding from yourself, for God's sake! And stop running from me. You know we'll have each other in the end, and you're a damned idiot if you don't realize that by now."

It was not his words, or even the way he almost spat them out at her, that truly horrified her. It was the fact that she *wanted* to go with him, wanted him to finish what he had started.

He kissed her again and again and again, whispering between his kisses, "Lorelei, come with me! Forget everything else and come with me. Or do you want me to *take* you with me? Should I sling you across my saddle like one of the Sabine women and take you until whatever it is, this fever between us, is sated? Wouldn't you like to find out if the wanting we both feel will *ever* be sated?"

His voice—*that* voice! No, he couldn't and she wouldn't believe that it could have been *he* who had— No! No! It was just because . . . because . . . Oh, but she couldn't stand this for another moment! What he was making her feel and making her *imagine* was quite intolerable!

With all the strength she still retained, and all the sanity that was left to her, Laura wrenched herself away from his touch and his encroaching lips that whispered lies, lies, lies. Between each kiss he had kept saying he wanted her, that he had to have her—but not *once* had he told her that he loved her.

"That's enough!" she panted. "You've had your fun and you've played your damned games, and now—now it's time for the play to end."

She backed away and he made a move toward her. Almost without her own volition she whipped the derringer from the pocket of her skirt and pointed it at him.

"I mean what I say, damn you! Don't try me any further, I warn you!"

"That's a convincingly deadly little toy you have pointed at me," Trent drawled. "I could probably get it away from you if I really wanted to try." His silver eyes slashed into the blue of hers. "But I don't think I'm in the mood to play this morning. Besides"—his voice became silken—"I do so enjoy these little exchanges of ours. I would hate to see them end over a stray bullet!"

Then he laughed. "Stop looking so grimly defensive, like a Rhine Maiden guarding the gold of her virtue! The game's over, as you told me. But only for the moment, Lorelei, only for the moment!"

She continued to watch him narrowly, not trusting him

or anything he said. He raised an eyebrow at her. "Well? Are you just going to stand there frozen into place like a marble statue until someone else discovers you and kisses you back to life? If not—I'll escort you safely to your door if you'll permit me."

"Just . . . just *go,* damn you! And for God's sake, from now on leave me alone!"

She watched him shrug and walk away from her, mounting his gray stallion in one easy, fluid motion. Now she felt foolish as she dropped her ineffective little gun back in her pocket. Would she really have used it on him?

"Adiós!" he called to her over his shoulder with a smile that boded no good for either of them she was to think later.

"Wonder what got into 'er?" Tom, the stable boy, said to Duffy after Laura, disheveled and disturbed, had flung the reins of her horse at them and then had positively run up the steps to the house.

Whatever Duffy thought, he kept to himself. But he was Irish and sometimes he felt he had the Sight. When Duffy dismissed the stable boy he thought, Ahh, so that's the way of it, is it? And I wonder which one of them gents it was that could make the young lady so hot and bothered— yes, and with her cheeks all flushed and her hair coming down too!

Below-stairs the usual gossip raged. There was nothing, no nuance of expression or signs of agitation, that the servants missed while being supposedly invisible as they served.

Upstairs, Laura was relieved to regain the comparative security of her room without encountering anyone on the way. She wanted a bath—she wanted to wash her hair— she wanted to clean away all thoughts of what had happened—and what *might* have happened!

At first, she didn't want to ring for Adèle. She didn't want anyone to see her. With shaking, fumbling fingers, she began to undress herself, but then came unbidden thoughts of his fingers doing it for her, unfastening one

little button after another while he kissed her down her
back, one kiss for every button—oh no!

He was like a demon after her soul that she *must* exorcise—like the strangely erotic images and thoughts that
suddenly seemed to flood her mind. Oh God, how she
wished that she might never have to set eyes on him again!
But on the heels of that wish she wondered where he was
now? And what was he thinking, feeling . . . *remembering?* She didn't want to know and she didn't want to care!
But she did.

Chapter 29

Trent Challenger, also known as the Duke of Royse, decided to call on Lady Westbridge. He needed to vent his anger, his frustration, and his lust on someone—and Sabina, pretty as a porcelain doll, was the perfect choice. Not only was she pretty, but she was most obliging, and *very* knowledgeable when it came to pleasing a man. He was currently paying for her nicely appointed apartment on Curzon Street, so he had the right to walk in on her whenever he pleased. And by God! Trent thought, today, she had better not have another lover in her bed!

As it happened, Sabina was in bed, in a charming state of deshabille. He liked her like this, Trent thought as he looked down at her—when she was still half-asleep, her eyes heavy-lidded, she was unlikely to talk too much.

She sat up, brushing strands of platinum hair from her face. "Trent! I thought you'd never get back!"

Without a word, he pulled the silken covers down from her shoulders and began to tease first one nipple and then the other. She, at least, was not only easily aroused but easily giving!

"Oh Trent, please do stop for now—I must talk to you!" She pushed his hand away, gazing up at him with what appeared to be tears welling up in her sky-blue eyes. "Trent . . . we just have to talk! Everyone is gossiping, and Reggie—well, Reggie is just furious with me."

Either not noticing or disregarding the sudden glacial coldness of his eyes, Sabina rushed on. "You don't know what it's been like for me while you were away, especially with the Season at its height! Everyone was wondering where you had disappeared to and why, and it would have placed me in the most awkward of positions to have to admit that even *I* did not know, and so Reggie insisted I remain *cloistered* here so that people might think we had gone away *together!* I've been miserable, just miserable! And we promised to attend so many different affairs together too! Oh, it was so thoughtless of you to do this to me. I feel so humiliated, so—"

"Come to the point, Sabina," he said in a voice as steely as his narrowed eyes. "What exactly are you trying to tell me? That I owe you an explanation for all my actions?"

"No, of course not, but my reputation . . . !" Tears rolled down her cheeks. "Don't you see that you have *compromised* me with your attentions and your escorting me everywhere and . . . and . . . oh, surely you understand something of convention and what is *expected* of one . . . and how very hard it would be for me to hold my head up in society again if—"

"Sabina!" The pronouncement of her name in the coldest, most dangerous tone of voice she had ever heard stopped her in mid-sentence, and her eyes widened as she looked up into his harsh, unyielding face.

He gave a short, ugly laugh that barely disguised the underlying steel in his voice. "My dear Sabina, there is something that you had better learn about me if you haven't learned it already. I don't give a damn about society or the opinions of others. What is more, I've made a habit of never doing what is expected of me nor do I care what others expect of me! I think we should get this much clearly understood between us. I'm not a polite, civilized Englishman, my dear—I'm a barbarian American, and that's a cross between a backwoodsman and a savage! Isn't that what you once told me *'they'* were all saying I was?"

Sabina suddenly realized he was going to leave her; and seeing the Duke of Royse and all her chances slip out of her grasp, she cried out to him in a frantic, broken voice: "Trent! Please don't go, please don't leave me, please, I beg you! I only said what I did because I felt so hurt, because Reggie—"

He turned at the door to stare at her with those icy gray eyes that always made her shiver. "Because Reggie *what?* You can tell your brother, my sweet, that if he has anything to say he can say it to me! And though I don't usually choose to duel with fools, I think that in this case I might make an exception."

Sabina erupted out of bed, wearing nothing but a flimsy nightshift that he had bought her. She threw herself up against him, entwining her arms tightly about his neck. "Don't leave me like this, Trent! You know how I feel about you. I promise I won't care what anybody else thinks as long as you still want me, and as long as you'll still take me everywhere with you! And I won't be frightened of Reggie anymore, either, as long as I know *you* still want me!"

He was in a mean, angry, cruel mood right now. "Are you ready to prove that, Sabina?" he queried harshly.

"Oh, Trent, Trent, I swear to you that I mean it! I don't care for anything but you! I only need you to want me."

"Let's find out right now if you mean what you say, Lady Westbridge!"

Suddenly he put one arm under her thighs and lifted her up. He looked around a moment, holding her in that position until he deposited her on the thick, red-patterned Persian rug between the bed and the window.

"Stay there, Sabina," he commanded. "I want to see you with your legs open."

Trent frightened Sabina when he was in this kind of mood! But she was mesmerized at the same time; fascinated to find out what he intended to do with her.

"I told you to spread your legs for me, didn't I? They're not spread widely enough." With his booted foot he nudged her thighs farther apart, and she started to whimper softly, her eyes fixed on his face, even while she obeyed his next harsh command and pulled the gauzy nightrobe well over her breasts.

He stood between her outstretched legs and slowly unbuttoned his tight buckskin trousers, and with secret pleasure she saw the evidence of his desire. And then, as he roughly pushed her legs upward, Sabina realized with a sense of shock that he meant to take her without even undressing himself completely.

He positioned her so that her knees were drawn up so far that they were on either side of her face and her legs hung down helplessly over his shoulders. His fingers began to play with her breasts, and with her open and exposed sex until, in spite of the discomfort of her position, she started to moan and writhe and beg him in choked whispers to enter her, to take her. Her heels drummed against his back until at last he did drive himself into her, and she screamed softly—first with pain at the initial roughness of his entry, then with exquisite pleasure that mounted feverishly as he thrust himself deeper inside of her; and she climaxed over and over again under his deliciously brutal assault.

Afterward, Sabina teased, "What a brute you are! Now I really believe that you are a barbarian savage." And then, just as he was preparing to leave, she called to him, "Are we going out this evening? Have you had time to look at all the cards and invitations you must have received?"

"No, I'm afraid not yet. But if there's something interesting to attend this evening, I'll call you on the telephone in plenty of time for you to get yourself ready, and we'll go together."

Somehow, and for whatever reason, Trent suddenly felt sorry for Sabina, and for the way he had used her to expend his own frustrations and fury. She was what she was, after all; at least she didn't attempt to pretend, or to deny her feelings. In her own way Sabina was honest.

As for Laura, Trent thought as he rode back to Royse House, the trouble with *her* was that she was unpredictable, and a damnable, teasing little bitch! She was afraid of herself, and wouldn't admit it. Unlike Sabina, Laura was dishonest—even with herself.

When Trent finally returned to Royse House and was on his way up to his suite of rooms, Miss Renfrew caught him halfway up the staircase to inform him that there had been a telephone call—she made it sound like a major event—from a certain Mr. Bishop. Oh, she was sure that was the *right* name, she had written it down and left a note on his desk in the study.

"He said that he was only calling to confirm an appointment you had with him for—Oh dear! Was it tonight or tomorrow night? No, I do believe it was for tomorrow night, but it's all written down . . . I *did* make sure of that! I'm sorry, Your Grace, but I really am not used to such things as *telephones!*"

Trent was unaccountably furious. Damn Bishop and his devious plots, anyhow. Right now he had enough on his mind—wondering what he was going to do about that damnable little witch Laura Morgan.

Reggie Forrester had been elated when he received the perfumed note from Francine asking him to visit her at his earliest convenience. Naturally he had hurried over, his mind filled with all kinds of wild imaginings of Laura completely at his mercy. But soon after he was ushered into Francine's private parlor, his mood of anticipation turned into frustrated rage at her first words.

"I'm afraid, Reggie-boy, that it didn't work out the way we had hoped for."

"What do you mean?" Reggie demanded, his face becoming suffused with angry color.

"Darling, I mean that our plan—clever as it was—did not turn out successfully."

Francine stretched languidly before she continued. "I think that we underestimated this Miss Morgan of yours! You said she was from America, but you *didn't* tell me that young women there are brought up differently from

ladies here!'' Seeing the confused look on his face, she
explained: ''Two men—big, burly bullies—armed with
cudgels ought to have been enough; that is, *ordinarily!*
But your Miss Morgan routed them. From what I was told
they felt themselves lucky to escape with their lives! One
of them thinks he might be crippled for life since she
kicked him in—shall we say a very *vulnerable* place.''

Francine laughed suddenly. ''Do you know, Reggie-boy,
I think I'd really like to meet this young Amazone who
can take care of herself so well. If she wasn't as rich as
you say she is, I could probably help her to make a fortune
with *me!*''

''But how could it fail!'' Reggie stormed, as he began
to pace back and forth across the carpet. ''I don't understand how on earth she was able to—''

''I think, Reggie,'' Francine murmured, ''that you
should be very careful in your dealings with Miss Morgan.
Or at least, try not to make her too angry with you!'' She
sat up from her reclining position on the couch and beck-
oned to Reggie with two slender fingers. ''Surely you must
know by now that in this life things do not always happen
as we want them to. And so instead of walking up and
down, like an angry schoolboy, why don't you find consolation with one of my girls? Since it's early yet, all the
best ones are still available.''

''For God's sake, Francine! What shall I do now?''

''It's obvious, isn't it? Either you continue to see Miss
Morgan on her own terms—or you give up the chase and
let one of the others have her.''

It didn't help Reggie's mood in the least to find out,
when he visited his sister later that afternoon, that Royse
was back in town. He had a feeling that Royse was merely
playing with his sister, using her for his convenience while
he stalked Laura Morgan! Well, maybe he could use *that*
arrangement to his own advantage by encouraging Sabina
to be friendly with Miss Morgan and, in time, to make a
confidante of her.

''Once you have accomplished that, dear sister, then

perhaps you might tell her how close you are to Royse—
the promises he has made to you, the *intimacy* of your
relationship with him! I'm sure you'll know what to say.
And remember, this is something that concerns us *both.*"

"But I can't *stand* her!" Sabina said petulantly. "And
I can't stand the way Royse looks at her—and *she* looks at
him, even though she might pretend she doesn't like him!
I know that she doesn't like *me*, either, so how could I
possibly—"

His sister had only been half-dressed when Reggie had
come in, unannounced, and had dismissed her maid peremptorily. They were facing each other in the small dressing room, and now he suddenly reached out to catch one
of her nipples between his fingers, twisting it cruelly and
making her swallow her words in a cry of surprised pain.
"You will do exactly what I tell you to do, Sabina. Do
you understand?"

She put her hands up over her breasts protectively as
she nodded sulkily. Reggie enjoyed hurting her. He always
had, even when they were both in the nursery; and she
had always been afraid of him. *She* knew, just as he knew,
that she would do exactly as he instructed her.

Chapter 30

"What on earth's the matter with you, my girl?" Lady Honoria asked with her eyes fixed unwaveringly upon Laura's face. "You haven't been your usual self for the past week, although the Lord knows you've had enough attention to turn any young woman's head! But I know the difference! You are not the kind to have her head turned, are you? That's one of the reasons why I like you! But now I want to know what's behind this strange moodiness of yours. You might as well tell me because you know I'll find out sooner or later!"

Laura felt trapped, there in the carriage with Lady Honoria facing her and Helena beside her. She cast an imploring look at her friend, who promptly spoke up for her by exclaiming: "But Belle-mère, *I* haven't seen any change in Laura! Perhaps it is just the strain—she is not used to the London Season yet, and after all—"

"Oh, nonsense!" Lady Honoria said impatiently. "I know better than *that!* Let Laura answer for herself!"

Laura, her cheeks flushing involuntarily, said boldly, "Ena's right, Ma'am. If I've appeared tired recently, it's only because I am not used to the frantic pace, with hardly any time in between for resting." Then she added hastily, "It's not that it isn't all very *exciting*, but—"

"Is it Royse?" Lady Honoria demanded bluntly, taking Laura off guard. "I know you've been seeing him with that silly little milk-sop Lady Westbridge, but you should realize that that doesn't mean anything. Men are strange creatures after all—unfortunately, we have to learn to live with them, but if we're clever enough, we can manipulate them. Although I'm sure you know that already—I've seen you with the others! Then again, Royse is a different kettle of fish, isn't he?'' Laura was too taken aback to utter a word.

"He's not easy," the dowager continued. "Which I could see for myself from the first. So what are you going to do about it, eh?"

"I . . . well, I really don't know!" Laura said honestly, wondering how Lady Honoria always managed to goad her into coming out with the truth.

"Then you had best think about it, my girl!" Lady Honoria sniffed, leaning back with her eyes closed to signal that the discussion had ended.

Looking out from the window of the moving carriage, and longing for the moment when she could be back in the privacy of her own room, Laura wondered about the blunt question that Lady Honoria had directed at her. What *was* she going to do about Royse? She didn't know what it was that existed between them, but she did know, all too well, that it was *there*. For her as well as for him—yes, she accepted that. But he couldn't have her and he wouldn't have her! He was too strong for her liking, and far too overbearing. She'd rather get herself engaged to somebody else, *anyone* else, for that matter, rather than let him imagine that he could have her once he was through running around with Sabina Westbridge. Reggie's sister had, strangely, tried to become almost too friendly with her of late; even to the point of starting to whisper confidences to her whenever an opportunity presented itself, although she tried her best to discourage it.

"Oh, but as you and Royse are such old friends," Sabina had said to her recently, "I thought . . . I had hoped that you might be able to give me some advice. He's the first American man I have ever encountered, you know, and I don't know how to deal with him, and with the rather compromising position he seems to have placed me in! He doesn't seem to understand—although of course he tells me he loves me, and has even mentioned *marriage* to me. What do you advise I should do? *You* know him far better than I do.''

"But I don't really," Laura had said briefly. "And if you really want my advice, what *I'd* do is tell him to go to hell!" Then she had added: "As we both should know by now, men will say and promise almost anything if it suits their purposes, so why get taken in by sweetly phrased lies? I certainly don't!''

Laura could not help but relish, with a certain maliciousness, the look on Sabina's pretty porcelain face when she had said that. She really couldn't *stand* Sabina!

"Oh, miss! You look so beautiful tonight!" Adèle said as she fastened the last button into its loop on the back of Laura's tightly fitting princess evening gown of white satin trimmed with dark blue velvet ribbons that almost matched her eyes. It was the night of the reception at Royse House, and Laura felt as if Adèle had been dressing her for *hours*.

"Oh, do look in the mirror. Mademoiselle will outshine every lady there, of that I am sure!"

Laura turned to study her reflection. She had made sure that her décolletage was low enough to show the slight rounding of her breasts, as it dipped into a deep vee edged by black lace studded with shining rhinestones. Puff sleeves reached to just above her elbow, ending in a matching ruffle of black lace and rhinestones. She had decided to wear diamonds and sapphires tonight—in her ears, in a choker about her neck, and on her wrists. Adèle had carefully put blue wings in her hair—but even if it *was* the fashion, Laura didn't like them.

"Oh, take these out, *do!* I feel silly with two painted wings standing out of my coiffure," Laura said. "Look in my jewelry box, Adèle, and find me the combs that match my necklace and earrings.''

The effect of the combs in her hair made her look like a Spanish dancer, Laura thought. Her mother had given these to her and they were real Spanish combs, one placed behind the other to complement the layers and coils and loops of her coiffure. "I like this much better!"

"Mademoiselle has a flair for what is right," Adèle murmured as she handed Laura her fan—painted silk with amber sticks.

Laura was about to ask for her cloak when Adèle said suddenly, "Oh, there is one more thing. Please wait just a moment."

She rummaged in Laura's velvet-lined jewelry box and triumphantly produced a thin strand of diamonds alternated with tiny sapphires, spaced along the length of the long gold chain. "Here! Oh, please let me just try this. I think it will be perfect." Deftly, Adèle looped the chain around and through Laura's elaborately arranged hairdo, then stepped back to admire the effect. The gold of the chain, tiny loop upon tiny loop, glowed; and the jewels caught the light as Laura moved her head to see herself.

"Adèle, you are a genius!" she said gratefully. "I can hardly believe that this is *me!* I suppose I had really better go downstairs to join the Countess and Lady Honoria before they send someone up here to look for me."

"Well! At last!" Lady Honoria exclaimed impatiently as Laura descended the stairs. "We have no time to waste! The carriage is waiting, and there's no doubt that we will be fashionably late, although I wish I had enough time to inspect what you have chosen to wear. I like your cloak, however! Come along now, come along!"

When they had been comfortably settled in the carriage and were on their way to Grosvenor Square, Laura thought, This is nothing, *nothing!* Another evening's entertainment. Even if His Grace the Duke of Royse deigns to dance with me . . . well, in front of all his guests he can't very well be as obnoxious as he usually is! She knew that Lord Anthony would be there, he had mentioned it. So there was no reason in the world for her to feel apprehensive—no reason at all!

The "small" reception turned out to be a grand and glittering affair. Lady Margaret looked quite lovely in black lace over gray satin with a tiara sparkling in her hair; and she was as warm and welcoming as she had been on the first occasion they had met. As for her stepson—Laura caught an occasional glimpse of his dark head with its unruly hair; and then turned her mind and her gaze away deliberately.

"Quite a select crowd," Lady Honoria commented approvingly. "Margaret knows how to arrange things properly, although I don't doubt that Royse had something to do with the guest list."

Lady Honoria insisted upon being seated, but she urged Laura and her daughter-in-law to mingle.

Helena was looking really lovely tonight, Laura thought. Her friend's ivory satin gown was heavily embroidered with an intricate oriental design, the colors matching the brocade inserts in the skirt and the corset-like bodice. Embroidered lace flowers barely covered Helena's creamy shoulders, and her ivory satin gloves were also embroidered along the seams.

"Ena—how beautiful you look!" Laura whispered just before she noticed that Ena wasn't listening to her, and saw Franco heading purposefully toward them.

Helena's face went pink when she caught sight of Franco heading toward her; and it was with relief that Laura caught sight of Lord Anthony and his sister.

"The Prince of Wales is here already!" Lady Evelyn whispered. "This is early for *him,* you know." She looked at Laura, her eyes dancing with mischief. "You must tell me what he is *really* like. He has never asked me to dance, and I've always seen him looking at you. There he is, at the far corner of the room with Lady Randolph."

Mr. Carruthers walked up to join them at that moment, making an evenly matched group who were all comfortable and at ease with each other. The general atmosphere, Laura found to her surprise, was pleasantly informal. Perhaps because there were no liveried footmen in powdered wigs standing about.

Laura concentrated her attention upon her friends and even danced with her brother once. And, as Lady Evelyn had predicted, the Prince of Wales *did* ask her to dance with him—and pressed her hand in a significant way while he held her closely against his rather corpulent body.

"As soon as you're married," he said, "we'll see more of each other! I would like to see much more of you, you lovely girl, if *you* wouldn't mind, of course."

Laura didn't know what she was supposed to say, or how she should respond; fortunately it seemed as though H.R.H. didn't expect an answer from her. Perhaps he took her silence as acquiescence!

His Grace the Duke of Royse did not ask her for a dance until the evening was almost ended. When he did, it was with polite formality and just as formally she gave him her hand as she rose from her chair. Oh, Lady Honoria would applaud her manners *this* time, Laura thought.

"Have you ever been to Cornwall, Lorelei?" She had expected almost anything from him, except this seemingly innocuous question.

"No, although I've heard it's very beautiful—wild and rugged and steeped with all kinds of old legends and history."

"It's a lot like Monterey," he said, surprising her again. "Black, ragged rocks and the ocean breakers crashing against them, throwing up fragments of white foam and salt sea spume. But you'll see for yourself when you come to Royse Park. From the west wing of the house, where I've arranged you will be, you can hear the ocean."

Laura flung her head back to look him in the face, her brows drawn together. "What in the world are you talking about! When I come to Royse Park—?"

"I thought you knew." He was smiling down at her in

a most *peculiar* fashion that she mistrusted. "Lady Honoria has already accepted the invitation to a house party at Royse Park. You needn't worry that I'm trying to lure you there for the purpose of ravishing you—there will be several other people present as well, friends of yours. The Count d'Arlingen, Lord Anthony Grey and his lovely sister, and—oh, of course, Reggie Forrester! No party would be quite complete without him, would it?"

"I know nothing about this!" Laura said in a low voice that was full of suppressed fury. "Nobody said anything to me, nobody consulted me."

"Oh, but I believe it was all arranged only very recently between Lady Honoria and my stepmother." Then he lowered his voice, before he said silkily, "You will come, won't you, Lorelei? Or are you afraid?" He looked down at her breasts and her face reddened.

"You're quite insufferable! And I don't feel like being baited by you any longer! Why on earth hasn't this waltz ended? It should have been over long ago!"

"I told the musicians to keep on playing until I gave them a signal to stop," he told her in his smooth drawl. "Have I tired you out?"

Laura recovered herself enough to say acerbically, "Yes, you have! I'm not only tired of dancing with you, but I'm tired of *you*, Trent Challenger—Your *Grace*! I don't know what kind of game you're playing with me or *why* you're playing it at all, but I'm tired of it—do you understand that? Tired of it!"

"Unfortunately," he said, his voice suddenly becoming grim and hard and harsh, "I'm *not* playing any games with you, Lorelei. Unfortunately for both of us perhaps. But—come to Cornwall anyway. I've already given you my promise that I won't attempt to ravish you—unless you seduce me into doing so."

"And the reason," Laura said in a fierce whisper to Helena later, "that the music went on and on was because he had told them not to stop playing until he gave them a signal of some kind! Oh, how I detest him!''

''Well, I don't think you do, really,'' Helena said placidly before she added with some anxiety creeping into her voice, ''But you *are* going to Royse Park, aren't you? Franco will be going, and you know very well that without you along, we won't be able to spend any time together! Laura, *please* don't be difficult!''

''I hate having plans made for me without my being consulted about them!'' Laura said, still angry. ''Really, Ena! I'm tired of giving in—especially where *he's* concerned. Why, he told me that he'd even arranged where my room was to be! He takes too much for granted, and it's high time that he . . . that someone taught him a lesson!''

''Then why can't that someone be you?'' Helena suggested. ''After all, Laura, you can't let him think you're afraid, can you? And as Belle-mère has already told you, almost everyone we know has already accepted their invitation to Royse Park. You know it would look very strange if you didn't go. Although of course''—Helena sighed with a cunning that was unusual for her—''I suppose that Lady Westbridge would be only too happy if you stayed away! If you could only have seen her face while you two were dancing!''

''I can see,'' Laura said grimly, ''that this is a conspiracy! But Ena, if I go with you, you have to promise me that there will not be any tactful maneuvering to throw me in Royse's way. I don't mind playing little flirtatious games with him in order to detach him from Sabina, who suddenly says that I am her dearest friend. But mind you, *only* in front of other people! I *won't* be alone with him,'' Laura added strongly. ''He annoys me too much, and puts me in a bad mood.''

Afterward Laura could not help asking herself why she had given way so easily. Was it because of Helena's pleas, or because Lady Honoria had told her bluntly that she would be a fool if she didn't go? Or was it because of the challenge that his very presence seemed to be for her? She didn't really know. Perhaps, Laura thought suddenly, perhaps she needed to find out. All she had to do was *not* remember a certain morning, very early and mist-gauzed, in Hyde Park.

Chapter 31

The London Season was ending. People were already talking of closing up their town houses, of country house parties and shooting boxes in Scotland. Laura realized she would miss it all—the excitement of going to see the latest plays, operettas by Gilbert and Sullivan; racing at Goodwood and Ascot; and especially driving her phaeton with her high-stepping chestnuts that Lord Anthony had helped her purchase.

"I can't believe that I feel I might actually *miss* London!" Laura had confessed to Helena. "But at least I was always kept busy, with no time to think! And now, I wonder—where shall I go next? After this *boring* house party, I mean!"

"But we *have* to go to Cowes for the Annual Yacht Regatta, of course. It's on the Isle of Wight. Belle-mère has reserved hotel rooms for us already. And after that . . ."

Laura noticed how downcast Ena had suddenly become, and the protest she had been about to utter died on her tongue.

"Ena?"

"Archie has written to me. He's been posted from Istanbul to Gibraltar, where he'll be Lieutenant-Governor. And . . . oh, Laura! He wants me there as his hostess! Not only *that*, Belle-mère says she cannot stand to be under the same roof as he, and so after we leave Cowes she's set on taking the waters at Baden-Baden. I don't want to go to Gibraltar, but I shall have to, I suppose, and I just don't dare tell Franco yet, and spoil our next few days together. I *do* wish you'd come with me! Archie did say I could invite any friend I wished for company. I *know* you don't like to plan things too far ahead, but—oh, Laura, at least promise you will *think* about it?''

Laura had promised to think about it, but in the meantime there were so many other things to think about! Packing, for instance. She hadn't realized just how complicated the preparations involved in leaving town to spend a few days in the country could be!

Lady Honoria sometimes reminded her of a general, Laura thought wryly. Marshaling her troops, ordering them into their various positions on the front line of battle.

''You cannot, of course, be seen in the same attire more than once!'' Lady Honoria explained to Laura impatiently. ''All the ladies will be changing into different clothes to suit different occasions at *least* four times a day!'' She nodded kindly on seeing the expression on Laura's face. ''My dear girl, you would do well to leave all these arrangements to me and Miss Edge. All that you will be required to do is to choose the correct attire for each occasion. You will need one or two yachting costumes, because I understand that Royse has his own yacht that he keeps in a small harbor adjacent to Royse Park; and then you will need several walking costumes, traveling costumes, and riding habits—not to mention one or two gowns suitable for the seaside, as well as evening gowns and morning gowns! Now, if you have any questions. . . ?''

''Oh no, Ma'am!'' Laura protested. ''Really, I think I have heard enough and I *will* leave everything to you, Miss Edge, and Adèle!''

''Very sensible of you,'' Lady Honoria commented. ''In this way everything will be organized before we start out.''

Laura had already learned from Ena that they would be accompanied by their own entourage of servants. Ladies' maids, grooms, and so forth. Good God! It struck her that they were embarked on an *expedition* rather than a simple visit to a country house, but of course she did not dare say so in Lady Honoria's hearing.

"We'll have to leave very early in the morning, I'm afraid," Helena explained to Laura, afterward, "but our luggage will have already been safely stored away in one of the baggage cars. We shall have a private compartment to ourselves—Belle-mère has arranged for it. And *then,*" she went on with a sudden tone of anticipation rising in her voice, "when we arrive at the railway station in Penzance, there will be carriages waiting to take us to Royse Park! Oh, Laura! I really do feel that this is going to be an exciting time for us both! Just think, so many different people thrown together in a house surrounded by parkland on the Cornish coast with its history of smugglers and wreckers and—"

"Ena, I'm beginning to think that you're the one who should be writing gothic novels, not I!" All the same, Laura could not help enjoying her friend's unexpected flight of fancy. "Let's see now, what can I remember reading about Cornwall? Oh yes! King Arthur. Camelot and the Knights of the Round Table—*especially* Sir Lancelot!"

"Oh yes, and Guinevere . . . and Merlin, with his magic and secret spells and . . ." Helena had begun to laugh, too, joining the game.

"And Morgan-le-Fay who managed to enthrall poor Arthur—and oh, of course Tristan and his Isolde . . . although I believe she was really supposed to be an Irish Princess called Isotta!"

"Laura, you have read so much more than I have that I can't keep up with you!" Helena protested, still laughing.

"Well, His Grace the Duke was kind enough to offer me the use of his library any time I please during our stay there. Now you can accompany me, Ena, and brush up on your history of Cornwall!" Laura teased her.

"Oh, but I never did like spending time in stuffy old libraries!" Helena said, her lips forming a little moue while she wrinkled up her nose at the prospect. "But Laura," she added with an anxious tone creeping into her voice, "you haven't forgotten our pact? You and I will go *everywhere* together, and Franco will join us, and—"

"Oh yes," Laura said dryly, "and then you and he will disappear somewhere together. What do you expect *me* to do then—look at old ruins and go wandering about the Cornish coast by myself?" When she saw the expression on Ena's face, Laura relented. "Oh, you know I don't really mind. And who knows what I might find, or who I might meet? The ghost of a smuggler shot by excisemen perhaps, or of a Spanish captain from one of the ill-fated ships of King Philip's Armada that were wrecked off the coast of Cornwall! Maybe a descendant of one of the lucky survivors who managed to swim to shore to be sheltered and succored by a lonely young woman!"

"Laura!" Helena said, shaking her head, "sometimes you *do* let your imagination run away with you!"

Laura's mouth curved upward suddenly in a smile that did not quite reach her eyes as she murmured, "I've been thinking, Ena. Not using my imagination, but *thinking!* And I've decided that I need to take a lover. Lord Anthony is far too staid and would be shocked, I'm sure; and Reggie, although charming, is far too obvious. So I've chosen the Count d'Arlingen—my mother's ex-lover. If he managed to please my mother for a while, then I'm sure he must be a good enough lover to please *me!*"

She laughed at the horrified look on Ena's face. "Oh, for heaven's sake, Ena dear, don't look at me that way! As if you didn't want to believe what I've just said. Because I *do* mean it, you know. I'm so sick and tired of all this gossip! Everybody says, or *implies*, that Royse is pursuing me so I intend to prove otherwise!" Then Laura added thoughtfully: "You know, Ena, suddenly I find that I've quite begun to look forward to this house party at Royse Park! It should prove *very* interesting."

"You can't be serious!" Helena whispered disbelievingly.

"Oh, can't I?" Laura retorted. "You'll see! And what's more, I'm going to pretend that I'm Sarah Bernhardt—and *act!* I'm going to be decorous and intelligent when I'm with Lord Anthony; flirtatious and friendly with Reggie; and ever so seductive with Michel!''

Helena remained speechless, her eyes wide.

''And as for Trent Challenger,'' Laura added, her voice hard, ''I intend to have as little to do with him as possible!''

Chapter 32

The journey from London to Penzance seemed interminable, although the train stopped a few times along the way, giving the passengers the chance to walk about and stretch their legs and also to obtain refreshments. As they drew closer to their destination Laura took out her notebook and began to scribble down notes of her impressions of the journey and the countryside they had passed through; merely to keep her mind occupied, Laura had to admit wryly to herself. She didn't like the direction in which her thoughts had been wandering far too often of late! But then, she meant to do something about *that,* as she'd told Ena before. She would either become engaged or have an affair; one or the other, it didn't make a difference as long as it kept *him* away from her!

Deliberately, Laura concentrated on making her notes, a sudden half-smile curving her lips as she wondered if she *dared* place the dark Duke of her gothic novel in a Cornish castle. Why not? Perhaps while she was sitting among the ruins waiting for Franco and Ena she should take along a notebook and sketchpad—and she could write more chapters of her novel. Frank would no doubt enjoy them!

She *missed* Frank Harris, Laura realized suddenly. He'd been invited to Royse Park, too, but he'd begged off, explaining that he had already made plans to spend the rest of summer and autumn traveling in Germany, Austria, and Italy. Why did he have to *desert* her when she needed his moral support? But—she'd promised to keep writing, and she supposed she would—if only to pass the time thinking about more of the dark Duke's evil doings—and the way in which he would get his comeuppance in the end.

She didn't care in the least how Royse would react when *he* read her novel or realized that everyone *else* who read it would guess who the dark-visaged Duke was! Oh—a pity Frank couldn't see the rest of her manuscript until after he returned to England—*unless* she decided to visit him in Italy before then. Hmm, that was an idea! Just then, before Laura could follow that train of thought further, Ena nudged her to say that they were almost at Penzance.

"I must say that for an American only recently arrived in society and new to this country, Royse certainly does things in style," Lady Honoria allowed grudgingly.

They had been met at the railway station at Penzance by no less than three carriages dispatched from Royse Hall to convey them there. There was one carriage for the ladies, a smart new brougham; and two other conveyances as well that were old-fashioned and roomy, one for the servants, and another for their mountains of luggage.

Let the curtain rise and the play begin, Laura thought as she looked out of the window; but soon the rugged beauty of the countryside, which was so different from the sedate and well-ordered, almost manicured landscape she had seen from the window of the train, held her complete attention. This terrain did indeed remind her of Monterey; alternately green with high trees casting their shadows over the road, then the sunshine of late afternoon bursting upon them as they climbed a ridge. There were black rocks among the twisted trees on either side, leaning away from the sea; and the smell of the ocean was strong, sharp—the wind chilling, tasting of a slight saltiness. The road curved around rocky hillsides and parched tors, then dipped and rose again until there was a slight descent into what almost seemed like a small valley with cliffs to one side and a densely forested slope on the other.

Laura leaned forward to the coachman. "Is the ocean on the other side of those cliffs?" she asked eagerly.

"Aye, miss," the man said. "And on the other side it's all rocky going down to the Strand, although there's a few ways of getting down now—stepping paths with railings that the last Duke ordered the workmen to put up. But the going's still mighty steep, and it can be slippery, too, when the wind starts blowing in real strong from the sea." He cracked his whip, and continued. "We're at the edge of Royse Park now, miss. Around the bend in the road there ahead will be the gatehouse, although it's still about a mile or so getting to the Hall itself."

The gatehouse was quite imposing, and obviously very old, Laura thought as they swept through an ivy-covered stone archway, then down a long and well-kept drive with parkland on either side and more forest brooding behind, to the left. The drive curved and wound about small groves and statuary covered with moss that seemed to be growing out of damp grass, then entered seemingly endless avenues of trees until they emerged into quite a different world. Ornamental gardens, bridges over a small stream that apparently ran right through the property, leading to gazebos, and now even fountains and a few peacocks strutting about to display their bejeweled tails. They even passed by another small grotto that was almost completely shrouded by shrubbery and overhanging willows where water gurgled out from the mouth of a stone satyr and into a pitcher held up by a nymph.

"Hah!" Lady Honoria exclaimed with a chuckle. "Now *that* makes me remember that in *my* time, those of us who were more adventurous used to sneak out to take midnight dips in just such little grottos!" Quickly recovering herself, she fixed the two young women with her gimlet eyes before adding sternly: "Not that I would advise either of *you* to do that. Times have changed, my dears, times have changed!"

Now the road was graveled and branched off in two directions, curving around a miniature lake with four swans, two black, and two white, floating on its mirrorlike surface. But it was her first sight of the house—or no, it looked more like a *castle*, Laura thought—that made an instinctive shiver run up her spine. Ivy-covered stone walls with pointed Gothic turrets and stone gargoyles guarding roof terraces suddenly loomed up before them like a dark vision against the sky.

She was shaken out of her sudden feeling of apprehension when Lady Honoria pronounced, "Here we are at last! And I hope our other two carriages are not far behind because we will soon have to change for a late tea."

Once the usual bustle and hubbub surrounding new arrivals had subsided and Lady Honoria was satisfied that all had been taken care of properly, they ascended the short flight of steps leading up to the ornate entrance hall to be warmly greeted by Lady Margaret herself. There was no one else about, and Lady Honoria remarked upon it, but Lady Margaret explained that the gentlemen had gone out to shoot in the woods, and the ladies, under the guidance of Miss Renfrew, had gone on an expedition to visit the ruins of an ancient priory that was nearby. They would all be back very soon, she assured them—certainly in time to take tea, which would be served informally in the small salon opening out into the conservatory.

They were escorted upstairs by the housekeeper, Mrs. Evans, and Laura discovered that she had been assigned to the Moorish Room. "All the rooms have different names," Mrs. Evans explained as she bustled ahead of them to open doors and make sure that the chambermaids had left everything in order. Ena had been given a room next to Laura's, and Lady Honoria was at the other end of the long, carpeted passageway onto which the guest rooms opened.

The Moorish Room, indeed! Laura thought as she looked about her. There was a huge canopied bed set in the center, with tasseled draperies that hung down around it, caught back by velvet cords; and the walls, instead of being papered or paneled, were draped by layer upon layer

of exotic silken fabric that gave her the impression of being
in some Bedouin sheik's tent! The predominant colors were
peacock-blue, crimson, and dark gold, and the nightstands
had clawed feet and brass surfaces, looking as if they had
been bought in a Middle Eastern bazaar. There were even
huge fat cushions edged with tassels that matched the bed
canopy scattered with artful abandon about the room, some
piled up against one corner of the chamber with a red-
shaded gaslight above.

In front of the bed there was a long, low, and heavily
carved wooden table covered with a profusion of fruits and
flowers in brass and silver bowls. Even the lamps on the
nightstands were of a Moorish design, and then as Laura
explored further, pushing aside heavily beaded curtains,
she discovered an opulent bathroom which was furnished
similarly to the bedroom, with the same colors predomi-
nating, and the same fabric-lined walls and ceiling. Patterned tiles had been used to create an effect of a Moroccan
bathhouse, with tiled steps leading up to a large, sunken,
oval-shaped bath. An oil lamp suspended on brass chains
from the ceiling above the copper-lined bath gave out a
red glow, and on either side of the heavily curtained door-
way there were shelves laden with oils and unguents and
soaps and crystal-stoppered bottles of perfume as well as
large, fluffy cotton towels.

This is too much! Laura thought wrathfully. Now he's
gone too far! She flung the heavily beaded curtains aside
again only to find her eyes drawn unwillingly to the bed.
That bed—with its tasseled canopy and its heavily embroidered bedspread that reached down to the carpeted
floor. This, she knew already and instinctively, was *not*
the kind of room that Lady Margaret or her late husband
could have conceived of. The Moorish Room could only
have been Trent Challenger's idea!

Who does he think he is, a . . . a sultan? And what
does he think *I* am—one of his willing concubines? Since
Laura's anger was growing by the minute, it was probably
fortunate that there was a knock on the door at that mo-

ment, and Adèle hurried in followed by three footmen carrying her portmanteaux and heavy trunks.

Adèle unpacked swiftly and efficiently; if she was surprised at this particular room, she gave no sign of it. The sounds of the other guests returning drifted up through the open windows and drowned out the crashing sounds of the sea for a while.

Who had rooms *where?* Laura wondered, still so angry that she had already made up her mind to act as outrageously as possible when Lady Honoria or Lady Margaret were not around. And as for Lady Westbridge . . . ! Well, the poor thing had best look out for herself, because she was going to be beaten at her own game! This house party, Laura thought, might prove quite interesting and quite amusing after all!

What would await her downstairs? Laura wondered pensively. She *knew* that she wasn't afraid anymore. This had actually begun to seem to her like a game of wits and wills pitted against each other—his and hers—and she suddenly started to feel a kind of excitement building up inside that made her ready for anything. *Anything,* and any challenge at all!

Why, the little hussy! Lady Honoria said to herself when she noticed that Laura, the last to arrive for tea, made her entrance wearing one of the new seamless gowns designed by Worth to cling extremely closely to the body so as to show off every line and curve of the female figure. The gown almost matched the dark blue of Laura's eyes and was trimmed with gold passementerie. The only jewelry she wore were sapphire and diamond studs in her ears and a single sapphire brooch pinned to the high neck of her gown. Helena, standing next to Franco, whispered in dismay, "Oh no! She couldn't have meant it—she wouldn't really do what she said."

"You'll have to tell me later exactly what you mean by that, my love," Franco whispered back, "but right now

I'm quite lost in admiration of my sister's performance—
not to mention her choice of a gown!''

After the sudden hush that had fallen when Laura walked
in, her train held *just* so, her head held high, everyone
began to speak to each other at once.

Laura crossed the room to go straight to Lady Margaret
to make her apologies for being tardy; and then, as Trent
managed to disengage Sabina's clinging fingers to stride
across the room toward her, Laura met him halfway with
a bright and far too obviously artificial smile. She held out
both her hands to him while she *gushed,* in an equally
artificial voice that could be heard by everyone in the room:
''Oh, Trent! I mean, Your Grace, I had thought you might
be too busy to greet me at all! Why, I assure you, I was
of half a mind to remain upstairs in my room, *pouting*—
until, of course, I suddenly realized how much time and
care you must have expended in choosing to give me *that*
particular room, the Moorish Room, isn't it named? So
comfortable and so . . . so very *opulently* furnished. I'm
sure I shall enjoy it during my stay here at Royse Hall!''

Laura knew at once from the tightening of the muscles
in his dark face and the narrowing of his icy eyes that
every barb concealed beneath her sugared words had struck
home. It was all she could do not to wince when his fingers tightened almost unbearably over hers.

''I owe you an apology, Miss Morgan, for neglecting
my duties as a host as well as for the *distress* I seem to
have caused you. You *must* tell me how I can make up for
it.''

He held her hands imprisoned for far too long while he
smiled down at her in a strangely *calculating* way, Laura
thought, before he whispered under his breath *''Putita!''*
''Little whore'' he'd dared call her in Spanish! Laura
caught her breath at his daring! And there they stood in
the center of the room, like actors on a stage, Laura
thought furiously, with an interested audience watching
their every move, their every expression.

''Do say you will forgive me!'' he then said, acting *his*

part to the hilt as well. "Perhaps if I promise to show you the stables and some of my new livestock after tea—will *that* help? And if it will persuade you to smile at me again, dear Miss Laura, I will also solemnly promise to show you our famous Moon Garden after dinner!"

Damn him for turning the tables on her! Laura thought, before she managed to say archly: "Oh, but Trent, since we're such old friends from the time of *my* childhood at least . . ." She heard Franco's smothered snort of laughter and ignored it as she went on in the same deliberately *simpering* voice. "Why, there's really nothing to forgive, I suppose! My goodness! I certainly didn't mean to act like a disappointed child here in front of all your guests— or to keep you from them. Now it's *my* turn to apologize." With a sharp tug to release his grasp on her, she added hotly and in a lower voice, "I think that makes us even!"

"But *I* don't think it does—not yet, anyhow!" he whispered down at her before letting her go, his smile as false as hers.

They had *all* been watching, of course, while keeping up a flurried flow of conversation and pretending not to notice the exchange. Lord Anthony stroked his luxuriant side whiskers thoughtfully; his sister, trying hard to hide her giggles, told him that she thought Laura had done magnificently! The Count d'Arlingen, on the other side of Lady Evelyn, said to her with a knowing smile, "Ah! So this was a *planned* performance, was it? In that case I think that they both did very well, although I feel that some of us are not as *understanding*, shall I say?" And his eyes strayed significantly to a pink-faced Lady Sabina who was whispering in her brother's ear. Michel Rémy, while appearing amused, had, in fact, bowed himself out of the picture. It was clear enough to him, having known Ginette, that the daughter took too much after her mother for his liking, or his peace of mind. But in the meantime, he decided philosophically, as he turned attentively toward Lady Evelyn to ask her a question, there were three more days to enjoy other guests in this magnificent country estate; and in those three days who knew what might transpire?

"Hmm . . . hmm . . . that little minx!" Lady Honoria had whispered to Lady Margaret as they watched the tug-of-war between Laura and Trent. "I warned her about playing dangerous games, especially with dangerous men! But I suppose the young have to learn for themselves. I think they have a lot in common those two, as a matter of fact!"

"I don't think it is a game with them any longer," Lady Margaret said thoughtfully. "I think it has become much more serious for both of them, although they don't know it yet."

"You little idiot! If we were alone I would slap your face," Reggie was snarling to his sister at the same time the dowager and Lady Margaret were having their exchange. "You had better remember what I've said, and stop sulking. Men don't like women who pout and show jealousy. Act as if nothing happened when he comes back to you, d'you hear? Act as if you're sure of yourself, you silly bitch—and leave the rest to me. She's already managed to put off two of her admirers, I think. *I'll* manage to put off the rest—and have her, too, in the end, don't you worry!"

Chapter 33

"Good God!" Lady Honoria said. And then she repeated again, which was very unlike her, "Good God! So *this* is the Moorish Room, is it? No wonder you—" And then she cut herself off as she continued to walk about the room, her eyes taking in *everything* as she gave an occasional snort or a curt "Hmphh!"

As she flung open the beaded curtains that led into the bathroom, Lady Honoria stood transfixed and was actually struck silent for several seconds. She had to breathe deeply before swinging around with a rustling of tafetta petticoats to face Laura before she could speak.

"I'm sure I don't know what's up between you two; and at *this* point, I don't think I want to know! A room out of the *Arabian Nights,* hah! For what purpose, I wonder? And you, my girl, should wonder too!"

Lady Honoria picked up her train decisively and prepared to leave. "If I've ever seen a den of prospective iniquity, *this,* my girl, is it! It's obvious he has *intentions,* but you had better find out what *kind* of intentions if you know what's good for you. First he makes a present to you of this mare he has just had shipped here from America— I can't remember what kind of a horse it is—some outlandish name—and now *this!*"

"Oh, the mare we saw in the stables is an Appaloosa and she's beautiful!" Laura said demurely. "But of course I didn't accept her as a *gift.* I merely accepted her as a mount for as long as I'm staying here."

"Oh, is *that* so? Well, my girl, just remember the story of the Trojan horse, and try to be careful if you can!"

Defiantly soaking in her sunken tub later with perfumed oil poured into the warm water, Laura almost felt like Cleopatra. "Be careful," Lady Honoria had warned her. Of course she would be careful! She was only—only playing a game, just as *he* was! And she would enjoy riding Beauty, that sweet little mare, during the next few days. He'd even promised her a Western saddle! Laura wondered suddenly and wickedly if she would dare to wear buckskin riding breeches instead of her usual divided skirts. That was, if she could talk Franco into lending her a pair of *his*. Why not? Why not *anything*?

When Laura stepped out of her perfumed bath, Adèle was waiting there with one of the huge fluffy towels. Sometimes Laura wondered what Adèle really thought about everything. And sometimes she felt like turning to her and asking her. At such moments she actually missed Filomena, who had always spoken her mind! But there was no time for feelings of nostalgia now—not when she was supposed to get dressed for dinner. "Country hours," Lady Honoria had warned her earlier; and that meant seven-thirty in the evening—such a ridiculous hour for dinner, Laura thought, as she was being laced into her brocaded black corset.

Laura was almost dressed when Helena burst into her room, saying anxiously, "Oh, Laura, please *do* hurry. We can't be late for dinner! It's just not . . . not . . ." And then her voice trailed away into a startled gasp.

"Oh yes, Ena, I know very well by now that it's not *done* to be late for a dinner party in the country—especially on the first night," Laura said coolly, while turning around to observe herself from every angle in the mirror. She had chosen black and silver—to suit the Moon Garden.

A black velvet gown with an *extremely* low décolletage held up only by narrow diamanté strips that went over her shoulders from the similar diamanté edging of her décol-

letage to cross over her all but bared back; a matching
trim edging her skirts and train. Laura had chosen to wear
her diamonds again tonight—about her throat, dangling
from her ears, and banded around her upper arms.

Helena recovered her voice at last, and said feelingly,
"Laura! You *can't*—I mean, surely you don't intend to—
oh, you *know* you're going to shock everyone including
my mother-in-law! I haven't seen *this* gown of yours before, but it reminds me of a portrait by Sargent called
Madame X!"

"I know!" Laura said. "I always did like that portrait,
so I decided to improvise on it! I had this particular gown
especially ordered for me at La Maison Rouff before I left
Paris. Aside from being shocked, do you like it?"

"Well, it's . . . it's *becoming,*" Helena managed. "And
of course you will put poor Lady Westbridge completely
in the shade, no doubt about *that!*" Recovering her sense
of humor, Helena began to chuckle. "I really can't wait
to see her face when she sees you—to see *all* their faces!
Oh, Laura, you really are incorrigible!"

"She goes from bad to worse!" Lady Honoria exclaimed in an undertone to Lady Margaret when Laura
came downstairs. "Although I must say that your stepson,
Royse, is *quite* as bad and seems to incite her into this
kind of behavior, what with that Moorish Room he had
her put in, and his invitation to take her outside alone to
see his Moon Garden!" And then, with a shrug of her
shoulders, the dowager added philosophically, "Well, I'm
sure we will see the results of all this tomfoolery within
the next few days."

As Laura had expected, there were a variety of reactions
to her daring choice of an evening gown. Lord Anthony
was genuinely shocked before his eyes started to wander
over her in quite a different way. Michel's eyes had a newly
interested glint to them; Reggie Forrester sent out melting
messages with his eyes that did not seem to be able to tear
themselves away from her; and of course Franco scowled
blackly at her to show his disapproval.

Of them all, only Trent had displayed no outward emotion at all, except for the lift of a raised, satirical eyebrow that told her he saw through her; and Laura damned him for it!

Dinner seemed interminable after her dramatic entrance, and Laura could only take small nibbles of each course. For once, she couldn't wait for the time when Lady Margaret would give the signal that the ladies could retire into the drawing room, leaving the men to enjoy their port and cigars while they sat around the dining table and discussed whatever men discussed on such occasions. She wished, in fact, that Trent, from his seat at the head of the table, would *not* look her over so very obviously, those silver-gray eyes of his seeming to plunge between her breasts. Seizing a moment when everyone else seemed occupied with what was on their plates, Laura couldn't resist the impulse to stick out her tongue at him, just like a street urchin. Of all things, he gave a burst of laughter before pretending that he had developed a cough.

Throughout the rest of the meal, Laura found that his eyes *still* kept wandering all over her, much to her annoyance and discomfort. When she caught a venomous glance from Lady Westbridge, however, Laura decided to smile sweetly back at him.

Damn her, Trent thought as he watched her actually manage to carry off, with a cool aplomb and insolence that Lady Westbridge could never match, that outrageous gown she had chosen to wear tonight. Although her gown was tightly buttoned up her back until just below the shoulder blades, he knew it could be unbuttoned *down* her back until it slipped from her shoulders and then from there down past her thighs, to lie in a black and silver moon-pool around her silk-stockinged ankles. But no, he thought savagely. He'd rather rip the goddamn thing right off her to save time!

Just as the ladies, signaled by Lady Margaret, rose and were about to withdraw, Franco came up to his sister and caught her wrist. "Laura, you *owe* me, especially after this latest exhibition of yours!'' He whispered urgently to her: ''Now listen—everyone will be in bed, and hopefully asleep by twelve. Helena has agreed to join me for a swim in Pan's Grotto after we've been shown the Moon Garden. She'll only dare it if *you* come, too—so you *must*. Understand?'' And then he let her go without giving her a chance to respond.

They all probably thought her brother had been giving her a lecture about her appearance, Laura thought with annoyance. Why should she be so obliging? But then she caught Helena's pleading look, and shrugged her shoulders with resignation.

At that particular moment, Sabina looped her arm through Laura's and whispered to her pleadingly that she *had* to talk to her!

While the other ladies settled themselves on couches and small gilt chairs, Lady Westbridge drew Laura to a corner at the far end of the room that overlooked a balustraded terrace.

''Oh, forgive me, *do,* but I don't have any other *women* friends but you to confide in!'' she said. ''And there's no one else I can talk to who would understand what I am going through. I know that *you're* not like most of the other women here, who are either jealous of me or condemning—and that is why I feel that I can safely *confide* in you without restraint! If you only knew how much I need a woman friend—a *true* friend! And, oh please! I beg you to promise, *promise,* that you will never say anything of this to Reggie because he would *kill* me—I know he would, with that violent temper of his!''

''I can't really say *anything,* can I, unless I know exactly what you are talking about,'' Laura said shortly, wishing that Sabina would not cling to her arm and lean up so closely against her. It was true that she did not like Sabina, yet there were times when she actually felt sorry for her; even thought of her as a victim of the society whose opinions she had been taught both to fear and to prize.

Laura was about to disengage herself politely from Sabina's grasp and her imminent confidences when, still holding tightly to Laura's arm, Sabina looked up at her with eyes brimming with tears, and said with a burst of honesty that surprised even Sabina herself: "Oh! How could you know how it is for someone like *me? You* have everything that I don't have—money, a family, security, and confidence in yourself! You can have any man you choose—but please don't take Royse from me."

She blinked back tears before continuing. "I know he wants you, as hard as that is for me to admit. But when I became his mistress it was because I thought . . . because he gave me to understand that in the end he would marry me! He told me that he believed in *trying* a woman out before he would ever commit himself. And so, foolishly trusting, I . . . I gave in; and afterward he kept telling me that I was the only one for him—the only woman he'd ever think of marrying! And . . . oh, and now I think I might be bearing his child and I don't know what to do about it!" A slightly sharper note came into her voice as she added: "If *you* hadn't come on the scene, he *would* have married me, I know!"

Laura was ready to detach herself from the whole unpleasant scene when Sabina whispered: "He bought me a house, you know, a pretty little place on Curzon Square—not in St. Johns Wood, where men usually set their mistresses up! He has been in the habit of visiting me almost every day—and of taking me home after we have been out somewhere and staying the night. He's a wonderful lover—so forceful, so demanding, and sometimes . . . oh yes, sometimes so sweet and kind and considerate! He's—"

"Why are you telling me all this?" Laura interrupted in a carefully controlled voice.

"I'm *confiding* in you," Sabina all but sobbed. "I've told you—there's no one else I can think of to whom I can talk as frankly and as openly as I feel I can speak to you! I don't dare tell my brother, and I can't bear for anyone else to know. I can't stand being humiliated by him like this! If this was the way he was going to treat me, he should *never* have asked me here!''

''I agree with *that*, at least,'' Laura said briefly and dispassionately as she moved away. ''What exactly are you asking of me?''

Lady Westbridge seemed nonplussed at her blunt question. ''I . . . I'm not sure . . .''

''Well, I'm glad at least that you didn't go all gothic on me and beg me to give him up!'' Laura said briskly, anxious to get this whole little tête-à-tête over and done with. ''But I can assure you of this much, Sabina—*your* wanting Trent is one thing, and *his* wanting you is another. And that's between the two of you, I think. But where I'm concerned, you don't have to worry. Even if I decide to have him it'll only be for a *very* short while—as long as it takes for me to become bored with him. And then, I promise I'll hand him back to you for keeps!''

''You don't really like me, do you?'' Sabina said in a sharp whisper.

''No more than you really like me!''

The two women looked at each other for a few moments, measuring each other. Then Sabina sucked in a deep breath and laughed shortly. ''Well, at least we know where we stand, don't we?'' The flood of tears that had appeared imminent just a few moments ago seemed to have dried up all of a sudden, as Sabina's sky-blue eyes looked coldly and calculatingly into the darker ocean-blue eyes of her adversary.

''Since we're being so honest with each other, are you sure that in the end you might not change your mind? Royse—*Trent*, that is—has *very* persuasive ways, as *I* know very well by now! I wonder if *you* know what you're getting into when you talk of playing with him? I've a feeling that it might be *he* who plays with *you*—before he comes back to me!''

''What on earth have you two been whispering about for so long?'' Lady Honoria suddenly called in an impatient voice. ''We were just talking of taking a turn about the garden or along the terrace since it's such a nice, balmy night, and with a full moon rising at that!''

"I suppose it *is* time to join the others, isn't it?" Sabina smiled up at Laura before linking arms with her again as they walked over to the small cluster of ladies who awaited them.

When the gentlemen finally joined them, smelling of cigar smoke, Laura noticed how Sabina made a point of going straight to Trent and touching his arm caressingly before she held on to it in that possessive manner she always displayed in public. Well, let her! Laura thought recklessly. Sabina could keep him for as long as she could hold him. But I, Laura told herself as she looked up to meet his eyes and hold them boldly before she glanced away, *I* am going to have him, even if it is only for one night.

It was Lady Margaret who suggested that perhaps they might all enjoy going out onto the terrace or perhaps into the conservatory, where it would be much warmer. When they went out on the terrace, the yellow-gold moon showed itself from behind one of the high rocky tors. An ocean moon, Laura thought, looking at it against the blue-black sky. She had moved away from the others to be by herself for a few moments, leaning against the balustrade to stare at the moon and smell the faint fragrance that hung in the air. And then, not even having to turn her head, she sensed that *he* had come up behind her. Boldly, his fingers brushed against her bared back and the nape of her neck before he said, ''Well, Lorelei?''

He had surprised her with the lightness of his voice as he leaned far too close, and Laura wondered what he had done with poor Sabina. But without turning her head, and without acknowledging his touch, she said, ''Well, what?''

"Well, lovely Laura, do you think you can stay awake until past midnight so that I may show you the Moon Garden at its best? It has to be seen and experienced when the moon is directly overhead.''

He leaned his elbows on the balustrade beside her, his

shoulder brushing hers. "I've enjoyed watching you in this gown tonight. It's definitely seductive—as I'm sure you know very well!"

His voice turned dangerously soft. "And since you knew very well what you were doing, what would you do if I decided to put my arm about your shoulders to keep you warm, like *this;* and then—since your gown is cut so low— my fingers happened to stray and explore what you've only half shown and almost promised to every man around the dinner table this evening?"

His fingers, at that particular moment, traced the mounded outline of her breasts and dipped impudently into the hollow between them before Laura recovered her wits and moved away.

"Hadn't you better go back to Lady Westbridge? I'm sure she's impatient for your return!"

"Oh," he said with a casual shrug of his shoulders and an equally casual glance to where Sabina must be waiting for him, "I expect she is. But Lorelei, after she's safely in bed it's to *you* I want to show the Moon Garden. Perhaps Pan's Grotto as well. And if you don't come down here to meet me, I'll just have to come upstairs for you in your harem chamber—and carry you down by force!"

Chapter 34

"I feel like a schoolgirl going out through the window on a forbidden expedition!" Helena whispered to Laura as, on bare feet, they crept down the stairs, out through a door that His Grace the Duke himself had obligingly left unlatched, and into the garden.

They were both clad, quite daringly, in brightly patterned Liberty silks, with nothing more than their beribboned chemises underneath. Helena's was more flowing, and Laura's silk gown was wrapped more closely about her body—almost like a Polynesian pareu, baring one shoulder. As a precaution, however, both of the young women had wrapped tasseled cashmere shawls about themselves—just in case!

"My God! I thought you were never going to come," Franco exclaimed as he suddenly grabbed Helena in his arms from where he stood in the shadows. His action elicited a startled gasp from her, before he stopped her mouth with a lingering kiss.

"Isn't this supposed to be called the 'witching hour'?"

Before Laura could respond, Trent seized her by the wrist and swung her about so that she almost fell against him. "Well-met by the moonlight, sweet Lorelei!" he whispered against her hair.

The same moon-madness seemed to have seized them all tonight. Franco, his arms still holding a yielding Helena, said, "Trent's going to show us the Moon Garden first, before we explore the Grotto."

"What do you think of our plan for a moonlit exploration of the unknown, Lorelei?" Trent's silver eyes looked down into hers for a moment before, all holding hands like children, they ran across the lawns.

"I have decided not to think at all tonight!" Laura declared breathlessly when they had finally been guided through what seemed like a dense maze of shrubbery along a narrow path and into a small clearing. She added quickly, avoiding his eyes, "But this place fascinates me! Why is it called the Moon Garden?"

"I'm told it's because this little space is shaped like the crescent moon, the symbol of Artemis or, as the Romans called her, Diana the huntress," Trent said. "This garden is supposedly located in this particular place so that it will receive the direct light of the moon when it's full. These white stones here that resemble Stonehenge in miniature and the silver water there also reflect the moonlight, while this marble slab, shielded by shrubbery and fragranced by flowering bushes and cushioned with moss—*that* is supposed to be for sacrifices to the moon. The moon, as we all know, is supposed to have strange effects and do strange things to the minds of some people!" Trent gave a shrug before he added: "Actually, this garden is really supposed to have been built over the sight of another and much older garden which belonged to the ancient cult of the worshippers of the moon goddess in the times when men worshipped the goddess and the horned stag was her mate for a year, and in a way her victim—because at the end of a year he would be slain and his blood spilled over the soil to make the crops grow."

Ena hugged herself closer to Franco. "After that speech, I don't think I like the feel of this place. I'd much rather go for a swim in the Grotto before it gets too late and we have to go back in."

"Shall we go with them?" Trent whispered, holding Laura about the waist and pulling her close to him. "Or will you be a willing sacrifice to the moon goddess first?"

Laura twisted herself free of his arms, and retorted acidly: "Unless *you* want to lie back on that marble slab and offer yourself up to Artemis as a willing victim to a crescent-shaped knife, I think we both would be much better off having a nice cold dip in this Grotto of yours!"

The moonlight was suddenly dimmed by a black wisp of cloud that floated across it; Helena and Franco had already disappeared, it seemed. Trent held Laura's hand, keeping her unwillingly close to him. He bent his dark head to say softly and caressingly against her ear, "Where's your crescent knife tonight, my lovely Artemis? Should I undress you to find out where you have it concealed? Or, if you want me as a victim, would you undress *me* and mount me if I lie back for you upon that marble slab?"

Laura tried to snatch her wrists away from his grasp, and her voice became coldly cutting as she snapped, "I think you go too far!"

"And *I* think we've both gone too far to draw back from each other *now*, Lorelei! You came out here of your own accord—I didn't have to drag you downstairs gagged and bound in your silk sarong! So don't disappoint me by attempting to play silly teasing games at *this* point, because I'm not one of those poor silly fools you have twisted around your little finger, bound with the silken strands of your hair!"

Suddenly, unexpectedly, he began to kiss her—fiercely, violently, bending her body back while he held her wrists pinioned behind her so that she was helpless to resist him.

In the end, who was the sacrifice to the moon goddess? He or she?

Laura didn't know by then, and didn't care, as he unknotted and unhooked her silken pareu so that it fell from her body before he kicked it impatiently aside, and then removed her chemise as well, leaving her naked before him. His lips and his fingers kept on searching her and exploring her everywhere before at last he picked her up in his arms and carried her to the marble slab—putting her down on her back with her legs dangling down on either side of it before he poised himself above her.

"Now *you*. I want you to undress me, very slowly, button by button, as I have just undressed you. And when you've done that, and I'm as naked as you are now, bathed in the moonlight, then I'll make love to you, Lorelei! Again and again. And you'll make love to me."

While he was whispering to her and she lay there like a somnambulist, she felt the roughness of his clothing against her skin—*exciting* it somehow. She felt drugged by the moonlight shining into her eyes until she was forced to close them; by the heavy scent of flowers—and by his lips, his tongue, his fingers that traced sensual patterns all over her flesh. He slid down over her, his tongue licking teasingly at her navel, then kissing her again, his kisses traveling lower and lower until at last his lips and tongue found her *there*, between her thighs, driving her almost crazy so that she jerked about and arched her back uncontrollably. And then he slid his body upward again with maddening slowness until her fingers could reach him.

He kept one knee between her legs, taunting her, inciting her all the while. Her breath came in little gasps while she unbuttoned his pleated linen shirt and pulled it out of his pants, kissing him deeply and willingly as she did so. And then, sitting up to face him, she slowly unbuttoned his pants, looking into his face, suddenly feeling as powerful as a moon goddess herself. When she freed his erect phallus and instinctively bent to touch its tip with her lips and tongue before she deliberately pushed him away from her.

"Very well, I've done *my* share for the moment, and now I think it's your turn again! I want you to stand up in front of me under the moon and to take your pants off and let me look at *you*."

Neither the words that she had just spoken nor the strange feelings that were emerging from somewhere deep inside her belonged to *her*, Laura thought with one part of her mind, as she swung both legs over to one side of the slab and watched him, standing there naked before her, his eyes reflecting the moon's silver. Perhaps that old legend was true after all! Perhaps the moon goddess who had been worshipped in this very grove by the ancient Celtic inhabitants of this area had decided to live again—at least for a night—through her! A feeling of power and of self-confidence swept through Laura's veins, and she came to her feet quickly and walked over to him. She stood before him as unashamedly naked as he was, letting her eyes travel his body with all its very different contours, before she put out her hand and began to touch him—tentatively at first, and then more surely, while he stood still, watching her with his moon-silvered eyes that she still couldn't read. She traced the planes of his face, her fingers lingered over his nipples, half hidden by the black-curled hair of his chest, then moved teasingly downward as his had done, stopping at his taut belly to go around to his back, tracing lightly down his spine. She felt the tightening of his muscles under her exploring touch until she brought her hands around again, her fingers touching him lightly between his legs.

It was only at that point, as if a spell had broken, that he grabbed her wrists and pulled them upward so that she was thrown against him. "That's enough for now!" he said harshly. "Where in the hell and from whom did you learn all those teasing, exciting little tricks that can play havoc with a man's mind as well as his self-control!"

"Is it me or is it the moon that is playing havoc with your mind?" Laura taunted.

"It might be a combination of both—or a moment of madness for which we'll both be damned and sorry in the end," he said, his voice roughening while he continued to look down at her uptilted face with his lips only inches from hers. And then he laughed softly, before he pulled her even more closely against him so that she felt all the hard length of him. "But what the hell, Lorelei! We're both gamblers, aren't we?"

Without another word he began to kiss her again. Her

mouth, her cheeks, the hollow where a little pulse beat in her neck, along her shoulders. And then, bending her so far back that she thought her spine would snap and she had to cling to his shoulders for support, he kissed her breasts. With her face turned up to the moon, her eyes were dazzled by its brightness, and she closed them, letting herself give way to the dark primitive tide of her *feelings*. Caught and carried away by her own senses, there were no more barriers left between them at this moment. He could do anything he wanted with her and she would *let* him, for as long as he continued to make her desire him.

"And now it's your turn, sweet siren," he said as he suddenly released her, holding her away from him, his hands on her shoulders. "It's your turn to stand like a marble statue under the moon so that I may admire you and feel you and perhaps bring you to life like a Pygmalion with his Galatea."

He *did* make her feel like a statue that he was bringing to life, Laura thought bemusedly as he stroked and traced every contour, every tip, every hollow, every hillock, every peak, every valley, and every curve and secret cavern of her body with his hands and his fingers until she could hardly stand it and could hardly stand up on her feet any longer, and she had to lean against him for support until, with a smothered oath, he suddenly swept her up into his arms. He put her down again on the marble slab, for all the world as if she actually were some sacrificial maiden. And then he entered her while her legs wrapped themselves around his back and her hands clutched at him and her mouth opened and she would have cried out loud if he hadn't stopped it with his mouth, and the tide rose and rose and rose inside her like the crashing of the ocean breakers pounding and pounding until it spumed upward and reached its height.

"It isn't over yet, you know," he said softly afterward, watching her face and her eyes that were now heavy lidded and blinking sleepily.

"Mmm? What do you mean?"

"I mean, my sweet Lorelei, that although *you* seem to be sated and quite satisfied for the moment, *I* am not. I mean, goddamn it, that I haven't had enough of you yet! And since you suddenly appear sleepy—I've just the cure for that!" At which he bent down, and before Laura knew what was happening, he had picked her up in his arms again, just as if she were a rag doll, she thought resentfully, to stride off with her through the shrubbery, he still as naked as she.

Now Laura began to struggle and protest in earnest. "I don't know what you think you're doing but . . . you're insane! No! Put me down!" And she kicked at him and tried to claw at his face.

"No?" Trent said in what she should have recognized as a particularly dangerous tone of voice. He stopped in his tracks, much to her relief.

"No! And I wish you'd put me down! I don't know if the moonlight has driven you crazy, but I at least am sane enough at this moment to remember that we left our clothes behind in that silly little Moon Garden of yours and that Franco and Ena are still probably cavorting in the Grotto, and that—"

"How many excuses you have, Lorelei! But if you're worried about your brother and your friend, let us by all means go and find them—although being found might not please them, you know! But you shall have your visit to the Grotto by all means," he added grimly, "since I promised to show it to you. And if you don't keep still," he said through his gritted teeth, "I'm going to set you down and put you over my knee and spank you! Don't think that you can try your Japanese jujitsu or your Chinese kungfu on me, because I've had training in both those forms of the martial arts!"

Oh damn, Laura thought regretfully, what have I got myself into *this* time? And then she thought, since he seemed to be heading back for the safe cover of the shrubbery that they had just left, well, at least this particular adventure will soon come to an end. As soon as I see Ena I'm going to have to remind her of the time, whatever it is! And then—I wish he'd put me down, damn him! What is he trying to do *this* time, make me feel helpless in his clutches? Just for the moment, Laura decided to remain acquiescent; or at least to pretend that she was. And as for what had happened between them earlier, she had already decided that she would try to put it out of her mind like so many other things before that she didn't choose to think about or to remember.

"This is the Grotto. To your left you will see Pan with his pipes and his nymphs and to the right there's old Neptune himself." Why did he have to sound so detached all of a sudden?

Dim lanterns on either side of Pan and Neptune lit the entrance to the Grotto, and Laura could hear sounds from within: splashing, Ena's soft happy laugh, and Franco's deep voice.

"Now you know that neither of them has drowned and they're probably enjoying their privacy," Trent growled in her ear, "but if you're insistent on a cold dip, I'll be happy to accommodate you, of course!"

Before she could guess what his intention was, he had taken her to the ledge where the water bubbled out from the stream that flowed through this rocky Grotto, and then, bending down, he practically *dumped* her in!

The water was deep enough so that she went down under the surface before she came up gasping and spluttering. After the balmy warmth of the air, the water felt like ice against her shivering skin; and its chill almost cut off her breath so that Laura could not speak for some moments. She heard Franco call softly, "Trent? Is that you?"

"Yes. And your recalcitrant sister! But we won't be here for long, so why don't you two pick up our clothes from the Moon Garden on your way back to the house, huh?"

In a fury, Laura treaded water as she pushed clinging wet strands of her heavy hair back off her face with one hand, while at the same time she tried to reach for him;

to catch and to claw at any part of his anatomy that she
could find. She wished . . . she wished . . . and then she
felt him slip down into the flowing, moving water to join
her and to join *with* her as he tugged her body against his.
And against her will *it* happened again—whatever it was
that drew the sensual sides of them both to each other.
She felt it as her hands went about his neck and he started
to kiss her—both of them lost in the undercurrent of the
flowing, rippling motion of the stream; both of them suddenly lost in each other as they made love in the water
that kept moving and flowing against them and between
them. Laura felt as if she were flowing, rippling all the
way inside of herself too. She moved with the water, she
felt part of it as he moved in her. Everything was happening instinctively and naturally now. She felt like a mer-
maid . . . she felt . . . she felt . . . she *felt!* How could
she have known or guessed before now how insidious the
touch of his hands on her skin could be under the water—
and how sensual. The water about her, and him inside her
. . . taking her with him as sensation followed sensation
until there was only feeling . . . no thought . . . just *feeling!*

Afterward, when they were both lying together on the
rocky ledge that jutted out over the water, Laura could not
help thinking that it was *over* for them both at last. Questions had been answered. He was silent beside her—was
he thinking the same thing? He'd had her several times
already—was he satiated now? *Bored?* And why did she
have an urge to reach out to him and touch him again to
relearn the feel of his hard-muscled body? Perhaps it was
because there was something inside *her* that was insatia-
ble! A hidden part of her nature she hadn't known existed
until it suddenly took control of all of her senses so that
. . . so that. . . . She sighed pensively when he sat up
abruptly to look down at her. Oh yes, it *was* over. For
him, at least! She couldn't read his eyes but his impatient
words told her so.

"Let's go back to the house now, Lorelei, before you

catch cold with that long dripping hair of yours covering your body to make you look like a wet Lady Godiva!'' His voice sounded impersonal now that *his* appetites had been sated!

But then, soon after he had tugged her to her feet, Laura discovered that she had been quite wrong in thinking he had finished with her!

He pulled her out of the Grotto, shivering and stumbling in his wake, and then he picked her up in his arms again as he had done earlier. ''I'm taking you back to your room to dry you off,'' he informed her. ''*First*, that is! And stop wriggling!''

''But you're . . . you're going in the wrong direction! Our clothes are lying scattered all over your Moon Garden!''

''So? Franco and Ena will pick up after us before they come in. But *you*, Lorelei, are coming with *me!*''

''Not like this, surely? Oh God, you're crazy, you're mad!''

''I suppose I am in a way. Does it matter?''

''You can't really mean it! You *don't*, surely? Oh, for God's sake! Here we are neither of us with any clothes on and you're going to take me into the house like this? And still dripping wet? I suppose it's the moon! Please do put me down!''

''I'm going to take you up to your room by the secret staircase. There already was one before I decided to convert that particular room into a Moorish boudoir, but I must admit it seemed convenient—don't you think?'' Still carrying her in his arms, he took long strides across the lawn bordering the ornamental lake. Laura closed her eyes, trying hard not to imagine that Lady Honoria might happen to look out her window at that moment.

This, Laura told herself sternly, is only a dream. A bad dream—and I'll wake up out of it soon enough! But then she thought, Oh God, supposing one of the servants . . . supposing *anyone* should see us! He *is* a madman, after all—I should have known it!

"Put me down, put me *down!*" she whispered urgently again, but naturally he paid no attention, caught up in this mad mood of his. She was better off closing her eyes, Laura thought, and imagining that this was not happening!

As it turned out there *was* a concealed, and very narrow, little stairway leading into the rambling west wing from a side entrance that was almost hidden by trailing strands of ivy—and yet another, wider set of stairs that was supposed to take one up into the west terrace. He pressed a button in the wainscoting that made a concealed door slide into it revealing a tiny and tortuously narrow flight of stone steps leading up to—to *her* room!

This was indeed like something out of a gothic novel— except that she could never have imagined this kind of thing actually happening, and to *her!* Returning to her Moorish bedroom in the arms of the Dark Duke of her unfinished novel! And when yet another well-concealed panel slid open right next to her bed, she was almost speechless with indignation. How *convenient* for the cunning, scheming bastard! How well he had planned all this, Laura thought furiously before he dropped her onto the wide soft bed with the kind of laugh that boded no good for her. Without warning he lowered himself down over her, stifling her first angry protests with his kisses until she protested no longer.

Chapter 35

"Oh, dear God! I'm as sure of what I saw as I know I'm standing here *telling* you, Mrs. Evans! And I can swear it's the truth on a stack of Bibles if I had to!"

Mary, who was the chambermaid for that particular guest wing of the house, was in a *state*—her fingers twisting and untwisting at the edge of her white apron as she stuttered the words out.

"Now, Mary," the housekeeper said patiently, *"think* about what you're saying, will you? And tell me again, only this time do try to be more clear! What exactly happened to upset you so much that you took a tumble down the stairs?"

Mrs. Evans wondered if the poor girl hadn't been injured? Was she suffering from a concussion perhaps?

"But, oh, ma'am! I was *that* shocked I didn't know *what* to do!"

"Yes, well . . ." Mrs. Evans said soothingly. "You must *tell* me, my dear—and come to the point, do!"

Mary's face had turned scarlet, and she looked down at her own fingers that were still pleating and unpleating her apron.

"I . . . I . . . well, ma'am, I went in as usual to stoke up the fire and open the window curtains in . . . in *that* room that's all so dark and foreign-looking, trying to be as quiet as I could, and then . . . oh, and then I happened to glance toward the bed for a second—*only* for a second, of course, to see if the young lady was awake and wanted breakfast—you'll understand what I'm saying, I hope, Mrs. Evans?''

"Yes—yes, of course I do! You were doing what you are supposed to do every morning when there are guests here at the Hall. But you must go on and tell me the rest of it as quickly as you can, you know, because there are things to be done, and Her Ladyship might call for me at any moment. So?''

Mary made up her mind to blurt it all out *now*, before she had any more time to think about it, and her words tumbled out one over the other.

"And when I looked at the bed I saw—well, I saw *them!* His Grace himself with the young lady from America, lying all tangled up together in the bed, and both of them with not a stitch of clothes on, and fast asleep like that too! And that's when I ran from the room, ma'am, not knowing what else to do, and got to the *other* lady's room—Lady Westbridge, that is—and *she* was awake and narrow-eyed and asking me in whose bed His Grace was sleeping in because—because he was supposed to be in *hers!* And . . . oh, Mrs. E., I'm not used to *ladies* talking to me so freely, and I didn't know what I was supposed to say, either, so I just ran out the room, and then—''

At that point Mary began to cry, and Mrs. Evans got up from behind her table to try and comfort the poor girl, while her mind puzzled over the question of what to do *now!* She knew how fast gossip spread below-stairs, and with so many visitors *and* their servants as well—heaven knew how far and fast the talk would go!

But before then, there was only one thing to do, of course, and she knew it—and that was to see Lady Margaret and explain matters to *her* as well as she could.

"What? *What* did you just say, Izzy?" Lady Honoria sat bolt upright in bed, her graying hair in a thick braid. "Repeat what you just said, if you please; and for heaven's sake don't stumble and stutter over your words! You said, I believe, that Royse—''

"Yes! Royse and . . . and Miss Morgan! They were actually discovered together in . . . in . . . oh! I don't know how to say it!" And then, catching the warning look in Lady Honoria's eye, Miss Edge rushed on: "In *bed! Her* bed. And . . . both quite *naked* too!"

"Well, I expect that if they were in bed together it's natural that they *would* be unclothed! Hah! I should have expected as much, with that full moon last night! And so! What else? Does Lady Margaret know yet? But then, I'm sure *she* wouldn't know what to do about the whole affair! I suppose that *I* had better do something about it before things go too far or news travels too fast—and to the ears of too many people!"

The two dowagers met and conferred briefly in Lady Margaret's suite of rooms and planned their strategy.

In the meantime, the subjects of all the gossip and conversation that morning were still asleep. Or so Adèle, who had dared to tiptoe into Laura's room to see for herself, informed Lady Honoria.

They were still sleeping because they had probably tired each other out! At least, that was Franco's theory when Ena, in a shocked whisper, told him of the rumors that were going around.

"Oh hell! Why should Laura worry about it? Why should Trent? Ena, my love—they're neither of them conventional people! In any event," he added in an offhand kind of voice, "there's bound to be an announcement made when they wake up. Trent's going to have her—*marry* her, he told me. So let anyone say what they please—and if they say *too* much I'm going to have to defend my sister's honor, I suppose—Trent can defend *his!*"

They were at breakfast, all of them prompt except for their host, the Duke, and Laura Morgan; and of course everyone whispered and speculated among themselves. Only the fact that Lady Honoria had not yet come downstairs prevented even worse rumors from circulating. That—as well as the fact that Franco Morgan was a man no other man wanted to meet face-to-face as an antagonist.

"I want to leave here! Oh, Reggie—I *do* want to leave!" Sabina pleaded with her brother in a whisper, although she pasted a smile on her face for the benefit of the rest of the company.

"But you'll *stay,* sweet sister, and see this out, won't you? Like the rest of us!" Reggie whispered back to her. "Why, it's quite like a play, isn't it? Keep up your *friendship* with her when she comes down, as she has to in the end. It's my guess she'll be angry with him by then, and ready to be reckless!"

"Oh, but Honoria, I really don't think . . . I mean . . . well we both *knew* this was going to happen; well . . . not quite this way, I suppose! In any case . . . they will have to wake up sometime . . . ?" Lady Margaret was visibly upset.

"Margaret! There are no ifs or buts or maybes in this situation—and well you know it! And everyone *else* knows it by now, I'm sure! They're all probably downstairs wondering what will happen next in this scandalous drama— and who to *tell* next!" Lady Honoria's voice was steely.

"Oh, yes . . . breakfast! I had quite forgotten what with all this . . . I suppose I really should be downstairs seeing to things!"

"In that case, Margaret," Lady Honoria said ominously, "while *you* are attending to matters downstairs, *I* will attend to matters upstairs!"

Laura had lost all sense of time, or even, for that matter, of the reality of things while she was being made love to— on the bed first and then on the floor beside the bed, *and* in front of the blazing fireplace, and then after that in the copper-lined, sunken bathtub—after which she had been massaged with oils from the shelves and had massaged him in her turn, actually taking a great deal of pleasure in it! And then he had carried her again to the bed and had made love to her yet another time! She didn't know when they had finally fallen asleep, holding on to each other with one of his long, hard, muscled legs lying possessively across hers, as if to keep her close as well as available to him for the next time he wanted her.

When Lady Honoria stalked into the room herself after only the barest of knocks, she took everything in at a glance. She remembered being quite daring in *her* younger days, but *this* was going a little too far, she thought grimly. There they were, the two of them, still fast asleep and still locked in each other's arms—lying half in and half out of the bedcovers! No wonder the poor little chambermaid had been almost hysterical with shock—and no wonder all of their fellow guests downstairs were buzzing with speculation!

As she stood looking down at the guilty pair, Lady Honoria, with a sense of shock, noticed that *he*, with his eyes still conveniently closed, had with one arm maneuvered her on top of him! Well! But *this* was really *too* much! She would not tolerate such abandoned behavior any longer. Why, any second now they would probably begin to make love again, and right before her eyes, at that! She had to put a stop to it at once!

"Hrrmph!" Lady Honoria cleared her throat loudly enough to rouse them both. Trent half opened lazy-lidded gray eyes, and Laura gasped as she slid quickly under the covers.

No use trying to hide herself at this late stage, Lady Honoria thought disapprovingly. As if they could! No, there would be *Consequences* to this piece of reckless dalliance!

"All right, miss! There's no use trying to hide *now!*" Lady Honoria pronounced out loud before she turned her gimlet eyes on Royse, to say in her most *forbidding* manner: "And as for *you*, young man, I must say that I am surprised at your rashness and your complete lack of discretion! I can only hope you realize that it is too late now to escape the consequences of this . . . this foolish disregard for convention! They're all talking about it downstairs. Your *guests*, do you remember that you have guests? Not to mention the servants, of course.''

Casually Trent sat up and stretched, but not before he had slid a hand under the covers and, under Lady Honoria's horrified gaze, proceeded to administer a short slap on Laura's rounded bottom that made her squeal indignantly. Then he yawned, as if nothing was out of the ordinary. "Oh hell! I suppose it *is* late. I'll be sure to apologize to all my guests, of course, but you see, Ma'am, we were celebrating our engagement; and I guess we got carried away.''

"Hah!'' Lady Honoria snorted expressively. "And *after* you have delivered your explanations and apologies to everyone *else*, then I am sure that we'll all have a great deal to discuss about making the proper arrangements for your *wedding*—now that you've already accomplished the *bedding!*''

And with that parting shot, Lady Honoria swept from the room with her tafetta petticoats rustling angrily, and banged the door closed behind her.

Wriggling out from under the covers and Trent's encroaching hands, Laura sat up with her hair tangled all about her and her eyes wide with shock.

"Dear God! *Now* look what you've got me into! I'm glad I didn't get a look at the expression on her face! You—you—I should have *known* better than to let myself be—be—''

"Seduced by me?'' he offered helpfully, lying back again now with his hands crossed beneath his head as he looked her over.

"You don't understand! You've *ruined* my life! I don't *want* to be married—*least* of all to *you!* And now—''

"Well, we're not married yet—and we can always say that we believe in long engagements, can't we? There's going to have to be an announcement in *The Times* for form's sake, I suppose, before we go to Cowes, and after that—who knows? There'll be lots of time for both of us to find out what it is we really want, lovely Lorelei!''

His words and his drawling voice had made her stiffen and start to grow cold inside, and Laura made a move to leave the bed—turn her back on him before she exploded. But then his hand reached out for her to pull her back on top of him as he whispered teasingly and, damn him, temptingly: "Since there's nothing to hide at *this* late stage—there's still time before lunch!"

Part Four

Endings and Beginnings

Chapter 36

There must have been something to that old legend, after all, Laura thought moodily as she stared out to sea. Why else would she have let herself be carried away by the sheer force of feeling and the wilder part of her nature that couldn't reason against desire? It was that side of her nature that had brought her to the predicament she was in now: forced by circumstance and her own willfulness into an engagement that would soon culminate in the usual marriage of convenience—unless she could find a way out of it! Out of a situation that she now found unbearable as well as obnoxious.

It seemed as if everything had gone wrong and turned sour for her after that one night in Cornwall—that one stupid escapade she had enjoyed well enough at the time, but now seemed likely to change her whole life!

A *mariage de convenance*—an *arrangement* entered into only because of convention, and as a belated sop to morality—meaning the moral standards and codes of *other* people, of course!

"Well, you were very clever, I'm sure—the way you managed it all!" Sabina's voice had been sugary-sharp when she "congratulated" Laura. "And now of course he has no choice but to do the gentlemanly thing and announce that you're engaged to be married!"

"But we aren't married *yet*, are we?" Laura had returned in the same acidly sweet voice. "So you still have a chance at him yourself. And who knows—*I* might change

321

my mind about all this! So you must feel free by all means to try to reengage Trent's attentions. I promise I won't mind!''

"He loves *me*—I'm sure of that much! He's told me so a thousand times at least! *You*, Laura dearest, are a *convenience*. He told me that, too—only last night! It has to do with *money*, lots of money, being kept within the two families, I believe? You know Trent is clever and can be scheming too!''

Could he? And *had* he been all during his pursuit of her, his sudden desire for her that he'd sated in one long night and a late morning?

It must be so, obviously, because they had hardly exchanged more than polite pleasantries with each other since then—and that only when they happened by chance to run into each other. Sabina certainly seemed to be well informed about everything—in addition to being the recipient of his affection. Laura remembered only too well what he'd said about long engagements. They *weren't* married yet—and probably never *would* be in the end, if things went on *this* way!

She had not had a chance to speak with Trent alone for the past two weeks, Laura thought resentfully now, for Lady Westbridge was constantly at his side. On one occasion while they were still in Cowes for the Annual Regatta and Ball, she had swallowed her pride and gone very late at night to his room in the hotel where they were all staying. But she had quickly discovered that Sabina had got there first, and was lying curled up comfortably close to him in bed!

Neither of *them* had known that she had seen them together, and she had not mentioned it. She had acted as if nothing was changed—although *she* had changed inside herself and her feelings had changed. Oh, but she despised him for a lying, smiling hypocrite! He had *wanted* her— only *wanted* her, never loving her, never once saying so, and he'd taken her, and she'd *let* him, Laura remembered shamefully. But he *loved* Sabina, had actually told her so! Damn him, damn him!

But at least he'd freed her to go her own way as she meant to and would, even if they were actually married in the end. A woman might be frowned on as a sinner—but a man was laughed at behind his back as a cuckold! The Duke of Royse cuckolded by his Duchess—she enjoyed the idea. Perhaps she would even write about it—write intimate details in the final installment of her novel that only she and *he* would know were based on fact!

Laura touched the heavy jewel-encrusted bracelet on her arm. *This* was only the beginning! A souvenir of sorts, and a token.

She had literally run into King Milos of Serbia on her way back to her own room that night after she'd closed the door on Trent and Sabina. And . . .

She remembered that a Parisian friend had once told her that he was a wild, bullish kind of a man, but a good enough lover; and generous.

She'd begged his pardon in French, in a breathless voice, and he'd come directly to the point in the same language, holding her by the shoulders.

"This is my lucky night! I win at baccarat first and now I find you! I don't care whose bed you've come from, little lovely, but I want you in mine *now!* And I promise you won't be disappointed afterward, eh? Come along, don't be shy!"

He'd taken her for a whore—and she'd acted the part and had gone with him to his bed—having been taught all too well how to excite a man. The bracelet was the result of *that* night; and she had learned besides that she didn't have to *feel* anything when a man took her, as long as she simulated feeling to please *him* . . . *Hadn't* she? Laura bit her lip for an instant before she thought viciously: I hope Trent asks me where this bracelet came from. I hope he *does*. Because then I could tell him—tell him every detail of what happened too! Her fingers gripped tightly at the polished mahogany rail before her, and she closed her eyes briefly, wondering why her revenge did not seem quite as sweet as she had hoped earlier when she had been set on retaliation in *kind*. Sauce for the goose—sauce for the gander! Why then were her emotions so mixed up? Because her emotions hadn't been engaged in what had happened, perhaps? Oh—damn him! And damn her own impulsive nature!

The night sky was like a black velvet tapestry, patterned with silver stars and a yellow crescent moon riding low above the horizon like a Viking death ship. And she, too, was on a ship—a yacht, actually, she corrected herself. The Royal Yacht *Britannia* as a guest of H.R.H. the Prince of Wales.

"I've been persuaded by Mrs. Langtry here to take a short cruise—show her what this little ship can do!" he'd said at the annual ball of the Royal Yacht Squadron that was said to be the most exclusive club in the world. "Mrs. Langtry hasn't seen the Rock—Gibraltar, you know—and since the Countess of Sedgewick's husband's there and he's eager to see her again, and *you* gentlemen want Cadiz— well, that's as far as I'm going before we have to turn back!"

Mrs. Lillie Langtry, the actress, had almost all of the Prince's attention these days, so Laura felt safe enough in accepting his invitation.

Ena had accepted too. Ena and Franco seemed to be on the outs again. Ena hadn't talked about it, and Franco walked about scowling and glowering, but Laura guessed that their latest quarrel had something to do with the fact that she was going back to her husband. God—men were so unfair and unreasonable!

Laura suddenly remembered something that Lady Honoria had said to her on that momentous occasion at Royse Hall when wedding plans were being discussed. "I know you think of yourself as a rebel, my girl, and I suppose you *are*, considering this morning! But there's one thing you have to remember, and you have to swallow, like it or not! This is a man's world we're living in. There's nothing

that you can do to change that, so you might as well accept
the fact. And it's *men* who talk the most, and the worst,
about women—over their port and their cigars and their
billiard tables as the case may be. That's another thing you
ought to keep in mind!''

Laura was alone on the deck now as the yacht steamed
slowly on its way—midnight-blue waters foaming on either
side of the *Britannia*'s prow. A faint aroma of cigar smoke
drifted up to her, along with the sound of masculine voices
and the clinking of glasses. They were supposed to be
playing cards, and *she* hadn't been invited to join them,
naturally! It wasn't fair, it wasn't fair! Laura thought in a
rage before she wondered if the Jersey Lily, as Mrs. Langtry was being called by some people now, had perhaps
been daring enough to venture into that man's province to
stand behind the Prince of Wales; or if Lady Westbridge
might have had the same notion, and might at this moment
be standing behind Trent with her hands resting possessively on his shoulders. Well, *she* wasn't going to demean
herself by going down there to find out!

Laura wished that Ena had not decided to go to sleep
soon after dinner and had begged off from taking even one
turn about the deck. She wished that Sabina had not been
able to inveigle an invitation aboard the *Britannia* by making up to Lord Dunhill, who had a villa, it seemed, in the
region of Andalusia—not very far from Cadiz where the
Royal Yacht would be putting in for a day or two after
leaving Gibraltar before she turned about to return to England. But had Sabina been invited aboard for Lord Dunhill or for the Duke of Royse?

Laura had begun to pace up and down along the deck,
with the train of her skirt lifted as high as possible so that
she could take long, angry strides that helped to vent her
rage. She stared down balefully at the engagement ring
Trent had presented her with—a diamond surrounded by
blue sapphires—and felt like tugging it off her finger and
sending it sailing into the sea. An *engagement* ring! And
if she let it happen, there would soon be a gold wedding

band on her finger as well—a slave ring that would put an
end to her freedom forever; but not *his* of course! After
all, men, *most* men, could flaunt their mistresses with im-
punity while they cloistered away their wives—how often
she'd seen it! But *she'd* be damned before she'd be caught
in a trap like that; in fact she meant to tell *him* so at the
first possible opportunity—that was, if he could possibly
manage to disengage himself from Sabina's clinging arms
and voluptuous body for long enough.

She must have been crazed to go along with this whole
stupid farce, Laura thought now—despising herself almost
as much as she despised *him*. First an engagement, with
the usual announcement in *The Times;* followed, after what
Lady Honoria would call a respectable period of time, by
a wedding held in some fashionable church; and then a
grand reception. Afterward, of course, a honeymoon in
some fashionable resort. Intolerable! And all this simply
because she was supposed to have been *compromised* by
him and because *he* was supposed to make amends and
do the ''honorable'' thing as a sop to convention and society. Well, damn his black heart and even blacker soul!
She would have none of it or of *him* either!

She suddenly stopped stock-still as a thought struck her;
and gripped her fingers tightly over the polished railing.
What had she been thinking of? *She* was no conventionally
bred English miss. She was, in fact, the child of parents
who were both hardly conventional! *She* didn't have to
care or worry about what anyone would say or think;
therefore, if she broke off her so-called engagement or did
something outrageous enough to ensure that *he* would
break it off—it would only be what he deserved! There he
was below deck, smoking his cigar and playing cards with
the Prince of Wales and his cronies while *she* stood here
on the deck alone, with only the wind to ruffle her hair
and a star-spangled night-sky above her as she watched
the gold crescent moon drowning into the blackness of the
ocean.

Suddenly, Laura felt as if she were drowning too. She

felt oddly *lost,* and somehow more alone than she had ever felt in her life before, with feelings inside her that needed to be shared. Then, with a start, she felt her wrist caught and encircled from behind and for a moment her pulses leaped and she almost said "Trent?" But of course it wasn't he—he was too busy with other things, other people. Instead, this was *Reggie,* who had come up softly behind her to catch her by surprise.

"Reggie! But what on earth are you doing out here? I thought you'd be playing cards with the rest of the men below deck."

"I'm afraid the stakes were far too steep for me to afford; and then, somehow, I had a feeling that I might run into *you* up here by some lucky chance since I wasn't too lucky at cards!"

The lightness in his voice changed into concern. "You don't even have a wrap. Shall I fetch one for you?" To his puzzlement, she only turned back to watch the sea without replying—but she made no attempt to remove his arms from about her waist either. Reggie felt bold enough to whisper with his lips close to her ear, "Will you allow *me* to keep you warm, Laura dear?"

He couldn't believe his luck when she leaned against him and said in a softly languid voice: "Oh yes, I think that *would* be nice—in fact I think I feel warmer already."

"Laura—oh God, Laura!" he burst out suddenly, seizing his chance. "If you only knew how much I want to kiss you—just to feel the softness of your lips the way I've imagined and dreamed about so often!" His arms tightened about her, pulling her closer against him.

"Why do you *ask* me, Reggie? Why don't you just . . . why don't you just *do* it? And *then* tell me if you really enjoy kissing me." She turned then, of her own volition, in his arms and tilted her face up to his with her eyes opened and looking straight into his—the starlight reflected in their dark blueness that was like the blue of the ocean.

By God! he thought jubilantly, this *was* his lucky night

after all! "I love you, Laura. You're so lovely, so lovely . . ." he said hoarsely and then he bent his head down to hers and crushed her mouth, taking his time tasting and feeling the texture of her lips before they opened at last to his hungrily seeking and probing tongue.

He bent her back against the railing while he kissed her to make sure that she could feel his hardness as he pressed even closer to her. And then, knowing women as well as he did, and having learned exactly how to please them and how to woo them well, he continued to kiss her, forcefully—and then gently and teasingly. When he heard her begin to murmur incoherent half-protests they both knew she did not mean, he began to stroke her—the outline of her breasts first—very gently and exploratively, with his fingers searching for and finding her nipples which had suddenly become hard and erect; lingering teasingly over their tiny peaks before moving elsewhere. He always concentrated on whatever he was doing at the moment, and he knew how to time each different move that would lead up to the final act and its culmination. He said now, in a passionate whisper, while his lips still hovered over hers: "How very much I love you! I could never say so before now because I didn't want you to think me just another fortune hunter! But I adore and worship you, lovely Laura, and I want you more than I've ever wanted any woman in my life! Please, my dearest, please, let me make love to you as you deserve to be made love to! Please say you'll let me! I want to worship your lovely body—touch and kiss and feel every inch of it! Tell me you will give yourself to me, darling! That you'll let me take you to my cabin so that I can show you just how much I adore you, and how happy I can make you if you'll only let me!"

She surprised him again! "Let's go to *my* stateroom, Reggie dear."

Laura had purposely chosen her own cabin because she almost hoped that Trent might come looking for her and see her with Reggie; just as she had seen him with Reggie's platinum-haired sister less than a week ago. But none of her thoughts showed on her face or in her demeanor as she gave Reggie her hand and let him take her along with him.

She let Reggie kiss her and caress her as they stood outlined by lamplight before the half-open porthole facing the corridor leading to the deck. She even let him undress her down to her chemise and lead her to her bed, pushing her gently backward so that he could lie beside her while he continued to caress and touch her.

She had a lovely little body, Reggie thought as he kissed each portion of her body as it became exposed to his gaze and his roving hands. He was amazed that she was so acquiescent and so willing. It seemed Royse must have trained her well! Reggie thought with a sudden stab of anger and envy—wondering if Royse had been the first man to have her. But damn all that, *he* was going to have her now!

Why couldn't she have gone through with it? Laura wondered, after she had dismissed Reggie, and lay, open-eyed and sleepless, in her bed.

Why hadn't she let Reggie make love to her as he had wanted to? He had tried so hard to give her pleasure, she knew that, and at some moments he had managed to excite her; but that was only when she closed her eyes and imagined that it was . . . that it was someone else: dark-haired, with ice-gray eyes; someone who was probably sleeping at this very moment with Reggie Forrester's sister.

Trent was, as a matter of fact, with Sabina; but only because he had excused himself from the interminable game of cards that H.R.H. so enjoyed, and had gone up on deck for a while before he'd gone below looking for Laura. Through one of the portholes she had carelessly left open, he saw that she was occupied—or being occupied by Reggie Forrester of all the men the bitch might have chosen—since it seemed all too obvious to him *now* that all she really wanted was a *fuck*—and any available man would do! *Damn* her! He had been of a mind to open her door and kill them both, and in fact he'd started forward, seething with pure, primitive rage before *reason* stopped him at the last second; and he had turned on his heel and gone directly to Reggie's sister.

Trent undressed quickly and angrily in the darkness of Sabina's cabin before dropping his body over Sabina's and smothering her startled exclamation with a brutal kiss.

"Trent! Oh—it's *you*, and at last!"

"Who else were you expecting? Dunhill? Anyway, I outrank him! And since *you* paid me a surprise visit and woke me out of a sound sleep at Cowes, I thought I would return the compliment, Lady Westbridge!"

"Your Grace!" Sabina murmured before her murmurs turned into incoherent sounds as he stripped her nightgown off her and began to take her roughly—something she always enjoyed!

So he'd come to her at last—it didn't matter why or how it had happened at this moment. He was here with her, and she meant to keep him here, and satisfied, until morning. Perhaps then that bitch Laura would break their engagement and he'd have to marry *her* instead!

The thought of becoming the Duchess of Royse excited Sabina enough so that her movements and her response to him became wilder and even more abandoned than usual. Oh, but he was a good lover, and like a wild animal tonight as he took her. She wished that he *would* marry her, or at least make her his permanent mistress; anything that would take her away and keep her safe from Reggie, who liked to hurt her when he was angry, and make her do all kinds of things she neither enjoyed nor wanted.

Sabina tried to fall asleep again after they had both been satisfied, but she couldn't. Partly because Trent didn't stay with her as she had hoped, and partly because she just *knew* that Reggie would be angry with her because she hadn't been able to keep Royse in her bed until morning.

But surprisingly Reggie came to her in an exceptionally good mood, soon after he had seen Trent leave. "Well— congratulations, sister dear! And *don't* fail to mention your little rendezvous to Miss Laura! Nor to let it drop to *him* the next time you two are together that his fiancée whiled away several hours of her time with *me* this evening. Oh yes—and she turned out to be quite hot and eager too!''

''What? Do you mean that she really . . . !''

''What else? I'm going to have her yet—have her and use her and keep her too; especially when Royse finds out what she's been up to. And *that*, sister mine, I leave to you!''

Chapter 37

Two arms of land seem to curve about the harbor port of Cadiz—all white-washed buildings and red-tiled roofs under the blazing Spanish sun. The Royal Yacht *Britannia* had dropped anchor just within the harbor, and would remain only long enough for the launch that was already on its way from the shore to pick up some of the Prince of Wales's guests who were disembarking here.

Laura wore a stark white serge yachting costume that reflected the sunlight, and a wide-brimmed yellow straw hat that kept her eyes and her expression shaded as she leaned her elbows on the rail next to Helena and watched the launch chug toward them.

"Are you coming with us?" Trent had asked her earlier in that cold, distant voice that put a barrier of ice between them.

"No. Ena wants me to stay with her and Archie for a while—and perhaps it's the best thing for both of us." She kept her voice expressionless. "In any case, you'll probably have your hands full, won't you, with Lady Westbridge? That is, of course, if Lord Dunhill keeps on falling asleep. Naturally I wouldn't *dream* of spoiling your fun!"

His eyes had shot splinters of slivered glass at her in that moment, almost making her quail for a moment. Then he had said, "Nor I *yours* with Reggie Forrester, sweetheart!" With a barely suppressed note of violence in his voice, he added, "Do you know that at this moment, I'd like to wring your neck, you cheating, conniving little bitch!'' The fury in his eyes was almost palpable, and Laura had not been able to stop herself from taking a step backward, hearing him continue in a sardonic voice: ''But I don't think you're worth it! You're no Desdemona; and I, my dear, am no jealous fool of an Othello!''

She felt herself disintegrating inside but she had to go on with this hateful, cruel new game now, even though she felt lost and suddenly isolated inside herself. But some strange compulsion to hurt, to strike out, drove her on.

Looking straight up at him, she said, in a languidly expressionless voice, ''Do you want your ring back, Your Grace? Especially since we seem to be going in separate directions and have our own different amusements . . .''

''Oh, no,'' he said with a short, caustic laugh. ''Keep it, sweet Lorelei, by all means—as a memento of a moment of madness!''

Suddenly he took her face between his fingers, startling her into a gasp before he bent his head and kissed her— roughly and brutally. Then he looked down at her contemptuously. ''Do try to take care of yourself, my sweet. And try not to give yourself to too many men too soon and too easily in the future, for your own sake!'' With that he turned on his heel and left her staring after him. What she really longed to do was to run after him or to call him back—but the pain inside her was almost too much to bear, and kept her frozen in silence.

''Laura!'' Her brother caught her by the arm and pulled her around to face him. He ignored Ena, whose face had gone first pink and then pale in turn. ''Laura, goddamn it!'' Franco said in a low, furious undertone as he almost dragged her aside with him, ''what in God's name do you think you're doing? You've gone too far this time, sister mine. Trent Challenger is the last man on whom you should attempt to play this kind of dirty trick! Reggie Forrester—my God! How Trent has managed to keep his self-control, I don't know, but you should count yourself lucky that he has, or you would have been thrown overboard by now, I assure you!''

"If Trent can have an affair with Lady Westbridge and flaunt her in *my* face," Laura said coldly, "then why shouldn't *I* do whatever I want! After all, we're living in a modern world now, aren't we?'' She went on a trifle wildly, "I don't want a man to feel he *has* to marry me because I have been *compromised*. In the hotel at Cowes, I found Sabina in Trent's bed with him and then . . . and then . . . Do you understand, Franco? I don't want to have a man as a husband who flaunts his mistresses in my face; I can't live with it, I won't tolerate it! What's sauce for the goose is sauce for the gander, after all! And . . . and . . .''
Her voice choked in her throat and she had to suck in a deep breath to try to prevent her emotions from erupting, shaming her in front of everybody.

Franco took her by the shoulders, his fingers biting into her flesh as he looked down into her face. "Jesus Christ, Laura! I didn't know how far it had gone with the two of you. You really love him, don't you?''

Laura shook her head fiercely, closing her eyes so that the tears wouldn't show while her teeth bit into her lower lip.

"The *hell* you don't!'' Franco growled roughly, and then suddenly he held her close to him in a fierce hug. When he released her, he said bitterly, "I guess we're in the same boat, you and I! Except that Ena *knows* I want her. She just hasn't the guts to do something about what *she* wants!'' His voice hardened as he said, "It seems I'm supposed to stay with you and be your chaperone. Believe me, it's not a job I relish, especially when there are other things I have to do—damn it! And by the way, the launch hasn't left yet, so why don't you swallow your stupid stiffnecked pride and go after him, Laura? Why don't you just go get in that goddamn launch and surprise all of them? Go after him—like a real woman would! I know that Trent wants *you;* and I think you know that too. Shall I take you down to the launch myself and dump you in it? You can blame me for everything later, when you and Trent settle matters between yourselves. I'll even promise to take care of Sabina for you—and Reggie as well, if it comes to that, damn his hide! Laura?''

''I can't. Oh, Franco, surely you see that it's too late. He must have seen me with Reggie and thought . . . Oh, but I *wanted* him to see us together, and to think the *worst*—and he did! Nothing *happened*, Franco, I didn't . . . But it makes no difference now—I know Trent well enough to realize that he could never forgive me—or *believe* me even if I told him the truth!''

The chugging of the launch started up again and Laura realized that they were leaving. Lord Dunhill, Sabina, Reggie, and *Trent*—who was leaving *her*, and leaving her bereft, although she would never, never, let anyone know it!

''In any case,'' Laura continued in a voice that was hard and cold, ''it's too late for regrets, isn't it? For all of us, I think. I have to go to my stateroom now and make sure I've packed everything I need before we dock at Gibraltar. And I should go to Ena too. She's *so* unhappy.''

''I'm unhappy too,'' Franco said quietly. ''I don't know if you realize it, Laura, but men have feelings too; and if Ena is unhappy I'm afraid that's *her* problem! I asked her again to come away with me but she chose her husband and his damn title and this life she leads! As I said,'' he added in that bitter voice of moments ago, ''it appears we have a lot in common. But let me tell you this—I'm not going to stay around to watch Ena and her husband together greeting their guests at public functions and attending receptions. As soon as I have you safely installed in their villa in Gibraltar, I intend to be on my way to Algeciras; and from there I will probably meet Trent halfway between there and Cadiz, at the *casa* of a certain gentleman from Madrid who has information that Mr. Bishop might find interesting.'' He gave her a stiffly formal bow. ''Call on me if you need me in the meantime, sister. But if you want my advice, you should ask H.R.H. to have you sent ashore too. Unless, like Ena, you enjoy being miserable!'' And with that, he walked off.

They dined formally as usual that night, although their number had been reduced by the four guests who had left at Cadiz. By tomorrow night they would be in Gibraltar attending a grand reception at the Pall Mall Club to welcome the Prince of Wales.

In the ornately furnished dining room of the Royal Yacht, Albert Edward, the Prince of Wales, was seated at the head of the table, and as usual he had had Mrs. Langtry on his left and the Countess of Sedgewick on his right. But Franco Morgan had been seated on the other side of Helena; by some unfortunate chance, she thought, as she played with her food and plied her fan, while she made an attempt at polite conversation with him in a stiff and stilted voice. Across from them, Major Eagan, who was another of the Prince's cronies, had been seated between Mrs. Langtry and Laura Morgan.

H.R.H. was in fine fettle that night in the small, cozy atmosphere; and so was Mrs. Langtry, it seemed. And after dinner the Prince insisted that they must all pair off and stroll about the deck to admire the starred night sky, and the moon which had not yet set. He, of course, had Mrs. Langtry on his arm almost immediately; and a moment later Major Eagan bowed and offered his arm to Laura. But this left Helena and Franco paired off together, the last thing that either of them wanted. However, since there was no help for it, Ena was forced to take the arm that he offered her with no more than surface politeness, and to promenade with him along the deck while wishing, with her head beginning to ache, that she could have retired to the safety of her stateroom instead of being forced to be so *close* to him again—feeling the hardness of his muscles under the light touch of her fingers on his arm as they walked.

Protocol demanded that each couple keep at a discreet distance from the others; and while the Prince of Wales, who had by now slipped his arm about Lillie Langtry's waist, walked ahead of them all, puffing on his cigar and whispering to her while she smiled up at him and laughed occasionally, the rest of them were obliged to walk extremely slowly, pausing every now and then to look over the rail at the rushing water and up at the stars.

Ahead of Franco and Ena, Laura and Major Eagan seemed to be engaged in animated conversation; and not only Ena but Franco, too, had not failed to notice how Laura had started to cling rather too closely to the dapper Major's arm as she walked with him, and that as she leaned over the rail she also seemed to lean far too close to him.

"God damn! I don't understand my sister any longer!" Franco grated suddenly. "She's acting like a slut, and seems to invite every available man in sight to her bed to try him out! Now it's Major Eagan—well, the poor devil. I only hope that I won't have to feel obliged to call him out when we get to Gibraltar." And then, quite unexpectedly, and without Ena knowing how it had happened, he had her up against the rail with the small of her back pressed painfully against it as he leaned against *her.*

"Well, to hell with my sister and her games and her fucking around. I'd like to fuck *you,* Ena; maybe for the last time, who knows? One more time as a keepsake before you go back into your husband's arms and your husband's bed!"

His words and the tone of voice in which he'd said them seemed to burn into her, and Ena gave a startled gasp which was almost like a sob before she managed to say, "Oh, Franco! No, don't! Don't, please, I beg you!" She put her hands involuntarily up against his shoulders as if to ward off any other cruel barbs he might fling at her, and he caught at them to pull her even closer against his body, the grip of his fingers hurting her wrists.

"Why don't you say 'Oh, Franco, yes!' for a change?" he almost snarled at her. "Or is the Earl of Sedgewick so good in bed that you want to keep yourself chaste for at least a day or two before he has you again? Well? Tell me,

Ena—if you're capable of any real honesty, that is.'' And then before she could say or do anything, he deliberately brushed his fingers across her breast and then dipped his hand into the low décolletage of her gown to explore between them.

"I know you're a coward, my sweet Countess, but you're still capable of arousing me, as I think you know too well; and I think from the hardness of those sweet little nipples of yours that I'd love to kiss again and again that you're getting that way too!'' His voice had dropped to a low, teasing drawl, and he added, *"Admit* it, Ena! Try to be honest for once—at least just once. I want you. I want you *tonight,* I want you *now,* damn it!'' His fingers still continued to play with her erect nipples while she made little sobbing sounds; she could not and did not want to resist him or what he was making her feel, and he whispered again, tauntingly: "Once more won't make a difference, will it, Ena, my sweet love? We'll go to my stateroom and then . . . and then you know damn well what is going to happen between us, don't you?''

Helena knew, as she should have known all along, that this was what she wanted and that she couldn't stop the rush of passion and feeling that was between them—any more than she could have resisted the way his fingers inside her low-cut dinner gown were touching her so intimately, so possessively, so familiarly. Oh God, even if the Prince of Wales himself had been watching, she couldn't have stopped him, and wouldn't have *wanted* to either. "Just once more,'' he had said, and oh, the thought was almost unbearable!

Trying desperately to save herself from abject surrender to his will and her senses, and with a note of desperation creeping into her voice, Ena said, "But . . . but H.R.H.! And . . . and Laura . . . what if she—''

"My sister can damn well look after herself from now on!'' Franco said harshly. "And let's hope for Major Eagan's sake that he's a cautious man. As for H.R.H., in case you haven't noticed, he and Mrs. Langtry disappeared below deck a long time ago, my sweet Ena! So, well? Are you coming with me? Or shall I rip your gown off your back right here and now and fling you down on the deck and have you under this starlit sky? Is *that* what you want, Ena? Because you know I'll do it!''

Oh, yes, Helena knew very well that he'd do exactly as he threatened. In fact, his fingers were already hooked in the deeply cut vee of her silk and lace gown! And there was no one else out here on the deck but the two of them . . . Reading the dangerous look in Franco's eyes and the moon reflected in them for a moment, Helena gave in, as she had known she would in the end—for in any case he had already started to rip the bodice of her gown down the front so that it had slipped off her shoulders to expose their creamy paleness and—what else *could* she do?

''Franco, no, please,'' she whispered to him frantically, seeing that he meant to go even further. ''Franco, not *here,* I beg of you! Downstairs in your stateroom—but please not out here in the open when there might be people watching!''

''And why not here? Whoever wants to watch, if it excites them, let them watch!'' he said, harshly startling her into backing away in what was almost a state of panic as she suddenly realized that he meant every word he had just uttered! He said softly and insistently, ''Now take off your shoes, Ena. Take them off!''

''My . . . my . . . shoes? But I don't understand. . . .''

''It doesn't matter. Take off those dainty little evening slippers of yours and throw them over the rail. I want you to go downstairs with me barefoot like a Spanish peasant girl!''

And then with a sudden, broken laugh, she did so, and flung them over the rail as he had asked her to do and turned back to face him before she said: ''Does that satisfy you?''

''Not quite yet, my love. *That* has to go over the rail, too, before you can look like a peasant girl!'' And at that he actually did rip her gown off her and fling it carelessly over the rail, leaving her only in her corset and chemise, her taffeta petticoat, and her black silk stockings. "And now—*now* we'll go downstairs," he said huskily, as his eyes traveled all over her. "And when I have you in my stateroom and on the bed, I'm going to lock the door and keep you there for as long as I wish—like a lovely highborn beauty taken captive by some rough and uncouth villain of a pirate who keeps her solely for his pleasure!"

And so he kept her in his stateroom and he pleasured her for most of the night until at last he carried her back in his arms to her own stateroom, to put her back in her own bed, sated and drowsy by now; and said in an expressionless voice as he looked down at her, "And now, Milady, it's time for you to walk the plank!" And then he turned about and left her.

Chapter 38

No wonder they referred to the Crown Colony of Gibraltar as the Rock, Laura thought. A huge craggy mountain reared abruptly upward out of the sea. Major Eagan had told her that Gibraltar was not only a free port but guarded the gateway between the Atlantic Ocean and the Mediterranean. It had always been something of a historical and impregnable fortress from medieval times to the present day; and the British had gained control of it after the signing of the Treaty of Utrecht.

"It's only about three miles long running from north to south and only three quarters of a mile wide, although you wouldn't guess it," he'd said. "But it's in a most strategic position, in spite of its proximity to Spain. Almost like a castled fortress, isn't it? And within that huge rock are innumerable caves and caverns and tunnels—thirty-five miles, in fact, some leading out to the ocean. You might be interested in exploring St. Michael's Cavern sometime—it has an interesting history, and a torture chamber that was used during the time of the Spanish inquisition!"

By the time all the formalities and ceremonies of welcoming the Prince of Wales were finally over, Laura not only had a headache from the firing of the cannons in salute, but she felt quite wilted by the intense heat and humidity. It was a relief to be indoors again and to feel cool again! The house that the Earl of Sedgewick had taken when he was appointed as Lieutenant-Governor was surrounded by what looked like a tropical garden; and it had thick walls to keep out the heat and ceiling fans in every room. Hers, thank goodness, looked out onto the garden; and with the windows opened there was even a slight breeze that drifted inside carrying with it the scent of flowers.

One of the soft-footed maids had come in to unpack for her and hang up her clothes in a capacious armoire. The two maids that Laura had seen so far were either Moroccan or Andalusian, she thought, and quite pretty. And the menservants she had seen were also Moroccan or Arabic. They were all young and quite handsome in their way.

Once her maid, whose name, Laura learned, was Ayesha, had helped her to undress, Laura lay back on the wide bed with a sigh of relief and closed her eyes as she started to let her tense muscles relax.

There was plenty of time yet before she had to get up and begin dressing for the reception at the Pall Mall Club; and apparently here in Gibraltar they still followed the Spanish custom of taking the afternoon *siesta*. Perhaps by making her mind a deliberate blank she could manage to fall asleep.

She had slept only fitfully last night, and now she felt— *deserted*, especially since Franco had politely turned down the Earl's kind invitation to stay with them in his house, and had insisted that he must take a boat to Algeciras, where he said he was supposed to meet a friend.

She shouldn't have come here, she felt suddenly for no real reason. Not even for Ena's sake. If anything, she should have gone back to Paris where she had been happy once, and filled with the sense of living life to its fullest without restrictions or bonds.

As soon as Ena is settled in, and I feel that she's comfortable, Laura thought, I must leave. Perhaps I'll join Lady Honoria in Baden-Baden or perhaps I'll go to Italy. I don't care where I go—*anywhere!* Perhaps even the Philippines, if my footloose parents are still there and haven't traveled on to some other exotic place! She still felt resentful and even a little hurt that Franco had been told by Mr. Bishop that they had not gone to India after all; why couldn't he have told *her?* Why was she always kept in the dark about everything? All these mysterious errands, and comings and goings, and sudden secretive trips made by Franco *and* Trent—did they think she was a silly little girl who couldn't be trusted to keep a secret? And why couldn't Mr. Bishop have enlisted *her* help in whatever devious schemes he had brewing anyhow?

She had asked him that same question once, and had told him quite directly that she was sure that she could do a much better job at gathering information, or whatever it was that he needed done, than any *man* he had working for him. He had donned that inscrutable expression that she called his poker face before he murmured over his steepled fingers, "Umm. Perhaps I'll think about it." And then he had given an almost-smile before adding, "The only thing is that you remind me almost *too* much of your mother, and I still remember a certain time when she actually blackmailed me into doing what she wanted—much against my better judgment! I have the feeling, my dear Laura, that you are still far too impetuous and headstrong for *that* kind of . . . shall we say, hobby?"

He pushed his chair back and stood up, bringing their conversation to a definite close. "You must realize that there are certain places where men can go, certain things that men can do that you cannot." And then he had thrown a bone to her. "But I do assure you, that should I need a female agent who might have access to valuable information, I will certainly, and with no hesitation, call upon you."

No, Laura thought now somewhat curiously, she didn't think that Mr. Bishop ever hesitated about anything that he wanted done. She had heard stories—little things her mother had let slip on occasion—and overheard conversations between her father and Mr. Davis, who was one of his oldest and closest friends. Her father had done almost everything, she knew. He'd been a gunfighter, a killer when he had to be—even a *guerrillero* to oust the French and their puppet emperor Maximilian from Mexico. And her mother—her mother had been whatever she *had* to be in order to survive; had done everything and suffered every pain and degradation a woman could suffer, and *still* had emerged triumphant in the end! And so would she, Laura thought, before sleep finally claimed her . . . so would she!

She had been dreaming . . . strangely uneasy dreams. Laura suddenly sat bolt upright in bed and looked around her. Nothing had changed in this room, the window was open, the breeze fanned her face with its perfumed touch, the ceiling fan whirred overhead, and there was no one here—no eyes watching her. Unless, she thought as she lay back in the soft bed, one of the gardeners had peered in through the window and she had sensed his curious gaze. She closed her eyes again with a sigh, wondering what Ena was doing.

The Earl and Countess of Sedgewick's rooms were at the far end of the rambling house that was built in a U shape around an overgrown garden with a small fountain and a pool in the center. Used to having Helena close to her to talk to and to confide in and to laugh with, Laura felt curiously lost and lonely again before she reminded herself that surely she and Ena would have some time to talk alone with each other before the reception. Of course Ena would come into her room all dressed and perfumed and bejeweled to ask her anxiously if *she* had finished dressing yet! Poor, confused Ena! Why hadn't Franco just grabbed her up in his arms and carried her off with him, husband or not? He could have had her if he'd done just that, Laura was sure of it. Ena, as sweet as she was, needed someone strong, needed someone to think for her—*and* to sweep her off her feet! Why hadn't Franco done that?

But then, Laura thought with an involuntary sigh, why

hadn't *she* done what she had really wanted to do in spite of everything? She had gone after Trent in the beginning with a laughing air of insouciance, almost on a dare she had made with herself; and then . . . and then, she had got him or thought she had! What had gone wrong after that? And, oh, *why* hadn't she continued to be strong enough to fight for what she really wanted—and to keep the man she wanted? Why had she done what she had out of childish spite and a need for *revenge* when she should have known, even when she saw Sabina in his bed, that all she had to do was to walk in there and send Sabina packing before she told *him* in a few well-chosen words that she did not intend to put up with this kind of thing any longer or at any time in the future either! It would all have been settled then, once and for all—and there would not have been King Milos who had given her this heavy bracelet she wore on her arm as an act of defiance; and there would not have been the misunderstanding over Reggie that she had deliberately continued.

Oh God, Laura thought, sitting up and pushing her heavy mass of hair off her shoulders. I have to stop this. I have to stop thinking of the might-have-beens and what I wish I had done, or what I should have done or *not* done. What's the point in it *now?* He's gone and I'll never have him back—I might as well face that fact.

For a moment she had an almost uncontrollable impulse to call for Ayesha and ask her to pack her bags again—to make her apologies to Ena and to Archie, and to leave the Rock on the next steamer to whatever destination it would take her. She was so *tired* of all her aimless wanderings, and her pointless explorations into sensuality. She had had her fill of Europe, and of different Seasons in different places, and of society and sophistication, and a way of life that insisted upon surface conforming while underneath the polite exterior *anything* was permissible as long as one was *discreet!* No, Laura decided, she wasn't like her parents who enjoyed traveling about constantly, and never seemed to put down roots anywhere; no, in that way at least she was different. She wanted, she *needed* roots somewhere; some place that she could call home; and even if she did have to travel elsewhere for a while—a place to come back to. Her father and her mother had their roots in each other, so that wherever they went they were home *with* each other.

Laura thought suddenly, Mama—Mama would tell me to go after what I *really* want. She remembered something her mother had told her once, laughing when they had been talking about her father. "There was one time when he had been living with Concepción in the little Hacienda; and when I arrived there I had to scare her away with a knife and poor Paco had to take her off somewhere or I would have killed her! And when your father arrived in the middle of the night, not knowing that *I* was there in his bed instead of Concepción, well . . . he was so *very* angry, and swore he didn't want me, of course! But then—hmm—I made him feel quite differently in the end, even though I must admit I had to pull a knife on him and make him shuck his pants for me while I held the knife-blade against his throat in order to convince him that he did! Oh yes, and I drew some blood, too, when he thought I was bluffing! But after that . . . well, after that," her mother had confessed in a softer voice, "everything was quite different!"

I'm *not* going to stay! Laura resolved suddenly. Ena has to learn to fend for herself—I'm either going to Spain to look for *him* or I'm going back home to Mexico or to Monterey—and then *he* can come looking for me! It was strange but somehow, and quite suddenly, she *knew*, intuitively, that it wasn't all over between them—that something had to be settled between them yet, both for him and for her.

"I have made Mademoiselle's bath ready, if Ma'mselle wishes a . . . ?" She hadn't seen or heard Ayesha come in, lost as she was in the tangled confusion of her thoughts.

Laura had never felt awkward about undressing in front

of another woman, or even one of her maids. But when she took off her chemise now, however, and stepped into the round copper tub, for some reason she felt a sense of discomfort as the girl's eyes traveled all over her. She shrugged her momentary feeling off then by telling herself that of course Ayesha was a Moroccan and not used to seeing the naked body of what she considered a white woman—especially not an American woman.

In any case Ayesha was attentive and seemed to take it quite for granted that she was expected to rub the sandalwood-scented soap all over Laura's body before she immersed herself in the water again, making sure that all traces of the soap had been washed off before she held out a towel and proceeded to rub Laura dry very gently.

Ayesha's fingers lingered over Laura's breasts, particularly her nipples, and then between her thighs when she soaped her, as they did now too. But what of it? Laura thought. It meant nothing. At least she felt pampered while she was being patted and stroked dry!

Ayesha spread a fresh towel down across the bed before she produced a bottle of oil, and she asked rather shyly: "Does Mademoiselle like to be massaged with scented oil? It will feel very good, I promise. When I rub in the oil it will disappear beneath the skin to keep it moist, and there will be just the slightest shine left on the skin—the gentlemen think it is most attractive!"

Why not? Laura asked herself with a mental shrug as she lay face down on the towel and let Ayesha's strong and yet gently knowing fingers massage the oil into every pore of her body. Her massaging seemed to dissolve the tenseness that was in her earlier, Laura soon found, as she began to enjoy this new experience. Ayesha stroked the oil into her skin from her heels up to her shoulders and then down her arms before she requested that Laura should please turn around. The oil smelled of jasmine and gardenia mixed together and felt so wonderfully soothing!

Once Laura turned over, the Moroccan girl began again

with the inside of her arms, down to the tips of her fingers, and then from her neck to her shoulders, before moving to stroke, very gently, her breasts, her fingers enclosing each one in turn and moving upward and then around, always barely touching the nipples.

"Mademoiselle has such beautiful little breasts and such pretty crimson nipples that stand up so," she murmured as she gave a little tug to each. "Mademoiselle has such a very beautiful body, so beautiful!"

Laura felt as if she were in some kind of languorous stupor while Ayesha's hands and fingers continued to massage her skillfully and knowingly—all the way down to her stomach and the dark triangle between her legs, then down her legs, up again, very slowly, until she reached her inner thighs and lingered there before her fingers began to stroke and touch her very gently. Then Ayesha took the bottle of oil and poured a little between her thighs, massaging it in with feather-light butterfly-wing touches that skimmed and dipped only a little way into her at first, then further upward.

"Mademoiselle is beautiful everywhere—yes, everywhere," Ayesha whispered as she continued the light stroking motion of her fingers that held Laura almost mesmerized until she suddenly had the strong sense again that *someone* was watching her; looking at her, observing everything that was happening. But there was no one to be seen when she sat up abruptly, fighting to regain control over herself. She had to admit, unwillingly, that Ayesha *had* managed to arouse a certain feeling of rising excitement within her with her subtle and knowing touch.

"Thank you," Laura was able to say at last, in what she hoped was an even voice. "That was . . . very pleasant and it made me feel very relaxed indeed. But now I think I should begin to get dressed for the reception."

Ayesha had a slight smile on her lips—a knowing kind of smile—before she bowed her head and stepped back.

"Of course, mademoiselle. And I will help you dress if you will tell me which one of your so-beautiful gowns you will choose to wear this evening." She added softly, "I'm here to do anything that Mademoiselle might desire me to do for her. It will be my pleasure to please Mademoiselle in every way."

My God, Laura thought as Ayesha began to lay out her clothes for her, moving swiftly and soundlessly about on her bare feet. I wonder what Ena thinks of all this—that is, if *her* maid is as obliging as Ayesha. She wished that Ena would join her soon so that they could talk. At this moment, puzzled and confused by feeling at the mercy of certain strong urges and impulses that seemed to lurk within her, erupting, it seemed, at the slightest provocation, she needed to *talk* to someone; she needed to confide in someone, and she wished that Helena would hurry and finish dressing.

Helena had been almost fully dressed, as a matter of fact, and she, too, had been looking forward to having some private conversation with Laura before they had to leave for the reception, when her husband strolled into her room, already immaculately dressed himself. Ena noticed that he had a flat package in his hand that was all wrapped in silver paper, and wondered as he tossed it onto her dressing table why he had decided, unusually for him, to give her a present.

Fatima, the Moroccan girl Archie had chosen to be Ena's personal maid, fastened the last button on her gown as Archie entered, "Well, sweet wife, how beautiful, how exceptionally lovely you look tonight!" he said in his Oxford accent, that she could never quite get used to. "The little bauble I bought for you today is going to add to your loveliness and will suit you very well indeed, I think."

"Thank you, Archie," Helena turned impatiently to Fatima who insisted on hovering about her. "You can go now, Fatima!"

"But *dearest,*" Archie said, "I am sure you will need Fatima's help again very shortly! As you'll soon realize.'' And then he walked around her, studying her critically in a fashion that made her suddenly uneasy.

"You see, my love," he said critically, "I'm afraid that I don't really like this gown you've chosen to wear tonight. And so you must let *me* pick one out for you. After all, a man should be able to choose his wife's clothes and to decide what she looks her best in, don't you think?"

Before Helena had a chance to protest he turned to Fatima. "Undress your mistress immediately, if you please," he ordered, "while I inspect her wardrobe for a suitable gown of *my* choice. Hurry—we cannot be late on *this* occasion. And—oh yes, of course, we must make sure that my wife's corset and her corset cover match the dress I will pick out for her, so you might as well take those off her, too, while you're about it.''

Fatima had already begun to unfasten the buttons that went up the back of her gown when Helena recovered herself enough to jerk herself away from the girl's fingers. "Archie! I don't know what has got into you, but there's really not enough time for me to change. Besides, I don't see anything wrong with the gown that I am wearing now!''

Her husband had been searching among the gowns that had been neatly hung up in her armoire by Fatima, and now, ignoring her angry protest, he took out a gown of dark, deep-gold brocaded satin overlayered with black lace.

"This is just the right gown for this evening, my dear. I do not care for that blue gown you're wearing. For one thing, it it cut far too low, and I don't want my wife parading herself about in front of my friends and in my club as if she's a whore advertising her wares!''

Stunned, Helena stared at him before stammering, "What are you saying? Archie, I don't understand any of this! And suddenly I find I don't understand *you* either. Ever since I arrived here you've been . . . Well, I've felt as if I don't really *know* you any longer!''

"Certainly not as well as Miss Morgan's virile young brother seems to have known you, eh?" Adding to Ena's nightmarish feeling, he continued softly, and somehow menacingly, "From now on, Helena, you're going to do *exactly* as I say, is that clear? You're going to be a good, obedient little wife, my dear, and I mean to make very sure of that!"

Helena opened her mouth to protest, but she was too shocked to speak. And adding to her shock, Archie suddenly stepped close to her and slapped her across her face—once, and then twice. "Stand still, damn you," he said harshly. "Let Fatima finish undressing you. D'you understand me? Or do I have to make it clearer?" And he raised his hand again in warning.

Helena obeyed mechanically, still too shocked to move or protest. Her face was stinging with the force of his slaps, and involuntary tears started before she began to whimper softly, like a hurt animal. Archie slapped her again, this time making her cry out aloud. After that, she stood there dumbly, her head spinning, locked in a kind of horrified trance. She felt the busy touch of Fatima's fingers as she slipped off her gown, leaving her standing there in a corset cover and taffeta petticoat, while her face flamed with pain and humiliation.

But it was to become even *worse,* as she soon discovered. "Bring my wife the present I bought for her," Archie commanded Fatima who, with a smirk, did as he told her. "Open it!" he told Ena harshly, and when she still seemed unable to move, he struck her again, this time across her breasts. "I think I told you that you will do exactly as I say, didn't I? Now open the gift I've brought you—at once because we don't want to be late for the reception, do we now?" Sobbing, Helena obeyed him.

Horror piled upon horror as Archie explained in careful detail, exactly what it was that he had bought for her, and what it was meant for, while Fatima unlaced her corset, leaving her in nothing but a thin silk chemise.

"It's gold of course," Archie said conversationally with a smile turning down the corners of his thin lips. "It's a chastity belt, my dear! And isn't it quite cunningly contrived? See the tiny gold padlock there. Only *I* will have the key to it once you're safely locked into it. In that way I shall be sure that you remain faithful to me in the future, won't I? Now turn yourself about and let me put it on you—you're going to look quite charming wearing this, I'm sure!"

He laughed cruelly at the expression on her face before he seized one of her silver-backed hairbrushes and smacked her hard across her buttocks, his hand against the back of her neck pushing her down with her face against her dresser while he laughed again at her smothered screams of pain.

"Archie—no! Oh please, no—I can't bear it—I beg of you, don't hurt me, *please,* no!"

"You must admit that you deserve to be punished. I could have done worse to you, remember that, but as it is, you're getting off lightly, and," he added warningly, "if you don't stand still while I fit this clever little contraption on you, I will have Fatima whip you until you will find it most uncomfortable to sit down again for a while. I do hope I make myself clear?"

Unable to stop sobbing with pain and shame and degradation, Helena kept her face hidden in her hands while she felt the thin gold belt being fastened tightly about her waist. Then the small section of fine gold mesh was drawn tightly and painfully between the lips of her vulva, and the two tiny gold chains attached to it were pulled up between her buttocks to be fastened again to her waist belt, then looped around once more so that the padlock rested against that most sensitive little mound just above her sex.

"Oh *God,* Archie!" Ena cried out pleadingly without daring to lift up her head or to move until he told her that she might. "You have drawn it too tight—I can't bear it—it's cutting into me and it hurts so much that I can hardly stand it. I beg of you, Archie, I beg of you, oh please don't do this to me—I'll do anything you say, I promise, I promise I won't do anything wrong ever again! But please, spare me this, *please!*'' She was crying loudly and helplessly and quite uncontrollably now, her whole body shaking with the force of her sobs.

''You may stand up now my sweet, faithless little wife, and walk across the room for me so I can see how well the belt fits you and how it becomes you. Be sure to look at yourself in the mirror before Fatima dresses you again—doesn't it look pretty on you? The gold against the creamy whiteness of your skin? In fact, my dear, I think you might, once you get used to it, even come to enjoy the feeling of knowing that you're wearing it under all your petticoats and your satin and brocade gowns! Why, you might even derive some pleasure from the way the padlock is placed, don't you think? Look how it nestles there just where it can give you the most delicious sensations. You see, I *can* be thoughtful and considerate of your pleasure!''

Still crying, Helena stood up and did as he told her to do. She paraded about the room like a whore in her gold chastity belt, which cut so painfully into her soft sensitive flesh, for the delectation of Archie as well as Fatima, who watched her with a small smile, her large liquid brown eyes lingering on the mesh. And then, almost numb by now, Helena stood obediently still before her mirror while Fatima dressed her again in another corset that was laced extra tightly on Archie's orders, and in the gown that her husband had chosen for her. She didn't know how she was going to bear this, how she was going to face people—to sit, to stand, to walk while she felt *it* between her legs, pressing up against her, paining her almost unbearably.

''And now,'' Archie said jovially, putting one arm about her waist, ''let's go and see if your friend is ready, shall we?''

Laura could sense at once that there was something

different about Ena. There was an almost feverish air about her, a highly tensed nervous quality; and she talked almost too fast, her eyes large and brilliant in her pale face with only spots of high color on her cheekbones. But there was no time to ask questions while Ayesha stood by, looking from one to the other, and while Archie waited outside the door. As she snatched up her lacy wrap, her fan, and her tiny silver-mesh purse, Laura wondered if Archie and Helena had had a quarrel. Ena's eyes *did* look suspiciously red-rimmed! Maybe they would find the time to talk with each other in private after the reception.

Chapter 39

There was definitely something wrong with Helena, Laura thought worriedly as the evening progressed. She had fidgeted, and had kept adjusting the folds of her skirt, and moving about all of the time that they were in the carriage that had conveyed them to the Pall Mall Club, while at the same time she kept twisting her small lace handkerchief between her fingers and pulling at it until it actually tore. And then even *after* they had arrived at the club, Ena continued to act strangely! Why, she seemed hardly able to sit still for more than a few moments in one place before she had to spring to her feet and walk about the room to greet friends in a brittle, *artificial* kind of voice that Laura was not used to in her. She had meant to try and get a chance to talk to her alone, even for a few minutes, but that didn't seem to be possible with Archie hovering closely all the time, asking solicitously if she was quite comfortable in this crowded room, or if the heat was affecting her too much. And then he had said that of course she must get used to it, because he couldn't bear the thought of letting her out of his sight after such a long separation!

Besides being assiduous in his attentions to his wife, Archibald Ayre, the Earl of Sedgewick, was equally considerate of his guest; and with Helena walking beside him he made sure to introduce Laura to all the most eligible young men in the crowded assembly room. Why then, Laura puzzled, did she keep imagining that some-

thing was wrong? Archie had whispered to her that since
Helena was not used to such heat and humidity she had
complained of a headache all afternoon, and he was worried about her, although she had positively insisted that
she could never miss the reception. But there was still
something that was not quite right here, and Laura could
sense it. She had never seen Ena so nervous or so fidgety
before! She studied the Earl covertly from behind the
screen of her long lashes.

He was a man of medium height with a long face and
an equally long nose, and a rather receding chin that he
covered by affecting a sparse, watery-blond beard that
matched his macassared blond hair, receding from his
forehead. It was clear that he appeared to be well liked
by everyone in the room, but somehow, for all of the
charm and gallantry he directed toward her, Laura could
not like him. Perhaps it had something to do with the
thinness of his lips and the way his eyes looked her over
when he thought she wasn't noticing. Having met him at
last, she couldn't understand why Helena had ever agreed
to marry a man she obviously didn't love and was unhappy with—unless, like poor Consuelo Vanderbilt, she
had been locked in her room on a diet of bread and water
with regular beatings by that great brute of a father of
hers to force her into it. But then she also couldn't understand why Ena continued to stay with Archie when
Franco had offered her everything she really wanted.

At that point in her thoughts Major Eagan walked up
to her, and Laura, immediately beginning a lively conversation with him, refused to be introspective any
longer; determined to try and enjoy the evening instead.

Later, when they had returned to the house, Ena still
seemed tense, and Laura was about to ask her whether
she could come in and talk to her for a while when Archie
forestalled her.

"I'm sure you understand, Miss Morgan, that while
you two young ladies have had so much time to spend
together for the past few months, *I* have hardly seen my

wife since a short while after we were married! You can't blame me for wanting to make up for that lost time, can you? It's time we got reacquainted, Ena and I.'' And then with a smiling glance down at Helena's white face, he added, ''Don't you agree, my love? I'm sure Miss Morgan will understand, since this is our first night together after all this time!''

He had begun, holding Ena tightly about the waist, to lead her down the long passageway which led to their suite of rooms, when suddenly, as if a thought had just occurred to him, he stopped, and turned around to Laura.

''By the way, since Major Eagan mentioned to me that you were quite interested in seeing St. Michael's Cavern and the old Spanish Inquisition chamber, I hope you don't mind that I took the liberty of arranging for us all to take a short excursion there the day after tomorrow?'' He added in a casual voice, ''Mr. Forrester might also be able to join us—now that he has seen his sister comfortably ensconced in Lord Dunhill's villa near Cadiz. I hope you will not mind. He told me that you and he are very good friends.''

''Of course . . . yes, of course,'' Laura responded automatically while her mind raced. ''It was most thoughtful of you to arrange such an interesting expedition.'' Reggie here? she thought. What has he done with his sister that he could leave her so soon? But then the thought came as bitter as gall into her mind: Sabina was probably with Trent!

Laura went to her room in a thoughtful mood, and as soon as Ayesha had helped to unhook her gown and corset, she dismissed the girl, refusing her offer of some light refreshments. After tossing and turning restlessly for a while, Laura managed to fall asleep at last, although her sleep was haunted by strange, image-filled dreams. In one of them Trent was making love to her until Sabina came and pulled him away and then they both turned and laughed at her while she lay there waiting and expectant.

In the morning, of course, the shafts of sunlight slanting across her bed and the sound of birds and perfumed puffs of breeze coming in through her opened windows made everything seem different—and *normal*. She had been overtired, and so had Helena no doubt. She must really stop letting her imagination run away with her, Laura told herself firmly as Ayesha brought her breakfast on a patterned brass tray and informed her in her soft voice that the Earl and Countess always took breakfast in their rooms and so did their guests—it was a custom here.

Ayesha said brightly that the Earl had planned to take her and his wife on a tour of the Rock, if Miss Morgan wished it of course. "You will enjoy, I think, the town and the shopping; and there are many, many interesting bazaars and *souks* where they sell lovely caftans and little trinkets which are very different from what the Mademoiselle might find in England."

"I'm not English," Laura explained patiently. "I'm from America and Americans are very different from the English!" Ayesha's eyes widened questioningly. "But I've always loved exploring new places and I'm sure I'll enjoy it," she added with a little laugh. "And don't believe everything you hear about America, please. We're really quite civilized there—at least in *some* places."

"I thought there were wild Indians and people shot guns at each other, and—"

"Oh, it's not as bad as all *that!*" Laura assured her with a smile. "We do have great cities, and railroads, and even electricity and telephones in America—in addition to a great many other things and other sights one can never see in Europe!"

The girl seemed quite fascinated and eager to learn more, but she had other duties to perform, and left reluctantly.

They set out in an open carriage, Helena and Laura carrying silk parasols. Archie acted as their guide, pointing out different places of interest. Laura noticed that Ena's face looked drawn and strained, and that she could not seem to control her nervous fidgeting and the twisting about of her fingers. "Ena dear, do you have a headache? You don't look well. I hope you're not just putting yourself out because of me," Laura questioned as she studied her friend with concern. There *was* something wrong with Helena, she was certain of it!

"Oh no, no! It's not a headache, it's just the heat—I'm not used to it, that's all!"

"But you soon will be, won't you, my love?" Archie said, turning to her with a smile and giving her a squeeze about the waist. "Why, I think I know you well enough to be sure that you are adaptable, and can become used to anything in time, eh?"

"Oh—of course you're quite right, Archie," Helena agreed almost too quickly, before bursting out: "It's just . . . just that I'm not used to . . . to this kind of climate and . . . but I'm sure that in the end I will become used to it, just as you say!"

"But of course you will, my love," Archie said. "Why, I'm quite certain that in time you'll quite *enjoy* it!"

For some reason, Laura thought that the little exchange between husband and wife was somehow weighted with secret significance under the surface words, but she couldn't say anything aloud, of course, although she became more and more concerned for Ena's well-being. She had also not failed to notice that her friend refused to meet her eyes, keeping them lowered to where her fingers continued to twist and turn about each other. Laura wished suddenly that Lady Honoria was here with them. Her blunt forthrightness would clear the air of the tension she could sense between Helena and Archie. Lady H. would get to the bottom of whatever was going on and settle everything! Perhaps I should send her a telegram, Laura thought. It was something to consider since she certainly didn't like seeing Helena look and act this way.

"Perhaps if Ena is feeling the heat . . ." Laura began to suggest, but then Archie said heartily: "Oh nonsense! Ena's been looking forward to shopping in these little *souks*, as they call them here, haven't you, love?" He gave one of her hands a squeeze, and Helena, still not lifting her eyes, nodded dumbly.

Soon they were walking leisurely through the crowded little winding streets that were lined with all kinds of stalls and shops. Archie recommended certain shops where he said they wouldn't cheat one *too* badly. He insisted that he wanted to buy a few silk caftans for his wife since all the ladies here wore these loose flowing garments at home because of the heat.

"And you, Miss Morgan, perhaps you would like to purchase some too? They're fashioned, you know, from silks and brocades and exotic Indian materials, and some of them are very beautifully embroidered."

As they wended their way through the crowded streets and alleyways, Laura noticed again how uncomfortable Ena seemed and how flushed her face had become. She would have suggested that they return to the house if she had not been a guest, and if Archie had not been so insistent that they must see all the sights.

After a while even Laura had to admit to being quite fascinated by the sights and sounds and exotic smells that were all about her—and the colorfully dressed crowds that jostled them as they passed.

On the fringes of the narrow, dusty streets, street vendors hawked their wares—live chickens, bolts of silk, and Chinese embroidered satins—while unfamiliar kinds of foods cooked over braziers on every street corner.

Laura was actually disappointed when Archie decided that he didn't care for the stench of so many people, and escorted them into one after another of the dimly lit little boutiques, as he said they were called here, where rolls of silk, and gold- and silver-encrusted caftans, were held up for their inspection.

In one of the shops, Laura saw an elaborately sequined

belly-dancing costume with row upon row of jingling gold coins on the skirt. "Oh! How beautiful!" She exclaimed. "It reminds me of the one I bought in the Rue du Caire in Paris—do you remember, Ena?" And then, catching herself, she forced a laugh and said to Archie, "You see, belly dancing was all the rage in Paris when I was there last. *I* took lessons although I could never persuade *Ena* to do so."

"Oh, but I think that's too bad," Archie said smoothly. "But then, my wife has never been daring or adventurous, have you, dear?" With a quick look at Ena's white face, he turned back to Laura, saying indulgently, "Will *you* buy it? Perhaps I wouldn't mind if you taught my wife how to do this belly dance! As long as it's in the privacy of our home, of course, and as long as I'm allowed to watch your lessons!"

Sorry she had brought the subject up, Laura said, "Oh no, I couldn't. I'm only a novice myself. Besides, it was just a *novelty* at the time, you know."

"Is that so? Such a shame," Archie said regretfully, but Laura noticed how his eyes flickered over her body for a moment before he turned back to Ena with what she now felt was *false* solicitousness, and asked her if there was anything here or in any other shop they had gone into that she would like.

I can't stand this anymore! Laura thought fiercely. I can't stand to see Ena looking like this, or to see the way she almost winces when he touches her, or holds her too tightly around the waist! He reminds me of a slimy slug with that pale hair of his and that pale complexion of his and the slyly insinuating way he talks and looks at me! She started to fan herself vigorously, and then put her hand to her forehead that was damp with perspiration, before she spoke in a suddenly faint voice:

"Oh . . . dear! I'm afraid that Ena is not the only one to be affected by this heat! Why, I actually feel . . . quite . . . quite *faint* all of a sudden. How silly it is of me, to be sure, but I . . . I—" And then she actually managed to sway slightly before putting her hand out against one of the shelves in the shop as if to support herself. She looked pleadingly up at Archie and whispered in what she hoped was a weak-sounding voice, "Would you mind if we went back to your house? I really don't feel that I am able to go on any longer!"

Her acting put an end to their afternoon shopping excursion, but when they returned to the house, Archie suggested immediately that Laura must go to her room and lie down. He called for Ayesha to bring cold cloths for her forehead and also perhaps a small glass of some stimulant. "A little brandy will do you good," he said, looking at her in a way she still did not quite like. "Do make sure that Ayesha helps you off with the corset that you women seem to insist on wearing, and you'll soon feel much more comfortable, I'm sure."

Laura had no alternative but to go to her room and let Ayesha help her undress down to her chemise, which was damp with perspiration, and then help her to lie down in bed as if she actually was the invalid she had pretended to be.

"It is better not to put the sheet over you, I think," Ayesha said with what seemed to be real concern in her voice. "If you are not used to the sun and to the heat here, sometimes gently brought-up ladies can become affected by it. I have seen this happen to many English ladies—and even if *you* are an American lady," she added quickly, "still you are not used to the climate here." She hurried away to bring Laura a carafe of cool water and the brandy that Archie had promised her.

Laura lay back in bed with her eyes closed, hoping that when Ayesha returned she would think she was asleep and leave her alone again. Think—she *must* think! In spite of Archie's politeness, his expressed concern, and his affectionate manner toward his wife . . . she had the funny feeling that Ena was actually terrified of him! And it was now obvious to her that she would not be allowed to talk with Ena alone—*Archie* would see to that.

Laura also discarded the idea of sending a telegram to Lady Honoria. After all, what could she tell her when all she had to go on were her own feelings? As she was still pondering what to do, there was a sharp knock on her door and she heard Archie's voice asking if he could come in for a moment.

Laura pulled the sheet up over herself before she said in a listless voice, "Yes, but please forgive me—I'm not properly dressed."

"My dear Miss Morgan, as my wife's best friend you mustn't stand on ceremony with me," Archie said as he came in. "And in turn, I feel that I need not stand on ceremony with you."

Laura really didn't like the way he kept looking at her as if he could see through the thin cotton sheet that she held up to her shoulders.

"I came here on my way to my office to ask if there was anything that I could bring back for you from town? Since we have a good doctor here who happens to be the Governor's personal physician, perhaps you would like him to visit you? Or perhaps he can give me a prescription for some headache tablets or a restorative tonic for you? I'd like to make up for this afternoon and my dragging you about in the heat and dust, you know. Do tell me if there's anything at all I can do to take that wan look from your face! Ena would be angry with me if she felt I'd neglected you."

Laura now disliked not only the way he looked her over, but also the slyly insinuating little speech he'd just made with that false look of commiseration on his face! If she could only . . . And then Laura suddenly had a brainstorm. She sat up with the sheet still clutched closely to her, and said in a rather *shy* manner, "Oh, yes! Since you have been so kind as to ask me, what I would really like to be able to do is send off a few telegrams. Is that possible? Is there a telegraph office here?"

"Telegrams?" Archie repeated in a surprised voice, before recovering himself quickly to say with a smile,

"Of course there is a telegraph office here. We are not that backward, Miss Morgan. But *I* could arrange to have your telegrams sent for you. As a matter of fact I think I have some forms in my study. As soon as you're feeling better, you can fill them out and I'll make sure that they're sent off."

He kept looking at her in a questioning way—in a somehow *considering* way, Laura thought with a slight feeling of unease. She sensed that he was playing some strange cat-and-mouse game with her—but then she intended to play *her* role to the hilt.

She dropped her eyes. "Oh, that's kind of you. Most kind!" Then she added a trifle uncertainly: "But . . . would it be too much to ask to send *three* telegrams out at once? And . . . and . . . today?"

"Of course not, my dear Miss Morgan, no bother at all, I assure you. And since I have some slight, shall we say, influence here as Lieutenant-Governor, I can certainly make sure that they're dispatched immediately." He added, as if he had suddenly been struck with an idea, "In fact, why don't I bring those forms to you right away—no, no, please don't protest, for it's no bother at all, I tell you! And let *me* fill them out for you and take them with me right now. How's that, eh?"

Stalemate? Laura wondered, but she wasn't beaten yet! "That would be wonderful, if you *really* wouldn't mind?" While he was gone she would have enough time to think of exactly how to word her telegrams, she decided—knowing now for certain that she didn't trust Archie any more than *he* trusted her.

When the Earl returned, he pulled up a chair close to the bed, and resting a notepad with the telegraph forms on his knee, he smiled at her indulgently. "Well? So now you have the Lieutenant-Governor of Gibraltar as your secretary, Miss Morgan—and I can write quite fast when I have to! Please give me your messages and the names and addresses of the lucky persons to whom they are being sent."

With every appearance of being overwhelmed with gratitude, Laura dictated her three telegrams. The one to her mother and father was in care of her uncle Renaldo, who would know where they were, and would get word to them at once.

"Dearest Mama and Papa, I'm in Gibraltar now but need you desperately at the wedding. You must leave at once or I will be devastated."

"Your parents?" Archie said, studying her searchingly. "They are in *Mexico*? It's rather a long way, isn't it?"

"Oh no, not from Vera Cruz. The Hacienda—one of the family estates, you know—is close to Vera Cruz, and I do so want them here in time, for Mama *must* help me in choosing a gown and that kind of thing!" Laura's voice sounded ingenuous, and the Earl nodded understandingly.

"Well, of course, naturally you would want your parents at your wedding, although I thought—" And then he cut himself off, saying quickly, "And now, the next one?"

The next message was short and was to be sent to her uncle Pierre telling him that she was holidaying in Gibraltar with the Earl and Countess of Sedgewick and wished he could be here to see how beautiful it was. But the next after that . . .

Under Archie's quizzical and rather impatient look Laura bit her lip and looked down for a moment before saying softly, "I'm afraid this particular telegram is . . . is very *personal*, you might say, and I confess that I'm embarrassed." She glanced up at him just in time to catch the slight narrowing of his cold eyes before he put on an avuncular air and assured her that she need not feel in the least embarrassed and he would never tell a soul about anything she wished to say in her telegram; that he would, in fact, forget all about it once he had sent it off. She had his word on it.

"Well . . ." Laura began hesitantly, *"this* one is to

. . . to *Royse.*'' She dropped her eyes again to look down
at her clasped hands. ''We quarreled rather *fiercely,* you
see, and he was so very angry afterward that he decided
to disembark at Cadiz! But oh, I *do* want to make up
with him now and tell him how very sorry I am to have
provoked him! You *do* understand, don't you? When people are in love they tend to be very edgy with each other,
I suppose! I know that now, and . . . and I want *him* to
know it too!'' She glanced at Archie, her hands still
clasped tightly together in her lap. ''You don't think I'm
being too forward, do you? I know it's the man who is
supposed to apologize, but oh, I do miss him so!''

She had caught him off guard, Laura could see that;
for he didn't seem to know what to say at first. And then
he shook his head and gave a short laugh. ''My dear Miss
Morgan, I'm flattered that you should entrust me with
your confidence when we've only just met, but I really
don't know what to tell you. After all, this is a matter
for the two of you. But if you feel that *you* were the one
at fault, then you must follow the dictates of your own
conscience.'' His eyes narrowed slightly before he asked,
''But do you know exactly where he can be reached at
this time? If you do not have an address for him, then
I'm afraid it wouldn't be possible—''

''Oh, but I do know!'' Laura said quickly. ''He will
be staying with Lord Dunhill at his villa in Cadiz; and if
he's not there, I am positive that he can be reached
through the Prince of Wales or someone else aboard the
Britannia, because I understood that H.R.H. intended to
spend a few days in Cadiz himself, and that *he* might
also be at Lord Dunhill's villa. Oh, please do try for me!
Please do, you don't know how *important* this is for me!''

''You women!'' Archie said, before continuing rather
grudgingly. ''Very well, then, I'll see what I can do, I
promise you. But please try not to make your message
too long, Miss Morgan!''

''Trent, my very dearest darling, forgive me! I'm so
sorry that we quarreled. I do truly love you. Please,

please come to me here on Gibraltar at once, for I need to see you so very badly. Always, your Laura.''

Trent would see through that gushing message, she knew. Even if he didn't care about her, she was sure he'd come even if it was just to find out what was wrong, and even if it was only because she was Franco's sister. Now she could only hope that Archie would actually have the telegram dispatched. He'd been reading it over with his eyebrows raised. He looked up, folding the piece of paper and putting it in his breast pocket, and then he rose to his feet. She could read nothing in his face even while she thanked him effusively.

The Earl of Sedgewick was thoughtful as he climbed into his carriage. He didn't know what to make of that last telegram with all its expressions of endearment and love. Perhaps, he thought meanly, Miss Morgan didn't want to lose her chance of becoming the Duchess of Royse after all. A typical rich American bitch, she was—and the arrogant type he hated. He frowned thoughtfully to himself as he wondered whether he *would* send that particular cable or not. After all, he was expecting his old friend Reggie Forrester here this evening and Reggie was expecting to enjoy Miss Morgan's company exclusively. So, still frowning, he pulled out the cable and read through it again while he tried to decide. And then he thought, Oh damnation! She had mentioned the Prince of Wales, and he mustn't forget that they were acquaintances, or that he had been told that the Prince had shown a decided *tendresse* for the bitch.

Archie leaned back against the carriage seat and gave a little smile as a sudden thought struck him. Yes! Yes, why not? Perhaps it would all work out for the best in the end, for all concerned. Either Royse would receive the cable or he wouldn't; and if he *did*, and if he was fool enough to be taken in by those lying love words after his fiancée had been with Reggie Forrester right under his nose . . . . what if he found her again with Reggie? Well, well! Then *that* would no doubt be the end of that!

After Royse walked away in disgust, as any real man would do, then Reggie could have his American heiress *and* her millions. The more Archie thought about it, the better it sounded!

Chapter 40

Sabina, Lady Westbridge, was almost beside herself with the anger and frustration that she had to keep hidden under the eyes of Lord Dunhill and the rest of his guests. Things had seemed to go so well and so smoothly at first, just as Reggie had predicted; but then, quite abruptly, Reggie had suddenly remembered some urgent business he had to take care of in Gibraltar of all places, and had left her with instructions to be sure and let that "certain bit of information" drop when she was next with Royse.

Well, it hadn't worked out, and she didn't know why. She had spent the whole evening chattering and laughing and flirting with Lord Dunhill, who had whispered to her later that he'd like very much to ask her to his room, but it couldn't be tonight, because he was far too weary and needed his sleep, although he had added that he was sure he could manage to make her happy on the following night! She had been relieved at the time, sure that Royse would come to her, especially because she'd whispered to him pointedly that she had something *very* interesting to tell him later when they were alone.

Sabina paced furiously up and down her room now, hands clenched at her sides. Oh, goddamn him, goddamn him, the bastard! She recalled with almost unbearable clarity everything that had happened and had *not* happened.

She'd waited up half the night for him, and he had strolled in very late when she was almost ready to fall asleep, reeking of alcohol and tobacco. His shadowed, dark-bearded face had seemed harsh and unfriendly in the flickering flame of a small oil lamp, a cruel look that seemed to be reflected in his eyes, making them turn red like the eyes of a great cat or some other fierce predatory beast.

"Sweet, sweet Sabina! Here you are—waiting as usual! I did not keep you too long, I hope, you pretty obliging little thing?" She gave a small gasp as he put out a hand and his fingers ripped open her thin silk nightgown. "So here *you* are," he murmured as if half to himself, "and here *I* am! I suppose we might as well do something about that, don't you agree?"

She hadn't liked either the strange tone of his voice or his words, but before she had time to say anything he sat on the side of her bed with his linen shirt open down to the waist and began to caress her familiarly before he stilled her excited murmurs with his mouth and mounted her.

In the hot daytime sunlight that now slashed into her room, her cheeks began to burn at the memory of her own abandoned response to the way he had used her. He had made her want him so much that even when he finally decided to take her without completely undressing, she hadn't protested—no, she had only begged him to do it to her over and over again. And when he had finished with her he rolled the long length of his body away from hers and pulled his pants back up, coming to his feet a moment later, and looking down at her, his face giving away nothing.

"And now—why don't you tell me what interesting piece of information you were so eager to give me before?" he growled.

For several seconds, she had been speechless with shock and a sense of shame, but when she saw him turn to leave her with an indifferent shrug, she sat up in bed and almost hissed at him in a voice filled with everything he had made her feel and shaky with the desire to hurt him.

"For a few moments there you almost made me forget what it was. But I *do* think you ought to know that my brother, when he left so soon after he had arrived yesterday, went straight to *your* Miss Morgan! I suppose they had made some kind of arrangement for a rendezvous while she's still in Gibraltar. What do you think of *that*, Royse? She's still your fiancée, isn't she?" She laughed almost hysterically before saying viciously, "It's obvious, don't you think, that she seems to prefer Reggie's performance in bed to yours? And he of course was quite impressed with hers! I suppose you trained her well!"

He seemed frozen in place as he looked down at her, his face unreadable; and then to her shocked surprise he merely gave another casual shrug of his shoulders as if what she had just flung at him didn't matter in the least.

"This is what you had to tell me?" he said in a cold, expressionless tone of voice. "I don't know why you dislike Laura so, Sabina, especially since she and you seem to have so much in common in your ways of yielding to any man that might come along." And with that, he left her, closing the door behind him with a final thud.

This morning, by the time she went down to breakfast, he had gone out riding, and her subtle questioning of one of the maids had elicited nothing. And when he had returned earlier this afternoon, he had left almost immediately again without a word to her!

Lord Dunhill had told her regretfully that Royse had received a telegram and had some business to take care of that was quite urgent. "I don't expect him back for some days and I don't know if we'll still be here then, although of course I told him that my villa was at his disposal. I like Royse, you know, he's a good fellow for all that he's American born."

So he'd gone—God knew where! She had lost him, Sabina thought—that was, if she ever had had him in the first place!

* * *

Trent Challenger, also known as the Duke of Royse,
was in a violent and almost dangerous mood by the time
he strode into the small villa where he had met Franco
earlier only to find Franco packing.

"Trent! What the hell are you doing here? I thought we
were supposed to meet—"

"I want you to tell me what in the hell *this* means,"
Trent almost snarled as he flung a piece of yellow paper
on the table.

"Your sister, according to Lady Westbridge, is anxiously awaiting the arrival of Reggie Forrester in Gibraltar—so perhaps you can tell me, since you're her brother,
why in hell she would have sent this to me." His fingers
jabbed at the telegram as he stared with icy eyes at Franco's amazed face.

Franco was in none too good a mood himself and so he
retorted just as angrily as he snatched up the offending
telegram. "How in the hell can I tell you anything unless
you give me a chance to *read* the damned thing?"

"Read it then! And tell me if that sounds like your
sister—because you must know her better than *I* do!"

Franco was frowning as he studied the cable. Then he
looked up with a shrug that covered his sudden feeling of
unease.

"I don't know what it means," he said slowly. "It just
might be that she means every word of this because—
damn it, Trent, I don't care if you glare at me with those
icy eyes of yours—but she *does* love you, you know. From
what I can gather, whatever she did, unforgivable or not,
was only out of spite because she went to your hotel room
in Cowes and saw you in bed with Sabina!"

"She did *what?*" Trent's face was granite-hard as his
eyes looked narrowly into Franco's. And then he said suddenly, "Why in hell didn't she talk to me about it? Why
didn't she confront me as any normal woman would have
done! And that is no excuse for what *she* did anyway! And
you know that damn well, Franco Morgan. She—"

"Oh hell, Trent!" Franco said disgustedly. "Come on,

you know as well as I do that my sister is no *normal* woman—unfortunately for us all perhaps!''

He glanced again at the offending telegram before looking up to add: ''You know, I'm not saying these aren't Laura's sentiments because I think they *are,* but . . . it's not her *way* of expressing them. I mean that Laura would most likely have done something impulsive—like catching the next boat to Cadiz to catch up with *you!''*

He met Trent's eyes as the same thought flashed into both their minds. ''Christ, Trent! If she says you must come *at once,* it might be a signal of some kind! If I were you,'' Franco added hastily, seeing the look on Trent's face at that moment, ''I wouldn't believe anything that little lying slut Sabina might have told you, because I happen to know that she's completely under Reggie's thumb and God knows what Forrester has up his sleeve.''

They looked at each other, eye to eye over the small wooden table for a few moments before Trent at last said sardonically, ''That was quite a speech, my friend!''

''Laura's my sister, damn it, even if we've had our disagreements and our quarrels! And *I* am going to find out what the hell's going on, whether you want to come along or not.''

''Who says I don't?'' Trent said in a deceptively mild voice, although his eyes stayed cold and hard, and the muscles tightened along his clenched jaw. He could sense that Franco's temper was ready to erupt just as his was, and he tried to keep his voice controlled.

''If we rode hard or hired a *diligencia* with fast horses, we could reach Algeciras before nightfall,'' Trent said. ''Then we could hire a fast launch to get us to Gibraltar— a smuggler's boat would be best, I think, and I know of a few.''

Laura . . . the little bitch! Why hadn't he been able to get her out of his mind? Why did her face, the memory of her in his arms, the feel of her skin, of her body yielding to him, have to keep on haunting him? And why had he at first felt a leaping of his pulses when he tore open that telegram from her and read it—before he realized that she probably didn't mean any of it. But in any case, Trent thought grimly, he was going to find out once and for all this time. He would either get her out of his system forever or get her back and *keep* her forever!

Trent hefted the portmanteau which was all he had brought with him onto his shoulder, before he said to Franco, "Well, are you coming?"

Franco eyed Trent, suddenly realizing that he had meant to go to Gibraltar after Laura all along in spite of his anger and his bitterness. He stuffed two pairs of pants, a couple of shirts, and a jacket into a smaller bag. "What are you taking with you?" Franco asked in a deliberately casual voice. "You'd better give me some idea, so I'll know wnat else to take along."

"The essentials, naturally," Trent said, his voice hardening into ice. "A bowie knife, two Colt revolvers, and moccasins. And I advise you to do the same—just in case." He was out for blood, and he knew it, Trent realized. And at this moment, he didn't care *whose* blood he spilled, Reggie Forrester's, Sedgewick's, or even Laura's for that matter, if he found out that she had been stringing him along!

Laura herself, at the same moment, was lying in her bed in a deep dreamless sleep. Earlier, after Archie had left, she had tried to see Ena but when she went toward her rooms she found Fatima, the buxom maid that she didn't like, barring her way.

"I am so sorry, miss," the woman had said, "but the Earl has given orders that the Countess is on no account to be disturbed. She's sleeping after she took some of the medicine that the doctor sent for her. Please, miss, it's best that you go back to your own room and sleep too. Ayesha will bring you tea—mint tea is very good for heat stroke, you know." And not wanting to press the issue. or to make things worse for Ena, Laura had walked away and back to her room, even more puzzled, and almost afraid. Ena was being kept a prisoner—it was more than obvious to her now. But *she* was not Archie's wife. No one could keep *her* from leaving this house if she wanted to, or from going somewhere, anywhere where she might get help for Ena! She realized how silly her story would sound to anyone, but perhaps . . . perhaps that nice Major Eagan might listen to her.

Ayesha had come in then, carrying an enormous tray with a slim-necked bottle of mint tea and a tiny silver cup without handles as well as a huge amount of tempting Moroccan delicacies.

"Surely the American Mademoiselle is not going out in the heat of the sun, and by *herself?*" Ayesha said, distressed. "It's not good for white-skinned ladies, our sun here! And the Mademoiselle surely felt ill from its effects this morning! Please do try some food—all Moroccan food, very good; and some mint tea, yes? And then I must fill the bath—it will make you feel better, I'm sure."

"But I am feeling better—*much* better," Laura said stubbornly, "and I want to go out to the nearest telegraph office. There's one telegram that I have to send that I forgot about earlier."

"But mademoiselle, there is no carriage here now," Ayesha told her in a soft voice, "And you cannot walk out for such a long distance in the sun—ladies do not *walk* here."

"I am used to doing whatever I want, I'm afraid, Ayesha, even though it may not seem respectable or wise to other people! So if you would please bring me that white foulard gown of mine and my walking shoes, and—no corsets, please, for I'm tired of corsets. I'm sure if you give me directions I can find my way."

Ayesha looked frightened and she lowered her voice to almost a whisper before she said pleadingly, "Please, Mademoiselle! He will be angry with me—very angry if something were to happen and if he knew that I had helped you to leave on such a hot day! The Milor' said that you would be going this evening to see the cave—please wait until then!"

Laura hadn't understood then—as she would later. It was only to please Ayesha that she drank her mint tea in the end, and another glass of brandy from the Earl's cellar that was to give her strength to face the sun. She was still determined to go out, though—as soon as Ayesha left her.

Laura had decided, after all, to send a cable to Lady Honoria on the chance, she hoped fervently, that she was still at Baden-Baden and could be reached there. But while she was planning what to say, she felt, all of a sudden, the room start to spin about her, dizzying her, so that she fell back across the bed and across the pillows wondering what was happening to her before everything turned as pitch-black as night and she was slipping down and down and down into a dark, endless tunnel.

As she lay there, oblivious to everything, sprawled across the bed with her chemise and her petticoat removed, Laura could not feel the eyes on her nor hear their voices either.

"Well, there she is, my friend. Yours for the taking!" Archie chuckled as he looked sideways at Reggie who could not seem to take his eyes off Laura's body. "And I can guarantee you that for at least an hour she will not know anything, nor realize what is happening to her. The drug that Fatima put in her tea is absolutely tasteless, of course, but very powerful!" And then he added, his lips thinning, "I hope you're generous enough to give *me* a chance at her as well! 'Fair exchange,' eh, old man? I've wanted the little bitch ever since I've been watching her through the holes I had drilled through the fretwork in the ceilings of her room. Tell me, is she good?"

"Oh, good enough, I suppose!" Reggie lied as he walked over to the bed and looked down at her—at her limp, outstretched abandonment.

"Is everything arranged for later on?" he asked.

"Of course," Archie said impatiently. "I told you that earlier, didn't I?" He gave a short, ugly laugh. "And don't forget Fatima. She's Ena's maid, and she's been a big help to me. I am sure she will enjoy helping you to tame your

Miss Laura—and suggest the quickest ways of doing so too! Fatima knows ways of hurting a woman that only another woman would know. But then—that you'll find out soon enough, I'm sure.''

"Archie, old man," Reggie laughed, "I must say that you are a true friend! And I promise you that you'll have your chance at her as soon as *I've* done with her the first time."

While Laura was still in a deep, drugged slumber, still quite unaware of anything happening around her, Reggie took her first—everywhere and in any way he pleased without resistance.

By this time Archie had ordered Helena to be brought in to witness what was happening to her friend—her lover's sister. Helena started sobbing hysterically, almost screaming out protests until Archie, poised over Laura's still body, said to Reggie, "Oh, go on! You might as well have the bitch while I have yours."

"No!" Helena cried out wildly. "Oh please, no!"

She felt Fatima twist her manacled wrists cruelly behind her, pushing her downward before she sank in a sobbing heap to the floor and then she felt Reggie unlock the chastity belt, mount her and shove himself up into her painfully. She was living a nightmare, she thought feverishly, feeling the pain of his thrusting and of his fingers on her nipples, the palms of his hands slapping at her sides as if she had been a mare. And in the meantime Archie was using Laura, and moving her this way and that—probing into her as Reggie had done before turning her over to enter her again in a different fashion.

By now Laura had started to moan and was trying to thrash about although Archie held her down firmly. When he had finished, he said over his shoulder to Reggie, "When you've done, old chap, and before she comes around all together, I suggest we all adjourn to *our* bedroom—what do you say to that, Ena? We can keep her secured there as I keep my wife when I'm not in the mood for her and then you can do anything else you want." He laughed. "Fatima knows how to use a whip very well, doesn't she, dear wife; and just where it does the most good too!"

For a while, after the drug had started to wear off slightly, Laura had imagined that she was having a nightmare, a terrible painful nightmare, and tried to wake herself up out of it—but didn't seem to be able to for some reason. And when she did wake she was still in the same nightmare and experiencing the same horror and the same pain. She couldn't escape, she couldn't, for some reason—and then she realized that her arms were chained above her head to hooks in the ceiling and that her ankles were similarly chained to rings set into the floor. And she saw Helena before her on her hands and knees and realized the pain and degradation Ena had been made to suffer. Then she was being *used,* as Helena was being used, by all of them and she couldn't prevent it! There was Reggie, and Archie, and Fatima, and even one of the menservants that Archie had summoned for her further humiliation. Fatima began to whip her, viciously—whipped her and hurt her everywhere—across her breasts, and her buttocks, and even between her open thighs until she screamed and screamed again, over and over, and could not stop screaming, before she began to beg for a cessation of this torture, and to promise anything, anything at all, if they would spare her any more pain.

"D'you hear that, Reggie old boy?" Archie said. "Why, she's getting almost as tame as Ena, don't you think? Did you hear what she promised? She would do anything, anything, she said, and isn't that nice, eh? Isn't that so *wise* of our little heiress!"

"Very obliging of her!" Reggie chuckled.

"Stand up, wife!" Archie suddenly ordered. "Stand up! I want Miss Laura to see what a well-trained bitch I've made of you in just two days!" Ena pushed herself up painfully until she was able to stand, still crying bitterly.

"And now," Archie said, smiling as he caught her by her hair, "and now, my little bitch, you can get on your knees again and crawl to your friend—do you understand what I mean? You will do the same with her as I've made you do with Fatima! I'm sure that after all she has been through, your little friend will enjoy some tenderness, don't you?''

"Oh no! Please Archie no, not that, not that!" Archie yanked her head back by her hair and slapped her viciously, before almost dragging her forward. Reggie began to chuckle again, enjoying everything that was going on, above all enjoying the fact that Laura was now his. Yes, yes, *his* bitch!

Laura only vaguely remembered what happened after that. She knew that after the final degradation, she had been released and had been allowed to collapse onto the floor, sobbing and writhing with pain. And she remembered promising anything—even to sign the papers that Reggie said she must sign, making her his wife and making her fortune his.

They had made her drink a great deal of brandy before she was taken to a small stone-walled, red-tiled cottage, where an old man asked her questions which she answered mechanically. Her wrists were kept tightly secured behind her back under the long cloak that she wore all buttoned up, with nothing underneath. She was thankful for the cloak with its hood that partially obscured her tear-stained face and her red-rimmed eyes and her swollen lower lip that she had bitten almost through in her agony.

Reggie, his arm around her, held her upright, as she could not help swaying against him, half fainting by now. As he led her outside she heard him say from what seemed like a distance away, "And now I shall keep my promise to you. We shall visit St. Michael's Cavern and see the Inquisition Chamber. You had better remember to behave yourself and to stay silent. You understand by now, don't you, my dear?" He slapped her lightly across her face, which was still swollen and burning with the force of his previous slaps, and she nodded dumbly.

Archie, she understood dimly, was returning to his

house and to poor Ena. After the visit to the cavern, Reggie had told her with a smile on his face, why, he had ordered a boat that would take them to Tangier and to the villa that he had rented there for their honeymoon. At this she began to sob again quite helplessly. He struck her again then, hurting her and hurting her until she begged him in a choked voice to stop—please, please, to stop; she'd be good, she promised, she'd be very good.

"I hope you will be, sweet Laura," he said, his fingers pinching one tender nipple painfully, "or you know what will happen, don't you?" And she nodded again, and let him lead her out into the small carriage he had waiting for them. By now she was almost beyond caring, beyond anything. All she could think of was avoiding more pain and punishment.

But one part of her mind wondered and *hoped*, before she thought dully, Of course he'll never come, of course he wouldn't—even if that telegram had been sent off. No, and now it's too late—I'm married to Reggie. There's no hope, no hope, she kept repeating in her mind; and she wanted to cry but was afraid to, in case she made Reggie angry again. This is the end, her mind told her—this is the end of *me*, the old carefree Laura Morgan, so sure of herself, so unafraid of everything or anyone. This is the end of the person I once was! God knows what I've become *now*, and what I will be made into later. With a kind of numbness creeping over her, Laura felt as if she had no feeling left in her, not even enough to make her care anymore what happened next. She'd never longed and prayed for death before—but now she did.

Chapter 41

The Earl of Sedgewick had just returned to his home after being witness at a marriage ceremony, and seeing Reggie and his half-dazed bride off to visit the caves. And now, he was planning to retire to his rooms and go to his hysterical wife, whom he had left under the care of his faithful Fatima, so that he could have some more sport with her. But when he was almost at the door to his rooms he heard a thunderous knocking at the front door and turned around, frowning with annoyance. Damn, he thought, who could that be, at this particular time of night? He was in no mood to receive visitors when there was his sweet little wife awaiting his pleasure. Whoever it was, and whatever they wanted, they could bloody well wait until tomorrow, he thought, calling to one of his servants to say that he had retired for the night and could not be disturbed.

The servant, Achmed, had barely time to unbolt the door before it was all but kicked open and one of the tallest and most dangerous-looking men he had ever set eyes on strode in. When he caught sight of the man's eyes, Achmed almost blanched and fell back a few steps, muttering a prayer to himself. He had never seen such eyes before! This one, whoever he was, was surely the devil himself in disguise, for all that his voice sounded soft enough and polite enough at first.

"You may tell your master the Earl of Sedgewick that

the Duke of Royse is calling on him and that I intend to see him. Do you think you can remember that?''

No, Achmed decided, he did not like the soft-voiced stranger nor the knife blade he sensed under his voice! This was the kind of man one would not wish to encounter on a dark street on a dark night and, indeed, the kind one would do well to keep his distance from at any time, anywhere. And then there was another gentleman just as angry and evil looking as the first who walked in just behind this man who called himself a Duke but did not look like one! Achmed backed off a few more steps, his eyes wide with fear. He did not like any of it, and he did not feel that he wanted to stand in their path either.

Trent snarled through his teeth, terrifying Achmed even further. "I don't want to hear any excuses, understand? Now you go and get your master or I'm going to find him. I hope *you* find him before I do.''

"Yes, oh yes! Yes, sir! My Lord Duke—I will go at once, of course! Please to wait! I'm going!'' He looked back over his shoulder as he scurried along the long passageway, saying, ''You see, you see, sir? I'm going!'' And then the man was halted in his tracks by that same voice— that voice that he already feared for some reason.

"Before you rouse the Earl of Sedgewick, I want to know where Miss Morgan is. *My* fiancée, and *this* gentleman's sister. And I want an answer right *now,* you understand, or I might have to use some persuasion on you to make you tell me. Well?''

The gray-steel eyes drew Achmed back like magnets dragging at his unwilling feet. He began to stammer, not knowing *what* to say or how much to say. He had not been forewarned that something like this could happen! Or that men such as these would come in search of the woman who had been there.

"But I am sorry, sirs, this I do not know! I am only a poor servant of this household and I know nothing except for what I am told. There *was* a young lady here, I think, although I did not see her more than once or twice, and then only at a distance, but tonight I was told by one of the other servants that another English gentleman had come, and that he and the young lady were to be married this very night. I swear that is all I know except that I *think* I saw them leave in my master's carriage, and that my master went with them, and then he came back alone and went to his room to rest, he said. And I was told not to allow any visitors into the house.''

''Well,'' Trent drawled in a particularly dangerous kind of voice, ''but you didn't *allow* us into the house, did you? We let ourselves in, my friend and I! And now—and *now,*'' he repeated, ''you had better go and find your master and tell him to come out here. At *once*—tell him!''

Franco, already furious with rage, found himself amazed at the self-control that Trent displayed. ''I don't believe a word of that man's story!'' His voice barely hid his anger. ''Laura wouldn't have—Christ, I think I know her a *little* better than *that,* for all the escapades she has got herself into! And I feel—no, I *know* goddamn well that they're hiding something—that there's something very wrong going on here involving Laura. By God, I feel like . . . !''

Trent turned to look at him with those ice-cold eyes of his, and that hard look on his face that Franco recognized all too well. ''You had better learn, Franco my friend, that if you can keep your rage hidden at times like this, you'll have the advantage—until the time is right to let it explode! Whether we like it or not, we'd do better to wait until Sedgewick comes out to meet us, and to hear what he has to say. After that . . . .'' His eyes became slivers of glass.

''Damn it, Trent! Laura's my *sister* and I've a right to know what's happened to her!''

''And goddamn it,'' Trent snarled in a voice that Franco could hardly recognize, ''if you lose your temper we might *never* find out! Don't your understand that? Laura may be your sister; but she's also *my* woman! The woman I *love!* Try to understand *that* too!'' And then he turned away as they heard a door open and close somewhere and footsteps coming down the long passageway.

Archie had been angry when Achmed first burst into his room without even the courtesy of a knock. It took him some minutes to make sense of what his manservant was babbling about; and then he swore angrily.

"You may show the two gentlemen into my study and tell them that I will be with them shortly. Don't, on any account, answer any other questions they might ask you, is that clear?"

"Oh yes, yes, Milor', yes! I know nothing, nothing at all," the man stuttered.

When Achmed left the room, Archie turned to Fatima and said curtly: "Look after her and keep her ready for my return. You may whip her a few times if her sobbing gets too loud." He looked over at Helena, smiling as he began to dress, enjoying seeing her completely subjugated and at his mercy. "So, Royse has come looking for Laura, has he? I suppose he won't like what I have to tell him. Although he'll believe it when I show him the marriage certificate! And then, just fancy, my love, *your* lover is here too. What do you imagine *he'd* think or say if I showed you to him just as you are *now*? Do you think he'd still want you now that I have marked you as my property? Shall I show him how well you can service Fatima, or shall I have him inspect the chastity belt you wear to keep you my property?"

Helena could only sob dryly, her chest heaving with the effort and her throat sore and raw from screaming. She could only look at him dumbly, without daring to answer in case she said the wrong thing. She was on her hands and knees with Fatima standing behind her, that hateful whip in her hand; its lash that could sting so painfully now stroking her between her quivering thighs and buttocks. Helena knew that she would not dare to move from the position she had been told to stay in, not until she was told she could. And, oh God, she could never bear to think of Franco seeing her like this!

Archie was buttoning his jacket as he gave her another

satirical smile. "I'll be sure to tell you what they say, my dear wife; and what *I* say to them!"

They had been shown into the paneled study by Achmed and offered brandy, port, and cigars, which they had refused. Achmed left with a look of relief on his face because he had escaped being slaughtered, or worse. At last, Archie Ayre, the Earl of Sedgewick, walked in, full of apologies.

"Royse! And—Mr. Morgan! Well! I say, if I had known that I should expect you, I should certainly not have decided to retire quite so early." He added deprecatingly, with a sidewise glance at Franco's face, "My wife has a rather delicate constitution, you know. The climate here does not seem to agree with her and so I try to stay with her as much as possible because I feel quite guilty for having *neglected* her for so long a period of time, as she has reminded me *far* too often already! After all, what man can resist the tempting picture of his own eager little wife waiting for him in his bed?"

At *that* point, Franco, who was afraid that his fury would burst its bounds at any moment, rose abruptly to his feet and said stiffly: "If you don't mind, sir, I would rather go outside into the coolness of the garden and smoke a cigar, since Royse has private matters to discuss with you."

And that left the two of them alone. Royse had risen to his feet when Archie entered the room, and he had not deigned to sit down again, even when entreated to do so. It rather intimidated the Earl to have to look *up* at Royse who stood some distance away from him, with long legs apart and his hands behind his back as he studied his host.

"A cigar for you? I'm sorry Mr. Morgan left us. I understand that both he and his sister have been good friends to my wife. Will you have some brandy perhaps? Port?" Archie turned away to pour himself a glass of brandy, only to find that his fingers trembled slightly. It was damned unnerving, he thought, to talk into that cold silence. Why didn't Royse *say* something, for God's sake?

He said aloud, moistening his lips: "Well—I suppose this *is* a rather awkward situation, eh? And I really don't know what to say, old chap! You must really try to understand *my* position."

"*Your* position? Ah yes, of course." Royse spoke in a peculiar kind of voice that Archie did not like at all. "Yes, please do, by all means, *explain* your 'position,' Sedgewick 'old chap'; and I hope you will hurry up with it because I don't care for beating around the bush, if you get my meaning?"

This time Archie found himself almost stammering as he tried to explain. "Well . . . well, I had *assumed,* that is . . . that is, I *thought* . . . but I suppose you are here because of that telegram Miss Morgan insisted I send to you? You must try to understand how very awkward this is for me; that is, to have to try and explain . . . er . . . well . . . if I had known . . . but then what *was* I to say when she begged me to send off her telegram, only having told me at the time that she had quarreled with you and wanted to patch things up?"

Archie was starting to recover some of his aplomb now and poured more brandy for himself without even realizing what he was doing. He looked into Royse's cold, rock-hard face that gave nothing away, and added hurriedly: "Believe me, Royse, I didn't know it was all a *joke!* Until Forrester turned up here and she greeted him with open arms! And *then* she confessed at last that they had arranged it all beforehand, and that she'd only wanted you here to envy their happiness! In fact, they insisted upon being married this very night, and would hear no arguments against it, so I took them to a Registrar and paid him to speed things up—forget some of the usual delays and formalities, you know? I have to confess that I even agreed to be one of the witnesses, but after all, what else could I do? They were determined upon it anyway, and I thought I'd make sure that it was all legal. I believed I was doing it all for the best, you understand!"

All the time Ayre was speaking, Royse had not said a

single word—had just continued to stare at him, and *through* him, with those ice-gray eyes of his. But now, as Archie finished his speech and his voice faltered away lamely, Royse finally spoke, evenly, but with something else running deathly cold under the surface of his voice that made Archie suddenly afraid.

"No, Sedgewick, I'm afraid I *don't* understand. I hope you will go into much more detail so that I might. As, for instance, why you should witness Laura's marriage to your friend Forrester, and arrange to expedite it, too, so soon after *you* had sent me a telegram from *her* begging me to come to her immediately? For your own sake, Sedgewick, you'd best not take me for the kind of fool you're used to dealing with!" The sudden note of violence that tinged that voice made Archie falter back a step.

He attempted to bluster. "Why look here, Royse! I really feel that I have been more than patient with you, and that I've given you all of the facts already! I can even show you their marriage certificate, if you don't believe me—I have a copy of it right here in my desk, as a matter of fact. I was asked to keep it safe until they returned from their honeymoon." Archie was reaching in his desk drawer where he kept a gun in case of intruders, when he froze with his hand still outstretched to open it.

"If I were you, Sedgewick, I wouldn't reach for your gun. I rather doubt your little toy can match up to a Colt .45 revolver."

Archie couldn't move or speak for some moments after that. Royse had been wearing the usual gentleman's black frock coat, but suddenly, in what seemed like a lightning-swift blur of movement, he drew a gun from under it—a long-muzzled, deadly-looking weapon that the Earl of Sedgewick had only *heard* about before from stories about the "Wild West."

"Used to be a gunslinger, as *we* call it, not that long ago," Trent Challenger drawled, shedding the Duke of Royse like a rattlesnake changing its skin to become himself.

Archie stood transfixed, staring at the ugly-looking revolver that was pointed carelessly and yet quite unwaveringly at him, while Trent continued dangerously: "Matter of habit, I suppose. Two guns and extra cartridges in my gunbelts. And a bowie knife for real emergencies. Think you can understand me so far, old chap? And now—better remember to move *very* carefully, huh? And only if and when, this baby says to—*comprende?*"

Even if he hadn't understood some Spanish, the meaning of the word would have been clear enough—*spat* out at him with savageness that made the Earl wince.

Archie straightened up very carefully when the gun muzzle moved as a signal to him; and then he moved just as carefully away from the desk. He could feel his heart pounding in his chest, and he knew that he had never been so afraid in all his life!

"For God's sake, Royse," he stammered, "you must be mad, quite mad, if you think you can get away with something like this! I don't know why you think you have to threaten me with that ugly-looking pistol after I've already told you—"

"I heard what you *told* me. And now I want you to tell me the *truth*. The whole truth, Sedgewick. If you want proof that I can *use* this weapon of mine . . ." Before Archie knew what was happening, he heard an explosion and felt a bullet actually nick his ear, making it bleed, before it embedded itself in the wall just behind him.

Franco heard the sound of a gunshot from where he stood in the garden just outside the front door, and as he kicked it open and started indoors, the sound still seemed to echo throughout the house. What in hell was happening? he wondered. Had Trent finally gone berserk? He had begun to stride swiftly toward the door of the study when he heard a scream. A high-pitched, terrified scream, followed by yet another that was suddenly muffled. Ena! his mind and his instincts told him. Now he *ran* in the direction from where the screams had come—in the direction of the rooms of the Earl and Countess of Sedgewick.

Fatima had just forced a gag in Helena's mouth before she began whipping her about her haunches again when the door burst open. She looked up, but before she could say or do anything, a wild man, holding a gun in one hand and a knife in the other, burst into the room, clearing the space between them in two long strides. He slammed the gun butt viciously across her face, breaking her nose and her jaw, and Fatima lost consciousness, sprawling on her back on the floor beside Helena.

To Helena, looking up through tear-blurred eyes, it seemed as if this couldn't possibly be real. *Franco!* Quickly he ripped the gag out of her mouth and cut away the cords that had been used to bind her. "Franco?" she whispered disbelievingly. "Oh God, Franco! I don't want you to see me like this, I don't want . . . I *can't* . . . oh, don't look at me—don't, *don't!*"

"Did *he* do this to you? Your *husband?*" He had pulled her up onto her feet and against him, ignoring her hysterical words, but she shuddered at the harshness in his voice as he repeated: "*Tell* me, dammit! Did *he* order this done to you?"

She began to weep uncontrollably, her body trembling against his, but she managed at last to say, "Yes, *yes!* He . . . oh, Franco! He found out about *us,* and he said I had to be punished for it, and then . . . and then he made me . . . he *made* me . . . Oh! You could not want me *now,* not after this, not after everything he's done to me and forced *me* to do as well! You *couldn't*—I know it—but oh, at least please take me away from here, away from him! Please, Franco, please! And don't look at me—*please* don't look at me!"

It was only then, when the first redness of his almost blinding rage had left him; while she kept begging him over and over again, brokenly, not to look at her, that Franco realized exactly *what* had been done to Helena. Her body was covered with weals that stood up against her creamy white flesh—and then, worse, he saw the damned gold belt with its cunning little chains and gold mesh that dipped down from her waist to cut cruelly between her thighs. It was at that moment he knew exactly *how* he would kill her husband.

It took a few moments before he realized that Helena was trying to tell him something else, her voice still choked and hoarse from screaming. ". . . and Laura! Oh God! Laura! Oh, poor Laura! They *drugged* her first, then afterward, when she was unconscious and couldn't move, then—oh, they did the same things to her that they did to me . . . *both* of them—Archie and Reggie! They made her into a frightened, cowering creature so that she'd promise anything, anything at *all*, not to be hurt anymore! Oh Franco! She was *forced* to marry Reggie because he wanted her money!'' She looked up at him, her face all swollen from tears and discolored by vicious slaps, and blurted out wildly: "Franco! It doesn't matter about *me* any longer, but *Laura*—you *have* to do something to help her! Before he takes her off to Tangier with him—before it's too late for her too!''

It was with an effort of will that Franco forced his voice into being soothing and gentle. "Ena, love! And you are *still* my love—I'm going to make you forget all of this, everything, you *must* believe that. I'm going to take you away from here and from *him*—'' and his voice turned viciously cold—"the *dead* man who *used* to be your husband.'' Then he lifted her up in his arms while she protested feebly that he couldn't want her like this, he would *never*, ever forget, and he carried her down the passageway and toward the study where Trent was with Archie. With fury burning like acid into his mind, Franco knew only that he wanted to get at Archie before Trent did.

All the servants seemed to have disappeared. Franco, still carrying Helena in his arms, kicked open the door to the study and saw that Trent had Archie up against a wall with his hands clasped over his head, babbling promises that were mixed with threats and oaths. He could not help but notice how Ena shuddered and turned her face away

when she saw *him*—that creature who was her husband,
the Earl of Sedgewick.

There was a little couch in the study and Franco laid
Ena down on it gently before he walked stiff-legged and
purposefully, his whole body seeming to vibrate with pure,
cold rage, toward Archie who cowered back with a high-
pitched howl of fear as he actually fell to his knees.

Unexpectedly, Trent put out an arm to hold Franco back,
without taking his eyes off Archie. In no mood to be
stopped, Franco was ready to fight even Trent at this point.

"Get out of my way, Trent. Goddammit! He's *mine!*
You hear me? And if you think you can stop me—"

"Damn you, Franco! You have a *sister*, remember? And
the Earl of Sedgewick who witnessed her *wedding* is going
to tell me where Forrester has taken her, before I let you
at him! If he seems reluctant, then you can *start* off by
cutting him up, little piece by little piece, with your knife.
But he's going to *talk* first, understand, Franco? Cover him
with your gun while I tie the whoreson's thumbs together
behind him. Remember some of those old Apache ways
of torturing a man to make him talk?"

There was such deadly menace in that voice, and in
Franco Morgan's face when he *smiled* suddenly—a mere
thinning and curling of his lips—that Archie cringed in
abject terror.

"I sure as shit do! Those 'paches knew a helluva lot
about torturing a man real *slow,* didn't they? So he'd last
a long time and *suffer* a long time before they let him die.
Let me see now . . ."

"No!" Archie screamed, white-faced and almost faint
from fear. He was actually in the power of two wild Americans who talked casually of torturing him to death!

The man he knew as the Duke of Royse came up behind
him now, and used the ball of twine Archie always kept
on his desk to tie his thumbs behind his back so tightly he
felt his circulation cut off. While he begged uselessly for
help, Franco held his gun trained steadily on Archie's

crotch and described in a quietly conversational voice some of the Apache Indians' favorite methods of torture.

"Should we cut his eyelids off first?"

"No! Oh please, please, I beg you, don't! Just let me go and I'll tell you everything!"

"Ena's told me what they did with Laura." Franco turned his head slightly as he said to Trent in a cold, tight voice: "They tortured her—just as they did Ena. And you've only got to turn your head to see what they've done with *her!*"

Helena, who had been lying huddled on the couch with Franco's jacket that smelled of him covering her and comforting her, turned her head suddenly to cry out in a barely coherent voice: "The caves! St. Michael's Cavern, to the old Inquisition torture chamber. I heard him say so! You must go to her *now*, I tell you! God only knows what he might be doing to her! *Hurry*—oh, you *must* hurry!"

They all left the villa together, Archie's arms drawn tightly behind him, roped by his elbows as well as his thumbs. Franco carried Ena, his jacket wrapped closely about her to cover her nakedness. There was no time to do more—and Ena needed to be seen by a doctor as soon as possible.

Trent had hired a carriage that was waiting outside for them; and the driver was the kind of man who would ask no questions as long as he was paid well.

Archie was made to lie face down on the floor of the carriage and Franco placed one booted foot on his neck to keep him down there. "You'll never get away with this," Archie cried out. "I'm Lieutenant-Governor here and there will be inquiries made should anything happen to me! As for anything else, there's nothing you can *prove*—and not even you Royse, *Duke* or not, could get away with *murdering* me."

"My friend and I have a different viewpoint," Trent snarled. "You won't be *murdered*, Sedgewick. By no means. *Executed* seems to me the better word. As for the inquiries and who might actually miss your presence—

well, we'll see, won't we?'' And then Trent tied a gag in Archie's mouth to silence him.

The Earl of Sedgewick sobbed and moaned behind his gag and writhed with pain as he lay face down on the dirty floor of the hired carriage, while Franco, his booted foot over his neck keeping him in place, proceeded to prick him with his knife, inflicting shallow cuts on his back and twitching buttocks and thighs—*through* his clothes. If only he'd been given a chance to *reason* with them! If only— And then he was made to turn over, facing up this time, and the words he wasn't allowed to utter became choked and mixed with his copiously flowing tears—all sticking in his throat while the knife continued to play its delicately intricate game with his helpless body.

Chapter 42

Major Eagan was puzzled as well as thoughtful when his batman announced the Duke of Royse. There had been far too many strange events that had transpired within the last couple of days that he could not understand.

For one thing he had heard that the Prince of Wales's yacht had actually turned about and was coming *back* to Gibraltar! For another, he had been informed by a telegraph message that came directly from the Prince of Wales himself that Royse was to be afforded every courtesy; and that whatever transpired, there was not to be any hint of scandal! Now what on earth did *that* mean? Major Eagan wondered; and what in the hell was really going on here? Perhaps Royse would enlighten him. Or could it be that all this furor had something to do with Royse's ex-fiancée?

The Major had to admit to himself that he had been more than a trifle shocked when he had heard about Miss Morgan's sudden marriage, and to Reggie Forrester of all people! She had seemed far too intelligent to make such a mistake and to be so precipitate while she was still wearing Royse's ring! However, the Earl of Sedgewick had assured him that there was nothing he need concern himself about since Miss Morgan had made her choice of her own free will, and had *told* him so, or he wouldn't have agreed to witness their wedding ceremony.

"And there's no accounting for a woman's choice, is there?" the Earl had said to him with a laugh that Major Eagan hadn't quite liked for some reason.

And now, damn it, he had to face Royse and tell him that his fiancée had just been married to another man, with whom she was even now exploring St. Michael's Cavern! It was a hell of a position for a man to be put in, he thought, before he went out to meet his impatient visitor.

"Well, Royse! If I hadn't heard from His Royal Highness himself that you would be calling on me, I would have said that I was surprised at your unexpected visit. However, I've been asked to cooperate with you in any way I possibly can, and naturally I shall try to do so!" Then the Major added cautiously, "You must understand, of course, that you'll have to tell me *something* concerning what this is all about."

"We need a doctor first. A reliable one who won't talk. The Countess of Sedgewick is in need of a *very* discreet physician—and urgently too. I'm afraid she might be hemorrhaging internally, from what's been done to her. You'll see to it at once?" Before the astounded Major could utter a word, Royse went on in the same hard, controlled voice, "And then I need a map of the caves, showing the exact location of that old Spanish Inquisition chamber—which is where Forrester has taken Laura to play the Grand Inquisitor at her expense!"

"But . . . but I was given to understand that they were just married—*tonight* in fact!" Major Eagan exclaimed. "The Earl of Sedgewick told me himself that he had been a witness at their wedding!" And then forcefully: "By God, Royse! Would you mind telling me exactly what is going on here?"

"I'm afraid," the Duke of Royse said distinctly, "that you might have rather a mess on your hands, Major—unless it's handled discreetly, as I hope it will be! But I don't have time now, to waste on lengthy explanations! I'll tell you this much, and what your doctor will tell you will bear it out—Sedgewick has been torturing and abusing his wife in every conceivable way since she got here! Whippings, a fucking *chastity belt* of all things, that she was forced to wear all the time—when he wasn't forcing her to

service her maid, the houseboys—even Forrester! And then
they did that to *Laura*, too, goddamn them! To force her
into marriage with Forrester.''

''By God!'' Major Eagan was hardly able to believe that
he had heard right, until Royse, the barely tamped-down
fury and impatience that had lain just under the surface all
this time erupting all at once, said in a voice that caused
even the Major to blench: ''Have you heard enough to
understand now, Major Eagan? I want a map of those
damned caves of yours. And I might as well tell you right
now, sir, that when Franco comes up here with the Countess of Sedgewick, and leaves her with you, he'll follow
me with Sedgewick himself. And there'll be only the two
of us and Laura who'll return. If you, or anyone else, tries
to stop us . . .'' And then he shrugged out of his jacket
and flung it aside; and the dumbfounded Major saw the
Colt six-guns he wore, and *how* they were worn; noticed
also, for the first time, the Duke's unusual footwear. Moccasins, he believed they were called.

None of his thoughts showing on his suddenly impassive
face, Major Eagan said stiffly: ''Here's your map, sir. I've
heard myself that unfortunate accidents often occur in those
caves—particularly if someone happens to lose their way
and wanders into one of the sea caves that open directly
onto the rocks and the ocean below them.'' His eyes met
Trent's for a moment before he added: ''When young Morgan brings the Countess up, I'll see that she's taken to my
own quarters. And I'll send my batman out for Dr. Mat-
thews. He's completely trustworthy *and* discreet, as well
as being an excellent physician.''

And then Trent was gone—running—as swiftly and
soundlessly as an Apache with wildness and fury pounding in his veins and in his mind. He had the map in his
vest pocket but he didn't need it now. It had taken him
only one glance to memorize what he wanted to know and
where he had to go to find Laura. His Lorelei—his love.

There were flickering torches in cast-iron sconces spaced
along the rocky walls that cast a flickering, almost eerie

orange glow like hellfires. And if anyone had seen Trent Challenger now they would have thought him some kind of terrifying apparition out of hell: a tall, black-haired, black-bearded man loping down the curving tunnels like a wolf, with those eyes that reflected the flicker of the torchlight, and his silent footfalls and the black silk shirt and vest and pants and the holstered guns all blending in with the blackness of the water-dripping walls of the caverns—the devil himself moving in on his latest prey.

After Franco left Helena with the Major, he went down again to the carriage to get Archie. As they made their way through the torturous passages of the caverns, Franco prodded Archie before him at knife point while Archie moaned piteously through his gag. He was in agony, but he wasn't allowed to stop in his shambling run, as they followed Trent who was already far ahead of them and in much more of a hurry.

"This is only the beginning," Franco snarled through his teeth. His knife, razor-sharp, had already slashed through Archie's black dress trousers to cut deep slashes that made a crisscross pattern over his buttocks. He could feel the blood run down his legs, soak down into his boots. Oh God! he thought despairingly. Oh God, save me, *someone* save me!

Laura was moaning brokenly behind the gag that Reggie had forced into her mouth when he'd brought her into the torture chamber used at the time of the Spanish Inquisition.

"I don't want you screaming, with the sound bouncing off the walls of every mile of these caves, my love," he'd explained, smiling. "Anyone who heard might not understand that we're only having fun and games on our honeymoon, eh?"

He'd told her that she must try the rack and the wheel to find out how those unfortunates who had been stretched on them might have felt.

"And then, dearest wife, you can write a novel set in the time of the Inquisition, and describe truthfully how its victims must have felt with these leather straps about their wrists and ankles to secure them.''

Laughing at her terrified look, he had added in a falsely consoling voice that he was only going to have a *little* more fun with her, and then he'd forced her onto the rack and fastened her wrists so that her arms were extended over her head. He did the same with her ankles, making sure that her legs were spread as widely and as painfully apart as possible before he'd actually given the wheel a turn or two. The sensation of being *stretched*—all extended and open—was unbearable.

Oh God—oh God! She would have screamed if it was possible—screamed out loud in her agony—but all she could do was to make choked, anguished sounds from behind her gag.

"Well—we mustn't overdo it the first time, must we?"

She heard her own moans and Reggie's voice from what seemed like the far end of the tunnel and wished she could faint, could die—anything to stop this nightmare from going on and on and *endlessly* on.

What *more* did he want from her? She'd already signed all the papers he'd put before her giving him possession of everything she owned. What *else* would he think of to do with her?

Her mind screamed soundlessly for release; for this to be a nightmare from which she'd wake up; for her lover, her *love* whom she'd so carelessly lost! *Why* hadn't he come? Trent—oh God, Trent! Hear my thoughts now, please! *Feel* them, and me—Trent, love me still, please hold me again and keep me—please! Trent . . . Trent . . . Trent . . .

Over and over she screamed his name in her mind— over the gloating, ugly words Reggie was using on her now and the pain of the way he handled her helplessly exposed body before he started to slash at her with expert skill, using the dogwhip he'd brought with him to keep his bitch well-behaved, he'd told Archie and they'd both laughed.

Oh, Trent, she thought. Oh why? Why didn't I know it was *you?* Trent . . .

When he knew that he was close to that damned torture chamber at last, Trent drew his knife from its sheath, his lips curling back from his teeth in a purely primitive, animal grimace of killing rage. The knife blade, reflecting the torchlight, looked bloodied already, as it soon would be. Soon now, he thought through the red mist in his mind. *Soon!* And then . . . *now!*

Trent—she kept saying his name in her mind like a talisman, He'll come for me—he will, he will! And then the dogwhip lashed between her legs, forcing her eyes open with the sheer agony of it—and suddenly, as if she really *had* conjured him up out of her mind—he was *here!* She saw him over Reggie's shoulder—dressed almost the same way he'd been dressed when she'd first set eyes on him, with the twin holstered guns snug against his thighs. But the look on his face, and in his eyes, was something she had never seen before.

''So, bitch—'' Reggie started to say tauntingly when he heard a soft, deadly cold whisper behind him like the sound of a rattlesnake just before it strikes.

''Turn, whoreson! Turn—because I want to see the look on your face while you're dying.''

Dropping the whip, Reggie swung around, unable to believe he had heard *that* voice. His eyes widened in sudden, abject terror as he looked at death. Gray-eyed death with a long-bladed knife.

''No!'' Reggie screamed. ''No—you don't—''

''You took my woman, Reggie Forrester. And you've abused her.''

Trent moved in with the bowie knife held before him, its blade flickering in the light like the tongue of a deadly snake.

''No! God . . . no! She *wanted* me . . . she—'' Reggie never had the chance to say anything else as the knife slashed viciously upward between his legs while a fisted blow to his neck and then his solar plexus cut off his wind and any sound he might have made as the knife did its work methodically and surely. All he could do with his eyes already turning sightless and rolling upward was to writhe against the floor a few times like a beheaded chicken before Trent finished him off in time-honored Apache fashion. He released Laura, lifting her into his arms, holding her hard and close against his chest while she kept sobbing and sobbing as her arms clung around his neck even before he took away the gag.

"I'd have given him a much slower death if there was time enough, my love!" he whispered to her fiercely. "But now I'll take you to Ena—yes, she's safe now, and there'll be a doctor to see to you both, while Franco gets rid of both Archie and *this!*" He kicked at Reggie's body contemptuously, as if it had been carrion, and took her away from her torture chamber—up into the fresh night air and the scent of flowers, his shirt wrapped about her.

They met Franco halfway—with Archie still being prodded before him, and still weeping.

Trent jerked his head into that place of horrors he had just left.

"There's not much left of him, but for Eagan's sake and protocol, you might clean up afterward, huh?"

"Ena's with the doctor now," Franco said briefly, his eyes skimming over his sister with a glint in them she'd never seen before. Then he took Archie to the sea caves and threw him to the barracudas that hovered below— waiting for any kind of offal that might come their way. Soon after, he did the same with Reggie's equally mutilated carcass.

Chapter 43

How could she ever *forget*, Laura wondered dully. How could she ever stop herself from living and reliving the nightmare of horror. And how could Trent bear to touch her again, or even to look at her again without remembering not only what he had *seen* being done to her but also what he had by now learned had been forced on her? How could *he* forget?

They returned to London on the Royal Yacht, and every night Laura would start up from her sleep, waking to escape from twisted, ugly dreams, sobbing bitterly and painfully.

Laura wondered sometimes what Ena felt and whether she had the same kind of nightmares; but they could not yet face each other directly because of certain shared memories. Dear God, she would think despairingly, what am I to do now? What am I going to do?

Oh yes, if she wanted to *console* herself, it was true that Trent held her in his arms every night to comfort her and murmured to her gently as he stroked her hair back from her face. But he had never once made *love* to her; never once kissed her and caressed her in the way he used to do before! And no wonder, Laura thought. How could she blame him, after all? It had all been *her* fault! He had rescued her, and now—now he was saddled with her!

Laura's manner was apathetic and even her voice showed only indifference after they had disembarked. Ena kept clinging tightly to Franco's arm as if she could not bear to let go of him, Laura noticed, wondering how it went with the two of *them*.

Franco and Ena had walked ahead of them, but suddenly they seemed to have disappeared. To keep her mind from wondering, Laura asked: "Where do we go now? And what do we do next?" She really felt like saying, "Why don't we put an end to this, Trent? You did what you felt you had to do for your pride, for your honor, but now, why don't you just let me go! I can go back *home*—Mama would understand, I know! I don't want you *this* way, Trent; not because you feel you *have* to!"

Her gloved fingers rested very lightly on his arm, but all the same she could feel his muscles tense under her touch before he said, with an inscrutable glance down at her pale face: "Since you don't seem to care very much either way, love, I hope you don't mind if I have made the arrangements for us."

There was something in his voice that made Laura suddenly look up sharply at him. "Arrangements? What arrangements? I'd like to know, Trent!"

But he only drawled infuriatingly, "A surprise, my love. And it wouldn't *be* a surprise if I told you ahead of time, would it now?"

"I don't know if I like surprises anymore. Trent, really, I'd rather know, please."

"Why don't you *guess*, Lorelei, as soon as you get on the train?"

And now he was tugging her along with him—actually *pulling* her, while she protested all the while. "Trent! Trent, what do you think you are—what do you *mean*, catching a train when we've only just arrived here?" But then he lifted her up into his arms right in front of the crowd of people who milled around. And suddenly, Laura knew that she didn't care *where* he was taking her as long as it was *he* who was taking her and holding her, and she put her face against his shoulder to hide the flush on it, while letting her arms clasp tentatively around his neck.

Traveling on the train to Cornwall seemed to Laura like

retracing the past as she looked out of the window of their private compartment. The only difference was that this time she was with Trent! Franco and Ena had been given the use of Royse House; and Franco was to book their passages for a week from now to leave England for the States. "They need time to themselves—and so do we," Trent had told her, looking down at her almost measuringly, Laura thought. She was afraid—and yet somehow unafraid as she began to remember her feelings the first time she had been with him. Oh God, but her mind was full of so many things!

When they arrived at Royse Park at last, and Trent had taken Laura up to her Moorish Room, still carrying her in his arms even as he kicked shut the door, she suddenly began to laugh—remembering her father and her mother. "And what in hell is so funny?" Trent demanded as he dropped her down on that wide, silken-covered bed she remembered only too well.

"Oh, I don't know! It's only that suddenly I was remembering how when my mother and father would have a quarrel, he would always pick her up in his arms afterward and carry her into their bedroom to settle it—just before *he* kicked the door shut! It took a long time before Franco and I realized exactly what was going on, you know!"

Trent said grimly: "And shall I tell you exactly what will go on right now and right here in this room? Or shall I surprise you, my darling Lorelei?"

She lay back on the bed, still laughing for *some* reason, perhaps for *no* reason at all! But there were tears, too—a release, stemming from her sudden joy. She held her arms up to him then and asked provocatively: "Aren't you going to undress me first? Or will you do it on the marble slab in the Moon Garden?"

"I'm afraid there's no full moon tonight, Lorelei, so this Moorish boudoir will have to do for now!" He began to unbutton her gown. "But there's always the consolation of that sunken bath, you know. That is—unless you'd rather we start *here?*''

He didn't give her a chance to answer, as impatient as he was to have her; and she relished his impatience and his fierce *wanting* of her. It wiped her mind from all her doubts, all her fears.

After he undressed her she sat up and, of her own will and wanting, helped to undress him as he stood before her, just as he had in the Moon Garden. As her eager, fumbling fingers revealed inch by inch every part of his body—from his chest and wide shoulders down to his hard muscled belly and lean flanks *and* the evidence of his desire for her—Laura kissed him everywhere and loved his man-god's body, and touched him everywhere with her fingers following the path traced by her eager, teasing lips that murmured against his skin, and against his hardness, until he couldn't stand it any longer and lifted her up to be held close against him, running his fingers up and down along her satiny skin before they lay down together, and he had *her* straddle *him,* and told her, with sparkling lights in his silver-gray eyes, to show him how well she could take *him!*

"Do you think you can ride me to exhaustion, my love? *Will* you?''

"Oh, but you'll find out—won't you? And perhaps *I* will too! Oohh! Oh, Trent! And I thought *I* was the one trying to please you . . . and . . . oh! I love making love to you this way—all the things I feel from you—and. . .''

"Will you just—oh, *Christ,* Laura!''

"Am I pleasing you?''

"You know damn well what you're doing to me! You're stretching my self-control to its limits, my little witch!''

"But I *want* you to lose your self-control! I want to be able to make you *feel . . . feel . . .* just the way I'm feeling now! Climbing and flying and . . .'' Her movements became more and more frantic before he heard her cry out over and over and felt her spasmodic contractions before she fell over him and he, too, could no longer hold himself back any longer, and could not help groaning as he held her more closely against him while his tightly muscled hips moved up to claim her and he felt her hands under him—taking all of him inside her.

Afterward he turned on his side to her and whispered roughly: "Oh God! Lorelei, my bewitching water-witch! You've actually made me fall in love with you, you know! And that's something I never thought . . ." And then as she touched him teasingly again and moved her body equally tantalizingly against his, he warned her: "You had better not forget, not *ever*, that you're *my* woman now—and mine *only*! Hear? And if I ever catch you so much as *flirting* with another man—"

"But why should I want to flirt with other men, darling, as long as *you* always keep me happy and *satisfied?*"

"I think," Trent said dangerously, "that this is just the right time for a nice hot bath in a sunken tub!" And even while he was speaking he was already tugging her up off the bed where she had been lying so languidly, seizing her by her wrists, overriding her murmured protests and her pretended attempts at pulling herself free.

"Oh Trent, really! *Again?*"

"Yes, dammit, *again!* But you can wash my back first— just as I've often wished I had you do that first time we met!"

"Oh! But you *would* remember that!" Laura said with a flash of her old fire, before she found herself pulled against him and held close again.

Then, still not releasing her, Trent said in a voice that was no longer light, but urgent and demanding, "I'm always going to want you, Laura-Lorelei. And to have you, and keep you close. Is that clear?"

"Oh, Trent—yes! Very clear. But—"

He cut off the rest of her words with kisses; and she felt again the infinite pleasure of his *loving* of her, and *knew* then, as *he* had already known, that there could be and would be no one else but each other for *them!*

"I suppose they *did* know what they were about, those

stiff-necked old Spanish ancestors of ours!'' Laura murmured, half in a daze of pleasure.

''*What* did you say?'' His voice sounded dangerous at that particular moment, and Laura whispered hastily: ''Nothing! Nothing at all . . . *mi querido!* Ah! *Mi amante, mi amor! Mi amor!*''

''That's *all* I want to hear!'' And then he took her—and took her again and again.

Epilogue

Weddings and Beddings

"Yes—oh, that'll be just fine, I think. And the flowers? But of course they are just beautiful and so *right* for the occasion, as you just said. I see that I can quite safely leave everything up to you, Monsieur Armand! You have such good taste."

The bride's mother, Virginia Brandon Morgan, bestowed a final, brilliant smile on the florist and the bemused-looking caterers before her husband strolled in, a cigar jutting rakishly from one corner of his mouth. Such a dangerous-looking man! Armand thought. Hopefully *he* would approve of the menu and the flower arrangements for his daughter's wedding reception! M. Armand felt quite tense for a few seconds, until he found out that Mr. Morgan seemed more interested in seeing his lovely wife *alone,* as he stated, rather than in the preparations for a wedding reception. And who could blame him, after all?

"Steve! Couldn't you have *waited?*" Ginny was all green-eyed witch in the seclusion of their bedroom overlooking the ocean in Monterey. "And I do wish you hadn't invited the Driscolls! I cannot *stand* Barney Driscoll!"

"No? But he seems to be fascinated by you, my love."

"Steve—oh, but I'm sure Franco will be able to take care of *him* as well as his Helena. I can hardly believe that . . . oh! I'm sure that Trent will make Laura happy and

407

. . . Steve! Do you realize that we might be *grandparents* at any time now?''

Ignoring the note of tragedy in his wife's voice, Steve leaned over her to hold her still before he whispered roughly against her lips: "For God's sake, woman! Why do you have to keep *talking* when I brought you in here for quite a different purpose, as you well know! Becoming grandparents isn't going to change *this* . . . or this . . . or—"

"Oh, Steve! Oh . . . stop it!"

"Do you really mean that?"

"No! No, damn you, and you know it!"

They were almost late for the wedding, which was to take place at the old Mission of San Carlos Borromeo in Carmel; something that neither Laura, nor Franco, knowing their parents' ways, could fail to miss.

"They've been at it again! I can always tell from the way they *look* afterward!" Laura whispered to Trent later.

"As soon as *we* can escape from this mob, I hope to hell that *we'll* be looking the same way! Damn! Did we *have* to go through all this just to get hitched?" And then, looking down into his bride's eyes, Trent said, in a different kind of voice, "On the other hand, I think I'd go through anything, just to make sure you're mine—and *stay* mine!"

"I thought . . ." Then Laura's voice trailed off and Trent, following the direction of her gaze, swore under his breath, before he laughed.

Lady Honoria had actually agreed to attend the wedding—she had to see *this* for herself, she had said. And now, she was, in her own inimitable fashion, looking the bride's father up and down while *he* kissed her hand with excessive gallantry.

"Hah!" she stated. "Let me tell you that I've seen more than enough of *your* kind of rapscallion in *my* time! And you have a pretty and intelligent wife too—so don't waste your time kissing *my* hand, Mr. Steven Morgan! Hah!"

"But Ma'am, I was only leading up to introducing you

to my old friend and colleague who has been *pressing* me to present him to you! Mr. James Bishop might change your views about the rest of us rogues and rascals.''

"You *didn't!*" Laura said disbelievingly to her father a few moments later. "Papa . . . even *you* couldn't have—''

"No?" Steve said, one rakish eyebrow tilted wickedly. "As your mother knows already—I'm capable of almost anything! And I've been waiting a long time to see Jim Bishop bested by a female. Not only has she got him cornered—she seems to have him quite fascinated as well!''

"*I* have a strange feeling that they might just have met each other before,'' Ginny said as she came up to them just then, to take her husband's arm and smile at her new son-in-law.

"In that case, maybe what they're doing back there is making up for lost time!" Trent grabbed Laura's arm impatiently before he added, uncaring of the interested eyes that were on them, "And that, my lovely Lorelei, is exactly what *I* have in mind as well! If you'll excuse us?''

"He's far too much like you!" Ginny whispered to Steve after the bridal couple had disappeared.

"Oh? And you, my green-eyed witch-woman will have a chance to explain that statement to me *later*—but not *too* much later, I warn you, if you don't want your gown ripped off your back before I put you on your back right here!''

They exchanged a smiling look of perfect understanding and underlying promise then, before they went, for the moment, their separate ways to see to their guests.